CW00447326

GODS of the LOST CROSSROADS

First published 2023
Rymour Books
45 Needless Road,
PERTH
PH20LE

© Robin Lloyd-Jones 2023
ISBN 978-1-7391662-0-5

A CIP record for this book is
available from the British Library
BIC Classification FA

Cover and book design by
Ingebjorg Smith and Ian Spring
Typeset in Bembo
Printed and bound by
Imprint Digital
Seychelles Farm
Upton Pyne
Exeter

Rymour Books is commited to the sustainable use
of natural resources. The paper used in this book
is approved by the Forest Stewardship Council

This book is a work of fiction. Names, characters,
places and events are used fictitiously. any resemblance
to persons, living or dead, is entirely coincidental.

To Gordon with very best wishes   Robin

GODS of the LOST CROSSROADS

Robin Lloyd-Jones

Robin Lloyd-Jones

RYMOUR

To my lovely wife, Sallie, without whose faith this book would still be an unpublished manuscript.

ACKNOWLEDGEMENTS

Thanks are due to Ian Spring of Rymour Books for championing *Gods of the Lost Crossroads* and for being a pleasure to work with, to Ingebjorg Smith for her wonderful and imaginative cover design, to my nieces, Julia Rardin and Catherine Grey for help and advice, to my children, Glyn, Kally and Leonie for their support and encouragement, to Jan Pester and his Vancouver book club friends, and to the Helensburgh Writers' Workshop for useful comments. Also to the staff at the Mitchell Library and the University of Glasgow Library, who rendered invaluable services while I was researching the book.

And most of all to my wife, Sallie, who has always been my best critic and whose help and support extends into every area of my life.

ROBIN LLOYD-JONES 2023

Crossroads are intersections of indecision where hard choices must be made, roads taken and not taken. In that sense all crossroads are places of loss, routes rejected, avenues abandoned, options left behind. Gods of the Lost Crossroads has the feel of a novel by Amos Tutuola (My Life in the Bush of Ghosts) or Ben Okri (Astonishing the Gods), magical realism with a political edge, a quest novel that raises questions about the conquest of fears as well as foes. The story goes beyond its Yoruba beginnings in the character of the shaman – and showman – Rainbow, into an epic otherworld, a spirit world that will be familiar to readers of magic realism, fantasy and futurism. But the crossroads is also where present and past meet, where memory and desire mix. The four quests mapped out in the narrative correspond to the four-cross-road and conjure up one of the original meanings of 'crossroads' as places of secondary importance, of isolation and desolation, of obscure corners and dangerous liaisons. The word emerged two centuries ago in the same decade as 'trickster', and they are related insofar as the trickster figure depends on a crossroads encounter, on chance, on turning a trick, on catching the mark unawares and on pointing the way ahead to empty pockets and heavy hearts. As someone acquainted both with African and with South American literature and politics, I found this playful and perceptive work of fiction to be a fascinating read, a quirky tale featuring a motley crew of characters, and an otherworldly story that addresses worldly issues such as slavery, colonialism, the challenges of street life, circus life, and intercontinental cultural struggle. Rather than root around for comparisons I read this as its own thing, a unique piece of storytelling that takes as its starting-point the historical novel – a time-travelling genre always open to invention – and then leads the reader on a journey through a warren of backstreets and byways to those troublesome locations where real history unfolds and unravels: at the crossroads of what's past and what's possible. Gods are plural – they too have their crossroads to bear.

Willy Maley
Professor of English Literature
University of Glasgow

AUTHOR'S NOTE

Yoruba, Rainbow's first language, is spoken primarily in Southwest and Central Nigeria. In this area, the 'Yo' is pronounced as in 'go', with the accent on the first syllable. The 'x' in Exu and Nataxale is pronounced 'sh'; for example, 'Eshu and 'Natashaly'.

1

In the bows of the small boat, Rainbow, a tall muscular African, peered nervously through the fog which drifted like lost souls across the water. The sun had not yet risen and the river was in semi-darkness. He turned to the two water-spirits.

'Is this the Dark River which flows from the other world? Have I reached it at last?'

The oarsman laughed and hawked up phlegm of much the same colour as the fog. His cough sounded like the barking of a baboon. 'Tell us your name first. You never told us your name.'

The other man, the one in the stern, rolled his eyes. 'He don't know where he is!' He raised the lantern and peered around. 'And nor do we, come to that! '

The muffled clank of a bell warned of a ship somewhere close. Rainbow slid his hand inside his shirt, flinching as he touched the markings made by the branding iron.

'Rainbow,' he said. 'My name is Rainbow.'

That was how he thought of himself now. He had taken his new name from the curving, seven-ribbed scar burned into his flesh. You have to protect your real name, leave it at home when you go on a dangerous mission, because a name is like the soft underbelly of a crocodile—a vulnerable part of you.

The oarsman prodded a swirl of garbage with his oar. 'Well, Rainbow,' he said, hawking up more phlegm, 'It's a dark river and no mistake. Dark with stinking filth. We call it the Thames.'

'How old do you think he is?' the one with the lantern asked, talking as if Rainbow wasn't there. 'I'd wager he's not a day over twenty.'

'He's big. Could be more.'

'No! Look at those eyes. All lost and scared like.'

'Ask him then.'

'No, you ask him. Anyway, what I'd really like to know is how he speaks our lingo. I thought heathens had some jabber of their own.'

'Ask him then.'

'No, you ask him.'

From the bows Rainbow said, 'King George taught me your

language.'

The oarsman's blade missed the water. 'Our King George? As was Prince Regent?'

Rainbow nodded. George King, in fact, he'd said his name was. But nobody could possess such powerful magic without invoking the powers of the world reversed—like Kako, the famous shaman once did when defeat at the hands of the Ijeru tribe seemed inevitable. He had approached the enemy backwards, hurling spears at his own warriors. The Ijeru had hacked him to pieces, but not before his deed had harnessed supernatural forces which ensured victory for his own people, the Obolu. Clearly, George King was the power-giving reversal of King George.

'King George!' the oarsman snorted. 'God Almighty!'

≈

So it was true. The George was a god. The George had been vague on that point, never actually claiming to be one, never denying it. The porters hired by the George at the borders of Obolu territory to carry his amazing belongings had thought he was. And they'd heard from the porters of the neighbouring tribe who'd got it from the ones before, that the George had crossed the Great Water on the far shores of which was the Other World. The George, they said, had emerged from the belly of a great sea-bird with huge white wings. And they said the George could make an object burst into flame by removing his eyes and holding them close to it.

≈

Only now did Rainbow begin to understand the true purpose of the George's visit to his tribe. With supernatural foreknowledge of Rainbow's spirit journey, the George had come to show him the ways and manners of the Other World. Of all the young men assigned by Chief Chimu to assist the George, Rainbow had been the most adept at learning the sacred language. The George had made him his interpreter, so that wherever he went to measure people's skulls or ask questions about their customs and beliefs, Rainbow went with him. Rainbow had spent two years in the company of the George, who had praised him for the speed with which he had mastered the language of the Other World.

The sailor in the stern wiped the moisture off the lantern window with his sleeve.

'King George!' he repeated, looking at Rainbow with a mixture of amusement and pity. 'I suppose it was enough to turn anyone queer what he's been through. Can't be no picnic on a slave ship. Never seen a cove so fevered up… not as lived, I mean.'

'Reckon that's why they heaved him overboard—in case the other darkies caught it.'

'What about us? What if we'd catched it?'

'Cap'n said it was our Christian duty to rescue him.'

'Talk about delirious!' exclaimed the other with a glance of wonderment at the figure in the bows.

'Bet he wasn't the only one that got chucked over the side.'

'Only one we saved, at any rate. Just as well if they were all as barmy as him.'

≈

The man in the stern moved into the middle of the boat and took one of the oars. The two men, or spirits, or whatever they were, pulled on the oars in silence, breathing hard as the current gathered strength. The boat headed towards slime-covered steps. Their words brought back to Rainbow vague memories, like a half remembered dream, of people all around him floating in the sea. He'd drifted away from them. Then, what might have been hours or days later, another ship had appeared and he'd been pulled out of the sea.

The one who sounded like a baboon swivelled on his seat. 'So we know your name, but who are you?'

Rainbow hesitated. He longed to say he was a shaman—well, that was the word the George had used—the shaman of the village of Mwanza. But he'd yet to complete his first spirit journey. He was still a novice, unworthy of the title. For three years he'd submitted to the rigorous training of old Ikpoom, the village shaman. He'd fasted, he'd spent whole nights staring unblinking at the stars and days on end rubbing one stone against another, round and round. He'd danced to the shaman's drum, round and round, round and round, but no swirling vortex had opened in his mind and sucked him into the long, dark tunnel which leads to the Other World. Just once he had felt himself starting the journey down the tunnel, then some force like a strong wind had opposed him until, exhausted, he'd turned back. That had been about two moons before the rains had failed and the rivers had begun to dry up.

'Come on, Rainbow! Run up your flag! Who are you?'

The man was panting, pulling against the current.

'Don't turn back' Rainbow shouted. 'This time I mean to go on!'

'Jesus, hark at him!'

≈

The boat drew level with the steps. The man—the Being—nearest to them grabbed an iron ring and held on. He jerked his head in the direction of the quay.

'Out yer get then!'

Rainbow jumped out. Except for the clothes which had been given to him by the captain, he owned nothing. That was usual, of course. Ikpoom had always made his spirit journeys unencumbered by worldly things. The boat pulled away from the steps with easy strokes now that they were heading downstream.

'Thank you!' Rainbow called after them as fog enfolded the boat.

≈

Cautiously Rainbow climbed the steps. Some unseen monster was hooting and wailing. Rainbow wondered if one of the tests or ordeals he'd have to pass would be to fight this beast. A cloaked figure began to materialise out of the fog, then faded away again. How long, he wondered, had he been away from his home? Time in the spirit world was not the same as in the world of mortals. Ikpoom would undertake spirit journeys months or even years long. Yet Rainbow, watching over the vacant, motionless husk of a man lying in the darkness of the hut, knew that Ikpoom was absent from his body for less time than it took the sun to travel from the blue mountains in the east to the rim of the savannah in the west.

≈

The steps led to a wharf cluttered with broken barrels. Half hidden under loose, rotting staves was a long-bladed knife, similar to the ones used by the fishermen on Lake Mwanza. Ikpoom must have left it there for him. Delivering up silent thanks to his master, he retrieved the knife and slipped it under his belt.

≈

A cat oozed from the shadows. Eagerly Rainbow stepped towards it. 'Are you here to help me?'

The cat arched its back and melted into a dark recess. Disappointed, Rainbow slumped onto a bollard. No wizard ever embarked on a quest into the spirit world without an Orisha Animal to help him. Ikpoom, over the years, had acquired four Orisha Animals—Rat, Ant, Snail and Raven. Sometimes they visited him in human shape, sometimes in their animal form, but there was no mistaking the surge of power inside you, Ikpoom said, or the clarity of the vision when your animal came to you.

≈

Buildings loomed up, tall structures grander than even Chief Chimu's palace. Chief Chimu represented power in the real world, and by his orders sacrifices were made to please the powerful gods of the Other World. It was all a matter of power. Rainbow trod, barefoot, in a puddle. The earth on the riverbeds had cracked and curled at the edges, then turned to dust, and the cattle and the children had begun to die. Under Ikpoom's supervision twelve goats had been sacrificed to Skyherd, Lord of the Clouds. And, when the rains still did not come, twelve cattle, chosen for the beauty of their horns, had been ritually slaughtered, their life-blood soaking the ground in imitation of the rain. This, too, had failed to end the drought. The last resort was to offer up human lives—not captives or slaves, but people of Mwanza, people Rainbow knew. At a certain hour, at a crossroads, both decided by an oracle, Chief Chimu's guards would seize twelve passers-by. But, before the human sacrifice began, the shaman of the village must make a spirit journey to the Other World and attempt to propitiate Skyherd. And so old Ikpoom had made ready to cross the Great Water to the Other World. There he would have sought out and overcome Nataxale, the Dust Devil, whose spirit now held sway throughout the land. And then the old shaman would have risen to the clouds and made offerings to Skyherd so that he would send the rain. But Ikpoom had died before he could begin his journey and it had fallen to Rainbow, the novice, to undertake the mission. He knew he wasn't ready for it. 'Only you can save us!' the eyes of the dying children, of their mothers, of the herdsmen, of the elders had said. And in those eyes, behind the hope, he'd thought he'd seen mockery and contempt, as if they knew he'd fail. And then there were Yaba's eyes. His young wife, his first and only wife so far, gazed at him with utter faith, believing implicitly in him, believing he would not let their little boy die of fever. That was what terrified him more than anything else. He'd wanted to shake her and shout, 'You expect too much of me!'

≈

Rainbow turned a corner and found himself staring at a wagon, pulled not by oxen, but by some other vast animal. Ikpoom had warned him that the Other World would be full of surprises, that the familiar would seem strange and the strange familiar. After the death of his teacher, Rainbow had consulted the Oracle. Should he make the spirit journey or not? The Oracle had said yes, unprepared though he was, he must go. Goat meat was cooking in the pot and Yaba was pounding millet in readiness for the evening meal, her song setting the rhythm of the work, when he'd slipped away, walking into the bush, seeking a particular hollow tree which Ikpoom knew to be an opening to the Other World. Sitting beside it in a trance, waiting to be drawn into the hollow and down the tunnel, he'd received what seemed like a blow on the back of the head and felt himself spiralling into blackness. Everything that had happened since then more or less fitted Ikpoom's description of the spirit journey to the Other World—the trials and torments in various parts of the tunnel, the arrival at a shore and the crossing of the Great Water.

A dog padded out of the fog—a short-haired, pink and brown animal. Rainbow addressed it respectfully. 'If, perchance, you are my Orisha Animal, I humbly request that you give me a sign.'

The dog shook its head and growled.

'In that case, you're my supper!' Rainbow said, slipping his belt round its neck, his mouth watering at the thought of tender dog meat, which normally was only eaten on feast days.

A dark, squat Being rose out of the ground and spread its black wings with a strange cry. 'Jasus, you gave me a fright!'

The bat—for that was surely what it was—nodded at the dog. 'Paddy would have come when I whistled, but it's thanking you I am, all the same, for holding him.' He climbed out of the hole from which he had emerged and placed some kind of metal lid over it.

Rainbow said, 'This dog is my next meal.'

'Holy Mother of God! Eat Paddy! Surely to God that's a mortal sin!'

Rainbow's grip tightened on the belt.

'Only one way to settle this,' Bat said. It searched the many pockets of its heavy, dark cape till it found a round metal object. Rainbow eyed it, wondering if it was a charm of some kind.

'Heads or tails?' Bat enquired.

Rainbow considered the matter. The brain was a delicacy, but the rump had the best meat on it.

'Tails,' he said, producing his knife to kill the animal and cut it in half.

'Woah! Hold up!' Bat cried.

At that moment the animal under dispute spotted a rat, broke free and charged after it.

Bat laughed. 'So much for your supper, my shaberoon!'

'Are you a spirit guide?' Rainbow enquired. I seek Nataxale, the Dust Devil.'

'Very dry spirits is it? Gin yer after, is it? Sounds like Mother Cleary you're wanting …down St Peter's Lane.'

'Is that the abode of Nataxale, the Dust Devil?'

'You got me there, Sambo. From round here, is he? Dawson's the only dust yard I knows of in these parts.'

Rainbow examined Bat more closely. His skin was Other Worldly, like King George's—like the mushrooms which grew in the underground caves near his village. How did he himself appear to Bat, Rainbow wondered. Ikpoom had told him the spirits would seem human to him only because he saw them with human eyes. 'Everything appears only in masquerade,' Ikpoom had said.

≈

Rainbow's hand was on Bat's arm, detaining him. 'You must take me to the Dust Devil.'

'Go to Hell!' Bat exclaimed, shaking him off and crossing himself.

'Hell? Where is that?'

'You can find your own effin' way without my help, I'm quite sure of that!'

Bat wanted his dance performed. That was it. Ikpoom had made Rainbow learn the dances of many, many creatures so that he could call up an animal spirit or appease one at a moment such as this. High-pitched cries pulsated from his throat as he swooped around Bat, gradually becoming another bat, letting it know that bats and men were interchangeable beings because they were both manifestations of the One Great Spirit; only the masquerade was different.

Bat edged away. 'Gawd save us! Where did you escape from?'

He took to his heels, the dog joining him and trotting beside him.

'Come back!' Rainbow implored.

Oh, well. Spirits could be fickle and temperamental. Ikpoom had told him as much.

≈

Cold and hungry, he wandered the streets. Disorientated by the fog, he found himself back at the steps where he had alighted from the boat. He groaned in despair. The water had receded, exposing three more steps. What hope was there if even here, even in the Other World, the rivers were drying up? He slumped on the top step, overcome by grief, thinking of the utter belief in him he'd seen in Yaba's eyes, thinking of his little Obobo tossing, and burning with fever. Every tiny downward creep of the water was his son's life ebbing away.

2

A woman's cracked voice intoned, 'Chestnuts all 'ot, a penny a score!'

A boy's sharp cry, a man's hoarse shout:

'Three a penny, Yarmouth bloaters!'

'Fine warnuts! Fine war-rr-nuts!'

By the light of the flickering flames around the square, Rainbow watched the market in progress. Everything in the Other World was so different. There was so much he didn't understand. And yet he was reminded of home. The spluttering brands beside each market stall were like the camp-fires lit by the herdsmen to keep the lions away.

≈

Another of the large animals he'd seen earlier clattered into the square, pulling an enclosed kind of cart. His eyes brimming with new sights, Rainbow stepped into the middle of the road, straight into the path of the horse. A running boy collided with him, knocking him sideways.

Cries of, 'The boy saved him! The boy saved the darkie!' were replaced by angry shouts.

'That's him! That's the little monkey what stole my fruit!'

Rainbow saw the boy who was really a monkey jump up, his wizened, old-young face pale with fear. 'No I nivver!'

He turned out his pockets and flapped the loose ends of his ragged shirt. 'I ain't got no apple... no fruit... See!'

His pursuer towered above him, mopping his brow with a large red handkerchief.

'It weren't me, mister, I swear! 'Sides, where's the hevidence. There ain't none, see.'

'Well... ' said the man uncertainly.

'We'd have seen, Ned, if he'd chucked anyfink away.'

'Aye, let the lad go. Saved the Ethiope, he did. Regular little hero.'

'S'pose,' said the costermonger, giving the boy one final glare before turning and trudging back to his stall.

≈

The on-lookers were dispersing. Rainbow stared intently at the boy.

'Monkey? Did they call you Monkey?'

'Maybe. And a reglar 'ero, too. A person what's a reglar 'ero usually gets rewarded wiv a pie.'

Rainbow remembered how King George conducted these affairs. 'But I have no trinkets or beads to barter for a pie.'

The boy stood on one leg, looking him up and down. 'We'll find a way, guv, don't you worry. You stick wiv me and we'll do all right.'

Rainbow beamed with pleasure. 'Little Monkey, my Orisha Animal. You have come at last!'

'Jacko's my name,' the boy said, blinking uncertainly.

≈

A young blood, dressed in violet, was rapping the side of a coach with his silver-topped cane.

'A florin for being bumped about in this tumbrel! Sixpence and count yourself lucky.'

'A florin,' growled the coachman, alighting and facing the dandy.

'Why a fellow'd fare better in a swill cart!'

'A florin,' repeated the coachman doggedly.

'Fight you for it. A florin or nothing.'

'Done!' the coachman readily agreed, rolling up his sleeves with massive hands to reveal forearms like a blacksmith's.

≈

Word spread that a fight was on and a crowd soon encircled the two combatants. The toff, as Jacko called him, made a small bow to Rainbow and handed him his cane, his immaculate white kid gloves and violet top-hat. Then, removing his velvet, cut-away coat handed that to him too before turning to face the burly coachman.

Rainbow knew how important a ritual exchange of gifts was in establishing a friendly relationship with strangers. What, he wondered, could he give in return to a fellow shaman, for there could be no doubting that was what he was. Clearly he had come on a similar mission to seek out and vanquish an evil spirit responsible for bringing some misfortune to his village. Rainbow passed the silver-topped cane and gloves to Jacko, rammed the hat onto his own head, then put on the coat, glad of its warmth. In buttoning the coat, Rainbow's hand brushed against something in the pocket of his baggy, seaman's trousers. He pulled out two apples.

Jacko grinned. 'Just thought you might be hungry, guv.'

Rainbow dropped them back into his pocket.

Jacko stood, hands on hips, head to one side, looking up at Rainbow.

'If yer could only see yerself, guv! Toff's coat, high collar an' all, an' no crabshells on yer feet!'

'Crabshells?'

'Gallies, boots. Where yer been all yer life?'

≈

Standing with fists raised, resplendent in a brocade waistcoat, the toff squared up to the coachman who had stripped to the waist, baring a thick, muscular torso. The toff, although of slighter build, was obviously well-tutored in the art of fisticuffs. He easily ducked the coachman's wild swings and eluded his attempts to come to close quarters, while delivering punishing blows to his opponent's face and body. The evil spirit was now bleeding from nose and mouth and breathing heavily. A thumping blow to the side of the head dropped it to one knee. It remained there.

'Nuff!' it panted.

They shook hands. The crowd fanned out amongst the stalls again. A young woman, her breasts pushed high, leant out of the coach. She had some kind of head-dress of bright parrot feathers. This must be the shaman's Orisha Animal. It gripped the edge of the window with long, red, parrot claws and squawked.

'You've bleedin' forgot all about me, 'aven't you?'

The shaman laughed and threw her a leather pouch which chinked in flight.

'Some other time, Polly.'

She softened. 'Any time, Cap'n Trevellyn, sir... Arthur. Whenever you please.' And she dwelt on the word 'please'.

Arthur Trevellyn waved a friendly hand, sucked his knuckles and strolled over to where Rainbow stood. He surveyed Rainbow with amused eyes.

'Why, damn me if people won't be askin' who's your tailor!'

Rainbow held out the two apples, one in each hand. Arthur took them, tossed one to Jacko and bit deeply into the other.

'Fair exchange!' he said through a mouthful of apple and laughed again. 'Violet's not quite the cheese any more, don't you know.'

Jacko said, 'You can't 'alf sling the mauleys, sir! Gave 'im a pastin' and no mistake!' And he danced around, throwing imaginary punches, re-enacting the fight.

'Oughta be celebrated wiv an 'ot pie, wouldn't you say, sir?'

'Capital idea!'

They moved piewards, the two shamans side by side, Rainbow wriggling inside his coat, revelling in the slipperiness of the silk lining; behind him, Jacko swaggering with the silver-topped cane and fancy gloves, nose in the air. Arthur stopped and looked Rainbow up and down again.

'No, I can't let you do it! Why, damn me, they'd drum me out of Fitz's if they heard I'd let you appear in that coat without the matching boots!'

Clasping Rainbow round the shoulder, he waggled a finely booted foot at Jacko.

'Lucky for you I've got big feet. Pull, boy! Pull'

≈

Rainbow clicked the heels of his newly-acquired boots together, wondering if that was how it felt to have hooves. He'd never worn anything on his feet before. In trying out a few experimental shuffles and stamps he felt something heavy in his pocket—the same pocket in which he'd found the apples. Miraculously, out came exactly the right gift to make in return for the boots—a silver fob watch. He presented it to his fellow shaman with a bow. A quick look flashed between Arthur and Jacko. Clearly he was wishing his own Orisha Animal could conjure up gifts like that when required.

'Splendid! Absolutely, splendid!' Arthur said, slapping himself with glee. 'Why, it even has my name engraved on it!'

Jacko coughed and grinned sheepishly.

The pieman said, 'I got beef pies, mutton pies, fish pies, eel pies, rabbit pies, apple pies, currants, rhubarb.'

''Ot eel pie, if you please, sir.'

Arthur turned to Rainbow. 'And how about our sartorial friend here?'

' 'E'll 'ave the eel,' said Jacko, prancing about with delight at his own joke.

'Toss you for 'em' Arthur challenged the pieman.

'You young gentlemen's all the same,' the pieman grumbled, but he agreed.

Arthur fished in his waistcoat pocket and produced a round metal object like the one Bat had.

'Heads or tails?' he challenged the pieman.

'But there is no dog! Where is the dog?' Rainbow wanted to know.

Monkey explained that Coin would decide whether the pies were to be a gift or not.

'Ah! The same as Benge!' Rainbow exclaimed, relieved at finding something familiar at last.

Jacko shook his head. 'What's all this 'ere bongo talk?'

Rainbow explained that Benge was an oracle like Coin. When important decisions were to be made, a cockerel was fed the magic poison, Benge. Sometimes the bird lived, sometimes it died, just as Coin chose to land one way up or the other when questions were put to it.

'Have you two quite finished?' Arthur demanded with mock severity.

He flipped the coin in the air, caught it in the same hand and smacked it onto his other wrist.

'Heads!' the pieman called.

Arthur lifted his hand to let the pieman see. 'Bad luck!'

'And I'll have a rabbit pie,' Arthur said.

'You an army cap'n'?' Jacko asked.

Arthur studied his white stockinged feet, which were rapidly acquiring a greyish tinge. 'Was. Seems we're not needed now we've seen off Bonaparte.'

'I'd like to be a soldier,' Jacko said. 'I could be a drummer boy.'

Arthur considered him with a grave expression. 'Could a street sparrow stand the discipline?'

'Monkey,' Rainbow corrected him.

'I could stand three square meals a day and no mistake.'

Rainbow turned up the collar of his violet coat and smiled at the victorious shaman.

'I expect you'll soon be crossing the Great Water, back to the other side now you've vanquished your foe.'

Arthur blinked in surprise. 'Er… Yes. Vauxhall Bridge gets me to my club… And that's where I should be now.'

He retrieved his silver-topped cane from Jacko and raised it in salute. 'Good luck to you both.'

Barefoot, he strode over to where the coachman was consoling himself with a tankard of ale, and where a florin and a pair of well-worn boots changed possession.

≈

With a mixture of envy and admiration Rainbow watched him go. 'I haven't even found my foe yet.'

Jacko admired the white kid gloves on his hands. Already they boasted a close acquaintance with eel pie, snot and a several varieties of street grime. 'You lookin' to get even with some bloke? What's he done, then? Somefink horrible, I bet.'

'He has caused my people suffering.'

'It's a when-debtor, that's what it is.'

'What's that? You must teach me.'

'You know guv, like they knows they're going to pay for what they done, but they don't know when exactly, so they're scared up somefink awful.'

'I see,' said Rainbow, glad he had such a knowledgeable Orisha Animal on his side.

'I was the George's interpreter for three years, you know. Now you will have to be my interpreter.'

'Got somewhere to sleep tonight, guv?'

'No. Do you know a good place?'

'Do I? I'll say I do! King 'o the Kips, that's me!'

≈

Jacko led the way down narrow lanes, past gaslights flaring over scraps of meat on butchers' slabs, past dens reeking with frying fish and barrows displaying nothing above a farthing. A little further on, Jacko stopped beside the entrance to an open yard in which an immense copper cauldron crouched on top of a brick-lined furnace.

'Oysters,' Jacko said. 'Native Pearls, Jerseys, Old Baileys, and whelks, of course. Boilings fourpence a bushel.'

He touched the cauldron, then placed a hand flat against the side of the furnace. 'Feel it. Stays 'ot all night.'

≈

They settled down, their backs to the warm bricks. Jacko pulled out a clay pipe and filled it with a pungent mixture from a small rusty box.

'Mundungus,' he said, in answer to Rainbow's stare. 'Horse shit, tea leaves… even got a bit o' baccy in it, this time… cigar butt a toff threw down. Strand's a good place for 'em, outside theatres, anywhere your toff's go.'

He sucked on it noisily for a while, before offering it to Rainbow.

≈

Rainbow puffed quietly on the pipe. So much had happened since he landed and not much of it made sense. He pressed his back against the warm bricks. Ikpoom hadn't warned him it would be as cold as this. Jacko's knees and elbows, Rainbow noticed, were like hard, black pads—a vestige, perhaps, of his monkey form. His thoughts slid towards Yaba. How many fingers' width had the sun moved, in real time, since he'd left her pounding the millet? He thought of her breasts rising and falling with each lift of the pounding-stick; and of her body, greased with fat, gleaming in the firelight when she danced. His stomach knotted in panic. What if he failed her?

Monkey nudged him. 'Cheer up, guv! We'll do all right together, you and me, won't we, guv?'

'Yes, I think we will.'

Jacko let out a sigh, snuggled closer and fell instantly asleep. Rainbow took off his violet coat and put it over the small curled up figure. Why Monkey had chosen to masquerade as a child he didn't know, but a child he undoubtedly was.

≈

The fog had cleared. A faint flush was invading the sky. Rainbow had been dreaming again that he was hiding in the reeds beside the river and that the Ijeru warriors were close, very close, and that …But he didn't want to think about that. Distractions like that weakened your shamanic powers. Only the greatest concentration and dedication enabled a shaman to struggle free of the Mortal World.

Jacko stirred and stretched. 'Effin good kip and no mistake. Told you I was the King o' Kips, didn't I? Come on, then, if you wants a tightener.'

Neither Ikpoom nor King George, Rainbow realised, had prepared him for conversations with Orisha Animals.

'Do we go to seek my foe, Nataxale?'

'Not right now, guv. Gotta make sure of our tightener, see.'

'What's that?'

'Listen, I'm telling you, we'll miss a good blow out if we don't look lively.'

'What do you mean?'

'Don't you know nuffink?'

'You must teach me.'

Jacko explained that the swill cart came round 'his street' at seven, which meant the skivvies and under-cooks in the big houses put out the scraps and leavings at about six. Since it would take about an hour to walk there, they'd need to start out now.

Rainbow nodded eagerly. An hour of walking in his newly acquired boots should hurt quite a lot. They were obviously an ordeal, a test, which shamans visiting the Other World must pass before they could succeed in their mission. Clearly, Arthur, having passed the test, had handed them on to him.

'Least the fog's away,' Jacko remarked. 'It's a help, though, when you wants to give the law the slip. Been on the street a two year or more and they ain't nibbed me yet.'

'These toffs you talk about... they must be very high up in the Other World.'

'They lives in a world of their own, if you asks me.'

'What about the toffs who are above King George, even?'

'Don't know who that might be, unless it's God. And gawd knows where he lives. Got a son what goes by the name of R Redeemer. Owns a pawn shop somewhere.'

≈

Jacko chattered away as they hurried through the grey, early morning streets, tangling now and then with little eddies of workers on their way to, or coming off, shift.

'I was a flue faker afore this,' Jacko told Rainbow. 'Lord love us...

a chimney sweep! Till I runs away, that is. Couldn't take no more beatings.'

Rainbow could hardly believe it. 'Who would dare beat such as you?'

'My master, for one.'

Rainbow was shocked that any shaman could behave like that towards his Orisha Animal.

'Got lost down a flue once. Went in from the top. Like a long dark tunnel, it was, wiv side bits a boy might go into by mistake.'

'Do you mean to say,' Rainbow demanded with rising anger, 'That your master sent you down the tunnel without going himself?'

'Always.'

'He must have been from the Ijeru. Scoundrels, murderers, the lot of them.'

'Thought I was dead when I dropped out at the bottom. Everyfink white. Shapes like ghosts. Only it was sheets to keep off the soot, see… Does your's wash off, guv?'

'My what?'

'The soot colour. Does it come off?'

'Maybe it fades when you're dead. I'm not sure.' Everyone here seems faded, Rainbow thought. Even the shaman, Arthur. How long must he have been here to have become so pale? It was a frightening thought.

≈

They reached Jacko's street. A tour round the 'dumpins' in the back lane proved most rewarding. Crusts of white bread, an apple which was hardly rotten at all on one side, a pool of rice pudding enriched with potato peelings, bones with meat on them and marrow inside them, and cheese rinds and cake crumbs soaked in gravy.

They squatted between the stone walls of two garbage enclosures.

'What a feast!' Jacko exclaimed.

Rainbow thanked his Orisha Animal for providing for him so magnificently. He could not recall having eaten as well as this since starting on his spirit journey. Not that he remembered very much about large parts of it.

Two boys, or likenesses of boys, bigger than Monkey, appeared in the lane and began rummaging through the garbage.

Jacko jumped up, bristling. 'This is my territory. Clear off!'

'Who says?'

Jacko hauled Rainbow to his feet. 'He says.'

The boys slunk away.

Rainbow said, 'In my country we offer strangers hospitality.'

'Yeah, they'll get a dose of 'ospital all right if I sees 'em again.'

Jacko made parcels of the scraps they hadn't eaten and handed them to Rainbow.

'Usually I scoffs it all down where I finds it. Can't keep nuffink on you... just gets took off you, see.'

Rainbow said, 'And now we must find Dawson's Yard... the place Bat told me about. He said it was near a place called Hell.'

≈

The gates of the yard were locked. Peering through the rusty bars, Rainbow could see heaps of dust and ash and various griddles and sieves lying about, but no sign of life.

'It's closed,' said a voice behind them.

The woman put down her basket of washing and drew her shawl around her ample body. 'On account of the clay pits being all worked out... 'Ere, keep away from my basket yer little basket! I knows yer game.'

'This is Prince Bongo from far Ethiope,' Jacko said. 'I'm his interrupter, don't you know.'

'What sort of animal's that?'

'I tells yer what he says.' He pointed to a red and white spotted neckerchief in her basket. 'And he was saying as 'ow a gift o' that kingsman might just stop 'im from turning yer into a toad.'

She seized Jacko by the ear. 'Little monkey! He said no such thing! Repent! Repent of your sins! I have seen the light and you, too, can be saved, for God is love!' She gave Jacko's ear a twist. 'What is God?'

'Ouch! Leggo! Love, misses, love!'

She released his ear and wagged a fat finger at them. 'Keep on as you are and you'll both go straight to Hell!'

Rainbow touched his hat in the way he'd seen the George do it.

'Much obliged, good lady, much obliged. Come on, Little Monkey, it seems we're on the right path.'

≈

They walked on.

'She mentioned clay pits,' Rainbow said.

'They mixes dust wiv clay to make bricks. Soot, too, sometimes.'

'In Mwanza we use straw for that.'

They reached an open space of trees and grass rather like the savannah that was familiar to Rainbow. Nearby, a Being was standing on a box, vigorously and loudly addressing nobody.

Rainbow asked, 'Can you tell us the quickest way to Hell?'

Drink, the preacher informed them. Drink was the surest way to Hell, and he pressed a tract upon them.

Inexplicably, the savannah was full of authorities on the best way to get to Hell. One, who impressed Rainbow with his sincerity on the matter, assured them that, while children worked in mines and mills and whole families starved, hell was here and now.

'Hell upon Earth! A living Hell!' he shouted, thumping his staff upon the ground. 'Hell is here and now, all around us and yet we hear not the bitter cry of the poor!'

If this was the place called Hell, Rainbow thought, his adversary could be any one of these Beings who passed by in masquerade, staring at him.

Through the trees of the savannah Rainbow saw a high, ornate building. It had a large window at the front in which was a picture made of glass. Around the head of the person in the picture glowed an aura like the one he had twice seen radiating from Ikpoom.

'Everything is connected,' Ikpoom would insist, again and again. 'When you learn to connect with the light of the universe, then you will see through the darkness and the shamanic light inside you will shine out of you—imperceptible to human eyes, but visible to all spirits of earth and sky and sea.'

Once, when Ikpoom was in a trance so deep that he seemed to have stopped breathing, Rainbow, watching beside him, saw Ikpoom's crown of light. Vibrating from the aura was a feeling of immense peace.

The second experience was when he and Ikpoom had started down the tunnel together, on a journey to the Other World. But Rainbow had dropped behind and Ikpoom had forged ahead. Just as the tunnel began to open out, the aura had blazed forth, surrounding Ikpoom's head in dazzling light.

Rainbow drew closer, looking up at the shaman whose Orisha Animal, a small woolly beast, lay at his feet.

'Interested?'

The Being who addressed him wore black. Its legs were hard and black and shiny up to the knee. It rubbed its hands together in the manner of the black dung-beetle.

Rainbow bowed. 'Who is that?' he asked, pointing at the glass picture.

'That is Jesus Christ, the son of God,' the dung-beetle replied.

'Oh, so this is the pawn shop, then?'

'Goodness me! The very idea!'

'But you said that was Hizu Kiristi.'

'It is, indeed, Jesus Christ,' replied the dung-beetle, who seemed to have difficulty pronouncing the name. 'God gave his only begotten son that we might live. We are saved by the blood of Christ.'

Rainbow nodded. He understood about human sacrifice and how the blood must wet the ground as if it was rain.

'So it always rains here, then?'

The dung-beetle looked startled. 'Well, quite a lot, anyway. But to return to what I was saying ...'

Rainbow was intrigued to learn that this god had sacrificed his own son in order to atone for the disobedience of mortal men.

The dung-beetle gestured towards the entrance. 'Come inside.'

≈

Stone columns rose from the ground, then fanned out overhead to meet and cross paths with the spreading canopy of the other columns. Every column, Rainbow realised, was connected to every other column by the criss-crossing pattern above his tilted head. Whoever had planned this place knew the truth.

'Tell me, this Hizu Kiristi... how many brothers did he have?'

'None. He is God's only begotten son.'

'And how many wives does his father have?'

'Gracious me! None!'

'In my country a man is measured by the number of wives and sons he has. Yet, you tell me this god has no wives and only one son, whose mother wasn't married!'

'Well, really! This is disgraceful! Heresy, treason, utter filth! Leave this holy church at once! Leave or I shall have you arrested! You should be thrashed, sir! Yes, thrashed!'

'But, I... '

'Go!'

Rainbow tried to placate the beetle. 'May you eat dung all your days and... '

'Go!' it screamed, purple in the face, stamping a black, shiny leg.

≈

Rainbow leant against a tree, wondering where he'd gone wrong. It was just as well. It showed how much he needed his Orisha Animal. The moment Monkey left, things went awry. Could it be that Jacko helped more than one shaman at a time? Or, maybe, monkey-like, he simply grew bored with one thing and went darting off to another. Perhaps Jacko might be lured back by a performance of the monkey dance. Usually, Ikpoom had been more miserly with praise than a field mouse with its store of grain, but Rainbow's monkey dance had earned his grudging approval. He removed his boots, realising as he did so that they could serve as the rattles he would need. Into one boot he poured a handful of sand—the wind sifting through forest leaves, the hissing of a snake, blood singing, branches shaking; into the other boot he dropped five pebbles—the underlying rhythm of life, the heartbeat of a monkey in repose or in the chase.

≈

Removing his violet coat and his top-hat, he placed them on the ground and began to dance, lolling, swinging, twirling, tumbling, squatting, leaping. A crowd collected. They cheered and gasped and laughed. When Rainbow stopped there was prolonged applause. Coins showered upon his upturned hat. Jacko appeared, grinned at Rainbow, gathered the coins on the ground and took the hat around those at the back, cajoling them to part with their money.

'I'll wager you've not seen the likes o' that afore. Why, performed in front of King George, he has! And King Bongo of Ethiope, too!'

≈

Jacko held out the hat, heavy with coins, to Rainbow.

'I knew you'd come,' Rainbow said.

'How much of the takings does your sideman get, then?'

'All of it, of course. They must greatly respect your powers, Monkey, to have paid tribute with so many oracles.'

'You're not makin' fun o' me?'

'Certainly not.'

Jacko stared into the hat. 'Nobody ever give me that much before.'

≈

They walked on, Rainbow hobbling badly.

'Boots troublin' you, guv?'

'I think I forgot to remove the pebbles,' Rainbow beamed.

Jacko jingled the contents of his pockets. 'We're flush, guv, and no mistake! We're going to get some decent scran in our bellies tonight and our 'eads down in a cushy lurk'

'Where do you think Nataxale is?'

≈

From the far side of a belt of trees drifted the sounds of blaring horns, voices raised in urgent command and the general din of a battle. At first, when the Ijeru had attacked in the dead of night, Rainbow had thought it was a bad dream. He'd called for his mother, but she wasn't there. The shouting, the running feet, strange men with painted faces, half crouching, with spears in their hands; his uncle, Koigi, screaming like Rainbow had never heard a man scream before; himself running, running for the concealing safety of the river reeds; the ground wet with blood; calling for his mother…

'And they got freak shows an' clowns, guv! An' all manner of wonders and wittals to make yer mouth water!'

'What?'

'The fair, guv! The fair! What are we waiting for?'

≈

Rainbow and Jacko plunged into the river of jostling, heaving bodies which flowed between the stalls and tents, a rabble as turbulent and as loud as the rapids at Iziwala after the rains.

'Gingerbread! Buy my gingerbread!' a freckled man with ginger hair was calling as he displayed little ginger replicas of himself. 'Hot as bricks, and rumble inside you like a barrow!'

Monkey made a ritual exchange of oracles for these effigies. There followed similar exchanges for jam tarts, a toffee apple and a hot potato. Then he was tugging Rainbow towards a stall on which stood a selection of clockwork toys. Rainbow understood the principal on which they worked because King George had a kilock which worked the same way and which every morning would make a terrifying noise which set the dogs barking and the hens and Chief Chimu's wives clucking. Jacko's eyes were fixed on a drummer-boy who beat his drum in little jerky movements.

'How much? ' Jacko asked.

The man behind the stall picked it up. He seemed to have been surrounded by clockwork things for so long that he moved in the same way.

'Too much for the likes of you. Beat it!'

He was right. Jacko's pockets were almost empty of oracles. The longing in Jacko's eyes was so great that Rainbow, remembering how that admirable shaman, Arthur, had conducted affairs, said, 'Toss you for it!'

The clockwork man slowly looked him over, his head travelling up and down in a series of separate movements.

'Take your swell's coat and boots if you lose. And here's my hand on it.'

They clasped hands.

'Only it's not me you fight,' said the clock-work man, 'But him.' He pointed to a hefty young bruiser with a broken nose and cauliflower ears who had been lounging at the corner of the stall.

'Fight?' Rainbow gasped.

'That's what you've given your hand on this very minute. First to toss the other to the ground.'

Already people were linking arms, forming an arena. The bruiser stepped forward, sneering at Rainbow through broken teeth.

'You've been had, guv,' Jacko whispered. 'Too late to back out now.'

The clockwork man laughed callously. 'Rule one—there ain't no rules. Anything goes.'

He raised his voice and announced importantly, 'Begin when I hollers 'time'.'

Rainbow kicked his opponent in the stomach, doubling him up.

'Hoi!' the clockwork man shouted. 'That's not playing the game!'

'But you said 'time'.'

'I did not!'

'What did you say, then?'

'I said begin when I hollers 'time'.'

Again Rainbow kicked the bruiser, this time in the crotch. He went down groaning and didn't look likely to get up. Jacko snatched the toy drummer-boy and darted off. The crowd, reckoning they'd had a good laugh, if nothing else, let Rainbow through to follow after him.

≈

When Rainbow caught up with Jacko, the boy's face was smeared with a variety of sticky foods. Nearby, a person was bawling, 'This way! This way! Feast your eyes on the Wild Man of Borneo what would like to feast on you! Your genuine cannibal, ladies and gents! This way! This way!'

'I know how to get in free,' Jacko said. 'Quick! Down here.'

Jacko stuffed the toy drummer-boy into his pocket then stood with his back to the tent, his eyes darting to left and right. There was a sound of rending canvas. Next moment they were inside the tent. Jacko leant against a metal door which swung open. His clutching hand pulled Rainbow in with him.

'Frigging hell!' Jacko exclaimed. 'I'm getting out of here!'

Drooling, leering faces were pressed to the bars of the cage. Jacko had said there'd be freaks. One of them, with a red bulbous nose like a diseased yam, blew quantities of snot into a cloth which, unbelievably, he then made a small parcel of and returned to his pocket. Rainbow was suddenly aware that Jacko had gone and that there was only one other spectator in the room with him, a dark-skinned man sitting cross-legged on a pile of straw. He was naked except for a grass skirt, a feathered head-dress and a necklace of human teeth.

'Who are your ancestors?' Rainbow asked in his own language.

'Come again, mate.'

Rainbow addressed him in English. 'Are you a shaman, too?'

'Sham? Who, me? Just bugger off!'

Through the rent in the canvas Jacko was beckoning urgently. Puzzled, Rainbow exited.

'That was a close 'un, guv,' Jacko panted when they'd put a good distance between themselves and the Wild Man of Borneo. 'Thought you was going to get all ate up.'

'I was certainly glad they were caged, Jacko. I wouldn't want them roaming free.'

'What are we waiting for, then, guv? There's plenty more to see.'

≈

Flushed with their triumphs at the stalls and booths, Rainbow and Jacko were swept along by a current of revellers to burst out on the edge of the fair. It began to drizzle. Rainbow tilted his head skywards, letting the drops splash over his face, tasting the moisture on his lips. How long had it been since he'd felt rain wet his skin, seen it darkening the ground and shining on leaves and grass?

He turned excitedly to Monkey. 'Do you think this means it's raining on the other side of the Great Water?'

'Dunno, guv. Sometimes I walks from one part of the city to anuvver and the pavemints is wet one place and not the next.'

'But it could be a sign, couldn't it?'

A white carriage, picked out in gold, drawn by a matching pair of pale animals like the one that had nearly knocked him down, and that Jacko had told him were called 'horses' pulled up. Out stepped a toff even more finely arrayed than Arthur Trevellyn. On his head was a tall, powdered wig and his face was powdered white. Rainbow's breath whistled through his teeth. Masks representing evil spirits were always painted white. White was the colour of evil.

'The devil take it!' drawled the dandy. 'Curse this damnably deuced rain!'

The evil spirit was cursing the life-giving rain, trying to make it stop. Who else could it be but the Dust Devil? Roaring with pent-up rage, Rainbow threw himself upon the vile enemy, rolling him in the mud, punching him, strangling him. Men in blue were running towards them from two directions.

'That's the treasonous heretic!' yelled the dung-beetle, pointing at Rainbow.

'That be the assassin!' shouted the dandy's footman.

'It's the Peelers, guv! Run! Leggo 'is throat and run!'

But Rainbow didn't even hear him. Jacko flung himself down beside him and bit his hand. With a cry of pain Rainbow let go. Jacko screamed into his ear, 'Run! Run!'

Rainbow allowed himself to be dragged by Jacko towards the anonimity of the crowd which squeezed and swayed between the rows of booths.

'Bad luck,' Jacko said when they had reached the safety of the throng. 'You nearly got 'im.'

'When will I have another chance like that? Tell me that, Monkey!'

Jacko shrugged. 'What I will tell yer is that we don't want to sleep on the streets tonight, not in this rain… Uhh!' And Jacko was sick over Rainbow's boots.

He stared at the vomit regretfully. 'That's the nuts I had and there's the… Oh, no! Look at me drummer-boy! It's frigging broke in the chase.'

He held out the headless, armless body and let it fall to the ground.

The drizzle had turned to a downpour and Rainbow was shivering.

'That Bat person you was on about, guv… Irish was he? Old soldier what works down the sewers now?'

'I don't know about these things, Monkey.'

'Well, I think I knows him. Muldoon's his name.'

≈

Jacko explained that Muldoon had told about a tupenny dosshouse or 'netherskon' he used in this part of London. But, when it rained, it was packed out and, if you hadn't been there before, you had to get a regular to speak for you and say you weren't the kind of person who would get drunk and start a fight, or slit the throat of the person sleeping next to you.

'I just hope he don't remember what I did last time I saw him.'

'And what was that, Monkey?'

'I tops up his bottle of grog with piss… So he wouldn't know as how I'd taken a pull at it, see. Nivver mind, maybe he nivver twigged.'

3

The nethersken was the first house Rainbow had been inside since his arrival in the Other World. The window which opened and shut, the staircase which led to a second layer of rooms... there were so many unimaginable marvels. Even mind you Ikpoom had impressed upon him that, here, he must expect things to be strange and inexplicable, he hadn't expected anything quite like this. Rainbow had supposed that only exalted beings inhabited places like this. Jacko assured him, however, that, when it rained heavily, ordinary people sometimes came into houses, too. And, to Rainbow's delight and excitement and Jacko's disgust, it had rained almost incessantly for the last two days and nights.

≈

Muldoon had taken a lot of persuading that Rainbow wasn't a dangerous maniac. The most convincing point in his favour had been the bottle of rum which Jacko had eased from the clutch of a drunk asleep in a back alley. While Jacko questioned Muldoon about something called the Peninsular Campaign—some recent Other Worldly war in which Bat had taken part—Rainbow imagined himself describing to Yaba all the wonders he had seen.

≈

The smell of toasted herring pervaded the smoky room. A large blackened cauldron hung over a smouldering fire. Barefoot children dodged between huddled adults.

Jacko prodded Rainbow in the ribs. 'Where've you slipped off to, guv?'

'What?'

'You was miles away.'

'Oh.'

'Reckon it's done,' Jacko said.

An assortment of strings and cords disappeared over the rim of the pot into its belching greyish waters. Jacko pulled on one of the strings and lifted out his two kid gloves, each knotted round a lump of penny dumpling. Bat opened the wings of his cape to dip a cracked mug into the cauldron.

'Nigh on a hundred dinners boiled in here the day.' he remarked, sucking nosily at the brownish broth. 'Rather be down the sewers, though. I stay down for days at a time now my Mary's gone… Not when it rains like this, though. Floods've drowned many a good sewerman. Yes, there's a lot goes on underground folk up top don't know about.' He chinked a bag around his waist. 'You'd be surprised what finds its way down a sewer.' Inserting thumb and forefinger into his mouth, he pulled out his teeth. 'Take these for instance… '

Rainbow was impressed, Neither the George nor Ikpoom had been able to do that.

Bat dipped his mug again.

'Rat drowned in there earlier,' Jacko said.

Bat grunted, unperturbed.

Jacko said, 'Not much difference twixt rat an' rabbit… to eat, I mean. 'Specially if you wait till the skin slides off the tail, that's when they're ready.'

'Where is your dog?' Rainbow wanted to know.

'If it's eating Paddy you're wanting, I've drunk him already… well in a manner o' speaking. The thirst was on me, so I traded him for a bottle of the hard stuff. Helps you forget, so it does.'

'Forget what? Rainbow asked.

'My Mary.'

'A wife?'

'My daughter. Just turned twenty. She was a reason not to get rat-arsed… Well, not totally, I mean.

Jacko said, 'What happened?'

'The wasting disease. She'd been fading for several years. Fading until she was no more.'

Jacko broke the silence. 'We're close to mucked out, guv. Three browns an a fadge is all we got left.'

Bat sucked in his broth and laughed mirthlessly. 'It's the ha'penny hang for you.'

In the basement, Rainbow had seen him with the other bats in tightly packed rows, hanging from straps, swaying slightly, mumbling and cursing.

'I wouldn't advise it,' Bat said. 'Not if you've got the extra penny.

Hard choice, though, between booze and a bed.'

≈

At Monkey's suggestion Rainbow had danced in the street and Jacko had seemed satisfied with the tribute of oracles placed in the hat he took round the crowd. But when the rain had started they'd earned next to nothing from it.

'He's the dabbest hand at the footwork I ever did see.'

Rainbow smiled. He felt deeply privileged to be asked so frequently to perform the dance of the Monkey. 'We shamans are the last humans able to talk with the animals,' Ikpoom had said. 'Indeed, we are the last ones able to talk with all of Nature, the plants, the streams, the air, the rock.'

≈

Bat took a swig from his bottle. 'I'm turning in. Had my fill o' the ha'penny hang, It's a proper bed for me tonight. Want to be sure of a place upstairs away from the leaks. Not that a little damp's anything to sneeze at, not for a sojer... Not that the friggin army wants me anymore.'

'Last time I was in a place like this,' Jacko said, 'I got shoved out of one good spot, then anuvver, till there was only places where the slates was all gawn.' He looked at Rainbow and there was pride and admiration in his voice. 'Won't 'appen this time, though.'

≈

In the crowded, stuffy attic, Rainbow lay on a thin mattress scratching himself. Beside him lay Monkey. In his sleep Jacko seemed so human and so childlike. The knowingness, the quickness of wit, the cunning and toughness all seemed to melt away. Did Orisha Animals dream? Of what spirits and monsters did spirits and monsters dream? Ikpoom had once warned him about the difficulty of returning from that dangerous tunnel, a dream within a dream within a dream.

≈

Rainbow tossed and turned, frustrated that he'd been so close to defeating Nataxale only for the Dust Devil's allies to save him. He'd let the people of his village down; Yaba, Obobo, everyone. He was no more than a useless novice incapable of such a quest.

Jacko stirred.

'Are you awake, Monkey?'

'Mmmm.'

'Do you think the Lord of the Clouds will look favourably on my mission?'

'Mmmm? Mmmm... Mission? One near here. A right ear bashin' and no mistake. Current bun at the end, though.'

Rainbow pondered his Orisha Animal's reply. Many of Ikpoom's most profound teachings were in the form of riddles. He'd have to meditate upon these words.

≈

Obviously, the bugs weren't bothering Monkey. Maybe they didn't bother Orisha Animals. Snails were sliming up the damp wall. Snail had been one of Ikpoom's several Orisha Animals... not that you always had a choice. You could dance an animal's dance and it wouldn't come to you; and then, apparently for no reason, another animal to whom you'd paid no respects would make itself known. Rainbow lay scratching, staring at the snails. If he got another chance to come to grips with Nataxale, he must not fail.

≈

Three slumbering bodies away, Bat was still awake, clutching a bottle of rum, sucking in, long and slow, then exhaling like a surfacing hippopotamus. In... and out. Bat had advised Rainbow and Jacko to do the same—put themselves to sleep with liberal quantities of cheap scoach. So what was the meaning of Bat? Bats could fly successfully in the dark. Wasn't being in the Other World, where everything was so obscure, its true meaning so hidden, like trying to find the way in the dark? Perhaps Bat was a sign that he, Rainbow, might succeed even though so little of the Other World made sense to him.

≈

Rainbow squashed a bug on his arm. He whispered across the huddled shapes whose every breath added to the alcoholic fumes in the air. 'Hey, Bat! Is there anything in these mattresses except bugs?'

'Flock, so they say. And they're right... flocks of vermin... zzrrrrr-rrrrr-zz... whooooo!'

In... and out. In and out. The last pools of the water in the lake, churned grey by thirsty cattle, were disappearing down a huge guzzling crack, zzzzrrzz Nataxale, a scorching, whirling wind, sped across the land, withering everything in his path, raising columns of red dust. Standing in two silent lines, covered from head to foot in the dust, were the people of Rainbow's village. He walked down the avenue of gaunt, motionless figures, greeting each one by name as he passed. They remained silent, their faces expressionless red masks. Only their eyes spoke to him, reproachful, accusing.

'Yaba! Obobo! It's me!'

But they turned their faces from him and joined the others in a long, low, collective moan of despair.

'Whooooo!'

4

The Kentucky Serenaders, who worked the Southwark area, were short of a man. Jacko heard this from a woman in the doss house. They were one of the very first minstrel bands in London, copying the new American style, so Jacko was told.

'What's America?' Jacko had asked.

'Foreign parts,' the woman told him.

Sometimes on a clear day, on a roof amongst the chimney pots, Jake had been able to see for miles around. Foreign Parts was probably all the bits beyond that. Then there was a place named Overseas, or Across the Great Water, as Rainbow called it. The Peninsular War and Napoleon Bonaparte had been in Foreign Parts.

'Might be worth a try,' Jacko said.

'Just the thing for your dark-skinned friend.'

'Why?'

'Because they pretend to be darkies and black their faces, but he's your genuine article.'

'Sounds silly to me,' Jacko said.

'I've heard that the five of them earn up to four shilling a week… each.'

'Sounds like a very good idea to me,' Jacko said, adding, 'When I was blacking my face in the chimneys I never got that much in three years! This afternoon at Southwark Hall did you say?'

≈

Jacko trotted beside Rainbow along cobbled, grey November streets, past dingy terraced houses. Huddled in a doorway was a woman wrapped in a shawl. There was something about her. Jacko's heart lurched. Could it be his mother? She would sit up, smile with joy at seeing him and welcome him into her arms. Then he noticed the empty gin bottle. Even if it was her, she might not recognise him or even care. It wasn't her anyway. Good thing, really… she would only have sent him back to Grimshaw. In fact, he was glad it wasn't her, that's what he told himself. So why had that empty ache started up again? He found he was holding Rainbow's hand. Rainbow didn't disapprove of him or despise him like other people seemed to. Filthy urchin, Godless little bastard, human garbage … being called things like that still hurt, even though he should be used to it by now. But Rainbow seemed to like him and admire him, although Jake couldn't think why. Being praised was a wonderful feeling, like the one and only time he'd sat in a tub of hot water and poured mugs of it over his head and down his back and all over his body. Jacko's heart lurched again. Supposing Rainbow sent him away like his mother had done?

Matthews, the leader of the Kentucky Serenaders, met Jacko and Rainbow outside the hall. Like the other three, his face was blacked up, his lips painted white and made to look much bigger than they really were. He wore white cotton gloves, a cut-away long coat and a battered top hat underneath which was a wig of fuzzy black hair. Matthews introduced them to the banjo player, the fiddler and the tambourine man. 'And I'm on the squeeze box and we all sing a bit.' he said. 'We lost our Mr Bones last week. Can you play the bones?' He waggled his hand like he was rattling bones held between his fingers.

'I can tell the future from the bones,' Rainbow said.

Jacko nudged him with his elbow. 'He means the future looks good for you if you take him on. He's the best dancer in the whole of London town, you know.'

'Well, let's see what you can do then. We'll play and sing 'Dem Happy Days is Just Ober de Hill,' and you dance to it. And then we'll do some patter. No! I think we'll play 'Jump Jim Crow.' The sheet music only came out this year. Now there's a song can whip its weight in wildcats!.'

Jacko said, 'Aren't we going inside, mister? It's cold enough to freeze the balls off a brass monkey.'

'I said meet me outside the hall, not inside it. We're street performers. The difference in the way you sound outdoors and indoors is like chalk and cheese.' Matthews' shrewd eyes roved over Rainbow. 'You don't look right. You don't look anything like a black man should.'

'You seen lots of them, mister? Jacko wanted to know.

'Well, no, but everybody knows what they look like and this isn't it. Your skin's too shiny. Here… rub some of this burnt cork on it. And make your lips bigger with this. And your hair… it's nowhere near wild and woolly enough! Get this wig on.'

The band played and sang, and Rainbow danced.

First on de heel tap,
Den on the toe
Every time I wheel about
I jump Jim Crow.
Wheel about and turn about
En do j's so.
And every time I wheel about,
I jump Jim Crow.

'Again!' Mathews shouted. 'Roll your eyes this time! Don't try and pretend you got a brain, just act natural!'

When the song finished, Mathews said, 'Not bad. With a bit of coaching we might get you looking like the real thing. Now we'll try some patter.' He turned to the other minstrels. 'Jim and Ned, give us the Coon patter, so he can see what's to be done.'

Jim rolled his eyes and fluttered his hands. His voice was loud and unnaturally high. 'Ah is wondrin', Mr Coon, what is de best time to bury a darkie?'

'Why dat queshun sure is hard, Mr Brown. What is de best time to bury a darkie?'

'In de late summer, Mr Coon.'

'An why be dat, Mr Brown?'

'Because it's de best time for blackberrying.'

≈

Matthews said to Rainbow. 'Now you do it. Take the part of Mr Brown, the one Jim was doing.'

Rainbow began, 'I am wondering, Mr Coon, what is the best ….'

No, no!' Mathews screamed. 'I want nigger talk! And roll your eyes for God's sake!'

He stared suspiciously at Rainbow. 'Where did you learn to speak the King's English?'

'From King George of course,' Rainbow replied.

Matthews snatched the wig off Rainbow's head. 'I've had enough of you wasting my time! Be off with you!'

They stopped at a horse-trough so that Rainbow could wash off the make-up.

'I'm worried, Monkey. Were those people all shamans who have failed in their mission and been unable to cross the Great Water back to their home village?'

Jacko was intrigued. His new friend an endless source of wonderment. 'And why would you think that, guv?'

Rainbow explained as best he could that, maybe, the unfortunate men had been here so long that their skin had faded. It was clearly some kind of ritual. They imitated their skins turning dark again to influence the gods into making it really happen, like when you do a dance imitating spearing a buck before you go hunting for one... and like the blood of human sacrifice wetting the earth in imitation of rain. At least it was reassuring that he had been told to go, that they did not think he needed this ritual.

'Not yet, anyway.' Rainbow said.

Jacko laughed with delight. 'Best one yet, guv! Maybe they were just jealous. About you being the real article and all... Look there, guv.' Jake pointed across a piece of waste ground. 'First Guy I've seen this year.'

≈

On top of a conical stack loosely constructed with timber, sat a grotesque figure which swayed and quivered and nodded its head at Rainbow in a jeering, sneering kind of way.

'Aha!' Rainbow bellowed, charging towards it. 'You didn't think I'd find you again so soon, did you?'

He jumped, caught Nataxale by the leg and pulled him from his perch. A boy who had been lurking nearby, watching them suspiciously, took to his heels. Nataxale swung a fist. Rainbow ducked, threw his adversary to the ground and leapt on him.

'Not so brave without your allies, are you?' Rainbow snarled, getting a headlock on Nataxale.

His opponent fought back, jabbing Rainbow in the eye with a piece of straw.

'Guv! Guv! Leg it, guv!'

From the far corner of the waste ground surged an angry mob, headed by the boy who had run off. Brandishing cudgels, they shouted things which were clearly not friendly.

'Papist!'

'Bleedin' Pope's poodle!'

'We'll learn yer to tamper with our bonfire!'

'Trying to save the traitor, Fawkes, he was!'

≈

Sobered by danger, Jacko and Rainbow raced through the streets pursued by the mob. At a corner, Rainbow came to an abrupt halt. In a parallel street, framed by the connecting lane, moving slowly along, antennae protruding, its curling, stripy, gold and brown shell on its back, was a human sized snail, a snail in half-human form.

'Snail!'

Jacko dragged him forward. Reluctantly, Rainbow followed his Orisha Animal through a labyrinth of filthy streets, chased by the yelling horde. They came to a fork in the road.

'We'll split 'em up.' Jacko panted. 'You go that way. Just keep straight on. See you where they join up.' And he darted off.

≈

Rainbow's boots were hampering him, but to stop and pull them off would mean losing his lead over the mob. The road forked again. Which of the two was straight on? He veered left and realised he'd gone the wrong way. Ahead, beyond a long row of railings, the street ended in a high, blank wall. Rainbow sped past the railings. The sun, filtering through the gaps between them, flickered …on-off-on-off, flicker-flicker-flick …like the rapid flapping of wings …his own wings… he was flying, looking down on himself. He could see what the running figure below could not see—that a narrow passage, just before the high wall, would join up with a street which would take him, the hunted him, back to the road he should have been on. Then he fell out of the sky, hit the pavement with a thump, picked himself up and was running again.

≈

He slowed. There was no sound of the mob behind him. He looked back. The street was empty.

'Guv! Over 'ere, guv!'

Jacko was waiting for him on the corner, grinning broadly. 'Reckon we shook 'em off.'

He strutted about like a cockerel. 'Did you ever see such sport? All them people! All chasin' just you and me!'

'Nataxale has many allies.' Rainbow replied, still breathing deeply.

A man shot out of a side street, spotted them, turned and shouted, 'This way! This way! They're right here!'

'Quick, guv, down 'ere!'

But another group was advancing up that way to meet them. They dodged right and right again. On either side of them, in parallel lanes, their pursuers were shouting and calling to one another.

≈

Near a deserted intersection, outside large wooden doors set in a high brick wall, Rainbow heard a cockerel crow.

'Root-a-toot-toot!' it crowed—except it wasn't a cockerel, but a little goblin with a large hooked nose and a hunched back. The glove puppet on the small stage was Exu in different guise, Exu the mischievous God of the Lost Crossroads. There was no mistaking that sly, impish expression. Rainbow had spent weeks, in a taboo state of fasting and sexual abstinence, carving Exu's mask from the wood of the sacred tree. That wicked, leering grin had grown out of the block almost by itself, as if it had been there all the time, waiting to be freed. And now Exu was beckoning to them from his gold and brown striped booth.

'Don't stand there dreaming, guv! Mr Punch could be the saving of us!'

'Is it the Beadle's men you're running from?' Exu squawked.

'Nataxale, the Dust Devil's men.' Rainbow gasped out.

'Ah, I know the Devil well. A horrid, dreadful bogey of a personage… You'll want somewhere to hide, then. Come round the back.'

≈

They squeezed between the wall and the side of the booth and crouched below the stage. Squatting beside them was a big, muscular, freckle-faced woman with an aura of flaming red hair around her head—the snail woman who'd been carrying her load on her back. She wore a faded red tunic and men's trousers and boots. She extended a hand still inside the Punch-Exu creature. 'Carroty Kate's the name.'

Rainbow shook hands with it in the manner King George had taught him.

'And I am Rainbow.'

'And I'm Jacko.'

≈

The interior of the booth, below stage, was lined with glove puppets and various stage props—a small gallows and noose, an assortment of truncheons and staves and miniature hats. There was barely enough room in the cramped space for Carroty Kate, let alone two more people.

'Mind where you park yer arse!' Carroty Kate bawled, snatching Punch from under Rainbow.

There was a rasping hoarseness to her voice, but an underlying warmth in it too, like coarse-ground millet mixed with fermented maize bran, such as the women served when an all-night watch had to be kept for a marauding elephant.

≈

Carroty Kate stuck her finger though a peephole in the canvas. 'Keep a look out, Jacko. Sing out if any horrid, dreadful personages, as Mr Punch would say, show up… and try and keep out of my friggin way.'

She busied herself preparing the puppets, cheerfully barging Rainbow aside with her bulk when necessary.

'Hooter lets out a belter in a few minutes, the factory gates opens and out tumbles my audience. That would've been your chance to slip out and disappear in the crowd.' She looked at Rainbow and laughed. ''Cept you wouldn't 'xactly disappear, would you? Best stop here a bit longer… Mind your bloomin' crabshells on Judy!'

Rainbow picked up Judy and examined her. 'And the others?'

'That's the Baby… the Doctor… the… '

'Stow it!' Jacko hissed.

Two men armed with knobkerries were scouting the street. The hooter sounded. The gates opened.

≈

Carroty Kate knelt, reaching upwards and outwards so that the puppet on her hand could beat the drum slung from a corner strut of the stage.

'I let Beadle do this bit,' she said in an undertone. 'More his style.'

'A real, proper drum,' Jacko breathed. 'Like sojers use when… '

Carroty Kate's beefy elbow nudged him into silence.

≈

B-b-b-boom, b-b-b-boom. The drum's beat synchronised with a throb inside Rainbow's brain. The man chained to him was banging his own head against the deck, again and again and again. When the man died, he'd remained chained to Rainbow for two days. Three feet of space between the floor and the deck above them, crammed in so tight they could only lie on their sides, one cup of water every three days. The thirst, the terrible thirst, and the loathsome stench. That had been the blackest part of the dark tunnel, the hardest trial yet.

≈

Carroty Kate swayed to and fro inside the booth, now with the Doctor on her left hand and Punch on the other.

'Why, I declare it's my old friend Punch. What's the matter with him? Punch, are you dead?'

Punch leapt up and whacked the doctor with a stick. 'Yes.'

Now she was the Doctor. 'Mr Punch, there's no believing you; I don't believe you're dead.'

Her right hand gave her left hand another tremendous whack. 'Yes, I am.'

'No, he's not!' Jacko shouted, quite carried away with it all.

Carroty Kate's eyes blazed a warning at him which somehow turned into a wink accompanied by a quick grin.

≈

Desperate to escape from the dark, confined space, Rainbow scrabbled at the canvas side-flap. The whole booth swayed.

'What now?' Punch shouted angrily. He popped down from the stage and rapped Rainbow on the head with his stick. 'Take that you nasty ghost! And that!'

'Ouch!' Rainbow cried, rubbing his head.

Punch popped up again and addressed his audience. 'That's the way to do it!'

The blows brought Rainbow back to the present. He watched Snail manipulating the puppets, trying his best to give her the room she needed. Punch, he knew, was a thing of cloth and wood, with Snail giving it movement and voice, and yet it was a two-way process. Punch would also be giving emotions and thoughts to Snail. When the millet was harvested in the fields outside Rainbow's village, the whole community made a huge fire and placed upon it a straw effigy of Dukobari, the spirit of the old year. Thus the old year, with all its mistakes and quarrels and rivalries, died, so that the new season, the year's new children and the new crops could start without blemish. Last year Ikpoom had entrusted Rainbow with Dukobari's angry, snarling mask and allowed him to dance the spirit's dance before it went to its annual death. When he had put on the mask he'd found it impossible not to bare his teeth in a snarl or to prevent his features contorting with rage. The relationship between a mask and its wearer, he'd discovered, was a dangerous, ambivalent one. After Dukobari was burned and the ashes of the fire scattered on the wind, Rainbow's state of ritual cleanliness could come to an end. Making love to Yaba after such periods of abstinence was a special kind of pleasure ...the explosive passion of the first time; on the second one the renewal of acquaintance with every part of her body; the sweet, languid pleasure of the third time to the first whispers of the awakening forest and the haunting, melancholy horns of the fishermen, calling to each other through the river mist.

≈

Punch was weeping as the Hangman erected the gallows. Pretending he didn't know what to do, he induced the hangman to show him by putting his own head in the noose. Jacko and Rainbow were hugging each other in ecstasy.

'Old Punch's going to get away wiv it!' Jacko whispered, pinching Rainbow's arm in his excitement.

'You're right! Trickster is more cunning even than the hyena.'

≈

The performance ended. A jubilant Punch, fresh from cheating death, held out Rainbow's top-hat, bowing and bobbing all the while, encouraging the crowd to part with its ha'pennies and farthings.

'Seems safe enough to come out,' Jacko said, peering through the peephole.

'Takings up today,' Carroty Kate said, tipping the money into the capacious pocket of her heavy grey-green military great-coat.

Jacko crawled out of the booth. He unhooked the drum from the front of the stage and slung it from his shoulder, marching up and down, imitating a drum roll with his tongue. Rainbow followed.

'You set up near a crossroads, I see.'

Carroty Kate, her voice even rougher after the demands Punch had made upon it, replied from the other side of the canvas, 'Crossroads is always good for business.'

'And pleasing to Exu.'

'You lost me there, Rainbow.'

≈

With Rainbow helpfully hindering her, Carroty Kate dismantled the booth. She packed the puppets and the props away in a large bag, rolled up the stripy canvas and arranged the frame poles on either side of it, making a neat but sizable bundle of it all. Bending, she swung the bundle onto her back in one easy motion. Much more sensible to carry it on her head like Yaba would, Rainbow thought. But, of course, the woman's essential snail nature was showing through. Seeing Jacko's round-eyed amazement at her strength, Carroty Kate laughed.

'Carried loads a bloody sight heavier than this. Carried my man's full pack many a mile when he was taken with the squitters or plain worn out with the fighting.'

'Fighting? Boney and them lot?'

'Peninsular War... Spain. Women wasn't meant to go. Some of us got across one way or another, though. We slept rough like our men did, marched every mile with them and more; foraged for them, cooked for them, nursed them. The regiment couldn't have done without us.'

≈

Rainbow nodded thoughtfully. It was clear enough what she was telling him. If she could carry her heavy load so lightly and willingly, he should do the same. The weight of responsibility for lifting the drought, for the lives of his wife and child, the burden of his special gift, he must accept and shoulder without complaint.

'Thank you,' he said humbly.

She laughed. 'I'm always on the side of the one that's in a spot of trouble… In Smithy's case that was all the bleedin' time.'

Her Smithy, she said, was a Romany, brought up around horses. He'd tried for a cavalry regiment, but couldn't get it, not even as a groom.

'So he 'ad to make do bein' yer poor, friggin foot-sloggin cannon fodder.'

She set off at a steady plod down the street. Jacko reached up and touched the drum on her back. 'That don't belong to our army, do it, Carrots?'

'Took it off a dead Frenchie at Badajoz. Those snail-eating bastards put up some fight. At the breach, our dead was in mounds as high as that wall back there. My Smithy came through all that with hardly a cut… then he went and got took prisoner, the bloody fool. Never knowed what 'appened to him. When the war ended, he never friggin' showed up.'

She kicked a stone out of her path. 'There was this old geyser in the workhouse, not long for this world… got the dolls off him for next to nothing.'

Her Smithy, she said, was likely to be in London, if he was anywhere. Working the streets with Punch and Judy enabled her to look for him and earn a living both at once. Several times a day she was able to gather a crowd around her and scan it for Smithy's face.

'Not a friggin' sign' of 'im and that's eight year since the Frenchies give in.'

≈

The light was fading when Snail broke the silence. 'Sorry to retreat into my shell like that… You two got anywhere for tonight?'

Jacko shook his head.

She turned to Rainbow. 'I got somewhere. Ain't much. You're both welcome.'

Rainbow looked at Jacko. Jacko nodded. 'Better than the street, I reckon. This time of year, anyroad… How do you make that voice, Carrots? The one you gives Mr Punch?'

Carroty Kate put a hand inside the pocket of her great-coat and pulled out a small flat instrument, like a folded piece of tin.

'What's that?'

'It's like a whistle in your mouth and you speaks through it. That's why they calls me a swatchel omi.'

'Don't get it, Carrots.'

'Swatchel… like swazzle.' She brandished the instrument. 'This is a swazzle, see. And an omi's what showfolk call a person.'

'I know that,' Jacko said crossly, blowing his nose with his fingers and rubbing them on his trouser leg. 'Give us a go wiv it, Carrots. Oh, go on, let us!'

She handed him the swazzle. Jacko put it in his mouth and tried speaking. Other than making him lisp, nothing happened.

Carroty Kate smacked him playfully on the head. 'Takes practice.'

'Wha' if I thwallowed it?'

'Oh, you wait till it comes out t'other end. S'what happened to the one in your mouth.'

Jacko spat it out, spluttering. Rainbow retrieved it from the gutter and handed it to Carroty Kate.

She wiped it on her sleeve, laughing. 'You should hear me fart when I've swallowed it!' And she gave several loud imitations which had Jacko doubled up, holding his sides. Suddenly he straightened. 'Friggin' Hell! Only left my gloves in the nethersken, haven't I?'

'Perhaps Bat has them now,' Rainbow said.

'Can't keep anyfink for long, that's me, guv.'

≈

With some of the takings, Carroty Kate bought three hot potatoes from a vendor, and a bottle of gin. They walked through the darkening streets past dimly lit windows, eating as they went, handing the bottle from one to the other. They turned into a narrow lane and stopped at a derelict, snail-damp, three-storied house, the windows of which were, for the most part, covered over with brown paper, old sacking or bits of board. Carroty Kate kicked open the peeling, half-hinged door. Steep, rickety stairs, peeling plaster, a corridor with loose and missing boards, doorless, gaping rooms smelling of rotting timber and damp, filled with huddled bodies.

'In here.'

≈

Two burly men, in workmen's clothes, sat on the bare boards playing cards. Carroty Kate removed her pack and advanced upon them.

'That's my corner!'

'Who says?' one of them smirked, barely looking up, studying his fistful of clubs.

'I say.'

The other man flipped a card with casual insolence. 'Well, there ain't nothin' you can do about it, so clear off!'

Carroty Kate yanked the bottle from her pocket and smashed it into the sneering face. The man crumpled to the floor amidst a pool of gin and broken glass. His companion leapt up with an oath and swung a punch at her. She blocked it with her arm, seized him by the balls and head-butted him.

A knife flashed, stabbing her forearm. Rainbow started forward, but Carroty Kate's teeth were already crunching on the bones of the man's wrist. The knife clattered to the floor. Seizing him by the nose, she twisted his head sideways and bit his ear off. He screamed, clutched at the wound and stumbled out of the room, pouring forth blood and oaths. Picking up the knife, she plucked the ear from between her teeth and pinned it to the wall.

'Where's the other man?' Her lips were red with blood.

'I let him crawl away,' Rainbow said.

Jacko was rocking to and fro on his heels, head in hands, a pool of urine spreading across the uneven boards.

Rainbow bent over him. 'Jacko?'

'Why did they fight? Why did they have to fight?'

'But they refused to go.'

Carroty Kate touched Rainbow's shoulder. 'He doesn't mean me and them. Best leave him be for the moment.'

Rainbow straightened. 'How's your arm?'

'S'nothing. The coat stopped most of it. Better in no time flat.' She looked past him at the crouching Jacko. 'But some wounds need time to heal.'

5

One end of the roof was open. Naked beams angled across clouds that spread across the dawn sky like flamingos' wings. A mop of flaming red hair and one bare arm was all that was visible of Carroty Kate beneath the spread of her military coat. The underside of the arm was so creamy white—like the underside of a snail and excitingly different from the mahogany hues of Yaba's skin. Desire awoke and swelled… then rapidly subsided as Rainbow imagined his penis nailed to the wall beside the ear. Only then did he remember that, to stay in a state of ritual cleanliness, he must observe strict sexual abstinence. He rolled over. Jacko wasn't there. A fragment of plaster rattled onto the floorboards. Jacko was sauntering along a beam, as fearless as a monkey. He grinned down at Rainbow, his black mood of yesterday forgotten.

≈

Rainbow watched him turn and run back along the length of the beam. Monkey, he knew, had many meanings for him. At this moment, Monkey was the embodiment of his need to find the courage to walk his own high, narrow beam—the beam that was the arrogance to believe he really was the one chosen to deliver his people from the drought and the humility to accept the wisdom of his Orisha Animals; the beam that was the narrow line between the need to blot out the terrible doubts implanted in his mind by the Dust Devil that this was not the Other World at all, and the need to understand the strangeness that surrounded him… The sensation of swaying and nearly falling was so strong that Rainbow planted both hands firmly on the floor. Jacko leapt lightly from one beam to another. 'Did you see that, guv? Did you?'

'Yes, Monkey, I saw.'

Jacko hung upside-down from the beam by his knees. 'You don't half say funny things at times.'

≈

A wide, yawning mouth slid above the great-coat.

'How would you like to be my Shallaballah, Rainbow?'

Rainbow stared uncertainly at Carroty Kate. 'Would it mean having sexual communion with you?'

'It friggin' well would not! You and me do the goose and duck? Last friggin' thing I want. Men! Soon as they open their trousers their brains fall out!'

Jacko swung upright, dropped lightly to the floor and stood poised for flight. 'At least we've got brains!'

He dodged the first flying boot, but not the second.

'Ah! Carrots!'

'About Shallaballah,' Carroty Kate said. 'He's the darkie servant in the story. Supposing you was to step out of the play as the real Shallaballah... might work. Worth a try.'

'And he dances a treat, Carrots, he does, so he does.'

Carroty Kate winked at Rainbow. 'And I need someone to take a hat round and bash a drum... Know anyone could do that, Rainbow?'

Jacko was dancing with excitement. 'The drum? Really, Carrots? Really?'

His face, blossoming with pleasure, suddenly closed. 'What's our cut?'

'Twenty per cent.'

'Thirty.'

Carroty Kate looked at Rainbow, who nodded.

'Agreed,' said Carroty Kate.

She beckoned Rainbow closer. Seizing him by the shoulder with one hand and by the end of the sleeve with the other, she gave a mighty tug. The sleeve parted company with the coat.

'What are you doing?'

She laughed. 'Shallaballah, the other Shallaballah, needs a violet coat just like yours. Now this sleeve.'

≈

A cold gust flurried along the street, making Rainbow wish for good thick sleeves instead of the orange cotton things Carroty Kate had replaced them with.

Jacko was proudly marching up and down, beating the drum. People were beginning to collect in little knots, waiting for the performance to begin. Carroty Kate's head appeared, framed by the stage. Then an arm, holding an empty bottle.

'Here, Jacko! Be a good lad. Run and fetch us three fingers worth.

Friggin' swazzle—always useless till it's wetted with a little gin… Mother Cleary knows me well. She'll put it on the slate.'

≈

When Jacko returned, Carroty Kate downed the gin in two gulps. It did, as she said, put her in fine voice. Rainbow, reading the faces of the audience, saw that Trickster's appeal was the same here as in his village. Everyone delighted in the upsetting of the established order, in the discomfiting of pompous authority, in seeing him break rules they secretly longed to break themselves. The puppet Shallaballah, wearing a similar violet coat to Rainbow's, with orange sleeves, made a brief appearance on stage. Then, as the puppet dipped out of sight, Rainbow jumped out, shouting 'Shallaballah!' and began dancing amidst the audience, who roared and stamped and showed their approval by raining coins around the booth even though the show had some way to go.

≈

They had walked three miles before Jacko asked, 'How much further?'

'Can't do me pitches too close,' Carroty Kate replied.'Or too recent.'

She usually did six or seven shows a day, she said, which meant, on average, about twenty-five miles of walking.

'Forced marches across Spain were a doddle compared to this,' she joked.

'Does he 'scape the rope and the Devil every time?' Jacko asked.

Carroty Kate smiled. 'Up to now he has… The next pitch is where there's… a pugi… pugifistical… you know!'

'Gypsy Morgan 'gainst Jem Ashley!' Jacko exclaimed, delivering an uppercut to his shadow. 'Morgan'll thrash 'im, even though Ashley's a bag of tricks and most of 'em dirty.'

≈

Rainbow stood beside their booth on Horsefair Common, where the prize-fight was due to take place. He could hear Carroty Kate mumbling drunkenly inside, fumbling with the puppets and cursing them for being awkward. It was too early to start the patter. When the fight was over would be the time to catch her audience.

'My wig! If it isn't Rainbow and little Jacko!'

Arthur Trevellyn stood in front of them, silver-topped cane in hand, resplendent in a plum coloured coat with exaggerated lapels. His companion, a young man of much the same age, dressed even more lavishly, stood aside, an expression of haughty disdain on his face.

Jacko grinned at Arthur. 'Thought you might show up, Captain, you being one for the fisticuffs and all.'

'And what amazing sartorial adventures has my old violet been having?' Arthur touched one of Rainbow's voluminous orange sleeves and started to laugh. 'Capital! Capital! …Ah! I've remembered something.'

He stepped forward and turned back the lapel of Rainbow's coat. Pinned to the reverse side was a metal object that looked to Rainbow like a talisman to ward off evil spirits, an interweaving of magic signs, in which the only thing he recognised was a pair of crossed swords.

'Regimental badge,' Arthur said. 'Sentimental value, don't you know.'

Rainbow unpinned it and offered it to Arthur, who clicked his heels and bowed.

'Much obliged.'

'Quite the white man, isn't he?' sneered his companion.

Arthur said, 'Wouldn't insult you, of course, by offering to pay for it, but perhaps something for Mr Punch… '

He felt in his pocket. 'Ah! That is… I seem to have… ' He turned to his companion.

'Er… Slogger, stout fellow, could you do the honours?'

Mr Punch called out, 'Whose that with a smell under his nose? Must be that dead mouse on his hupper lip.'

Arthur laughed heartily. 'Good day to you, Mr Punch! A fine judge of a moustache, I see. Meet Captain Carlton-Syms.'

Carlton-Syms turned his back on Punch, but produced a handful of coins and contemptuously tossed them in Rainbow's direction. Rainbow saw them floating through the air, as slow as eagles on the hover, winking in the sunlight as they turned. Seven oracles, each with a different trajectory. 'Everything is connected,' he heard Ikpoom say. 'Everything is part of a greater whole and the whole is in each part.' The arc of each winking disc moved to the music of the universe, in harmony with the swoop of a bird, the curve of the swords on the talisman, the shape of Arthur's lapels. With the revelation of the pattern came an exact knowledge of the speed and path of the oracles. His flashing, sky-cleaving hands caught all seven before a single one hit the ground.

'Slit my windpipe! Did you see that, Slogger?'

≈

A single raised eyebrow briefly relieved Carlton-Sym's bored expression. 'Tolerably amusing. Now, do come on, there's a good fellow. I'm putting a pile on Ashley and I want to get it down.'

'Slogger, poor fellow, everyone knows Morgan has the beating of him.'

Arthur turned to Rainbow. 'And who are you backing?'

Over Arthur's left shoulder, in a deserted corner of the common, was a massive tree. Its bark was like the wrinkles on an elephant's skin.

'Backing?' Rainbow echoed. How long it seemed since he'd touched a tree. 'That tree... what name does it have?'

Arthur shrugged and glanced over his shoulder. 'Um... an oak, I think.'

'Are you coming or not?' Carlton-Syms demanded.

Arthur gave a cheerful wave. 'Better toddle.'

≈

Rainbow ran towards Oak, this venerable elder amongst trees with huge twisting branches like rivers of time... branches bare of leaves... like the trees around Mwanza. Oak was reminding him of his mission to end the drought. He leaned against its vast girth, feeling its energy surge through him, absorbing its inner stillness, his mind travelling down its labyrinth of roots, seeking its firmness of purpose. Sometimes, in the hour before dawn, when the nocturnal animals had returned to their lairs, before the sun signalled the start of the daylight clamour, Rainbow would slip into the silent forest to receive the wisdom of the trees. Even in the presence of the Old Ones it was difficult not to think of the warmth and closeness of Yaba's body, the soft cry she gave as he stole from their bed.

Rainbow sighed. 'Oak, Oak, even as you give me strength, you remind me that I, too, have roots.'

≈

When Rainbow returned to the booth, Carroty Kate was completely befuddled.

'Nine year,' she mumbled. 'Only been lookin' for 'im nine friggin' years, 'aven't I?'

He helped her get ready. The crowd around the boxing ring sounded like a bush fire fanned by the wind. He'd heard a crowd like that once before. When Chief Chimu's father died, his sons fought to the death in the arena until only one remained alive. That way, there could be no rivals, no treason, no plotting for the throne or internal strife. This was the way of the Uboku and it made Chimu all powerful and a mighty warrior in the eyes of his people, a strong leader who was capable of defeating the Ijeru.

≈

The crowd was dispersing, a-buzz with how Jem Ashley had beaten Gypsey Morgan in the nineteenth round of a bloody battle. Jacko darted out of the throng and snatched up the drum.

'Did you see the squelcher in the bread-basket as finished Morgan? Don't see nobody stopping Jem, not that one... 'cept maybe Tom Cribb.'

'Beat the bloody drum!' Carroty Kate shouted. 'And let's get on with the effing show!'

Inside the booth, Rainbow clung to the framework, trying to steady it as Carroty Kate lurched from side to side, making the whole thing rock perilously.

'Trust you to be friggin' awkward! Get on my 'and you friggin' useless sod! Go on!'

She fetched Punch a smack across the head. 'I'll learn yer to be difficult! Now get up there sharpish or you'll feel my 'and again!'

Up went Punch only to take a swing at Judy, miss her completely and hit the stage so hard that his stick broke.

'I want another stick!' Punch shouted.

'Well, you can't have one!' Carroty Kate yelled back. 'Get on with the show.'

'I want another stick!' Punch shrieked.

'You can't have one!'

'We'll see about that!' And Punch, descending from the stage, set about Carroty Kate with the broken end of his stick.

Rainbow grabbed her hand, preventing her from hitting herself. Punch snatched up a new stick and up they went, Punch and Judy. 'Little bugger!' Carroty Kate snarled. 'I'll get 'im for this.'

≈

And she did—because Judy killed Punch and threw his body out of the window.

≈

The crowd, already put in a black mood by Gypsy Morgan's defeat, let out a roar of anger. The booth was knocked on its side. Rending canvas, splintering wood, feet kicking and crunching, hands ripping and tearing. Carroty Kate sat amidst the ruins laughing, oblivious to the kicks and blows. Slowly she toppled over and rolled out of sight beneath a cart. The crowd, with nothing left to smash, drifted away, satisfied they'd had better entertainment than usual.

≈

Out of the wreckage rose Rainbow, shaking himself like a dog. Loud snores rose from the direction of the cart. Rainbow's worried frown eased a little. Then Jacko was beside him, holding the remains of a drum.

'Look Rainbow, look what they gone and done!'

The skin of the drum hung in loose flaps; the frame was broken beyond repair.

'Nuffink good ever friggin' lasts.'

He stooped, snatched up a leather bag, the one which had held all their takings, then threw it to the ground in disgust. 'Not a farthing left!' Jacko shifted bits of wreckage with his foot, looking for anything worth salvaging. His eye was caught by a splash of red. Not blood, but sealing wax. A letter had been folded, tied with string and the knot stuck to the paper with red wax. A large, ornate J was inscribed on the stiff paper. Jacko couldn't read but he did recognise his own initial, similar in shape to a fishhook, or the hooks that the meat carcasses hung from in the market. The letter must have fallen out of someone's pocket in the frenzy around the booth. Suppose it was for him? Perhaps his mother had sent it! She couldn't write, of course, but she could have paid one of those street-corner scribes to do it. Jacko picked up the letter. That was it! She had heard that he was working with the Punch and Judy show, and she had asked around and found out what Carroty Kate's regular pitches were, or guessed where she was likely to be and…

Sauntering towards them was Arthur, accompanied by Carlton-Syms and a bulldog of a man with cauliflower ears and battered nose who was soberly, but fashionably, dressed.

'Lost a packet myself, Jacko,' Arthur announced cheerfully. He looked straight at Rainbow. 'But enough left to make it worth your while to go ten minutes with Ben here.'

He put an arm on the shoulder of the man with the battered face. 'I've never seen hands as fast as his, Ben. He's a natural.'

Jacko said. 'Thinks you'll be a dab 'and at the bare knuckle game, guv.'

'So,' said Arthur, 'I'd like to see how you shape up with Ben, Ben Bugler, former contender for Champion of All England.'

'Now in semi-retirement,' Ben Bugler added.

'But still able to give all but three or four in the country a licking, I'd wager.'

'Me?' said Rainbow.

'Only ten minutes, old fruit. Money's yours even if you lose.'

'How much?' said Jacko.

'Twenty guineas.'

'Blimey! We could do wiv that sort of mellish, so we could, guv.'

'You think I should do it, Monkey?'

'I do, guv, I do. He can't hurt you too bad in ten minutes.'

Rainbow nodded his assent to Arthur. Ben Bugler stepped forward and shook Rainbow by the hand.

'I've hired this for half an hour,' Arthur said, leading the way towards a beer-tent which had been on the point of closing down for the day.

≈

Tables and benches had been pushed to one side. Sitting astride one of the benches, his weight on a thick ebony staff, was a man in his middle years, wearing a long, black cloak with a yellow lining. Carlton-Syms gave him the briefest nod, sat down next to him, took a pinch of snuff and assumed an air of boredom. Bugler removed his cravat, fancy shirt and jacket and stood, stripped to the waist, fists raised. If anything, he looked bigger with his clothes off than he did with them on. Rainbow followed suit, removing his boots as well.

'Begin!' Arthur commanded.

≈

Rainbow was well practised in capoeira, the Uboku style of ritual fight performed by shamans in which feet and head were used as well as hands. To have only a pair of fists to avoid seemed ridiculously simple. Trained in total focus and concentration, he knew from tiny signals in his opponent's eyes, even before Bugler knew himself, when a punch was on its way. And he was fit. Several hours of dancing a day had made him fast and light on his feet.

≈

After five minutes, Rainbow was unmarked while Bugler was blowing hard, his body blotched, blood trickling from one nostril. With one minute to go, Carroty Kate blundered in, distracting Rainbow. Bugler's punch sank into Rainbow's midriff, doubling him up. Carroty Kate, befuddled by drink, leapt forward, roaring, and, with one massive blow, floored Ben Bugler. Laughing heartily, Arthur helped Ben Bugler to his feet. 'What amazing Amazonian is this, Jacko, who rescues young men in distress?'

'This is Carroty Kate, the… er… swatchel omi.'

'Ah! Good show! I mean bad show. That is to say, I don't mean it was a bad show… Sorry to see it wrecked.'

'That old bugger Punch got what was coming to him,' Carroty Kate growled.

Arthur pushed Ben forward. 'Meet Ben Bugler. Would have been the champion if only he'd had a left hook half as good as yours, by Jove, yes! What do you say, Slogger?'

'I say the whole thing's prodigiously tedious.'

Smiling sheepishly, but taking it in good part, Ben Bugler made an ironic bow to Carroty Kate and shook Rainbow warmly by the hand. 'He's a good 'un, sir. Oh yes, he's a good 'un alright. With a bit of training, he'll do.'

Arthur nodded thoughtfully. 'The puppet thing's completely finished, what?'

Rainbow paused in the act of pulling on his coat. 'Exu is never finished, he simply puts on another face.'

'Ah! Yes. Quite so. The fence I'm riding at is that you'll be looking for work, I shouldn't wonder. Fact is, I'm leaving town for a bit. Me tailor's hounding me with his damnable bills.'

Carlton-Syms raised one eyebrow. Arthur turned to the middle-aged man on the bench. 'This is Mr Barnaby Thackston. I'm joining his travelling circus, don't you know.'

≈

Rainbow stared in wonder at Barnaby Thackston, his eyes riveted to the ornate black staff, topped by an ivory bird—the symbol of the god of thunder. He was looking at Xango the Thunder God. He'd spent a sleepless night longing for home, fretting about Obobo, worrying that he'd fail, but now he was in the presence of the Thunder God.

Arthur was laughing ruefully at his own forgetfulness. 'Er… Barnaby, what exactly is it I'm doing?'

Xango raised his staff in a dramatic gesture. 'Heroic Episodes Involving Our Brave Lads in the Defeat of Bonaparte.'

'Ah, quite so. I was wondering, Barnaby, if you could use these good people in some way.'

Xango beckoned to Rainbow.

'Rainbow,' Arthur prompted him.

'This Rainbo… His coat reminds me of what Grimaldi wore for his Lord Humpty Dandy burlesque. Did you ever see him sing 'Hot Codlins' Captain Trevellyn? Wonderful!'

'I hear tell he's going to retire this year,' Arthur said.

'More's the pity. Greatest clown I ever saw.'

'I was thinking,' said Arthur, 'You haven't got a boxing booth this year, have you?'

Barnaby nodded thoughtfully. 'Boxing booth… yes… '

He dropped his cigar butt on the ground. Instinctively, Jacko started forward and would have picked it up, but for Carroty Kate's restraining hand.

Barnaby lit another cigar. 'Yes, a boxing booth with Rainbow would be quite an attraction. You're hired, Rainbow. I've got plans for you, bigger fights in mind, but for the moment you can cut your teeth in the booth.' He turned to Jacko. 'Can you play the accordion, boy?'

'No, sir.'

'Are you crippled in any way?'

'No, sir.'

'Pity. There's nothing more guaranteed to catch an audience's sympathy than a cripple playing an accordion, especially if it's too heavy for him.'

Jacko pulled two of Punch's truncheons from his pocket and beat a tattoo on the table.

Xango thumped the ground with the staff. 'The little drummer boy! By thunder! That gives me an idea! You're hired.'

Arthur said, 'Nothing like the roar of the grease paint, the smell of the crowd, what?'

Xango looked pained. 'And you, madam… '

'Carroty Kate's the name, sir.'

'Yes, I've got plans for you, too. Yes, I see it all, by thunder!'

Rainbow glowed with happiness. The shaman, Arthur, and the Thunder God knew of his mission to defeat Nataxale. They were going to make sure he was ready for the battle. After thunder and lightning came rain. Clearly, Xango, too, wanted to see the downfall of Nataxale, the Dust Devil. Perhaps Xango would lead him to Skyherd. Not for the first time Rainbow tried to imagine how Skyherd would look in human form… Like the swaggering Carlton-Syms, perhaps, disdainful of all beneath him, or like Chief Chimu, but even more powerful. How long would it be before he was deemed worthy to enter Skyherd's presence and what would he be like?

6

A thin, pale young man stood in front of his father, General Reginald Stanhope. The General, dressed in country tweeds, was seated behind the mahogany desk in his study. On the walls were a stuffed and mounted tiger's head, prints depicting hunting scenes, and several racks of fishing rods and sporting guns.

'I might have known you couldn't be trusted to spend your allowance in a manner befitting a gentleman!'

Robert bit his lip. Father meant he should have been up in 'Town', staying at Fitz's Club, cutting a dash and generally indulging in high-spirited rake-hellery such as young men of his age were supposed to do. Father would have been proud of a son like that. He was guilty of innocence which, in Smart Society, was a crime of the worst order. Everything had been going so well until Father came home after three years in India, on secondment to the East India Company. When Father was abroad on military duty, Beechwood House was a happy place—just himself and Mama and Gwen the cook, leading a life in which creating paintings was preferred to killing animals, and making jam more important than making war. Even worse, Father had announced his intention to retire. Now he would be at home most of the time.

'And on top of everything else,' the General bristled, 'You refuse to join my friends in our Autumn shoot… all of them wealthy, influential people, might I remind you!'

'I take no joy in slaughtering animals, sir.'

'It's expected of you, Robert.'

'Why?'

'Because you are a gentleman.'

Robert longed to reply, 'How silly of me to forget that violence and killing are what a gentle man does.' But all he could manage was a shake of his head.

'It's high time, Robert, you joined my regiment. As you know, it's always been my intention that you should do that. The army will make a man of you, by God! Enough of this shilly-shallying!'

Shilly-shallying—was that all that three years of studying under the Royal Academician, Henry Washburn, meant to Father? The contempt on Father's face was what hurt most. That withering contempt which reduced him to an absolute certainty that he was a misfit, an oddity, nothing but a failure. It hadn't helped that father had wanted to send him to a boarding school with boys of his own age, but Mama had insisted that he was too delicate to go. Robert would never forget those weeks of meals eaten in silence, the slamming doors and Father's and Mama's angry voices floating up to his bedroom while he wheezed and fought for breath and twisted in agony, knowing he was the cause of the friction.

≈

Washburn had taken a house in rural Oxfordshire, near to the Stanhopes. Robert, who was almost never without a pencil and sketchbook in hand since early childhood, had persuaded the well-known artist to take him on as an apprentice. In return for tuition in portrait and landscape painting, Robert had spent hours in Henry Washburn's studio scraping down old canvases, stretching new ones on frames and priming them, grinding and mixing pigments. Occasionally, as Washburn began to think him worthy of it, he had been allowed to fill in parts of the backgrounds to Washburn's own paintings.

The General rose from his chair. 'I did not consent to this useless daubing of yours. It's time to put an end to it and join the regiment.'

Robert's legs were trembling so much he could hardly stand up. A week ago, when Henry Washburn had praised his painting of Beechwood Chase by Moonlight, everything had seemed wonderful. And now... He desperately wanted his father to think well of him, but he could not, he simply could not give up painting and he would rather die than join the army.

The General read Robert's expression. 'Well then, for as long as you choose to ignore my wishes I shall stop your allowance. Furthermore I will not have you under this roof. Unless you change your mind I want you gone before the end of the week.'

≈

Robert stood outside Fitz's Club where Father had been a member for years. He bent to pick up his one leather valise but half-way there straightened again. The trouble was that the club would be full of hearty army officers, ex-army officers or would-be-army officers with whom he had nothing in common and whose conversations revolved around killing things—birds, animals, natives, Frenchies. They could enthuse over the fine points of distinction between one fox-hound and another, but they wouldn't know a Gainsborough from a Raeburn. No doubt, like his father, they regarded painting as 'useless daubing'. But here he was, standing outside Fitz's club, trying to pluck up courage to go in and ask for a room. Three years ago, to mark Robert's twenty-first birthday, his father had given him a life membership to the club, which entitled him to a free room whenever he was 'in town' and meals that were, at least, not exorbitant. Robert had never made use of his membership despite travelling to London on several occasions to tour the art galleries—yet another way in which he had disappointed his father, another sign that he was not a 'man about town,' a manly man, as he was expected to be, as sometimes, no, as most of the time, he believed he should be. With only his meagre savings and the slender purse his mother had managed to slip into his pocket, Robert had reluctantly come to the conclusion that Fitz's Club it would have to be for a night or two until he could find somewhere cheap but respectable or until he could find employment. It would take years, of course, to establish himself as painter. To get commissions you needed contacts, patronage, the favour of influential people, none of which he had. Henry Washburn, not wanting to anger his neighbour, the General, had declined to write Robert a letter of introduction.

≈

The journey from Beechwood House had been a long, dark passage of guilt and doubt—guilt at being the cause, yet again, of a quarrel between Mama and Father, guilt that it was all his fault and that he was, as Father said, a poor apology for a son; and doubts about his ability to make a living in London. Even if he'd had the right contacts and introductions, he didn't feel ready to launch into a career as portrait and landscape painter. He had planned to do at least another two years apprenticeship with Henry Washburn. He needed more time to perfect his technique and to find his own style. In his pocket was a caricature he had drawn during the coach journey. It showed an exaggeratedly crusty and dyspeptic army general pointing and saying, 'Never darken my door again!' To exaggerate and parody the painful scene made it easier to bear. Or was it just a way of avoiding the reality?

≈

A robust young man, perhaps a couple of years older than Robert, bounded up behind him and began pirouetting around the valise, executing what Robert took to be the latest dance step. He wore a brocade waistcoat and violet trousers, but no coat and, curiously, on his feet were heavy workmen's boots. Robert noticed that the knuckles of his left hand were bleeding.

The young man clapped his hand to his head. 'Don't tell me you're a member of Fitz's! You've got to be as thick as two planks, totally mad and permanently in debt before they let you in, and I'll wager you're none of those! Trevellyn's the name, by the way. Arthur Trevellyn.'

Robert shook the proffered hand and mumbled. 'Robert Stanhope. I've been a member three years but haven't er… haven't made use of it until now.'

'Stanhope. Know that name. Not related to General Stanhope, by any chance?'

'Well, yes. He's my father.'

'He was the Colonel of my regiment when I joined as a young subaltern. Not a bad old stick in his way. Strict but fair. In good health, I trust?'

'Yes, thank you. What an amazing coincidence!'

'Not really,' Arthur grinned. 'Everyone knows everyone in the army. And most officers belong to Fitz's. It's a small world… and your mother? Used to hold tea parties for us young subalterns. She knew just how lost and green we were, though we pretended otherwise. Such a dear, kind, gentle lady.'

Robert remembered those tea parties when the house filled with rumbustious young men. The regiment had been temporarily stationed near Oxford while on extended manoeuvres. He'd hidden whenever they came, dreading being made to field in their inevitable games of cricket, dreading being exposed as utterly hopeless at stopping, catching or throwing a ball.

As they talked, Arthur steered Robert towards the entrance to the club and past the lordly doorman whom Robert had felt sure would immediately spot he was a fraud and refuse to let him in, but who merely tipped his hat to Arthur and smirked at some bantering remark the latter threw his way. Arthur oversaw the signing in and commandeered a porter to show Robert up to his room—something Robert knew he would have been far too diffident to do himself.

'Well, we'd better get togged up before putting our snouts in the trough. See you in the dining-hall, old fruit!'

≈

It was three in the afternoon, the fashionable hour for lunching, when Robert peered into the dining-hall, trying to summon the will to brave the waves of hearty laughter and noisy high spirits. A waiter in a military style monkey-jacket caught his eye and pointed to Arthur who sat at the far end of a long table, near the window. Robert made his way between rows of tables, aware of eyes upon him, of a sudden hush in the clatter and din of the meal. A young buck had tilted back his chair, half blocking his way, and was surveying him with a languid insolence.

'Tradesmen and butcher's boys use the back door.'

'I… I'm a mm-m… '

Arthur shouted half-way across the hall. 'I say, lay off the poor blighter! He's all right! Come on, Stanhope, come and join me here.'

A supercilious eyebrow rose heavenwards. 'Damned bad form, Stanhope, appearing here in that ill-fitting weskit. Damned bad form.'

'Sorry,' Robert mumbled.

Stiff with embarrassment and misery, he blundered to where Arthur sat.

'Mustn't mind him,' Arthur said as Robert squeezed in beside him, thankful that he was at the end of the table and there was only Arthur next to him.

'Hugh Carlton-Syms, Slogger Syms, best cricketer a fellow's ever seen. At school together. Same house, same form.' Arthur made an imaginary stroke with an imaginary bat in his hand.

'You might as well know, Arthur, I'm a complete dud with a ball of any sort.'

Arthur clapped a hand on his shoulder. 'Not to worry. Takes all sorts… she's a lovely person, your mother.'

≈

All appetite lost, Robert picked at something he was unaware of ordering. The heads of buffalo, ibex, sambhur, tiger and rhino adorned the walls. Into the oak panelling was carved, with varying degrees of skill, a welter of names—a privilege, Robert learned from Arthur, accorded to those who could traverse the underside of Great Table without touching the ground.

≈

Robert explained that he had come to London to try to establish himself as a painter.

'It's not going to be easy, though.'

'The Pater says, to be half-way decent, a picture's got to have something four-footed in it.'

Robert smiled. 'I'll bear that in mind, Arthur. In the meantime, I need to find a job.'

'My hat, you must be short of the readies! A job, by Jove! The very last resort!'

Robert said he was thinking of trying to get a position as an illustrator with the *London Illustrated Chronicle* but that first he needed to accumulate a portfolio of relevant drawings to show his prospective employers.

'I don't quite know where to start, Arthur.'

'Draw what draws a crowd,' Arthur advised. 'You know, race meetings, fairs, accidents, anything that's got blood and guts. There isn't a person in this room wouldn't look at that.'

≈

Gusts of laughter, in which Robert had no part, swept through the dining-hall. He looked across at Carlton-Syms. Father would have much preferred him for a son. Father's angry, dismissive words were in his ears. 'You're a disappointment to me, Robert, a big disappointment!' Why wouldn't he be when he was a disappointment even to himself? Robert sat with a grin fixed to his face, only half hearing Arthur's account of how Slogger had scored the winning runs in some cricket match or other. The diners were becoming rowdier by the minute. Anyone who got up to go was pelted with bread rolls and subjected to a barrage of good-natured insults—a gauntlet Robert could never bring himself to run. At a nearby table, a group of some dozen well-wined diners had stripped back the damask tablecloth and were spinning a knife on the polished mahogany surface.

'Finger of fate!'

Robert broke into a sweat.

Yells of delight. 'Hollis! It's you, Hollis!'

Several tables away, Hollis protested it wasn't pointing at him at all.

'No shirking! Up you get!'

Hollis put his chair on the table, stepped up and, balancing on one leg, downed a quart of ale to loud cheers. The knife spun again. Robert began to wheeze with anxiety. It swung towards him, slowing, slowing, then stopped. Arthur pushed Robert back and leant forward so that the knife was pointing at himself. Another wild cheer.

'Trevellyn! You're the one, Trevellyn!'

Arthur stood up, grinning broadly. 'I utterly decline! And furthermore, I declare everyone at that table to be poxy gander-faced ninnies!'

'Scrag him! De-bag him!'

≈

Robert pressed himself into the corner, trying to become invisible as the room erupted into a mass of howling, struggling bodies. Tables were overturned, crockery and silver crashed to the floor. Arthur's trousers sailed through the air and draped themselves over a moose's horns. Yelling lustily, a group charged to Arthur's defence. The battle swept to the other end of the room. Not far from Robert's corner, the window was half open. The dining-room was on the ground floor, so it would only be a short drop to the pavement. Seizing his chance, he climbed out.

≈

As Robert gained the pavement, Arthur tumbled out of the front entrance, followed by his trousers and boots.

'Stanhope?'

Blushing, Robert pointed to the open window.

Arthur slapped his thighs. 'Capital! Capital!'

While he dressed, Arthur stared at Robert thoughtfully. 'I think Mrs Budge's lodgings will be more to your liking… Use it myself now and then. Good little bolthole when the old funds run low. You know what a devil it is, riding it out till one's flush again. Decent enough. She's isn't a bad old trout, really. You can usually charm her into letting you pay at the end of the month.'

He gave Robert a friendly punch on the arm. 'By which time your paintings will be selling like hot cakes!'

'I'm not so sure about that… Thanks, Arthur, for, you know, that business with the knife.'

'All good fun. Your obedient, humble and all that tosh. Well, must dash. Yes, dashed if I mustn't dash! See you again, old fruit!'

Robert wanted to say, 'I hope so, Arthur. That would be nice.' But the words wouldn't come out. That he should so very much want to see Arthur again, an army-type, of all people, was confusing.

7

Overcoming his reluctance to move deeper into the jostling crowd, Robert pressed towards the illusionist. He was following Arthur's advice to 'draw what draws a crowd' and was at the annual Autumn Fair in Hyde Park. A couple of quick sketches of the illusionist, then a man with caged birds. For a penny one of them, a jackdaw, could be induced to talk. After a brief conversation with the caged-bird man, and guided by the sound of a mechanical organ, Robert found his next subject, an Italian organ-grinder and his wretched monkey. The poor animal was chained and clearly half-starved. What upset Robert was that everything about it was against its true nature—the way it had been forced into a soldier's red jacket meant for a doll, and a pill-box hat tied upon its head; and its mournful prancing to the organ's brash mechanical noise, its anxious eyes constantly upon its master. Robert couldn't bear to watch. The teeming lanes of booths and stalls suddenly seemed oppressive and claustrophobic. Pushing free of the crowd, he walked to a quieter part of the park.

≈

He sat on a bench in the shade of a beech tree, trying to forget the dancing monkey. Arthur's second piece of advice had been a good one, too. He had found lodgings at Mrs Budge's place, which suited him so much better than Fitz's Club. Robert hoped he would see Arthur again. He wasn't quite sure, though, how it would happen. The obvious thing would be to go round to Fitz's Club and see if he was in, or leave a note for him at the desk, making an arrangement, but he couldn't bring himself to go back there.

≈

At the other end of the bench an old woman sat clasping a walking stick. He began sketching her gnarled hands, finding an affinity between them and the corded, nobly stick. Behind him, beyond a large round boating pond, a game of football was in progress. Every time the ball crashed into the bushes nearby, he flinched. The beech tree under which he sat reminded him of home, of Mama, of Beechwood Chase.

'Excuse me,' said a boy's voice.

Robert turned to see a boy of about ten standing beside the bench.

'Cadey, my govern… er… that is, my tutor, says to ask you, please can we have a piece of your paper.'

Beyond the boy, a woman in a long blue cloak, about the same age as Mama, perhaps a bit younger, stood smiling pleasantly. Robert obligingly tore a blank sheet from his sketch-pad.

≈

Robert watched her fold the thick paper into the shape of a boat. The boy launched it on the pond where it was soon blown out of reach. He lobbed stones at it, making suitable cannonading noises, crying out with delight at the near misses.

The woman stepped closer and smiled at Robert. Her sweeping gesture took in both the sea battle and the football. 'Boys are never happier than when they're trying to hit or kick something, are they?'

At that moment, the football struck the tree and rolled towards Robert. Grumbling to herself, the old woman tottered off in the opposite direction from the offending footballers.

'Hoof it back!' came the distant shout.

Robert's heart sank. Past humiliations flashed through his mind, remembered jeers rang in his ears.

'Oh, let me! Please let me!' the boy cried, pouncing on the ball.

Robert waved him forward.

'Good one!' the woman applauded. She held out her hand. Robert wasn't sure whether he should kiss it, or shake it, or what. Blushing, he put his sketch-book into it.

'Thank you!' she said, laughing, and began looking through it. 'These are good. I'm Mrs Thomson, by the way.'

'No you're not! You're Cadey!' the boy called from somewhere up in the tree.

A little shrug, an indulgent smile.

'And I'm Robert Stanhope.'

'What leads you take an interest in the likes of an illusionist and… what's this one?'

Robert peeped over her shoulder. 'A chestnut vendor.'

He told her how he hoped to work for the *London Illustrated Chronicle*. She peered into the branches of the tree.

'That's high enough, Dickon!' Turning to Robert, she said. 'I'll wager, Mr Stanhope, that few readers of the *Chronicle*, if any, know or care how much people like your vendor here earn, or that old woman who was sitting next to you.'

As Cadey Thomson stretched forward to hand back the sketchbook, her long, blue cloak fell open. Robert saw that she was wearing some kind of baggy trousers and that she was clearly uncorseted. Seeing his surprise, she laughed.

'My father was Giles Thomson, the radical—and he had radical ideas about bringing up his children. He campaigned against slavery and that included the enslavement of women by men.'

'It's been abolished now, though, hasn't it? I mean African slaves and that sort of thing.'

'No, it has not!'

Cadey explained that it is only the trade in slaves which has been abolished, not slavery itself, and only in the British Empire, beyond whose boundaries were many unfortunates.

'We are a long way from ending this barbarity. The Arab traders do a thriving business and the Spanish and Portuguese sea captains grow rich by transporting these wretched captives to the colonies, our colonies.'

Robert said, 'You speak of your father in the past tense.'

'He was one of those cut down at St Peter's Fields.'

Robert had only the vaguest notion of the event. About three years ago there had been a demonstration of some kind at a place near Manchester.

'Ah yes, when the mounted yeomanry charged the mob.'

'Mob? Now there's a loaded word. Take note Mr Would-be-Chronicler, words like that can be more lethal than a primed pistol. Why, one could charge a mob without shame, without fear of recrimination, could one not?'

'Was there much violence?'

She let out a bitter laugh. 'Oh yes. And it was all from the yeomanry. You see, our enlightened rulers say they disapprove of violence, but what they really mean is that they want to own the rights on its use.'

'Your father was killed at St. Peter's Fields?'

'He died two weeks later from his wound.'

She talked to Robert about her father, about 'Orator' Hunt, Samuel Bamford and the other radicals she had met. At his group meetings, she told him, the women voted along with the men. Robert felt safe talking to her. Her plainness and unfeminine garb put him at ease. Clearly he wouldn't be expected to indulge in those false compliments, which always seemed to him so uncomplimentary in their assessment of the recipient's ability to tell fact from fiction. Nor would he have to act the dundering rake to impress either her or the world at large. Robert realised that for several minutes at a time he'd forgotten to be miserable.

≈

Cadey smiled at Robert. 'We must be going. I think it's about to rain and I don't want Dickon catching a chill.'

'Oh Cadey!' complained the voice in the tree, 'You're my tutor, not my mother!'

'Anyway, it's time for your lessons.'

'What's for supper?' Dickon asked from somewhere in the branches.

'Wait-and-see pudding.'

'Will you read to me afterwards?'

'Yes, if you want.'

Robert said, 'My mother always read to me. I loved it.'

Dickon dropped from the branches. 'We went to the fair yesterday. The Wild Man of Borneo, that was the best bit.'

'Good luck with the *Chronicle*,' Cadey said, taking Dickon by the hand and setting off. Robert watched them go. On an impulse, he called out. 'Do you come here often?' He felt silly as soon as he'd said it, but she turned and said, 'Yes, quite often.'

'Perhaps I'll see you again, then.'

'That would be nice, Mr Stanhope.'

Robert felt suddenly happy. Now he had two friends—Arthur and now Cadey. Well, he thought of them as friends. He thought of Arthur quite a lot, in fact. Perhaps leaving home hadn't been such a terrible thing after all.

8

Robert sat at his desk in 'the Hackery', the rather dreary room allocated to the junior members of the art staff of the *London Illustrated Chronicle*. He had shown his sketches to the head of the Art Department and had been hired on the spot. The other three desks in the room were unoccupied. The iron stove glowed and whispered. Gilbert, Bob and Jerry were out recording various events and would, no doubt, contrive to meet up in some public house. They had stopped asking him to join them. It was obvious that he was the misfit of the Hackery. Robert was working up his sketch of the caged-bird man. There'd been thrushes, goldfinches, larks and starlings in his cages, and a solitary jay. Jays were becoming rarer in Beechwood Chase. Father shot them at every opportunity because they took the pheasants' eggs. Many a time rows of dead jays hung from a fence. They were such beautiful birds with their subtle cinnamon colouring and wing patches of brilliant blue, barred with black. Robert changed to a finer nib. His quills were nice for letters, but, for this kind of work, the new steel nibs were better. His pen hovered above the pot of Indian ink. Cages kept you safe, though… especially if you were an exotic species different from the rest.

≈

Robert paused, his pen hovering above the drawing. He had returned to the boating pond several times, at the same hour as before, in the hopes of seeing Mrs Thomson… Cadey Thomson… again, but she had not been there. He dipped his quill in the inkpot, then paused again. He wished he could tell his mother he was happy in his new life. It would be a lie. Probably, only when he was totally immersed in his painting was he truly happy, and he hadn't done much of that lately. The last one, in fact, had been the small watercolour of Beechwood Chase—a winter moonlight scene after the style of Samuel Palmer. He'd tried to achieve the same mystical beauty of Palmer's landscapes. After the style of… that was the trouble. His work shouldn't be a copy of someone else's. His painting must come from inside himself, not from some outside source. Mama had once said to him, 'Every person is unique. You have only to be yourself to be original.' But did he really know who he was?

To be fair to himself, there was a difference between being influenced by someone and slavishly copying them. He gave a guilty start as, inside his head, he heard Father roar, 'Stop daydreaming, boy! I can't bear the sight of you mooning around like that. Go and do something useful. Go and hit a ball about or something!'

'Stanhope, isn't it?' A middle-aged clerk was addressing him.

'What?'

'Are you Robert Stanhope?'

'Yes.'

'Sir Charles wants to see you in his office now.'

Robert scrambled to his feet. What could Sir Charles Makepiece, owner and editor of the *London Illustrated Chronicle*, want with the likes of himself?

≈

In a room considerably more comfortably and lavishly furnished than the Hackery, Robert sat facing Sir Charles across a large, leather-topped desk.

≈

'What I am about to say might come as a shock to you, young Stanhope, so take a deep breath.'

Panic rose inside Robert. Mother's dead, he thought. He's going to tell me news has just reached him that Mother has died.

'I want you to cover the war in Peru.'

'What?'

Sir Charles wanted him to send back eye-witness accounts and drawings of the campaign. The struggle for independence in South America had been going on for more than ten years, first in Venezuela, then in Colombia and Ecuador. Now it was reaching its climax in Peru, the jewel in the crown of the Spanish Empire, their richest possession to which they clung with the utmost tenacity. As the final scene in the drama approached, the appetite of the British public for news of the conflict increased—an appetite which was sharpened by the decision of Bolivar, the Great Liberator, to form a Foreign Legion to reinforce the Patriots in their struggle against the Spanish Royalists. For the past six months Bolivar's agents had been in Britain, recruiting officers and men from the thousands who found themselves unemployed at the end of the war against Napoleon.

'Hasn't been done before,' Sir Charles said. 'The *Chronicle* is breaking new ground sending a civilian to a theatre of war.'

It was usual, he said, to rely on official dispatches released by the War Office. But these were too discreet, too dull and lacking in pictures.

'What about one of the others… What about Gilbert?' Robert said. He was white and shaking. 'Gilbert would do it much better than I.'

Sir Charles Makepiece spun the large globe which stood in the centre of his spacious office. 'Chance of a lifetime, young Stanhope. An increase in salary, too.'

'Yes, sir. Thank you, sir. It's just that… ' Robert's voice trailed away.

In particular, Sir Charles wanted Robert to follow the fortunes of the newly-formed British Brigade, privately raised by Brigadier Cochrane-Dyat and financed with Patriot money. Before the month was out, the brigade would be sailing for Peru.

'The point about the *London Illustrated Chronicle*, Stanhope, is that it's illustrated. Gilbert Baxter is nowhere as good an illustrator as you. You're the best we've got. Well, the most suitable, at least. Not fair to send men with wives and children. Besides, it stands to reason, your father being a General and you a member of Fitz's Club—clearly you know a thing or two about military matters, which is more than can be said for the others.'

Only a few weeks ago Robert had hardly been outside Oxfordshire, except for the occasional short visit to London, and now he was expected to go to the other end of the world .

'Who would write the reports that accompany my drawings?' Robert asked, more to gain time than anything else.

'You would, of course. You're good at writing, I hear. Long letters to your mother, I believe. Very commendable. So there you are.'

'But I… '

Sir Charles nodded at his black-suited clerk who rose from his seat and opened the door.

'So there you are.'

'I… I need… may I please have some time to think about it?'

'If you must. This time next week, then.'

Robert slumped onto his hard wooden chair in the Hackery. 'War Correspondent' was the phrase Sir Charles had used. Yes, Father could almost be proud of that... well, less contemptuous, at least. Robert could still see his face the day... the day he'd been dismissed from his own home. Peru was so far away. Let Father be disappointed in him for turning down the opportunity. Let Sir Charles think the less of him. He was not going. After all, Mama would worry about him desperately. And to be plunged into a military world, day and night with no escape... It would be Fitz's Club multiplied a hundredfold, surely the nearest thing to Hell on Earth. No, he was definitely not going.

≈

It was Robert's morning off. He was at Horsefair Common sketching the great oak he'd heard about. He had filled a whole sketch-book with its grotesque carbuncles, whorls and knots, its rain-filled hollows and secret recesses, its massive confusion of branches, the great split down its central trunk where it must have been struck by a thunderbolt. Now he sat in the crook of the huge tree, reading his pocket-sized edition of 'The Tempest.' When Shakespeare wrote the play, the oak was already a century old. Poor Caliban. Why should he be the one branded as a misfit? It was his world, after all, which had been invaded. Rejecting the jellied-eel sandwiches provided by Mrs Budge, he took an apple from his pocket and bit into it. What was that joke which had so delighted Arthur? What's worse than finding a worm in your apple? Finding half a worm! Apparently there'd been some big boxing match on the Common several weeks ago. No doubt Arthur had been there. Robert had braved Fitz's Club and asked at the desk about Arthur, only to learn he was riding with a circus. He must remember to entertain Mama with that little titbit in his next letter. Maybe he wouldn't mention just how much he missed Arthur.

≈

Behind him. and beyond some bushes, he heard a voice he recognised. At least he thought he did. It was loud and insistent and slightly hectoring, not the well modulated tones he remembered. Scrambling out of the tree, he rounded the bushes. There, standing on a bench with a gathering around her, was Cadey Thomson. This week Robert's free half-day had fallen on a Saturday, and the Common was a popular place on a Saturday for promenading, courting and generally 'taking the air,' so the crowd around Cadey was quite a sizeable one. She was wearing pantaloons and a brown jacket which made no concessions to the latest fashion. The topic of her discourse or harangue was the iniquity of sending pregnant women to jail.

'You're the one should be in jail!' bellowed a red-faced man.

'Easy to see who wears the trousers in your house. I pity your poor bleedin' husband, I really do!'

Somebody kicked the bench, nearly causing her to fall off. A roar of laughter went up. Several others joined in this entertainment until Cadey toppled to the ground, landing awkwardly. Robert ran forward and helped her to her feet. Trying to shield her from the jostling and the elbowing, and with jeers ringing in his ears, Robert led her to a small coffeehouse on the edge of the Common.

'Thank you, Mr Stanhope.' She smiled wryly. 'By rights I should be a little vexed with you. You see, a lot of my tracts and lectures set out to show that women are the equal of men, that, in many instances, we are better off without them. But I was glad you were here today and I'm grateful for what you did.'

'I think I'm shaking more than you are, Mrs Thomson… '

Cadey became aware that he was staring again at the way she was dressed.

'You stare, Mr Stanhope. Is practical clothing to be the prerogative of men?'

Her eyes were wide and frank, like her mouth. Robert stammered out some inadequate reply. She laughed heartily, almost like a man, at his discomfiture.

≈

She fixed Robert with an amused gaze. 'You don't know what to make of me, do you?'

'I… I… Well, that is to say… no, I don't… you certainly seem to have inherited your father's reforming zeal. Who else are you goading into pushing you off benches?'

Cadey smiled. 'Well I do have a seat on the board of Warberton's

Private Asylum for the Insane. I take pride in being a thorn in their flesh. The insane are treated as if they are no better than common criminals. It's a disgrace in this day and age.'

She told him that, at the time of her father's death, she had been in Lord Hawksmoor's employ in the dual role of his housekeeper and governess to Dickon. It was he who had procured for her a seat on the board of the asylum. Dickon, she said, was Lord Hawksmoor's nephew from a branch of the family in India. When his parents both died of fever, he was sent back to live under the protection of his uncle. Minagh was the family name. Hawksmoor was the name his uncle had chosen on receiving a peerage—after his estate in Yorkshire. Robert wondered whether it would be improper to ask about her husband. Where was he? What had happened to him? He supposed she would tell him when she was ready to.

'Nice boy, Dickon,' Robert said. 'He's certainly has a lot of influence behind him.'

'Yes, and now his uncle has used his influence to buy him a commission in Cochrane-Dyat's British Brigade.'

'Oh my pippin! You mean the one going to Peru?'

Cadey's expression was grim. 'The very same. He will be joining one of the cavalry regiments in the brigade, the British Light Horse.'

'But, he's only... what... ten? 'Tell me it's not true, a ten-year-old commanding a squadron of cavalry!'

Cadey thumped her cup onto the table, spilling coffee into the saucer. 'In this mad, man-organised world, that's how it works, apparently. The Brigadier has the authority to sell commissions to the highest bidder whenever a vacancy occurs.'

'For his own personal profit?'

'Of course.'

'With no regard to age or military training?'

Cadey's voice was bitter, scornful. 'Oh, a passing thought, perhaps. Breeding is what counts, you see. It seems there's no finer preparation for being an officer than the life of a country gentleman—commanding inferiors, plenty of riding, hunting, shooting.'

≈

'Even so... ten! But why?'

'Lord Hawksmoor thinks it's time he saw something of the world, something of real life, that it will make a man of him.' Her voice trembled with emotion. Whether it was anger, or something else, Robert wasn't sure.

Cadey leant forward. 'And I'm going with him, Mr Stanhope. I shall be accompanying him as his tutor to ensure his education is not completely neglected in this claustrophobic, immature, all-male world called the army.'

'Immature?'

'Men, as individuals, don't grow up till they're over forty... if then. But, put them in a group—a club, a regiment, whatever, and they never grow up.'

'You don't like men?'

'Not much. And you? My guess is you don't like them much either.'

'I... I... Well, I'm not a very clubbable, hearty person, if that's what you mean.'

'Good. I think you and I shall get on very well. Dickon likes you, anyway.'

'Will I see you before you go?'

'Oh yes, bound to.'

Robert walked with her to the edge of the Common and watched her into a cab. The thought that she would be sailing for Peru had momentarily weakened his resolve to decline the great opportunity Sir Charles Makepiece was offering him—only momentarily because, if he went, there would be no chance of seeing Arthur.

9

The French soldier clutched his chest, swayed, then fell from the topmost battlements of the fortress city of Badajoz.

Barnaby Thackston lit a fresh cigar 'Enough sawdust in the pit for you?

The soldier brushed down his uniform. 'Just right, Mr Thackston.'

From somewhere Joey the Clown produced a fake cigar, ten times the size of Barnaby's. He strutted round the ring imitating his boss's mannerisms so exactly that it drew sniggers from the circus hands.

'Quite enough of that!' Barnaby bellowed, waving his cigar in the air, as if copying Joey.

≈

At one end of the Big Top, a replica wall had been constructed from interlocking wooden boxes. When the moment came to breach the citadel's defences, under cover of the copious smoke which accompanied the fake explosion, a section of the wall could be pulled away. Thackston's Circus was rehearsing 'The Storming of Badajoz'. They were three days out from London and heading into Hampshire. Yesterday something had gone wrong. The British troops had failed to breach the wall. Result—a rather unconvincing surrender on the part of the French and a little corner of England which had its own unique version of the event.

≈

High in the back row of seats, Rainbow looked down into the ring. The soldiers in the arena, with their stamping and parading, were not unlike the warriors of his own people. How many times, he wondered, had he watched them dancing and chanting and beating their spears upon their shields in unison? He was always the one who stood apart from his age-mates, the one who was different, the lonely one. He knew it was the price he had to pay for his special gifts and for being the one chosen by Ikpoom under the guidance of the gods and the ancestors. Sometimes he longed to be like the others… except that, when he tried to imagine it, he knew the truth of Ikpoom's words: 'Once you have started on The Journey, the most arduous journey a man can undertake, no other path will satisfy you.'

Rainbow descended the aisle between the seats to where the cavalry would charge past and where Carroty Kate sat at the edge of the ring. Her old army tunic, trousers and boots had been temporarily exchanged for a dress, chosen by Barnaby with a showman's instinct for what would not alienate the women in the audience, yet be sure to win the men. A demure brown wig hid her natural glory. Carroty Kate leaned forward to catch Barnaby's attention as he walked by. She patted her wig, 'Do I have to wear this dead moggy on me 'ead?'

'Aye, lass. They'll think your real hair's a wig. The wig's much more convincing... Sure you know your part?'

'Yes, Mr Thackston. But... '

'But what?'

'Badajoz was nothing like... like what we're doing here. Nothing like it.

'And not like we had it yesterday, either.' Barnaby growled, chewing his cigar.

'I was there, Mr Thackston. Saw it with my own two eyes. This is all too... too... I dunno... too prettified.' She rose to her feet, thumping the ringside barrier with a brawny arm, setting her frilly puff sleeves aquiver.

'Those scaling ladders... within minutes they was so slippery with blood and brains nobody could friggin' use 'em. And the wounded... they didn't lie around in poncy poses, they suffocated to death under piles of other poor bastards... did you know that, Mr Thackston?'

Barnaby studied the tip of his cigar. 'People come because they want a good story. They want to feel proud of being English, to cheer heroes and boo villains. They aren't paying for a history lesson, lass... Just remember that.' He raised his voice. 'We'll have the entry of the cavalry again. Are they ready this time, Captain Trevellyn?'

Carroty Kate turned to Rainbow. 'When Smithy came through all that, I thought... I thought... '

≈

The cavalry swept into the ring, circling it three times, sabres drawn, Arthur performing feats of horsemanship in the limelight, splitting turnip-heads fixed to wooden cut-outs of French dragoons. He wore an especially dashing uniform, designed by Barnaby.

'Good! Good! That'll do!' Barnaby barked through a megaphone.

Arthur trotted up to Barnaby. 'Spiffing uniform, Barnaby. Enough to make the doorman at Fitz's green with envy.'

Barnaby blew a couple of smoke rings and chuckled.

Arthur plucked at the hairs of the moustache he was growing, his eyes roving roguishly over Carroty Kate. 'Women can't resist a man in uniform, isn't that right, Kate?'

Carroty Kate tossed her head, allowing a flash of red to escape from the wig. 'Well now, Captain, if that thing between your legs is your manhood, I might be interested, but if it's only your horse... '

The horse shook its head and snorted. They all laughed.

Arthur said, 'Kate, I'm sorry I didn't tell you sooner. Frightful ass. Forget my own head next.'

'What?'

'Something I heard at my club... there was a batch of British prisoners not released until last year. Seems they were working in the Spanish opal mines and the owners thought they were onto a good thing with free slave labour and hung on to them.'

'Was Smithy one of 'em?'

'Sorry, Kate, that's all I know.'

'But he might of been one of 'em. Bloody hell! All those sodding years looking for the bugger and he was still locked up!'

Barnaby raised his megaphone. 'The show begins in one hour!'

≈

The Big Top was packed. The country folk from the surrounding villages had enjoyed the clowns and now they bubbled with anticipation of the main event. Barnaby, wearing his Hamlet costume stood in the centre of the ring.

'And now, ladies and gentlemen, we take you back to the year of our Lord, eighteen hundred and twelve. Who but the men of England, with hearts of oak, can free Europe from the stranglehold of Napoleon Bonaparte? In Spain, the advance of the Duke of Wellington... ' he paused for the cheer he knew would go up at the mention of the name. 'His advance cannot proceed unless the impregnable fortress of Badajoz is captured.'

A bugler sounds the alarm from the top of the tower. French soldiers dash to line the ramparts. Into the arena, led by a little drummer-boy, march the British infantrymen. In the ranks is a jaunty soldier with one arm in a sling. A woman runs forward and embraces him.

'Oh John, my John, come safely back to me!'

'That I will, Meg, 'cos I love you.'

≈

From the battlements a deadly fire pours forth. Gaps appear in the lines of the British, but the little drummer-boy, swaggering at the front, bearing a charmed life, keeps a steady beat and on they come, unfaltering. Then, with a loud 'Hussah!' they charge the wall, swarming up ladders—only to be repulsed. The crowd groans with despair, then roars on the brave lads to another attempt. This time a smaller group dares the bullet-swept terrain. They carry a bomb, round and black with a smouldering fuse. And the drummer boy is with them, his drum rallying them, giving them heart. One by one they fall. And each time, the bomb is taken up and carried onwards. But the deadly hail has mowed them all down. Their bodies lie below the wall, even that of the little drummer-boy. The bomb hisses uselessly in the open. The audience weeps. A single faint tap on the drum, then another and another, growing louder sends a sigh of hope sweeping through the Big Top. The drummer boy crawls with agonising slowness towards the wall, dragging the bomb with him. He'll never get there! Not before the fuse reaches its end. But here come the cavalry, sabres drawn. A handsome officer sweeps the boy into his saddle, hurls the bomb at the base of the wall, wheels his horse and gallops away. An almighty explosion rends the air.

≈

When the smoke clears the breach is plain to see. Our plucky soldiers pour through, cheering. Fierce hand-to-hand combat ensues in which the British bayonet is triumphant. A gallant band fight their way towards the top of the tower. Amongst them is John, fighting the enemy with his one good arm. Only he reaches the top. He lowers the French colours from the flagpole and runs up the Union Jack. As he does so, a cowardly Frenchman creeps up and knocks him on the head with the butt of his gun. John slumps across the battlements. The Big Top is hushed. Meg is picking her way through the dead.

'John! John! Oh, where is my John?'

''E's over there, Meg!' a country voice shouts.

'Not there, Meg, t'other way!'

'Higher, go higher, Meg!'

And so they direct her to her John. She gives a cry of anguish, then gently lifts his limp but faintly stirring body from the battlements.

'Meg, my Meg! I knew you'd find me!'

Out springs the same dastardly Frenchman and attacks her. They struggle, the foreigner forcing his unwanted attentions upon this flower of English womanhood in a way that has the country folk of the Big Top in uproar, booing and yelling their indignation... and then their delight as Meg throws the man to the floor, jumps on him, picks him up as if he was no more than a rag doll and tosses him over the side.

Outside the Big Top, at the back, the boxing booth was placed between the roundabouts, powered by boys looking for a free ride, and the Grotesque—a man with a lopsided, bloated face and twisted body. Barnaby had decided not to open the booths and side-shows until the Big Top events were finished. Thus he himself was free to be Rainbow's bottler and Arthur and Carroty Kate his seconds. Barnaby arrived and approached Carroty Kate, all smiles.

'I liked that extra bit of business you put in with Joey... when you jump on him before you throw him over the wall... keep it in from now on.'

Carroty Kate winked at Rainbow. She'd already told him how Joey had thought he could take liberties with her while pretending it was part of the act, but had got more than he'd bargained for.

'You want me to give him a drubbing every time from now on?'

'Yes, exactly like tonight.'

≈

Barnaby allowed himself to be helped into the raised ring. 'Step up! Step up! Your money back if you go five minutes with the Lion of Africa. Double your money if you knock him down. Step up! Step up! He'll box you, not eat you! You, sir, you look as though you don't scare easy... Or you, sir. Now there's a fine set of muscles! Want to show your girl what you can do?'

The young farm labourer who climbed into the ring with a mixture of bravado and sheepishness was strong, but unskilled, all rushes and wild swings. Rainbow coped with him easily enough, punishing him sufficiently to slow him down, but letting him win his money back.

'God dammit, Rainbow! This isn't a charity I'm running.' Barnaby growled at the end of the five minutes. 'More aggression. You've got to act like… like you're a lion and they're your prey.'

'But I don't know them. I wish them no harm.'

Barnaby chewed the end of his cigar. 'All that talent and the killer instinct of a butterfly! More aggression, by thunder, more aggression!'

Rainbow nodded. Xango was right. Xango and Arthur had told him he must prepare for what lay ahead, harden his hands, learn to move about the square shape they called a ring, get used to fighting with the noise of the crowd in his ears. Only then would he be ready to meet Nataxale.

'When will it be?' he asked.

'The big one? When I say and not before. When the money's right… Step up! Step up! He'll box you, not eat you! You, sir… '

≈

Thackston's Travelling Circus was at sleep. But, two, at least, were awake —the lion prowling its cage, and Rainbow, watching it cross and recross the shadows of the moonlit bars. Who or what was Africa? Rainbow wondered. 'The Lion of Africa', Barnaby had called him. King George had spoken that name, but he hadn't understood what he'd meant. The lion rumbled softly—a sound which carried great distances across the savannah, making the baboons flee, gibbering with fear, for the trees and the high rocks; making the night-watchman of the village check the thornbush defences; making Yaba draw closer in bed. Yaba. Was she watching over him at this very moment, or perhaps tending to Obobo? Was the goat meat still simmering, awaiting his return? How long till he could be with them again?

≈

Rainbow saluted the lion and moved on, passing silently through the temporary village. A midget, riding a saddled dog, flitted across the gap between two lines of tents. He paused outside the caravan shared by the

Grotesque and the Bearded Woman. Exu, who inhabited the borders of things and the crossroads, the liminal areas of life which are not quite one thing nor yet another, was here in this circus, walking the boundaries between illusion and reality.

≈

In the makeshift stables, the stable-lads lay curled up in the hay. Even the elephant was lying down in its enclosure of straw bales. Where was Jacko? He'd said he'd find a place somewhere in or near the stables. Rainbow hunted around, finally spotting Jacko sitting dejectedly inside an empty horse-box.

The boy stared down into the straw, his voice harsh with the lump in his throat. 'Thought you weren't coming... Not that I care. All one to me.' Tears welled up. 'You don't need me no more, do you?'

Ikpoom had not prepared him to deal with this aspect of Power Animals, but one thing was clear—the child in Monkey needed comforting.

'What would I do without you, Jacko?'

'Well... well, there's some as seems to manage fine and dandy wivout me... like my old lady.' He burst into tears. 'What took you so long? I thought you wasn't coming.'

Rainbow lifted Jacko onto his lap and held him tight. 'It's all right, Jacko, it's all right. We'll take care of each other, that's what we'll do... Look, I've got a pie.'

Jacko ate with his fingers, cramming it in till his cheeks bulged. With barely more than a mouthful left, he hesitated and looked guiltily at Rainbow.

'Go ahead and finish it, Jacko. I'm not hungry.'

≈

Jacko lay with his head in Rainbow's lap while Rainbow plaited a straw giraffe for him. His thoughts returned to the letter in his pocket with the big J on it and the red sealing wax, the one from his mother. Arthur would read it for him if he asked him. But there was no need for that. He could guess what it said—that she loved him and missed him and that she would come and get him very soon once a few problems were settled. The letter would start with the words: My own dear little boy... My own dear little boy that I long to hold and comfort...

'Here, this is for you, Jacko.'

'Blimey! What sort of animal's that when it's at home?'

'It's a kiraffy… I think that's what the George called it.'

'Some kind of long necked mouse, by the looks of it.'

Rainbow laughed. 'No, it's taller than an elephant.'

'You're having me on!'

'But you didn't believe the elephant till you saw it.'

'Still don't. I has to pinch meself whenever I sees it… pinch me… self… He drifted into sleep.

≈

Rainbow plaited another kiraffy so that the first one wouldn't be lonely, remembering how he used to plait animals out of the river reeds. The straw rustled as Jacko stirred, then went back to sleep. The reeds were rustling, too. He didn't want them to rustle, to whisper of his presence to the Ijeru warriors. He knew his mother was there on the river bank. He could hear her pleading with them, their rough laughter. Slowly he parted the reeds. She let out a wild scream… Only it was Jacko who had screamed. He sat upright rubbing the soles of his feet.

'Fuckin' straw jabbed me.'

'You were dreaming?'

Jacko nodded. 'I was in the chimleys again. When you're new at it… You're in this dark, narrer place, see, and you goes slow 'cos… 'cos you're scared.'

'I know how it is.'

'So he sends an older boy up after you wiv a pin to jab your feet and make you shift double quick.'

'He must have been a terrible master.'

'He was, guv… When you comes down wiv the skin hanging off your knees and elbows, he rubs in winniger… to harden 'em up, see… that's worse than any beating.'

'Go to sleep now, Jacko. You're safe, I promise.'

Rainbow placed the two giraffes side by side so that they were nuzzling and comforting each other. Somewhere in the distance a clock struck twelve. Twelve was a number that seemed to crop up all the time in the Other World. The dung beetle had mentioned the Twelve Apostles; in the oracles called coins there were twelve pence in a shilling; a day was divided into twelve parts. They even had a special word for twelve, 'a dozen.' The spirits, beings and Orisha Animals of the Other World bartered for eggs and other things by the dozen. It was a constant reminder that there were twelve villagers who would be sacrificed if his mission failed. And Yaba might be one of them.

≈

He was dreaming of his village, of the Ijeru with spears and climbing boys with pins, dreams mingling and flowing together and meeting at the crossroads where Exu, the great trickster presided.

10

Water. Water gurgling and gushing. The river Itzwala had come to life again, flowing through the land so that the cattle might drink from it and the women fill their water-jars. It could not be so, he had yet to defeat Nataxale and make his gift to Skyherd. He must not fail. Then the squeaking of the 'iron cow,' as they called the pump on the village common reminded Rainbow where he was. A bowl of steaming porridge was being placed beside him. Rainbow sat up.

Jacko grinned at him. 'Carrots says you're to get yourself outside that.'

Arthur appeared, razor in hand, his face half lathered. 'What's that frightful row? Someone killing a pig at this hour?'

'It's the pump,' Jacko said.

'When a fellow's used to his barber shaving him, he needs to concentrate on what he's doing. Nearly cut myself... What's this, Rainbow, not had your cold bath yet, or run round the common? You're in training now, you know.'

Rainbow smiled. 'Ikpoom and Monkey and Snail are my shield and spear.'

'Sounds biblical,' Arthur said, stroking his chin, so that his hand became covered in soap. 'Never was one for the Good Book, or any other book for that matter. Bit of a duffer at that sort of thing.'

He regarded the razor in his hand. 'Well, better get ready. On the march in a jiffy or two, I shouldn't wonder. Winchester is where we're making for, I gather... A chance to see more of our countryside, eh, Rainbow? What do you think of it?'

'Everything's so green,' Rainbow replied, eating the porridge with his fingers.

Jacko sighed. 'Yeah, including certin people not a million miles from here.'

≈

From Hannibal the elephant, striding at the front, to the hay carts at the rear, the circus stretched along the Winchester road for more than a quarter of a mile—covered animal-wagons, carts loaded with tentage and seating, private caravans, mobile stalls and boxes for the show horses

—all bumping along as fast as they could in order to reach Winchester in time to claim the best ground for the fair on the following day.

≈

Directly behind Hannibal, two shire horses pulled the wagon which carried the huge canvas bundles which were the Big Top. Nestling on top of these were Rainbow, Carroty Kate and Jacko. Rainbow sat apart, hunched up, tense and uneasy. Rooks circled overhead, occasionally returning to their rookery in the bare branches of the trees... branches with long bony fingers like skeletons. The drought in his homeland was so severe that all the leaves had fallen from the trees. It had been like that, too, the year the Ijeru raiding-party had descended on them because their own cattle had died... The raiding-party which... Rainbow thrust the thought away.

Carroty Kate moved up beside him. 'Feeling all right?'

Rainbow shook his head.

'What's up, then?'

'The old crocodile is stirring in the mud.'

≈

The sound of Jacko drumming on the side of the wagon reached them.

Carroty Kate grimaced. 'Drives yer bleedin' mad, that does.' She gripped the bottle. 'It's bloody hard having him around.' She raised her voice. 'Jacko! I'll shove those sticks up where the sun don't shine, if you don't pack it in!'

Jacko shrugged, clambered down from the slowly moving wagon and jumped up onto the caravan directly behind, belonging to a Welsh couple that did the William Tell act—he with the crossbow, she with the apple on her head.

'Can I look at your crossbow?'

'No!'

'Oh, go on, let us, please!'

'No!'

Carroty Kage took a swallow of gin. 'It's the not the noise he makes. It's that... that he puts me in mind of my own boy... he's much the same age an' all.'

'Your boy?'

She nodded. 'Gave 'im up three days after he was born. Three days

≈93≈

is all I had.'

'Did you give him a name… in those three days?'

'William,' she said and gulped down her gin. 'After Smithy. Couldn't keep my babby what with 'im being a sojer. It's like this… When a sojer's sent overseas, not your bloody officer, in course, your plain friggin' sojer he has to leave his woman behind, abandon her, you might say. Not even your church-wed wife gets a single farthing to her name from the paymaster and, in times of war, it's nigh on friggin' impossible for a sojer to send back money.'

Unless they had relatives, she explained, or something saved, most of the women left behind had a choice between prostitution, the workhouse or starvation.

'Any judy as I knows'd choose a stretch in jug rather than the workhouse. Wouldn't 'ave been no life for a babby. And there was my man. I was afraid he'd die if I weren't with him. Many a night in the mountains only the warmth of my body's kept him alive. And women are better at progging nor men.'

'Progging?'

'You know, foraging for scran… for food. Most times you never gets the rations what reggerlashuns says you should. You 'as to find what you can. It's hard looking at Jacko day on day and thinking on my own flesh and blood… ' She paused as the wagon trundled past a group of mummers walking to the Winchester Fair. Ashley's circus had overtaken them an hour or more ago, they said. They gave their names according to their parts in the mumming—Pepper Britches, Pickle Herring, Bold Slasher, Tom Fool, the Recruiting Sergeant. They talked of places in terms of the food they'd been offered on doorsteps—pie and cake land, a bread and cheese neighbourhood, snossage town.

'Speak us a line for luck!' Carroty Kate shouted down.

Bold Slasher flung his arms wide and proclaimed in a loud, flat voice, 'So battle to battle you and I must play, to see who on the ground shall lay.'

Rainbow said, 'Is it the devil, Nataxale, to whom you speak?'

'No,' Bold Slasher replied. ''Tis religious, kind of, though. All our plays have a death and a resurrection in them.'

Rainbow nodded, his interest caught. 'Ikpoom, of whom you have, no doubt, heard, has experienced death and resurrection many times.'

Bold Slasher shrugged, raising his voice as the wagon began to leave him and his companions behind. 'I speak of the death of the sun and of the seasons.'

'You oughta be a prize-fighter wiv a name like Bold Slasher!' Jacko called after him. He puffed on his clay pipe before shouting across to Carroty Kate, 'Did you know, Carrots, Giles Ashley what owns the circus is Jem's bruvver... You know, Jem Ashley as mangolated Gypsy Morgan.'

'And that's the truth,' declared Barnaby, drawing level with the William Tell caravan. He was mounted on one of the 'cavalry' horses.

'Something for you, Jacko.' He held up a small wooden object.

Jacko reached down and took it.

'Well done, lad.' Barnaby said gruffly. 'That's a prime drummer-boy you do. There's some say I'm hard to please. That's as may be, but when I am pleased, I like to show it.'

'Thanks, Mr Thackston, thanks!'

Jacko examined the little painted clown, weighted so that it rocked up again when pushed down.

'It's a little-get-up-man,' Barnaby told him. 'And if you open him, there's a surprise or two.'

Jacko removed the clown's top half and found another clown inside and, inside that, was an even smaller clown which contained a little tinder-box.

'And how is Joey today?' Carroty Kate asked with a nudge for Rainbow that nearly knocked him off the wagon.

Barnaby directed his horse round a large, steaming elephant turd. 'Thought he'd be pleased about keeping in that bit of business you cooked up together. Seemed quite upset when I told him.'

'Oh, that's just his manner, Mr Thackston,' Carroty Kate assured him. 'Too many pratfalls have addled his brains. He's as pleased as... as Punch about it, really.'

'Funny man,' Barnaby said. 'And I don't mean funny like a clown. His father was a clown too, you know. Went mad. Used to pretend to be mad in his act. Funny thing was, when he really was mad, he wasn't funny at all. Nobody was ever as funny as Joseph Grimaldi, of course.'

Barnaby looked up at Carroty Kate. 'And there's a present waiting for you in my caravan, Kate.'

Carroty Kate snorted. 'Oh yes? Another little get-up-man, is it?' She tried to catch Rainbow's eye, but he stirred uneasily and hung his head.

≈

The circus came to a brief halt, wheels as close to the edge of the drainage ditch as possible, to let the Winchester to London mail coach come bowling by from the opposite direction.

'Passed Ashley's ten minutes back!' the coachman shouted, recognising Barnaby.

'Looks like we're catching them up,' Barnaby said, kicking his horse into a trot. 'I'd better get everyone to close up.'

≈

Soon after that, they topped a rise and saw Ashley's Circus strung out ahead of them. A much bigger concern than Thackston's, with many more animals and more and bigger wagons.

'I bet they won't let us by,' Carroty Kate said. 'And that could mean trouble… Oh, my gawd! That fool of a Taffy's only gone and let Jacko get his paws on the crossbow!'

≈

The Welshman in the caravan behind them seemed unaware that Jacko had fitted a bolt into the bow. At least the safety lock was on. The caravan jolted over a pothole. Jacko lurched sideways, his clutching hand somehow releasing the locking device. The bolt sped away, narrowly missing Carroty Kate and struck Hannibal in a tender part of his backside. Trumpeting with pain and rage, the elephant careered down the road.

≈

In the next dip in the road, the rear section of Ashley's entourage was drawn up so as to block the way and prevent any overtaking while the main body raced on to Winchester and secured the best pitches. Perhaps Barnaby would have backed down from a fight, possibly he might have made a deal or reached a compromise, but from the moment Hannibal's bulk struck an Ashley wagon, splintering it and overturning it, the battle was on.

Thackston's men gave a wild cheer and rushed forward. The main body of Ashley's outfit, seeing their own folk under attack, turned back and, snatching up any weapons that came to hand—crowbars, tent-poles, whips—laid about them. Rainbow, Carroty Kate and Jacko leapt from the wagon and joined the fray. Carroty Kate, wielding an axe-handle, felled their Strong Man with one blow, then set about the Fattest Man on Earth who was sitting on Joey. Rainbow, attacked by three dwarfs with daggers, was hard put to it to avoid injury. Jacko, grabbing a bundle of netting spilled from a cart, clambered on top of a caravan and flung it over them, enmeshing them. The rampaging Hannibal put such fear into four horses attached to an enormous van that they bolted, smashing everything in their path. Aroused by the combat, a whole menagerie of wild beasts added their roaring and howling to the din.

≈

Carroty Kate it was who, time and time again, rallied Thackston's forces, her flaming hair a banner around which they grouped and fought. But the little army, outnumbered, began to fall back. In the retreat, Carroty Kate became isolated. Surrounded by a dozen or more roughnecks, she flailed at them, a red tornado, spitting fury. They were closing in on her, preparing to rush her and overwhelm her when Rainbow saw her plight. Punching and kicking, he battered his way through the cursing, yelling circle to her side. Back to back they held off their assailants until Arthur's cavalry, armed with staves, drove them off.

Carroty Kate spat out a tooth. 'Thanks, Rainbow.' Her breasts were rising and falling beneath her military tunic. 'But for you I was a gonner. I'll not forget this… Oh, my gawd, fire!'

≈

A flanking movement of Ashley's men had reached the wagon containing the Big Top and set the canvas alight. Everyone fell back to put out the flames while Arthur's mounted troops held back the enemy. Under Barnaby's direction, buckets passed from hand to hand between the water in the ditch and the flames. The Grotesque, the Bearded Woman, the midget's pregnant wife, William Tell's children, everyone worked to quell the blaze. Even Hannibal, who had been consoling himself with the contents of an upturned toffee-apple stall, was pressed into service. Instead of squirting Joey, as he usually did in the ring, he sprayed the flames. With the extinguishing of the fire, the battle petered out. Both sides withdrew, leaving a debris-strewn middle ground between them.

≈

People stared, almost in disbelief, beginning to count the cost. The wounded lay all over the road amongst the remains of broken vehicles and equipment. Rainbow put an arm on Carroty Kate's shoulder.

'Is Jacko all right?'

She chuckled. 'The little-get-up-man! Every time he was knocked down he just bounced right back, grinning like he was really enjoying it.' She laid a hand on Rainbow's broad chest. 'Rainbow, thanks again. You're a good man.'

≈

Barnaby, on horseback, was picking his way through the wreckage, his face blackened by smoke.

'Little Billy, the Lee brothers and Jim Johnson will have to be taken to a bonesetter,' he said grimly. 'And the Big Top's in no condition for the fair.' He raised a fist in anger. 'Ashley had no right to block the road! By thunder, he's going to pay for this!'

Riding into no-man's land between the two circuses, he shouted, 'Ashley! Come out here, Ashley! I've a proposition for you.'

After a few minutes, Ashley's private carriage appeared from behind a chaos of other vehicles, dragged by six sweating men. Giles Ashley lolled in the seat, a younger man than Barnaby, well built, swarthy and ostentatiously dressed. Beside him sat his mother, dressed in the Spanish style with a black lace mantilla over her head. She seemed so small and frail, Rainbow thought, to have born two hefty sons.

Ashley's beringed hand rested on the carriage window. 'Make it quick, Thackston. I intend to be at Winchester, even if you can't cut it.'

'What's the matter, Ashley, can't you afford horses these days?'

'Damn you! One of your poxy lads cut 'em loose. Your proposition, what is it?'

'A challenge. I've got a man can beat your brother in the ring any day… providing it's fair and square.'

'You must be meaning my kid brother what's twelve.'

'I mean Jem, as you well know. And I'll wager ten thousand guineas on it.'

'Ten grand! My, my! You do like to lose big! All right, it's on! Who's your man?'

Barnaby smiled mysteriously. 'Nobody you would have heard of. He fights under the name of The Lion of Africa.'

11

The carriage bounced towards London. Jacko was up top beside the coachman. Inside, Carroty Kate was asleep. Arthur was stroking his fledgeling moustache and studying his Racing Gazette. Rainbow watched him from the opposite corner of the carriage. He had seen the George's books with similar marks like little black ants on them. They were the same sort of thing as the spoor of animals—signs that told you things if you knew how to interpret them.

≈

The fight had been arranged to coincide with the Newbury Races. three week before Christmas. Now, though, it was to London they were travelling. London was where Ben Bugler, mine host of the George and Dragon, had his gymnasium.

'He's the man we need,' Arthur had said, and Barnaby had agreed with him. If anyone could give Rainbow a chance of beating Jem Ashley, it was Ben Bugler.

≈

Although the Storming of Badajoz was a crowd puller and the Big Top could be patched up sufficiently to allow the show to go on, Barnaby had decided to let his key performers, Arthur, Carroty Kate and Jacko, go to London with Rainbow—Arthur to fix Rainbow's accommodation and food and generally take care of him; Carroty Kate and Jacko because Rainbow had insisted they accompany him. Arthur had backed up Rainbow on this.

'From what I saw of Carroty Kate in that little skirmish, she knows the lot when it comes to fighting foul… and I mean the lot. If anyone can teach Rainbow to look out for Jem's nasty tricks, it's her.'

Barnaby had nodded in agreement, adding, 'Besides, what we take at the turnstile is irrelevant now. I've had to go to the money-lenders for the ten grand. If we lose, I'll have to sell up to pay it back.'

≈

Jacko's head appeared, upside-down, at the window. 'Pie face, here, says… ow! I didn't mean it, ow! Leggo! Our nice, kind, driver says Giles Ashley fixes all his bruvver's fights for 'im.'

'Fixes is the right word,' Carroty Kate said, waking up.

'Do you think we'll see Bat again?' Rainbow asked Jacko.

'Not if he sees you first!'

Jacko's head disappeared. Carroty Kate took a swig of gin. 'Don't you look at me like that, behind your paper, Captain friggin' Trevellyn, as if I'm some bevvy omi. You may have been on a campaign or two, but what do friggin' officers know? You never slept, soaked to the skin in the open, in winter, did you? Not a friggin' officer, not friggin' likely!' She raised the bottle. 'This's what gets you through it... Gets you through a lot of things.'

Arthur lowered his gazette. 'Ah! I say, that's a coming on a bit strong, isn't it?'

'S'pose you'd prefer honest Meg, wig an' all, to me, wouldn't you? Let me tell you, Meg wouldn't have lasted a week in the Spanish Campaign.' Carroty Kate took another swig of gin. 'And I'll tell you why... 'Cos she'd've known sweet Fanny Adams about fighting foul. You fights with your man, you fights the enemy, you fights bloody army regerlashuns, you fights the other women for the best places, the best... I don't know what, you fights the weather, the bloody country... and if you don't grab the whole friggin' lot by the balls, you're done for, do you hear me? Done for.'

Arthur's face brightened. 'I say, Rainbow, a friend of yours out there.'

'What?'

'Other side.'

An arc of rainbow joined earth and sky.

'Read of your good book in verse... what was the other one? Oh yes... Richard of York gained battles in vain. About the only thing I remember from school... except, amo, amas, amat—I love, thou lovest, he, she or it loves.'

Carroty Kate and Rainbow stared at him as if he was a being from another world. Rainbow slid across the other side of the carriage and looked out of the window. The smell of burning flesh was suddenly in his nostrils. His hand went to the seven-ribbed scar on his chest. He saw the branding-iron coming towards him. He gripped the edge of the window. Had he cried out aloud? Perhaps not. Arthur had returned to his gazette as if nothing much had happened. The branding iron, like a crocodile, had emerged from murky waters and taken him unawares. That the mark upon his chest had meaning and significance for his mission, he did not doubt. If only he could find Nataxale. Rainbow knew from Jacko all about the punishment Jem had meted out to Gypsy Morgan. Morgan, of course, had been slow on his feet. All the same, in what condition would he be to fight Nataxale after tangling with Jem?

≈

Arthur stuck his head out of the window. 'Hey, Jacko! Come down here and give us a song!'

Jacko swung through the opening. Imitating Barnaby, he said, 'Joseph Grimaldi. By thunder, we'll never see his like again! So I gives you the song he made famous, I gives you 'Tippety Witchett'!'

When Rainbow had been rehearsed in the chorus, the song rendered twice over, the bottle of gin emptied and a final chorus sung, Arthur announced with an imitation fanfare, 'And when we get to the George and Dragon, Jacko, young fellow-me-lad, a capital good feed awaits you!'

But Jacko was fast asleep, his head resting on Carroty Kate's shoulder, snoring.

'That's Jacko for you,' she said. 'A boy what can keep his trap open longer'n his blinks.'

≈

The second floor of the George and Dragon Inn had been converted by Ben Bugler into his gymnasium. Here sporting bloods, Corinthians and young gentlemen of The Pugilistic Club paid handsomely to say they'd been given a bloody nose by the former contender for champion of all England. And here Ben set about passing on his hard-won skills to Rainbow—a task into which he threw himself wholeheartedly. Nobody, he said, wanted to see Jem Ashley humbled more than he. Jem had gouged out the eye of Ben's sparring partner, Prothero, ending a promising career as a prize-fighter. Although gouging, butting and biting were within the rules laid down by that old exponent of the 'Noble Art', Jack Broughton, many fighters agreed before a contest to fight with fists only. Prothero had shaken hands with Jem Ashley on such an agreement, but had been gouged all the same.

'Deuced unsporting,' Arthur commented. 'The Pugilistic Club took the fellow's picture off the wall.'

'It's him that needs taking down,' Ben growled. 'And I mean to make sure Rainbow's the one who does it.'

≈

For several hours each day Rainbow sparred with Ben or men selected by him, concentrating first on defence, learning how to slip, block and parry punches, how to escape from a corner, how to use the ropes to his advantage. Then, shifting to the attack, he learned Ben's repertoire of feints, double feints and counter punches.

'I'm afraid of teaching him too much,' Ben told Arthur one day, as they watched Rainbow working with a series of sparring partners.

'If he stops to think about it, he'll lose that... that animal instinct, that lightning speed.'

'The Lion of Africa, he's well named.'

'Except for the killer instinct, sir. He don't hate Jem Ashley like he should... like I do. In that respect, begging your pardon, Cap'n Trevellyn, he's a lamb, not a lion.' He leant forward, shouting to the man in the ring with Rainbow. 'Rush him, Clem, try and close with him and grab him... And you, Rainbow, don't let him. That's when Jem's at his most dangerous.'

Rainbow acknowledged the instruction with a wave, dancing out of trouble.

≈

As Ben had explained to Rainbow, under the Broughton code, a round lasted until a knockdown occurred—which meant a round could be only a few minutes long or more than half an hour. To prepare for the latter, Ben had arranged for three sparring partners to take five minutes each in rotation until Rainbow had fought continuously for half an hour. And when the professional pugilists had finished, Carroty Kate would step up to the scratch and attack him with every trick she'd learnt in the back alleys of her childhood, in prison yards, workhouse and barrack rooms.

≈

Rainbow crawled from the ring, unable to stand after Carroty Kate had kneed him in the kidneys.

'Elbows low!' she barked. 'Didn't I tell you? Elbows low in a clinch!'

Rainbow groaned. 'One minute with you is more punishing than one hour with the champ!'

'Let's see yer 'ands, guv,' Jacko demanded, seizing one and examining the knuckles before rubbing in first brine, then vinegar, Rainbow's sharp intake of breath bringing the usual cackle of laughter from Jacko.

Ben wiped Rainbow's face with a wet sponge. 'Well done.'

And Carroty Kate thumped him on the back. 'You look as though you could get yourself outside a jug of beer. See you downstairs in the snuggery.'

≈

Rainbow sat with a tankard of foaming ale in his hand, talking to Carroty Kate. A glass and a bottle of gin stood on the oak table at her elbow. A log fire purred in the grate, casting flickering shadows on the stone wall. Any woman drinking in the George and Dragon would normally be taken for a prostitute. In her cast-off military clothing, not many thought that of Carroty Kate. One who did had two black eyes to show for it—the first for insulting her by offering her money, the second because the amount was insultingly little. Rainbow could hear the inn sign creaking in the wind outside the pebbled glass bow-window. He felt reassured by that sign. It depicted the George killing a giant spiny-tailed lizard, the kind of lizard that throve in dry, dusty conditions, one of the few that didn't go into a comatose state until the dry season was over and the rains came. Undoubtedly the spiny-tailed lizard was an ally of Nataxale and here was the George killing that reptilian creature with a long spear. It had not been easy, at first, to see the likeness between the man on the sign and the George, but it was there if you looked hard enough.

≈

Behind Rainbow a laconic voice drawled, 'Well, look who we have here. Damn me if it isn't Trevellyn's nigger.'

Rainbow turned. It was Carlton-Syms, the person who'd tossed him the coins the day the Punch and Judy booth was smashed. Several other young bloods had gathered to watch the fun. Rainbow was subjected to a sneering scrutiny. 'Hmm, not a bad specimen. I dare say he'd have fetched a tolerably good price on my uncle's plantation... Stand up, let's have a proper look at you.'

Carroty Kate grasped Rainbow's arm. 'Stay where you are,' she said quietly.

Rainbow remained in his seat.

'Insolent dog! Perhaps a damned good whipping will teach you some respect.'

Someone tossed Carlton-Syms a riding whip. Carroty Kate snatched it from his raised hand and struck him across the face with it.

Carlton-Syms let out an oath. 'If you weren't a woman, I'd... By God, you'll regret this!'

'Piss off! I know your sort.'

'And you, you trollop, can take your confounded ugly phiz to the devil!'

There was a smattering of sycophantic applause from his cronies. Carlton-Syms swaggered out of the snuggery, turning at the doorway to fling a final supercilious stare at Rainbow.

'As for you... me money's on Jem Ashley. English grit will beat your kind any day. Black on the outside, yellow inside.'

Rainbow bowed, confused that a friend of Arthur's should speak to him like that, puzzled that someone should try to insult him one minute, then compliment him the next by comparing him to Xango, the Thunder God, with his cloak that symbolised the black storm clouds and the yellow lightning. Perhaps this was another test of some kind.

≈

The moon cast the shadow of a chair-back across the floor of the bedroom. In the bed, a few feet away, lay Jacko. With regular meals and regular sleep, he'd begun to fill out and lose that scrawny look. His hair was free of lice and the sore on his lip had healed. Jacko turned towards Rainbow. 'Guv?'

'I thought you were asleep.'

'Tell me about your mother and father.'

'They're both dead.'

'Did she love you?'

'Yes... I'm sure yours does too.'

'I could go back any time, you know. She begged me wiv tears in her eyes. Not me, guv. A life of adwenture for me... begged me, she did, straight up.'

'She must miss you very much, Jacko.'

Jacko grunted and curled up in a tight ball.

≈

Rainbow lay listening to the creaking of the inn's timbers, the whinnying of a horse in the stables below and Carroty Kate moving about in the room next door, bumping into things and roundly cursing them for their clumsiness. Everything was taking so long in the Other World. He comforted himself with the thought that, in his village, perhaps only a few days had passed. He missed Yaba terribly. Under the blankets his hand encountered his stiff penis. No! He would endanger his whole mission! Those shamans who had painted themselves black haunted his thoughts. What had they called themselves... wastrels, no, minstrels. They must have failed in their missions, maybe succumbed to various temptations. And now they were trapped here for eternity, fading, fading. Flinging the blankets aside, he rolled out of bed, stumbled from the room and fled down the corridor.

≈

In the deserted gymnasium, by the light of a pale moon, Rainbow pounded the heavy punch-bag which hung from a beam. With grim fury he slammed his bare fists into it, again and again, attacking his own weak flesh, his unbidden, dangerous desires, until sweat dripped from his face, despite the coldness of the night.

≈

Several days later Arthur was standing at the bar of the George and Dragon, a glass of claret in hand, when he was buttonholed by an elderly, red-faced man with a prominent hook nose and one arm missing.

'Young Trevellyn or I'm a Dutchman!'

Arthur automatically came to attention, gripping his claret as if it were the hilt of a sword. 'Yes, sir!'

'Thought I'd drop in to see how your man was doing. Wouldn't let me into the gymnasium.'

'Top secret stuff, sir.'

The Brigadier, still with his finger in Arthur's buttonhole, said, 'Always in trouble with your gambling debts, if I remember rightly, young Trevellyn.'

'Yes, sir.'

'Good show. Like a young officer with a bit of spirit.'

'Yes, sir. Thank you, sir.'

'Heard of Simon Bolivar? Foreign johnny. South American.'

'A boxer, sir?'

'The Great Liberator, you blithering idiot, you nincompoop.'

'Yes, sir. Sorry, sir.'

'The point is… That's not the Lion of Africa, is it, the one got up in that extraordinary way?'

'Yes, sir. The very man himself.'

'Fetch him over, there's a stout fella! Thinkin' of a wager, you know.'

≈

'Who's that?' Rainbow asked Carroty Kate as Arthur beckoned him over.

'Yeah, I knows him, buggered if I don't. That's the old cockroach hisself. Brigadier Cochrane-Dyat to you, Rainbow. I seen him at Vittoria, or maybe it was Orthez. Anyway, that's the old die-hard all right.'

The Brigadier, who never shook hands with anyone he didn't consider a gentleman, glared as Rainbow offered him his hand.

'Looks fit enough. Fine teeth. Does the fella speak English?'

Rainbow grinned. 'Shallaballah!'

'Upper Volta region, I'll be bound,' Brigadier Cochrane-Dyat muttered. 'Out there as a young man. Good types, splendid fighters, gave us no end of trouble. Not like those ninnies to the south who'd sooner carry a hoe than a spear… Remember Colonel Parker, Trevellyn?'

'Won the Cheltenham point-to-point in '17, sir.'

'That's the johnny. Was out there recently. No game to speak of at all, apparently. Something to do with the rains. Didn't bag one decent thing. Talkin' of which, I'm shootin' on Lord Roseberry's estate this afternoon, better be on me way.'

Arthur saw the Brigadier to the door.

'My hat, Rainbow!' he exclaimed on his return. 'You look worse than when Carroty Kate's just hit you, if that's poss… Steady on!'

Rainbow sat down with a thump. The George had used the same word. He had called the wild animals 'game.' If they had moved out of the area, it could only mean the drought was getting worse. Those emaciated, dust-covered figures, those reproachful eyes—his friends, his loved-ones. Why was his mission taking so long?

≈

'Well, Ben, is it a go?' Arthur asked several days later. 'I know he's been very moody these last few days. How's he shaping?'

Ben Bugler rubbed his granite chin. 'If he had just one mean streak in 'im, he'd be Cock o' the Walk one day… But he don't and that's that. And Jem Ashley's an animal and that's the difference between 'em. He's worked hard, Cap'n Trevellyn, I'll give him that. Reckon he could do with a day off.'

'Capital idea!' Arthur said. 'An outing might be just the ticket.' He called across the gymnasium. 'Rainbow, old fruit, how about I show you a bit of London town? What would you like to see?'

Rainbow's eyes lit up. 'King George. I'd like to see King George.'

Arthur twiddled the ends of his growing moustache, encouraging it towards the desired curvature. 'Hmm, let's see… Ah! The very thing! Buckingham Palace. At least you can see where he lives. Can't promise much more than that, though.'

≈

In an open chaise and four they clattered through the cobbled streets —the first time Rainbow, Jacko or Carroty Kate had ever been in such a conveyance. Then, when the chaise was unable to proceed further because of a gathering crowd, they got out and walked until they reached a broad highway by the sides of which the crowd was waiting for something to happen. A double row of soldiers in scarlet jackets held them back.

≈

There was a stirring in the crowd further down the road.

'Here they come!' someone shouted.

Cavalry, with plumes bobbing in their burnished helmets, trotted past, followed by a magnificent carriage drawn by six grey horses.

'Who's in there?' Jacko asked Arthur.

'Why, it's the King, of course.'

Rainbow's face lit up. 'Do you mean King George?'

'Who else?'

Those fading shamans, the minstrels, were in Rainbow's mind again. He desperately needed to see the George and ask for his help. Rainbow was leaping in the air, waving. 'George! George! Sir it's me!'

Carroty Kate was laughing. 'Perhaps he'll invite us to tea, Rainbow. Oh, dear, and me not dressed for it!'

'You think so, Carrots?'

The carriage was nearly level with them and showed no sign of stopping.

'Here, George! Here!' Rainbow bellowed.

People were staring at him.

'I say, steady on, Rainbow!'

Rainbow shook off Arthur's restraining hand and began pushing and elbowing his way to the front of the crowd. He reached the wall of scarlet soldiers, one row facing inward, the other outward. He remembered a bit of foul play Carroty Kate had used on him. The soldier dropped his gun and staggered about the road with his hands between his legs, cannoning into those around him. Rainbow was through the gap in a flash and running beside the royal carriage.

'Rainbow, don't do it!' Carroty Kate roared above the crowd's indrawn breath. But Rainbow was already poking his head through the window.

'Mister George! It's me! I need your... You're not the George! Hey! This isn't King George! This is an impos...'

From all directions soldiers flung themselves upon Rainbow, pinning him to the ground.

'He don't mean no harm!' Jacko kept shouting at them, only to be roughly pushed aside.

Manacled, Rainbow was dragged away.

12

The chair gripped every part of Rainbow's body. A clamp attached to the backrest immobilised his head. Included in this device was a metal mouthpiece which pressed downward on his tongue, gagging him. An attendant of some kind stood behind him. Rainbow knew he was there because he could smell him.

≈

Three people sat at the table in front of Rainbow. Lounging in the middle seat was a florid man with small, rhinoceros eyes. Flanking him were a young man, hunched over his papers, eyes down, and a tall woman with large hands. From the brightness of her aura and the way his thumbs tingled, Rainbow knew her to be a special person, someone important to his own mission. Possibly she was Yansam, the Water Goddess, consort to Skyherd, but he wasn't sure. The padded flaps on the head restraint had been lowered to cover Rainbow's ears so that the words spoken were muffled and meaningless. Yansam, if indeed that was who it was, was speaking. He could tell from her aura whenever she glanced at him that she was sympathetic towards him.

'Dr Roth, I have serious reservations about committing this patient to an asylum.'

Dr Roth snorted impatiently. 'You heard his answers to my questions, Mrs Thomson. They exhibited a marked want of reason and an insufficient hold on reality.'

'And yet the test passage you read him, he quoted back verbatim—something very few in full possession of their faculties could do.'

'A mere trick.'

'But he comprehended its contents, did he not? Admittedly his views on it were… well, unusual, eccentric even, but that does not make him mad, Dr Roth.'

Dr Roth pulled a watch from his waistcoat pocket, sighing heavily.

Cadey Thomson rapped the table. 'I know you consider half an hour a day to be more than sufficient to discharge all your duties as head, the very well-paid head of this asylum, but surely this man deserves… '

'And you, madam, you erroneously consider a seat on the board gives you the right to interfere in my business. That seat, madam, was an act of charity on the part of a patron who should have known better; an excuse, madam, to give you a stipendiary, not a license to meddle in medical matters of which you are entirely ignorant.'

Rainbow observed that her vibrations had changed to a darker hue. 'I have every right, Dr Roth, to comment on practices which belong in the dark ages.'

≈

Rainbow was finding it difficult to swallow with his tongue held down. The saliva was building up again. He gulped convulsively, nearly choked and got it down. Yansam glanced at him, compassion in her eyes.

'That damned chair, for example—it's barbaric. I'll warrant you treat your hounds better than that.'

The doctor's bored gaze wandered back to Cadey Thomson. 'The Tranquilliser. Designed it myself. By restricting musculatury movement, it lessens the frequency of the pulse and the flow of the blood to the brain. That's science, Mrs Thomson... not something women have a natural capacity for. Best to leave these things to us men. Yes, best left, Mrs Thomson, lest your interest in the abnormalities and perversions of nature found within these walls be construed as indelicate and unseemly.'

He placed the tips of his fingers together with a satisfied smile as if to indicate the matter was now closed.

'Your pompous male opinions count for nothing with me, Dr Roth.'

The faintest snicker wafted towards Rainbow on the attendant's foul breath. The young man at the table bent even closer over his papers.

Dr Roth half rose from his seat. 'No doubt, madam, you're used to opinions expressed in coarser language such as may be heard in the low taverns I'm told you frequent.'

She regarded him coolly. 'The Radical Debating Society, Dr Roth, meets in the 'White Hart Inn' because it is for artisans and working people and it meets where such as they feel at ease.'

He dismissed her explanation with a contemptuous wave of his hand. She shrugged and tried to catch the young man's eye.

'Anyway, we stray from the review of this case. I am far from certain he should be detained here. A fine in the public courts would have been more appropriate.'

Roth grunted. 'At least, madam, I can accommodate you on your first point. Warberton Private Asylum for the Insane is an institution established for gentlemen and a Negro is barely civilised and certainly not a gentleman. In that respect, I grant you, he does not belong here.'

'And why, pray, do you think he is uncivilised?'

'Because, madam, a Negro cannot blush. Only humans can blush. An inability to blush is clear proof both of lack of moral sense and of not being fully human.'

Cadey gave an ironic laugh. 'I suppose you reach that thoroughly scientific conclusion from your extensive consideration of the matter, which is to say, that for a 'consideration' and to please your political masters, you agreed to lock away this unfortunate man.'

Dr Roth sprang up angrily, knocking over his chair. 'Clearly you do not understand the nature of the situation.'

'Oh, yes. I understand all too well that if a man insults the king he must be insane. It cannot possibly be allowed that the insult was uttered rationally or that it was deserved. What is it they say about our glorious king? ...a bad son, a bad husband, a bad father, a bad subject, a bad monarch and a bad friend.'

Roth banged the table with a gavel, trying to render her words inaudible. 'Enough, madam, enough!'

'Furthermore, Dr Roth, a private asylum is so much more discreet, is it not, than a public institu… ?'

'The review of this case is closed! And may I say, madam, I consider you have wasted my time insisting on it.'

'I was within my rights.'

'Rights, pah! There's too much talk of rights these days… Most of it from traitors and dangerous revolutionaries.'

'Sir, I'll have you know… '

Roth brought the gavel crashing down. 'I see no reason to revoke the committal papers of this man here before us. Those in agreement raise a hand.'

The young man kept his eyes lowered, but raised a hand.

Roth smirked. 'I exercise my casting vote to commit this man to an indefinite period of incarcer… of treatment in this asylum.' He nodded towards the attendant. 'Wheel him out, Grundy.'

≈

A long corridor, stone floor, stone walls. It was difficult to keep track
of time. The windows being small and barred and high up, Rainbow
was unable to observe the passage of the sun. Lamps burned day and
night, making it a place of perpetual light—except when Grundy
decided he should be plunged into perpetual darkness for lengths
of time impossible to measure in the cell where not even the sound
of the big clock striking filtered through. Time had no meaning any
more. Time in this place was different from time in the Other World,
which was different from time in the Earthly World. Strapped into the
Tranquilliser, Rainbow watched men in loosely fitting grey clothes
like his own go by, some with vacant, apathetic expressions, others
with brightly burning eyes. Had he been able, Rainbow would have
danced for joy. The other day, Yansam had spoken up for him—that
much had been clear, even though his ears had been covered. She
must have realised that Ikpoom's death had interrupted his training
as a shaman, leaving him ill-prepared for his mission. Obviously it
was she who had arranged this continuation of his training so that he
might defeat Nataxale. After all, drought was her enemy too. The hours
spent in the Tranquilliser, the random beatings, the chaotic behaviour
and seemingly nonsensical babble of those around him, the light-
headedness and feelings of not being tethered to anything, caused by
the constant purges and emetics, all bore a marked resemblance to the
methods used by Ikpoom. After keeping him awake for days and nights
on end, Ikpoom would suddenly confront him with weird dances
which gave new and disturbing meaning to the old stories whose
truths he'd thought beyond all question; and out of the darkness would
appear a bird with a lion's head and other bewildering and dismaying
juxtapositions. The purpose, Rainbow came to realise, was to break
down the familiar connections between one thing and another, to
demonstrate that the boundaries between categories of things are not
fixed or immutable, that facts, time, space, everything was like a liquid
to be poured into any shape you had the power to create.

'When everything you know can be dismantled and reassembled in

≈113≈

different ways,' Ikpoom had told him, 'when you yourself are dismantled and reassembled, then you will be ready to interpret the Other World.'

≈

Yes, it was hard. Of course it was. Almost to the point of being unendurable at times. But Rainbow knew how privileged he was to be in this elite school for shamans. It was an honour equivalent to being chosen to be one of Chief Chimu's bodyguard. Already this chair had taught him so much. His confinement was a metaphor for his restricted understanding of reality so long as he remained shackled to the Earthly World; and the muffled words he could hardly hear symbolised the need to reinterpret, to find new meanings.

≈

How many days had passed, Rainbow had no idea. The big clock was striking seven. Whether it was seven in the morning or seven in the evening, he didn't know. Released from the Tranquilliser, he sat on a bench in the corridor. What would Yaba be doing now? Was little Obobo still fretting with fever? Were all the villagers waiting impatiently for his return?

'It's not easy!' he cried out in his own language, his voice echoing down the corridor. 'It takes time! I wasn't ready!'

'Now then, Number Seven, what's all the noise?' Grundy demanded, touching the bulge beneath his coat. 'We'll have to call out Dr Payne if you don't mend your ways.'

≈

Further down the corridor an old man, in the same grey uniform Rainbow was so proud to wear, was sweeping the floor. The broom's twigs rattled and scratched, rattled and scratched, a sound like the reeds on the river bank. The old crocodile was stirring beneath the surface. And Rainbow, like the impala drinking at the water's edge, would be seized and dragged into the muddy depths. Run, impala! Flee for your life! But the quivering impala could not move. Hiding in the reeds, the little boy could hear his mother's screams.

'No! No!' Rainbow moaned.

Yansam's voice rang down the corridor, haranguing some unseen person. Rainbow writhed and trembled on his bench, banging his head against the wall. Not yet, please not yet. He wasn't ready to grapple with the monster that writhed inside him.

≈

Yansam rounded a corner and walked towards Rainbow accompanied by the young man who'd sat at the table with her. Her vibrations were no longer visible. The monster, the crocodile, is devouring my powers, Rainbow thought.

'Dr Byng, seven sick patients this morning, seven! There must be changes.'

'But Dr Roth says… '

Rainbow's heart lifted. Seven. On his chest seven scars from the branding-iron; seven chimes from the clock; seven, the number given him by Grundy. It was more than coincidence, of course, that the word should hang in the air like that, in his mind, on the lips of two different people. He was glimpsing some bigger pattern—a sign that the training given by his new teachers was beginning to work. When he'd encountered it before, Ikpoom had explained that coincidences of every sort occurred with growing frequency as one's inner being found closer harmony with the great universal spirit which connected everything. His fear and despair vanished like the river mist in the morning sun.

'This place,' the Water Goddess was saying, 'Is a museum of the unwanted. The only thing wrong with many of your patients is that they have greedy, scheming relatives. And you connive in this, Dr Byng.'

'But Dr Roth says… '

'And there's a significant number here, not because they're insane, but because they've threatened the values of our society in some way. Well, let me tell you, Dr Byng, I don't accept a great many of its rotten, corrupt values. Does that make me insane?'

'N-no, c-certainly not, Mrs Thomson.'

She smiled and nodded at Rainbow as she drew level with him. 'How are they treating you… er… Rainbow?'

He beamed at her. 'I am privileged to be here. I cannot thank all the medicine-men enough for what they are doing.'

Dr Byng looked flabbergasted.

Cadey Thomson scowled. 'It's that man, Grundy. He's been intimidating them again. I shall take this up with Dr Roth.'

They passed on and turned a corner.

≈

A fellow apprentice in this elite school sidled onto the bench beside Rainbow.

'Number Ninety-five, that's me. Can't remember the name I left outside. What they got you in for?'

'The Water Goddess arranged it for me… to help me defeat Nataxale.'

'I see. Well, I wish you luck.'

'What about you?'

'I'm here because I won't admit I'm insane… Clear proof, they say, that I suffer from delusions. And then there's the solitary sin, of course.'

'What's that?'

Number Ninety-five explained. Rainbow remembered how proud he'd been when little Obobo, encouraged by Yaba's hand, had achieved his first erection. They'd called the neighbours in to show them what a virile man their son was going to be.

'Sorry, what were you saying?'

'I was saying that, as far as Roth the froth is concerned, masturbation makes you mad. Therefore all madmen masturbate… thus making themselves even madder. And, if you deny you're doing it, that's just another delusion—proof that you have been doing it. I'm telling you, it's enough to drive you insane.'

≈

Number Ninety-five wandered off, weeping. A tall figure appeared in a doorway and stood looking at Rainbow, his head softly radiating colour. He moved, making the colours undulate and elide. Here, without a doubt, was a shaman of advanced powers.

'Who's that?' Rainbow asked Grundy who was now wearing Rainbow's violet coat and smart boots. A green triangular patch had been stitched onto the right breast of the coat—a sign, Rainbow gathered, that the wearer was not a neophyte in this establishment, but an imparter of the power.

Grundy gave a disparaging laugh. 'Calls himself Tupac Amaru. Thinks he's the… I forget the word… sounds like a flower… the carnation of some emperor from your history books. The things he comes out with! He'll haunt this place for the rest of his days.'

'Seven is your number,' Tupac Amaru said, looking straight at Rainbow.

'Yes,' Rainbow replied.

Grundy took Tupac Amaru by the elbow and steered him down the corridor.

'Next time your sister visits, tell her how much you enjoyed that cake she brought you.'

'But I never tasted it.'

'Oh, you did, Tupac, you did. You've simply forgotten. Do you want Dr Payne to jog your memory?'

'No, no. It was delicious. I shall ask my sister for another.'

Tupac Amaru returned. 'This body I inhabit is not my own.' He struck himself violently on the chest as if to prove his point. 'I am the rightful Emperor of all Peru and I am on a spirit journey to seek the help of King George in restoring the Inca Empire to its former glory. Instead they put me in here.'

'King George is a good man, I know him well. But beware impostors.'

'Come with me! Journey in spirit with me to Peru.'

'I have things I must do here.'

The Inca Emperor's aura blazed bright. 'Your story ends in Peru. It ends as it begins... with the number seven.'

He glided away, his aura trailing colours like a meteor.

≈

A bench, a long corridor, stone floor, stone walls, elusive, bending time. Tap! Tap! went a branch against the bars of a window... a bare branch... a bare branch like when the Ijeru came raiding and... Tap! Tap! it insisted. 'Open your mind to me!' Tap! Tap!

Rainbow jumped up. 'No!' His cry echoed down the corridor.

'Now, now! None of that!' Grundy growled, seeming to pop up from nowhere. His hand slid into the gap in the front of his coat, his violet coat. 'Or else I'll be obliged to fetch out Dr Payne, and he won't like that. It's your cell for you, Number Seven.'

≈

Rainbow appreciated the absolute darkness of his cell which, as his instructor had intended, assisted his meditation. And the subject for his meditation was the chain which ran from the iron collar round his neck to a ring on the wall. It had seven links. In his journey to the Other World, in the darkest part of the tunnel, there'd been seven links in the chain joining him to the dead body… a body whose weight he'd had to strain against every time he wanted to move, always there, like some putrefying extension of himself, an unbearable presence until he'd turned over and looked it in the face. Rainbow rattled the chain, groaning, seeing what he didn't want to see—that he was chained to a dead weight from his past, something he must face.

'Help me, Monkey! Oh, please help me, Monkey!'

The door of his cell opened. Grundy stood there, cat-o-nine-tails in hand.

'Stow your whid!'

Rainbow rolled on the floor groaning, his neck tugging at the chain.

Grundy eyed him dispassionately. 'Still a sight too frisky. It's the steamy for you!'

≈

In the bath house, Grundy closed the hinged side of the wooden tub and fastened the catch.

'That'll steam the stuffing out of you, you see if it don't.'

Grundy held a greenish pill between two filthy fingers. 'Open wide.'

'Inform me, please, as to the magical properties of this potion.'

'You gets it 'cos the last Number Seven got it and there's been no change of orders. Number Seven—green pill. So open up.'

Ikpoom, too, had demanded unquestioning obedience. Rainbow received the pill into his mouth and swallowed it.

≈

Only Rainbow's head stuck out from the hole in the top of the tub. Already the heat was building up. Close by, another shaman was trying to empty a basin of water, using a sieve. Rainbow recalled similar tasks set by Ikpoom. Sweat was running down his face. Like the steam escaping from the tub, his mind was beginning to drift. Yes, the meaning of Monkey… Why had Monkey come to him in the form of a child, a child with an ache in his soul? And now he knew why, because he could hear Jacko calling to him to come out of hiding. That little boy concealed in the reeds beside the river, while the Ijeru warriors raped his mother, had never emerged from hiding. All these years he'd crouched in the reeds, unheeded by his own adult self. And now Jacko was calling to him. The scared, hurt little boy in the reeds stood up. Sobs racked Rainbow's body, his tears mingling with the sweat. He reached for the child's hand and drew him close, hugging him, holding him tight, telling him it wasn't his fault, that he was only a child who couldn't have fought them all, reassuring him, healing his own spiritual wound.

≈

In the middle of the night, an explosion shook the asylum. All around, people were hammering on doors.

'Rainbow? Where are you, Rainbow?'

'Here!' he called, able to step close to the door because Grundy hadn't chained him.

A sledgehammer battered down the door.

'We're Cap'n Trevellyn's men,' said a man, lowering the hammer.

Rainbow shielded his eyes from the sudden light. The voice he recognised as belonging to Meg's John.

'What's happening, John?'

Out of a cloud of smoke, Arthur appeared. 'Sorry to spoil your little holiday, old fruit, but it's time to get back to some serious training.'

Accompanied by Arthur and a dozen men, Rainbow allowed himself to be hurried along passageways, through a hole in the side of the building and out into a moonlit park.

≈

They stopped behind some bushes to catch their breath. Arthur unslung a haversack from his back and pulled from it Rainbow's coat.

'Yours I think, Rainbow.'

Rainbow put it on over his thin asylum uniform.

John said with a chuckle, 'Some dub-cove with keys was sportin' it on his hide. We chained him up in the place you was in.'

'Better move on,' Arthur said. 'There are carriages ready for us on the other side of the park.'

≈

Jacko was waiting in the front carriage, stinking it out with his pipe. Rainbow climbed in and embraced him.

'Give over, guv!' Jacko mumbled, flushing with pleasure.

Barnaby was there, too. 'You got him out then, Captain Trevellyn… Just one thing… When I said, 'Same drill as for the Storming of Badajoz', I meant with the scaling-ladders, not breaching the wall!'

Arthur laughed and slapped his thighs with delight. 'Always was a prize galoot! Capital! Absolutely capital!'

John's face loomed at the carriage window. 'Just wanted to say good luck for when you fight Ashley. Knew him when he was a kid. Nat was a bully then and he's a bully now. Hope you teach him a lesson.'

'Nat?' queried Jacko. 'You mean Jem, don't you?'

'Nathaniel Jeremiah Ashley,' John said. 'He was always Nat when he was nipper. Called himself Jem when he became a milling-cove. Reckoned it sounded tougher.'

'Like a whirlwind with his fists, he is,' Jacko said.

'Nat Ashley,' Rainbow said, his eyes widening as the truth dawned on him. 'Nat Ashley… Nataxale… It's him!' He leant back in his seat, relief flooding over him. He'd found Nataxale.

≈

Arthur clambered in beside Rainbow and Jacko, calling out to John who was in the driving-seat, 'On you go, John! Storming of Badajoz accomplished with flying colours!'

He turned to Rainbow. 'Didn't like what I saw in there. Hasn't weakened you too much, I hope. Only twenty days till you step into the ring with Ashley.'

Rainbow's fist smacked into his palm. 'Oh yes, I'm ready for him! I'm ready for him all right! I'm healed, I'm whole. The lion has picked out its prey and is ready for the kill!'

13

In an upstairs room at the Lame Nag outside Newbury, Rainbow was sitting up in bed. A light breakfast on a tray awaited his appetite. Today was the day he was going to fight Nataxale. At last he was about to take the first real step towards fulfilling his mission. Ben Bugler had instructed him to rest all morning and eat moderately. In the early afternoon he would be taken by carriage to the Newbury race-course where, even now, a crowd was gathering. Coaches packed with singing, shouting followers of 'the noble art' had been passing by all morning.

≈

There was a knock on the door. Xango the Thunder God entered, an uncertain expression on his face.

'I have something to tell you, Rainbow. Well, I won't beat about the bush… the fight's off.'

Rainbow stared at him, stunned. Barnaby related what had happened. Jem Ashley had killed a man in a quarrel over a woman and had gone into hiding. Lord Chichester, the purse holder and marshal responsible for the proper conduct of the contest, had returned to Barnaby Thackston his ten thousand pounds and, along with it, Giles Ashley's purse for the same amount, which was forfeit when his brother did a runner.

≈

Xango held out a leather pouch clinking with coins. 'Your share, Rainbow. You've worked hard, Not your fault it's been called off. What with the damage to the circus and the interest on the loan… well, I wish it could be more.'

Sick with disappointment, Rainbow shook his head. 'Keep it. I don't want it.'

'Are you sure?'

'Yes, I am sure.'

'Well, the circus needs every penny it can get right now… That is, if you are sure.'

Rainbow was too downcast to reply. He had been so close to coming face to face with Nataxale at last, only for him to fade away like smoke from a fire.

Xango touched him on the arm. 'Don't take it too hard, Rainbow. There will be other fights for you. Better be going. There's a pile of arrangements to unarrange. And, by thunder, I'll be giving Giles Ashley a piece of my mind.'

≈

When Xango had gone, Rainbow covered his head with the pillow and beat the bed with his fists. Where was Nataxale hiding? He didn't even know where to begin to look. What was the most unlikely place that Nataxale would be? Because that was where he would be. Rainbow stared into the white pillow. As close as he could bear to be to the Land of Clouds, the Upper Realms, that was where Nataxale would be found.

≈

There was another knock on the door. This time, Arthur came in.

'I heard the news,' Arthur said. 'Must be a hundred times worse than having a horse refuse a fence. Terrible let-down.'

'Thank you for all your help. You understand the importance of my mission.'

'Oh, tosh! Your obedient humble and all that.'

Rainbow said, 'I must find Skyherd's dwelling place where the earth touches the clouds and where everything is white. Do you know where that place is?'

Arthur pulled up a chair beside the bed. 'Hmm… Could be Peru.'

'The same place where the great shaman, Tupac Amaru, comes from?'

'I wouldn't know about that.'

'Where in the Other World is it?'

'Yes, in the New World somewhere. Not sure exactly where. We only did the red bits on the map when I was at school… but it's a long way by boat.'

Arthur poured himself a glass of claret from the tray. 'Fact is, Rainbow, there's a filly getting a mite too serious about me, so I've decided to clear off for a bit… in point of fact, to sign up.'

'Sign up? I don't understand.'

Arthur held his claret up to the light. 'Deucedly poor vintage, if you ask me… Yes, sign up. Remember the old buffer with one arm—

Brigadier Cochrane-Dyat?'

'The person you were talking to at Ben's place?'

'The very one. He put a couple of thou' on you to win the fight. Slogger, on the other hand, bet against you. But that's not the point. Dashed if I can remember what the point is. Oh yes, the Brigadier had a little shindig last night. He's raising a brigade to go and help the Peruvians fight some war or other.'

Rainbow reached for an egg on the tray. 'Tell me about Peru.'

'Actually, there was a Peruvian officer there last night, guest of the Brigadier. He said much of his country is so high you think you must be looking at the clouds.'

'And you are going there, Arthur?'

'Haven't told Barnaby yet. But, yes, actually.'

'And I'm coming with you.' Rainbow announced.

'Good show!' Arthur exclaimed. 'That is, are you sure, Rainbow? You've a promising future here as a prize-fighter, you know.'

Rainbow shook his head. 'Nataxale was the one I came to fight, no other.'

'Are you sure? Fame and fortune are yours for the taking if you stay.'

'I'm sure.'

Arthur regarded him quizzically. 'Well… if that's really what you want… They're only taking officers and men who've seen action, but… Yes, I have it! Apparently we're going to be short of grooms. How do you fancy that?'

Arthur explained what was involved. Rainbow nodded his approval.

'In that case,' Arthur said, draining his glass, 'Better get down there at crack of dawn tomorrow—say elevenish? The boat sails the day after tomorrow. Anyway, better go. Meeting a friend downstairs.'

≈

The friend was Robert. He had left several messages for Arthur at Fitz's Club and, when Arthur had dropped in there two days ago, he'd picked up Robert's most recent note. Robert said he was being sent to Newbury by the *Chronicle* to report on the match with Jem Ashley and, knowing Arthur's 'pugilistic leanings', he presumed he would be there too. 'So how about getting together for a drink?'

'Peru! You're going to Peru?' Rebert exclaimed.

Arthur grinned. 'Seems safer than here. A woman scorned and all that.'

'Isn't that amazing!' Robert heard himself say. 'I'm going too!'

14

Robert waited on the quayside at Tilbury, outside the shed which was the recruiting office of Bolivar's Foreign Legion. He'd arranged to meet both Arthur and Cadey here at half past eleven. He'd arrived half an hour early and now it was half after noon. So like himself to be early, in order not to impose on anyone; so like Arthur to be late. Somehow, with Arthur, it was a virtue, part of being carefree and such fun to be with. But where were Cadey and Dickon?

≈

Robert paced up and down outside the shed, hardly noticing the throng of soldiers, the shouted orders, the clatter of hooves on the quayside cobbles as horses were led on board the waiting ships, and munitions, arms and supplies were loaded. Cadey had seemed pleased when he'd told her that he, too, was going to Peru; and Arthur had looked enormously surprised and said, 'Good show!' when he had appeared at Mrs Budge's to say goodbye to Robert and to present Mrs Budge with a bunch of flowers. Robert knew he should be sketching the activities all around him, but he felt too agitated to do it justice. He was leaving without saying goodbye to Mama. There hadn't been time to return to Beechwood House. Even if there had been, would he have done so with Father there? It would be the first Christmas he'd ever spent away from home. He'd written her a letter telling her of his decision. Although he knew it was unlikely a reply would reach him before he sailed, he couldn't help hoping. And where was Cadey?

≈

A coach drew up near the British Brigade's recruiting shed. Out stepped Arthur, resplendent in his new uniform, followed by an Amazon of a woman with a mop of flaming red-hair, a cheeky looking boy about the same age as Dickon, and a tall, well-built African wearing fashionable boots and a violet coat which, unaccountably had orange sleeves and a large green triangle sewn onto it.

Arthur bounded towards him like an overgrown puppy. 'My tailor's just finished altering my new toggery. Isn't it just the cheese?'

Robert could see that the immaculate uniform of the British Light

Horse had been designed more with an eye to its scenic effect than to its suitability to a campaign in the mountains. Scarlet jacket with light blue facings and gold lace piping on collar, cuff and sleeve, scarlet pantaloons with broad gold stripe, indigo sash and shiny knee-length boots.

Robert was composing a letter to Mama in his head. 'It seems, Mama, that in these newly-formed regiments, each colonel has been given a free hand as to the uniform. Apparently, the rivalry to be the one who cuts the finest dash at ceremonial occasions, at society balls and at the morning promenade has been intense. Some colonels have even dug into their own pockets and used their private incomes to ensure their regiment can strut like peacocks in their fancy plumage. If only you could have seen it, Mama. A recital of the many hues on show along the quayside would sound more like a description of exotic birds than of regiments at war.' Yes, no doubt he could write divertingly about it all, but how could he reassure Mama about this venture when he was so full of misgivings himself?

'Well, what do you say, Stanners, do I cut a dash or do I not?'

'I'd say, my dear Arthur, that the lilies of the field would feel distinctly drab next to you.'

'Well,' said the scruffy boy, 'I'd say it wasn't that different from the fancy outfit what Barnaby rigged you out in.'

Arthur guffawed good-naturedly, then slapped his head. 'A thousand pardons! I haven't introduced these good folk... this is Carroty Kate, this rapscallion is Jacko and here we have none other than the Lion of Africa himself, Rainbow.'

≈

Rainbow's scalp prickled. This was a very special Being of great importance to his quest, even more so than Yansam, the Water Goddess. Could it be Skyherd himself? Everything is in masquerade, Ikpoom had insisted, so there was no immediate way of telling whether this pale, thin youth was Skyherd or not. But that overpowering instinct, which all shamans had, was seldom wrong. Dare he hope... and so soon? And yet, there were doubts. The Being's aura, for one thing—it was fluctuating and incomplete, not blazing bright and fully formed in all its aspects as Skyherd's would surely be. Mister Stan Hope, Arthur had said his name was. Mister Hope, the hope of rain to come. It was forbidden of course to address him directly as Skyherd. That privilege was only allowed after The Gift had been made. Now Skyherd was speaking. His voice was not loud like Xango's, but soft like gently falling rain. He was telling them he was going to Peru, the Land of the Clouds, so that he could tell everyone the story of great happenings in the New World. Skyherd was creating a myth. The Mortal World needed a new myth before the rains could come. Perhaps the old myths were losing their power to connect people to the gods or to set them on the path to finding the larger whole. Skyherd had come to re-assemble, to re-member the dangerous body of knowledge which had been banished from the Mortal World.

≈

Arthur pointed to five ships, sails furled, berthed nearby.

'Those are all ours. BLH—British Light Horse to you—have been allocated the Good Hope, the one at the end. We take up quarters below decks tomorrow.'

Jacko sounded suspicious. 'Good Hope... Oh gawd, I ain't going to be preached at and saved again am I?'

'It's named after Mr Hope,' Rainbow explained. 'It's going to take him... all of us to the Higher Realm, to the Land of the Clouds.'

Jacko grinned. 'I don't know where you get 'em, guv, but you come out wiv some good 'uns all right, so you do.'

Robert said, 'What about the other ships, Arthur?'

Arthur explained that Cochrane-Dyat's brigade consisted of several regiments. The British Light Horse, the one he and Slogger were joining, was only one of them.

Robert's heart sank. 'C-S?'

'Yes, didn't I tell you? Fitz's Club's been buzzing with the news. Quite a few joining up, actually.'

≈

When they reached the recruiting shed, Carroty Kate said, 'I'll wait out here.'

'I wish you could come with us,' Rainbow said. 'I don't know what I'll do without you.'

'They ain't recruiting the likes o' me and that's that.'

There was a moment's silence.

'Well, go on then!' she said, propelling them towards the door with a hefty shove. 'Don't stand there like two floppy puppets waiting for a hand up your bums!' She turned her broad back and was soon lost in the throng.

'Goodbye, Carrots!' Jacko called, fighting back tears.

Rainbow put an arm round his shoulder. 'We are going to have lots of adventures together, Monkey, and we shall triumph.'

'Suppose,' Jacko sniffed. 'Well, blow me down, guv, look who's here!'

A short, barrel-shaped man, wrapped in a military cape of midnight blue, stepped forward.

'Bat!' Rainbow exclaimed happily.

Bat flapped his wings, eyeing him uneasily.

Arthur slapped his thigh. 'Sergeant Muldoon, or I don't know a horse from a kipper!'

Muldoon came to attention with a stamping of feet. His hand, half raised in a salute, fell to his side.

Arthur laughed. 'At ease, sergeant, at ease… So what are you doing these days, you old reprobate?'

'Workin' in the sewers, sorr… well, till recent, sorr.'

'Your daughter… Mary. She was sickly, I recall. How is she?'

'Good of you to remember, sorr. There's not many occifers as would. She died, sorr. Couple o' months back, sorr.'

'Sorry to hear it.'

'Sorr.'

'Yes, sergeant?'

'Sorr… now my Mary's gone… I heard tell of sojers being needed in Americky… not our bit, sorr, the jungly bit. So I comes down here, sorr… only… '

'Yes, sergeant?'

'Sorr… they say… they say I'm too old to go.'

Arthur tapped his boots with his silver-topped cane. 'Hmm, can't have that… By Jove, I think I've got it! Mr Stanhope here is accompanying the regiment. Not used to army ways. Needs an old-timer like yourself, Muldoon, to tell him what's what. I could get you in as his batman… what do you say?'

'Batman? Yes, sorr. Thank you, sorr.'

'Bat has powerful magic,' Rainbow announced. 'He can send his teeth to bite his enemies.'

Muldoon stared at him. 'Jasus, the blarnified blether off him!'

Jacko shook his head in disbelief. 'You're only talking to the Lion of Africa, 'im what would of thrashed Jem Ashley if he hadn't scarpered!'

A look of respect crept over Muldoon's gnarled features. 'You're him? Let me shake your hand.'

Arthur turned to Robert. 'All right with you, Stanners? Thing is, if you're to have any standing in the regiment… bad form not to have a servant.'

'You know best, I'm sure, Arthur.'

'Capital! That's settled then… But none of your old tricks, Muldoon. I'll be keeping my eye on you.'

'Yes, sorr. Much obliged to you, sorr.'

Robert drew close to Arthur and said into his ear, 'Why is Rainbow staring at me like that? He has hardly taken his eyes off me since he got here.'

Arthur laughed. 'You'll soon learn, Stanners, there's no accounting for the things he says or does. A good man, though.'

'And, Arthur, do you know anything about a Major Minagh joining the regiment? A very young major… only ten, in fact.'

Arthur slapped his thigh and laughed again, apparently unperturbed by the thought of a child holding a senior rank to him. It was how things were.

'It's news to me, Stanners.'

≈

The British Light Horse had a desk at the far end of the shed. Several officers were lounging about in uniforms similar to Arthur's. Arthur drew Jacko forward, vouching for his character and explaining that he wanted to be a drummer-boy.

'I can drum the legs off a turkey,' Jacko declared, whipping out two drumsticks from up his trouser leg and beating a tattoo on the desk.

'Cavalry regiments don't have drummer-boys,' the Sergeant said, winking at Arthur.

'But… But…'

'Luckily for you,' the Sergeant continued with another wink at Arthur, 'This is a Patriot show and Patriot cavalry does have drummer-boys, though gawd knows why.'

He dipped a quill into an ink-pot. 'Name?'

'Jacko, sir.'

'You call me Sergeant… What's your surname?'

'I ain't nivver been a sir, sir… er… sergeant.'

'Lord love us! What did they call your mother?'

'None of your business what folk called her. It weren't true.'

Arthur, chuckling hugely, said, 'Did anyone ever address her as Mrs something?'

Jacko thought for a bit. 'When she was up before the beak… Mrs Jackson… would that be it… sergeant?'

'Good enough. Put your mark there, drummer Jackson.'

The recruiting sergeant held out two indigo sashes. 'Batmen, grooms and other non-combatants are not eligible for uniforms, but must wear these.'

Rainbow took the proffered sash and tied it round the outside of his violet coat.

'I gets a uniform, don't I, Sergeant?' Jacko wanted to know.

'You do. Report at that shed over there at fourteen hundred hours. And, after you've got kitted out, the Drum Sergeant will take you in hand.'

'Fourteen hundred hours! But that's in two months time!'

'Are you deliberately annoying me, or does it just come natural?'

'No, Sergeant, I swear!'

'You'll get me swearing, if you don't watch out!'

≈

An officer, dripping with more braid and tassels than the others, approached Robert.

'Mr Stanhope?'

'Yes.'

'I'm Colonel Summers-Cox.'

Jacko nudged Rainbow. 'And some 'asn't by the looks of him!'

'You've been assigned to us for the purposes of mess facilities, rations, accommodation and so forth.'

'For the voyage or for the whole… ?'

'For the whole bang shooting match,' Summers-Cox said, and his tone implied the unspoken word 'unfortunately'.

He turned to Arthur. 'I'm making you responsible for him' With his swagger-stick he rapped the shoulder of the young officer standing next to Arthur. 'And you, Hollis, too. Good. Carry on.'

Robert hurried after him. 'Excuse me, Colonel, has Major Minagh reported for duty yet?'

Summers-Cox consulted the list in his hand. 'Minah… Let me see… No, not that I know of.'

≈

Robert leant on the rail of the Good Hope's upper deck, watching the bustle on the quayside below. He abhorred war and he would take no part in romanticizing or glorifying it. He made a vow to himself that he would record only the truth as he saw it. He wondered where Cadey and Dickon were. There wasn't much time left before they sailed. Perhaps they were on another ship, but Cadey had said she would insist that Robert was allocated to the same ship and would request Lord Hawksmoor to put in a word to this effect. At least he was on the same ship as Arthur.

≈

Muldoon appeared at his side. Robert had already prised out of him the fact that he'd enlisted at the start of the war with Napoleon and fought throughout the Peninsular campaign and then in France. He had, he cheerfully confessed, been promoted to sergeant several times only to be reduced to the ranks again for drunkenness.

'What did you do when the war ended?'

'Mary, my daughter, was poorly, sorr, very poorly. When I weren't caring for her, I was Inspector of Public Buildings.'

'Yes, I heard you telling Arther… er Captain Trevellyn that she died recently. Sorry to hear that.'

'Thank you, sorr. I got a picture of her, sorr.' From his breast pocket he produced a drawing such as might have been done by a street artist. 'Looks like her mother, so she does. I thinks of 'em both when I looks at this. Both gone now.'

'She's lovely,' Robert murmured 'Er, this Inspector of Public Buildings …Sounds like a good job. Was it well paid?'

Muldoon's bloodshot eyes regarded Robert with what might have been pity. He shook his head. 'I was unemployed, sorr… 'Cept when I was a timber merchant.'

'Well, that sounds… '

'Selling matches in the street, sorr.'

'Oh, I see.'

'Then I went down the sewers.'

'Sewers? Aren't they very… Did it affect your health at all?'

'Rats were the only thing, really. Never had a day's illness 'cept when one o' them varmints bit me. Some's so big as would frighten a lady into asterisks to see of a sudden. Not easy, though, when the army's been your life for so long, to… to… '

'To be a different kind of person. Yes, I can believe that.'

Muldoon's eyes bored into Robert's hip pocket wherein lay a silver brandy flask. He rubbed his throat. 'And this old sewer, the gin-lane, the beer-alley, is in need of flushing out, if you get my drift, sorr.'

Robert smiled. 'It's only apple juice… Er… Would you fetch my scarf, please, Muldoon.'

'Bless you, sorr. Young gen'lemen don't say 'please' to their batman. Not in the army. You has to speak sharpish and cuss me like Cap'n Trevellyn does, sorr.'

'Oh dear. I'm sorry, Muldoon. I'll try. But I'm only loosely attached to the army. Artists don't have to do that sort of thing, do they?'

'Looks better if they do, sorr… I'll get the scarf. Can't 'ave you getting a chill. Reminds me of my Mary the way you need wrapping up. Bless you, sorr. She was much the same age as you when she died.' And with that, he clattered down the gangway.

≈

Muldoon returned with Arthur following behind him.

Arthur spread his hands. 'Summers-Cox says we're to brief our squadrons on the general situation—what the war's all about and so forth… and, well, the whole thing's about as clear to me as a London pea-souper… Pay attention, Muldoon, you might learn something here.'

'Sorr.'

Robert tried to explain it as simply as possible. The Patriots, the long-term settlers in Peru, versus the Royalists who were the army of occupation and government officials who reported direct to the monarchy in Spain.

'You're on the Patriots' side, Arthur, in case you're interested.'

'Good show!'

'Rather like the American War of Independence, Arthur, only on that occasion it was we who were the ones trying to hang on to our colonies and the Americans who wanted to run their own affairs. You see…'

Arthur held up his hand. 'More than enough! As long as the men get their pay and their ration of grog, they'll be happy with that. Must toddle. Can't be late on parade my very first day.'

≈

Non-combatants already being on board, Rainbow watched the embarkation parade from the deck of the Good Hope. The bands of no less than three regiments had combined to play the brigade aboard the five ships. And here they came, marching along the quay, strutting in their new finery, plumes bobbing, metal and leather gleaming in the sunlight. Amongst the drummers was Jacko, his chest swelling with pride as he twirled his sticks with the best of them. All this pageantry, which even Chief Chimu could hardly match, marked the start of the final phase of his mission. But he was leaving Snail behind.

≈

The first company of the British Light Horse, on foot, was starting up the gangway, making it bounce and ring under their tread. Robert was drawing the scene, his very first entry in his new sketch-book, when he saw Carroty Kate, running across the space between the crowd and the marching column.

'Smithy! Smithy!'

One of the soldiers stepped out of line. Carroty Kate flung her arms round him.

'Smithy! At last!'

'Get bank in the ranks!' bellowed a sergeant. 'Fall in at once!'

Smithy held her tight, weeping. 'Oh, Kate, you have found me only to lose me. I have taken the oath. I have made my mark.'

'Don't friggin' leave me, Smithy. Not now.'

'Kate, my Kate... I... I shall be shot as a deserter if... '

≈

Rough hands seized him and were dragging him up the gangway. Carroty Kate's cry of agony was drowned by the cheering of the crowd and the crashing martial music with its promise of victory and glory. Robert heard the order given to raise the gangway. It was all he could do to prevent himself running down it and off the ship before it was too late, before vast oceans separated him from home and from Cadey, before he was caught up by terrible conflicts in unmapped wastes.

15

About an hour later, Jacko received a message via Rainbow that Robert wanted to see him in his cabin.

'Sir, did you see what happened with Carrots and her Smithy?' Jacko asked when he arrived in Robert's cabin. 'Can't we do anything, sir?'

Robert told him he had tried to find out what had happened to Smithy but nobody he'd asked knew the answer. 'I'll keep trying and let you know. Anyway, what I wanted you for was to run an errand for me.'

Robert didn't say so, but he wasn't sure he could trust his batman not to get drunk if he went ashore.

'Not allowed off the ship now, sir. Marines guarding the gangplanks and patrolling like this was a convict ship.'

'Officers can come and go, though, and I count as an officer on this little jaunt. I can give you a note authorizing you to go ashore on my behalf.'

Robert explained that, on checking his painting materials he had discovered he was short of burnt umber. It was, Jacko learned, a natural mineral which, when roasted and ground up and then mixed with oil, provided painters with a rich reddish-brown pigment. There was a place only half an hour away where it could be obtained. It was expensive though. Robert gave him the money and told him to be sure to be back in time before the Good Hope sailed that evening.

≈

Jacko jogged along the quayside, then turned down a lane. It was a new experience for him to be trusted with money. It felt good. It was a lot of money, more than he'd ever held in his hand in his whole life. He thought of all the things he could buy with a sum as big as that. In fact, he could live off it for weeks. He'd seen his cramped quarters in the Good Hope, shared with fifty other drummer-boys, barely room to sling his hammock, dark and smelly; and he'd heard accounts of what the food would be like aboard ship and it wasn't encouraging. It would be so easy to keep the money and not go back to the Good Hope. He could find Carrots and be with her. But Mr Stanhope had seen some good in him and he had trusted him. Jacko spat on the cobbles and turned another corner. You didn't survive by becoming soft and sentimental. In the narrow, sunless street a bulky figure suddenly barred his way.

'Don't rob me, mister, I'm just a poor boy who… Oh, Carrots! You gave me a fright and no mistake!'

≈

Jacko was never sure whether he would have kept the money or not, because Carroty Kate made it clear right away that her one and only concern at that moment was to get aboard the Good Hope and be with her Smithy. As they hurried through the evening streets, following Robert's directions to the shop that sold burnt umber, Carroty Kate and Jacko hatched a plan.

16

Three hours before the Good Hope was due to sail, and with the late afternoon sun slanting through the rigging, Jacko and Rainbow appeared on the well-deck. Imitating Barnaby Thackston, Jacko acted as Rainbow's barker.

'Who wants to say he's gone a round with the Lion of Africa? Who wants to say they've helped him train for when he meets Jem Ashley? You, sir, you look like you don't scare easy.'

Before long, instead of lining the rail, most of those who weren't fully occupied with their duties were crowded round the well-deck, facing the makeshift ring. They'd all heard of the Lion of Africa, but nobody had seen him in action. This was an opportunity not to be missed.

≈

When a large part of the crew and of the British Light Horse were gathered to watch Rainbow, Jacko slipped, away, put on his street clothes, hurried to a point near the stern and waited. Soon, a small rowing boat appeared out of the gloom with Carroty Kate sitting in the bows. Jacko lowered a rope. Carroty Kate began climbing up it, her feet against the hull of the Good Hope, finding purchase on the rough timber. Jacko turned his head. A loud, domineering voice, an officer's voice, a voice that sounded familiar, was shouting orders for the assembled crowd to disperse.

'You were not given permission! Get below decks or you'll be flogged!'

Soon, the deck would be filled with people making their way down to their quarters. Jacko peered over the rail. Carroty Kate was about two thirds of the way up. With her bulk and in her heavy greatcoat she was finding it hard work. She was resting on a ledge above a porthole.

'Hurry up, Carrots!' he whispered down to her.

A couple of soldiers were swaggering towards him. Jacko saw from the stripes on their sleeves that they were sergeants, the kind of people who noticed when regulations are being broken. As a precaution, Jacko had made a crude fishing rod. He leaned over the rail, rod in hand, using his body to hide the rope.

One of the sergeants laughed as they passed by. 'I doubt he'll get anything on the end of that except an old boot!'

'Come on Carrots!' Jacko urged when they were gone. 'Come on you old boot!'

Carroty Kate reached the rail and heaved herself over it and onto the deck. Jacko untied the rope from the rail and let it drop into the water. He heard Carroty Kate gasp. Walking towards them, nose in the air, was an officer. The collar of Carroty Kate's army coat was turned up and her flaming red hair was piled beneath an army cap. She quickly turned her back to the advancing figure. To someone who didn't know her and who wasn't very observant she might have passed as a soldier, but the person bearing down on them was Carlton-Syms. Jacko did the first thing that came into his mind. He jumped onto the rail and balanced along it towards Carlton-Syms.

'Look at me! Look at me!' he called out. 'Penny to see me dive from here, sir?'

'Certainly not! Get down, you fool!'

Jacko pretended to slip and fell on top of Carlton-Syms.

'Sorry, sir. Very sorry, sir… Oh look, sir, you dropped your snuff box.'

Jacko handed Carlton-Syms the silver box which his practised fingers had eased from a pocket. Out of the corner of his eye he could see that Carrots had hidden herself away.

'Haven't I seen you before somewhere?' C-S demanded.

'Me, sir? No, sir.'

'Hmm, that's as maybe. But I'll be watching you. Whose servant are you?'

Jacko took a chance that, in a newly formed regiment, together for the first time, Carlton-Syms wouldn't know everyone's names yet.

'Captain Jack Dash, sir.'

Carlton-Syms grunted and walked on, receiving the salutes of those scurrying past.

≈

When all was clear, Jacko called softly. A cap from which escaped a riot of red hair slowly rose above a large coil of rope.

'You can't swim, can you, Jacko?'

'I can so. Yard behind the gasworks. Gets flooded. Copied the frogs, didn't I?'

≈

Jacko led Carroty Kate down a hatchway and into a place where spare sails and ropes were stored. There they waited in the darkness until Rainbow joined them. Using a route that avoided the main passages, and with Jacko bringing up the rear, Rainbow led the way down to the middle part of the lower deck where the officers' horses were stabled. He showed her into an empty stable. In it were candles, lucifers, food, water and a bucket for her use.

'You'll be safe here, Carrots,' Jacko reassured her. 'The grooms won't tell on yer.'

'Reckon that's about right, Jacko. Other ranks stick together. And if an officer comes down here, I'll hide in the straw.'

She kept asking, 'Where's Smithy? When am I going to see Smithy?'

Jacko couldn't bring himself to tell her the truth which was that Smithy's punishment for breaking rank in the parade was an indefinite period of solitary confinement, in irons, in a cell deep in the bowels of the ship.

17

The ship's sails, replete and hard-bellied, dazzled in the morning sun. The ship heeled, tilting the coastline of Ecuador into view—the green foothills of the Western Cordillera running into white sand dunes, seen across a green ocean, white capped.

Robert lowered his eyes to the smaller canvas on his easel and to the sea of greens on his palette, greens almost as pale as the cabbages in their Oxfordshire garden, greens as blue-bright as dragon-flies' wings.

≈

Muldoon leant over Robert's shoulder and peered at his painting. His breath smelt of rum.

'You're not what I'd call a religious painter, sorr.'

'Oh?'

'There's some painters, sorr, religiously keep the second commandment—thou shalt not make unto thee any likeness that is in heaven above, or that is in the earth beneath, or that is in the water under the earth.'

'You approve, then?'

'Yes, sorr. I've never met a young gen'leman afore as paints.'

An excited yelping of hounds broke out in the direction of the stern.

'Wish it was my feeding time,' Muldoon said gloomily. 'They say as the Brigadier's hounds is better fed than us.'

'All the same, you're glad to be back in the army, aren't you?'

Muldoon grunted, unable to deny it, but not wanting to relinquish his chief occupation and pleasure—complaining. Robert extracted from the basket at his feet his pen, paper and glass ink-pot with its silver lid. When he reached their destination he wanted to have a letter ready. It would be delivered to Mama by courtesy of the *London Illustrated Chronicle*. Sir Charles Makepiece, as well as pioneering the use of civilian reporters in a war zone, had also been at the forefront of using carrier pigeons to receive news from distant parts and to keep in touch with his reporters. Thanks to well-organised relays of pigeons, Robert's letter would reach Mama some twenty times quicker than if it had gone by ship.

'The Charlotte Anne,
Off the coast of Ecuador,
11 February, 1824

Dearest Mama,

As you see, I am indeed on a different ship, the change-over at
Panama having gone smoothly and the fifty-mile trek across the
isthmus from the Caribbean to the Pacific effected with reasonable
efficiency. I shall leave it to the sketches and caricatures which I
send with this brief note, to describe life on board my new floating
quarters. You can tell which of the handsome young men at the
captain's table is me. I'm the only one not in uniform… '

Robert told his mother that the sort of ragging he'd thought would be
his lot in the officers' mess to which he was attached had not been so
bad after all. In part this was because Arthur had protected him from
the worst of it. He would draw the fire away from Robert by acting
the giddy goat, making outrageous claims about his hunting prowess
or deliberately provoking retaliation in some way. However fierce the
scrum, he always emerged grinning. And Robert, to his surprise, had
won a certain popularity amongst the officers because of his humorous
cartoons about shipboard life and caricatures of some of its leading
lights. He had really meant them for his own amusement, but Arthur
had spotted one of Carlton-Syms as a puffed up bullfrog and gleefully
posted on the mess notice-board. C-S, of course, had been furious,
puffed up with fury, in fact. Ridicule, Robert realized, was a potent
weapon. That caricature had led to requests for others, and now his
cartoons and caricatures were a regular feature on the notice-board,
enjoyed by the bored officers, starved of their usual entertainments.

≈

Only once had things threatened to get really nasty. Robert had feared
a crowd of rowdies was about to burst into his cabin in the dead of
night and carry him off to undergo some humiliating ordeal. As he
lay tense and dry-mouthed in his bunk, straining to catch the voices
whispering and sniggering outside his door, there was a sudden hush,
followed by the sound of the group dispersing. Robert had opened his

door a fraction and peered out. A tall figure was standing, arms folded, back to the door.

'Rainbow, is that you?'

'It is only a wretched person who has no gift for Skyherd.'

'Er… well… I'm much obliged to you.'

≈

'What do you think he meant by it, Mama? Whatever his reasons, I'm certainly glad he's on my side. I suppose C-S, clearly the ring-leader, could easily find an excuse to have him put in irons. I rather think it's not so much Rainbow's imposing appearance that deters C-S as the enormous popularity of the man whose Joseph coat is something of a marvel. And it is well known he would have been matched against Jem Ashley, but for the latter's disappearance. At first I thought he said he was a 'shy man'. Although there is an indefinable air of dignity about him, he is certainly not shy. It turns out he was telling me he was a shaman. I confess I had to look the word up in my dictionary—'A priest or priest-doctor among various northern tribes of Asia. Horace applied it to similar personages in other parts, for example a medicine-man.' So there we are, as Sir Charles would say.'

≈

Robert put down his pen. He could imagine Mama reading his letter in the kitchen, the smell of baking bread filling the room. Would she show it to Father? Would she read him snippets from it?

Arthur strode towards him along the deck. He stroked his moustache, now well beyond the fledgeling stage, and held out a map.

'Ah… It's like this, Stanners… Ah… Well… exactly where are we?'

He spread out the map on the deck.

'What I don't understand, dear fruit, is why the ship is travelling this way and yet the map says we should be going that way.'

Robert explained that the top of the map was always north, so to match it up with their southerly course he must reverse the map.

'Rum business, very rum! Rummer still when we cross into the other hemisphere, I shouldn't wonder… I say, take a look over there!'

≈

A fast frigate was overhauling the more sedate Charlotte Anne. After an exchange of signals, the Charlotte Anne hove to while a boat was lowered from the frigate. A shrill whistle sounded. Seamen were scampering about, no doubt doing useful, nautical things.

'By Jove!' Arthur exclaimed. 'I do believe someone's going to come aboard.'

He craned forward, leaning over the rail. 'Can't quite make it out... Like the cut of his togs. Wonder if he plays cricket. Who's that child with him? Probably the ship's boy with the baggage.'

Robert slid open his telescope. 'Let's see... Oho! I've got news for you, Arthur—your cricketing major is a woman! My pippin, I know her! It's Mrs Thomson... and that's Dickon.'

Arthur snatched the telescope from him. 'God's teeth, you're right! She's in some kind of trousers, by god... And the child! It's wearing the uniform of the British Light Horse!'

Muldoon shuffled his feet behind them. 'The new major's ten years old, sorr... Nephew to Lord Hawksmoor, so the Brigadier's batman tells me, sorr.'

Robert fixed Arthur with what he hoped was a severe expression. 'Below the age of borrowing money from, Arthur.'

'The thought never crossed my... Here they come! Ye gods, she's plain! The size of her hands!' His appalled tone gave way to one of grudging admiration. 'Still... make a jolly good wicket-keeper.'

≈

The pinnace was alongside the Charlotte Anne. The young major, unable to reach the bottom rung of the rope ladder which had been lowered, had to be lifted by Mrs Thomson. He gained the quarter-deck directly below Robert and Arthur. The sergeant of the assembled guard bellowed something totally incomprehensible to Robert which produced a well-drilled rattling of muskets and stamping of feet. In the ensuing silence the squeaking of Dickon's very new boots as he crossed the deck towards Colonel Summers-Cox seemed magnified tenfold.

'Major Richard Minagh reporting for duty, sir.'

Arthur leant towards Robert. 'The very minor Major Minagh and nanny.'

Cadey looked up and fixed Arthur with a glinting eye.

'Oh dear,' Arthur breathed into Robert's ear. 'A dose of castor oil for me.'

And then she saw Robert and her severe expression softened.

≈

'But how did it happen?' Robert wanted to know, an hour later. They were sitting in sheltered corner of the upper deck. 'I was really worried when you and Dickon didn't turn up.' Distraught would have been a more accurate description, but he felt he couldn't say that.

'Chicken pox. The poor boy went down with chicken pox the day before we were due to sail. Lord Hawksmoor's doctor advised against sailing, and the Brigade's Medical Officer practically ordered us to delay our departure.'

'I see.'

'I tried to get a note to you, Mr Stanhope, obviously without success.'

'Still, you're here now. I've felt in need of an ally at times.'

≈

They chatted amicably. To Robert their conversation about paintings and books and the wildflowers still to be found in London was like water to a man crawling across a desert. Somewhere in the midst of it they were calling each other Robert and Cadey.

Robert said, 'Doesn't it surprise you, Cadey, that our government, despite strong protests from the Spanish Ambassador in London, did absolutely nothing to discourage the open recruitment of regiments like this one?'

There was an edge to her laugh. 'Nothing surprises me any more about decisions taken by men.'

Robert said it wouldn't have surprised him if they'd come to fight on the side of the Spanish Royalists rather than of the Peruvian Patriots. After all, the British ruling classes were suspicious of republics and the Spanish had been Britain's allies against the French. Moreover, Miranda, Bolivar and the other founders of the Patriot cause were, in many respects, akin to the radicals who were being suppressed in England.

'You omitted something from the equation, Robert. All that you say signifies nothing compared to the prospect of commercial gain. You are forgetting we are a nation of shop-keepers. It is in our interest to break the monopoly of trade between Spain and her colonial empire.' She smiled. 'Besides, a romantic cause is very appealing… as long as it's far enough away.'

'You may be right, but I'm surprised anyone on this ship is prepared to die for that.'

Her eyes held Robert's. 'They're not being paid to die for a cause—they're no use dead. They're being paid to kill for it.'

Robert knew she was laughing at him in a gentle sort of way, but he didn't mind.

≈

A bugle was calling the regiment to fall in on deck. Someone... a woman was being dragged forward.

'Oh my pippin! That's Carroty Kate!'

She was being tied, face to the mast and stripped down to her thin chemise.

'What are they going to do to her, Muldoon?'

'By Jasus, they're for flogging her.'

'That's terrible! Terrible!'

'A stowaway,' someone said.

'Now who do we have here?' Carlton-Syms purred. As Adjutant of the Day, he was the one in charge

He looked Carroty Kate up and down 'I do believe we've met before... Corporal, a hundred lashes and don't hold back!'

Carroty Kate gave a defiant laugh. 'There's nothing you can teach a woman about pain, Cap'n Friggin' Syms! Not a woman of the regiment.'

The drummers began a loud, continuous roll. Amongst them was Jacko, his face white with distress. Amongst the onlookers was Cadey, biting her lip with agitation. Robert knew the struggle which must be going on inside her between roundly expressing her absolute disgust at such barbarism and keeping quiet for the sake of Dickon, so newly arrived, so keen to make a good impression amongst his fellow officers.

≈

A trooper called out the strokes as the corporal, a big, strong man, wielded the lash.

'One... Two... Three... '

Robert gripped his sketch-book, his knuckles white, as the lash tore her flesh, drawing blood. Not a sound escaped from Carroty Kate. Robert, glancing wildly around, saw Rainbow at the rear of the assembled men, standing head and shoulders above the rest. Any second, he was going to charge to Carroty Kate's defence, committing some grave breach of military discipline that might cost him his life. Robert found himself stepping forward, sketch-book in hand, and shouting in a voice he hardly recognised as his own:

'A minute if you please, Captain Carlton-Syms! I wish to capture this scene for posterity.'

The corporal paused, lash raised. C-S stared disbelievingly. Robert did a lightning sketch.

'Yes, I think readers of the *Chronicle* will recognise you, Captain. Let's see... what would be a fitting caption? ...The gallant Light Horse in action, displaying its customary chivalry? ...And you, soldier... What's your name? The public back home will want to know the name of the hero who strikes a blow for freedom against such intimidating odds.'

Blushing furiously, the corporal lowered the lash. Murmurs of approval ran round the deck. Carlton-Syms laughed a loud, false laugh.

'How many lashes was that, Trooper?'

'Four, sir.'

'We were going to stop at ten, anyway. Just giving her a fright. You didn't really think that... ' He laughed again, even louder. 'Release the woman!'

His face a mask of rage, he strode from the deck. Weak at the knees, Robert sought Cadey's approving eyes.

≈

Drumsticks beat a tattoo on the door of Robert's cabin.

Robert smiled to himself. 'Come in, Jacko. Thanks for finding the time to see me. I know a soldier's life is a busy one.'

Jacko's eyes swivelled to the plate of cakes with pink and yellow icing.

'You shall have the cakes, Jacko, after you've told me what's going on with Carroty Kate. How is she?'

'Breathin' fire, sir, so they say. She's in solitary till we land.'

'That's good, isn't it? The bit about breathing fire, I mean.'

'Reckon so. She's a tough 'un and no mistake.'

'I take it she hid herself on board because she's trying to follow her Smithy. But how did she do it? How did she get off the Good Hope, across Panama and onto the Charlotte Anne?'

Jacko tapped his nose and winked. 'That would be telling. Let's just say she got friends what helped. Ain't done her much good, though.'

'It was a terrible flogging... And to do it to a woman!'

'Oh that! No, I don't mean that, guv... sir. I mean Smithy ain't on board. Not this one nor the first one.'

He stared longingly at the cakes. Relenting, Robert pushed the plate in front of him. Cheeks bulging, Jacko explained that Smithy had been confined to a punishment cell in the depths of the Good Hope for breaking ranks and speaking to Carrots during the embarkation parade. During his incarceration he had contracted some kind of fever and had been transferred to the fever ship which always sailed down-wind of the fleet. Then, as they neared Panama, the fever ship had crammed on sail and left the rest of the fleet behind. On the word 'Panama', cake sprayed from Jacko's lips. He retrieved the pieces from Robert's shirt and returned them to his mouth.

Robert said, 'So they haven't managed to meet up yet?'

Jacko shook his head. 'Smithy don't even know Carrots is wiv us, Mr Hope.' He laughed. 'Mr Stanhope, I mean. It's sort of catching. Rainbow's always going on about you in that way of his... you know, like his mouth's a runaway horse.'

'Where's Smithy now?'

'Dunno for sure. Word is he don't plan to hang up his clogs just yet. Carrots says there ain't a fever inwented could kill off Smithy... And, thanks Mr Stanhope, sir.'

'Oh, well, I'm sorry there weren't more cakes.'

'I mean for standing up to Carlton-effin'-beggin'-your-pardon-Syms the way you did. But for you... '

'I didn't stop to think, you see. If I had... Anyway, you've filled out since joining up. How are you liking the army?'

'Discipline's hard, sir. But a boy can stand that provising how there's a hot meal and a place to kip on the end of it... Bleedin' hell! I'm late for practice!' And he bolted from the room.

It was a warm tropical evening—too warm for the formal scarlet dress uniforms being worn in the mess. The occasion was a party for the officers of the Light Horse to mark the crossing of the Equator. The sailors and lower ranks were celebrating in their own way with general skylarking which included Neptune presiding over the ducking of anyone who had not crossed the line before. On some ships this was a ritual extended to everyone. Aboard the Charlotte Anne, however, it had been deemed bad for discipline for officers to lose their dignity in front of the men. Even the Brigadier was honouring the party with his presence. Being an ex-cavalryman himself, the Brigadier took a keen interest in the BLH and had elected to sail with them rather than in any of the other ships. The chatter around Robert was of hunting and the merits of various sporting guns the officers all seemed to have brought with them. The only officer absent was Richard Minagh, Dickon, it being long past his bedtime.

'Another toast!' Arthur cried, raising his glass. 'To the senoritas of Peru, may they all get the scarlet fever when they see us!'

At one end of the long, portholed room was the glass case containing the Brigadier's stuffed right arm. It was dressed for the occasion in the sleeve of a scarlet mess jacket. At the start of the voyage, Arthur had tried to make Robert believe that anyone entertained in the mess for the first time had to shake hands with it.

Seeing Robert looking at it now, Arthur said, 'Tell you what, Stanners, I'd rather shake hands with that thing than with Nanny Thomson. Puts the fear of God into me, that woman does.'

'I see she isn't here.'

'Probably tucking up the infant. Mind you, the mess is strictly men only… Thank Heavens.' He shouted across the room, 'What do you think the hunting will be like when we get there, Slogger?'

Carlton-Syms pretended not to hear. Robert had noticed that only Arthur was permitted to call C-S 'Slogger' in recognition of the fact that they had been in the same form and 'house' at school. With his other brother-officers C-S was civil but reserved, freezing out any attempts at familiarity which later might be regretted. He knew, and they knew, that before long he would be their superior officer—not because of ability or aptitude, but because his family was wealthy and he would be the highest bidder for the next vacant post of major. Of late, even Arthur had been getting a touch of the frost.

≈

C-S pushed forward, scowling at Robert. 'What's a miserable little adjective-jerker doing here? The party is for serving officers only.'

Robert fanned his invitation under C-S's nose. 'From Colonel Summers-Cox himself.'

'Oh, him,' C-S said dismissively, 'I might have known.'

The Brigadier proclaimed in a voice for all to hear, 'In a month, no less, the French shall have a taste of our steel!'

'Brigadier!' hissed Colonel Summers-Cox, 'It's the Spanish Royalists we're fighting now!'

The Brigadier blasted him to damnation as a pedantic, nit-picking ninny, a tirade which was enjoyed by all. Robert had gathered fairly quickly that Summers-Cox was regarded as too earnest. He actually took war seriously. He tried too hard, apparently not appreciating that a true gentleman, while allowed to be a gifted amateur, should never be seen to be trying at anything—such bad form, fitting only for those who had to impress by their own grubby efforts rather than by their breeding, their fine instincts and natural gifts.

≈

C-S, seeing Summers-Cox temporarily downed, seized his opportunity.

'Colonel, your ruling about officers not submitting to old Neptune's attentions out there… it applies only to officers, does it not?'

'Yes. Why?'

'Because Stanhope, here, is not an officer. Surely he shouldn't be skulking in the mess.'

'But he's a gentleman, Captain.'

'The ruling, which is in writing, sir, specifically states 'officers'.'

Summers-Cox sighed, shrugged and walked away. Amidst yells of delight, Robert was grabbed and propelled out of the mess towards the waiting mob. A cheer went up. A friendly cheer. Robert's intervention on behalf of Carroty Kate had not been forgotten. For the first time in his life, Robert realised, he was actually a bit of a hero, respected by other men, and the terrors of the ritual evaporated. Whereas some people received a ducking and others had their heads shaved, all that Robert was requested to do was to look through a telescope at the Equator and pretend he didn't realize he was looking at a cotton thread stretched across the lens.

'I see it! Yes, I clearly see it!' Another cheer went up.

It wasn't until later that Muldoon told him he had a black circle round his eye and that the eye-piece of the telescope had been smeared with soot.

≈

In the space below decks allocated to the cavalry horses, Rainbow was renewing the straw in the stalls. He was glad to be alone. The other grooms were involved in some rite of passage similar to when the young men of his tribe made the transition from puberty to manhood… something about crossing a line called Equator. Apparently it didn't concern him.

'He got to of crossed it afore if he come from darkie land. Stands to reason… Christian folk our side of the line, savages t'other.'

Rainbow put down his pitch-fork and picked up the wooden puppet head he was working on.

Snail had said, 'Go to the end of the bleedin' world and the dolls'd still turn a penny for you.'

So Rainbow had offered to carve the figures for her.

≈

As he sharpened his knife his thoughts turned to the Brigadier, the cockroach in human form. He had spoken of someone who had seen evidence of the drought. If only he'd been able to find out more. How recent was this report? Had things got worse since he'd left his home? When he found Nataxale again, if he defeated him, the rains would come, but not until he'd made his gift to Skyherd at the proper time and the proper place. If he defeated Nataxale 'If' was a difficult word to sleep with at night. Time was gnawing at his confidence. A horse whinnied and kicked the side of its stall. Rainbow calmed it. When the frightened beasts needed quieting in a storm, he was the one the other grooms looked to. 'We are the last people on Earth who can speak with the animals,' Ikpoom had said. And 'faded' was a difficult word to sleep with, too. He kept thinking of those minstrels and he'd heard Bat saying something to Skyherd about fading, about how people could fade away in the Other World.

≈

Being back on board a ship awoke so many memories of the dark tunnel he'd travelled to reach the Other World. He opened the door of a stall and began to rake out the soiled straw. Suddenly he was in a dark, confined space which reeked overpoweringly of vomit and excrement and that sharp tang which fear and despair give to human sweat. A chestnut mare nuzzled him. He rested his head against its neck, drawing strength from it. As he plied his rake, Rainbow contemplated the state of Skyherd's aura—still faded, but gaining in brightness, though not yet the aura of a god capable of summoning massed ranks of clouds with which to saturate the parched earth. Nataxale's minions, headed by Carlton-Syms, were constantly harassing Skyherd, in an attempt to weaken his aura. And as for that evil spirit's treatment of Snail—Rainbow relaxed his fierce grip on the rake, recalling how he and Jacko and Smithy had outwitted them all, hiding her all those months on the Good Hope; then getting her off it and onto the Charlotte Anne. At least Yansam, Skyherd's consort, was here now. He'd always known she would come. Until such time as the nature of the gift he must make to Skyherd was revealed to him, what could he do to be of service to the Rainmaker?

18

Spread out below was the broad Rimac Valley, wooded along the banks of its river and bright with green irrigated patches. About three miles away Lima looked like a toy city, appearing neater and better planned when viewed from above. Robert dismounted and fondled the neck of Manco, his piebald gelding, thankful for their pact of mutual tolerance.

≈

As soon as he knew he was going to South America, Robert had begun to worry about the horse he'd have to ride when he got there. Only cavalry horses, trained for battle, were being shipped over. All other four-footed transport would be purchased on arrival. On the voyage across, he'd had nightmares about being astride some monstrous animal like the one onto which, terrified, he was daily hoisted by Father.

'Show him who's the master!' Father would shout, angry even before Robert was in the saddle. Robert could still recall his misery as, daily, it proved beyond doubt to be the horse.

≈

A couple of days before disembarking, Robert had been sitting in the hot tub while his batman washed his back. As if reading his thoughts, Muldoon had said gruffly, 'Don't you worry, sorr. When we get to Peruvia, Cap'n Trevellyn and I will pick out a quiet 'un for you.' And then he'd added, 'A good quiet 'un's as rare as a green dog these days.' Which Arthur had interpreted for Robert as meaning, 'I expect a little extra drinking money for my trouble—on top of the little profit I'm going to make from this deal without telling you.'

≈

Robert unloaded the basket-cage with the two homing pigeons which would carry his very first sketches for the *Chronicle* on the first stage of their journey back to England. Setting up his easel, he began sketching the view of Lima. Manco tossed his head and whinnied. Several teams of horses were dragging cannon to the top of an adjacent hill. More target practice, Robert supposed. Soon they'd be shattering the tranquility he had ridden out here to enjoy. A wind sprang up, causing Robert to shield his eyes against the dust. When he looked again, a long line of dragoons, or perhaps they were hussars—Robert didn't know the difference—were winding down a nearby side valley, the red plumes on their tall shakos bobbing to the rhythm of the their mounts. One of them was the eminently detestable C-S. Soldiers, like columns of red ants, were marching up the valley. And now, neat blocks of blue ants, followed by white ants were crossing the river and advancing from the opposite direction. They were shooting at each other! The cannon opened fire. Robert jumped to his feet. He was witnessing his first battle!

≈

The artillery on the nearby hill was pounding away and, in the intervals between their cannonading, the faint sound of musketry could be heard from the valley. Puffs of smoke issued silently from the neat lines and squares, followed by the muskets' crackle. More than half the action was hidden from view by a belt of woodland beside the river. Of the bits Robert was able to observe, he could discern no obvious pattern. There were men running in all directions, cavalry charging, manoeuvre and counter-manoeuvre. Clouds of gun-smoke, carried on the wind, billowed across the landscape, obscuring the view; figures kept disappearing into hollows then reappearing in different colours. Robert pulled his telescope from the saddle-bag and put it to his eye, discovering that, when the broad but blurred canvas is exchanged for a small circle of accurate detail, one learns even less.

≈

Into his circle of vision galloped C-S and company, sabres drawn, the pounding hooves of their mounts raising clouds of dust which mingled with the smoke in swirling eddies. First one, then another toppled from his saddle and sprawled on the ground. Robert expected to see some horses go down, but none did. He saw C-S fall, roll and lie still. Then the smoke and dust became too dense to see anything.

≈

Swinging the telescope to another part of the field of battle, he saw a head severed in two by a sabre, a bayonet enter a stomach. With a shaking hand he lowered the telescope. Emitting blood-curdling cries, a wedge of red-coated cavalry charged out of a wood on the far side of the valley, surprising their opponents in their right flank. Inexplicably, instead of engaging the enemy, they passed right through them, crossed the valley and continued on and up the hill in Robert's direction. He trained the telescope on them. Hunting pink; in front of them a pack of hounds. And... there! Some kind of South American hare, losing ground fast to its pursuers. The hare darted right through the battery of cannon on the adjacent top. On it loped, down the rounded ridge which joined Robert's hill to the other one. Baying hounds poured between the cannon. The gunners ceased their swabbing and their ramming to stand and stare as the hare met its death on the ridge.

'Tally-ho! Tally-ho!'

Huntsmen were leaping the silent battery and sweeping down the ridge to mill about in circles at the scene of the kill. Robert buried his face in Manco's neck, overwhelmed by the carnage below, confused about C-S.

≈

A hand clapped Robert on the shoulder. Arthur was grinning down at him.

'If it isn't our intrepid news-hound! How goes it Stanners? How are you and that heap of bones getting on?'

'Manco? You might say we're rubbing along all right... Particularly with regard to the tender flesh on my thighs.'

'Good show! And what stirring pictures are readers of the *Chronicle* going to get served up with their devilled kidneys for breakfast?'

'Oh! I... I forgot to make any sketches. I mean I got so carried away with... Oh dear! And my very first battle!'

'Battle?'

'Well, I suppose it's just a skirmish to you.'

'No, no. Battle it is. And a very important one. Definitely worthy of a report back to old Charlie Makewar.'

'Makepiece.'

'Yes, exactly.'

≈

Arthur dismounted Scaramander and stood beside Robert while the rest of the hunt trotted off at a slow pace.

'Er... shouldn't you be down there, Arthur? I mean shouldn't you all be taking part in the battle?'

Arthur bent to inspect his horse's hoof, coughing hard.

'A chap can't fight in hunting pink, don't you know. It's not done. Not the thing at all.'

'I think C-S may be dead, or at least hit and badly injured. I saw him go down, along with a number of others.'

Arthur removed his hunting hat and lowered his head. 'Yes, I was nearer than you… I saw it all.'

Arthur was clearly moved by the loss of his friend. He walked away, his face buried in his hands. Presently he returned and said in a voice trembling with suppressed emotion,

'Would you write his obituary, Stanhope?'

'Me? But I… '

'It would be awfully decent of you, old fruit.'

Robert nodded his agreement. He had detested Carlton-Syms, but Arthur had known him since boyhood. He'd do it for Arthur.

≈

Arthur took Robert's telescope and turned away to survey the scene.

'What's going on down there, Arthur?'

'History in the making.'

'But Arthur! This is my first big test as a reporter and I don't know who's which from when's what!'

'Cheer up, don't look so worried! Nobody ever knows the full story. At best even the generals only have a rough idea of what's happening. Utter bamboozlement is the order of the day and… ' The battery opened up again. Arthur raised his voice above the roar of the cannon. ' …And most dispatches are like a barber's cat, all wind and piss… and yet I was always having my knuckles rapped at school for putting the cavalry or the guns a few yards out of position when tested on some past battle or other. Odd that, very odd.'

He laughed and punched Robert on the arm.shouting, 'In this case, I'd say your guess is as good as their's.'

'Really?'

'Oh yes, with my expert help, that is… Anyway, time to get back to Lima. You can safely say that our side won and that a good time was had by all.'

As Robert was about to mount Manco, Arthur put his hand on his arm.

'I say, Stanners, may I touch you for a loan. I had a run of bad luck at the cards last night.'

'How bad?'

'A couple of thousand… Oh, not our money, not the real thing, the local stuff.'

Robert handed him the paper money issued by the Spanish Viceroyalty of Peru over which had been franked 'Republic of Gran Colombia': Bolivar's dream of a united Venezuela, New Granada and Peru.

'A thousand thanks, Robert… well, a couple of thou', anyway.'

'I have been deeply touched, Arthur, that you should ask me.'

They both laughed at their standing joke.

≈

They passed a small adobe hut. A young woman smiled and beckoned to them from the doorway.

Arthur said, 'Maybe we should stop here for a bit. I wouldn't mind a spot more rest after the chase… And… And, of course… You know… the shock… such a close friend. And you could write your report here while it's fresh in your mind.'

They dismounted—Robert painfully aware that he was, as Father would say, 'giving a good imitation of a sack of potatoes.' Arthur gesticulated and fanned the senorita with his newly-acquired bank notes until some kind of deal was struck. Arthur pointed to a table and chair under the shade of a tree.

'Why don't you sit there? 'I'm going inside for a… Ah! That is to say, for a siesta.'

≈

Robert worked on his report for Sir Charles and on the accompanying sketches, doing them on thin rice-paper, which, when folded, could be fitted into capsules which were then attached to the legs of the pigeons. Completing his task, he released the two birds and watched them circling before winging on their way to the port of Trujillo, carrying his very first effort as a war correspondent. Wild animal noises were coming from the hut. Robert hoped Arthur was not going down with some tropical fever.

≈

The wind stirred the leaves overhead. Beechwood Chase—the birds, the flowers, the dragonflies, the animals, the hours within its secret shady places which had been so much part of Robert's childhood. But everything was changing—the countryside, the new cotton mills, the demands of the radicals. His own dear country, it seemed, was at one of history's crossroads every bit as much as this seething continent in which he found himself.

≈

Arthur's head popped out of a window. 'Finished?'

'Yes. The pigeons are on their way, on the first leg of the journey.'

'Leg? They're not walking it, are they?'

'First stage… And before you ask, no, they're not going to act it out.'

Robert explained that these birds had a homing instinct and that, when released, they would fly back to where they had been hatched and reared. They could fly 600 miles in a day.

'They don't all get through, of course—which is why I've been instructed to write my reports in triplicate.'

'Good show! How about getting started on poor Slogger's obituary, then? Leave you to it while I get a bit more of the… Ah… of the old blanket drill.'

The head disappeared. Robert dipped his quill into his inkpot, withdrew it and dipped again. What could he write about someone who had done his best to bully and humiliate him? How could he say something nice about an arrogant, utterly self-centred philistine? 'Hugh Carlton-Syms had all the qualities required of an army officer,' he wrote.

At first it was a struggle, but soon he was translating into obituese with reasonable fluency. Stubborn pig-headedness became 'admirable determination.' Insulting behaviour to those he considered his inferiors: 'a champion of our finest traditions.' Total disregard of his men's welfare: 'a robust approach to the manly business of soldiering.' And, as for his shameful neglect of duty due to hours spent currying favour with those in a position to further his career: 'a keen analyst of military priorities and a sharp awareness of the overall strategy.' But he could find no way round the fact that C-S had ordered the flogging of

Carroty Kate, although it seemed that Carroty Kate had suffered more over Smithy than over her flogging. She'd been hoping, even expecting to find him waiting for her at Trujillo, the port of embarkation, only to find that, being pronounced fully recovered, Smithy had been ordered on ahead with an advance scouting party.

≈

But where was Arthur? He was certainly having a long siesta. Robert started making sketches for a large oil painting which would recreate the battle in its full panoramic sweep, recording a historic moment for posterity. 'The Battle at Rimac Ford.' Yes, it had a good ring to it. He worked feverishly, caught up by the multiplying possibilities, each line, each mark on the paper suggesting a dozen more. In the background, a snow-clad chain of mountains curved across the skyline—a curve which was taken up and continued by a white-clad column of soldiers. Yes, that worked very well, and he could put in drifting gun-smoke… there… no, just there, in a subtle echo of that curve. And the wood from which the red foot-soldiers were emerging—it was so verdant, so bursting with renewal of life despite the carnage taking place beneath its branches. Add some blossom here… and here, exactly matching the red plumes on the shakos of the close-packed troops. And another column of soldiers, bayonets fixed, to balance the clumps of thorns… It wasn't how it had really been, but it was true to the composition, to the logic of the picture.

≈

He had filled a complete sketchbook before Arthur finally appeared looking, Robert thought, more tired than when he had begun his siesta. He grinned at Robert and hauled himself into his saddle. Robert showed him Carlton-Syms' obituary and was gratified that he seemed hugely pleased.

≈

As they entered Lima an open carriage was bouncing along the road towards them. The passenger looked familiar to Robert… very familiar. The carriage drew to a halt.

'C-S!' Robert squeaked.

Carlton-Syms snatched the whip from the coachman and flicked it an inch from Robert's nose.

'Trust a dandiprat like you to let the side down, going about like some common tradesman on that piebald thing, fit only for the knacker's yard. Really, Stanhope! You have no style... Why are you staring at me like that?'

Arthur was rolling about in his saddle, clutching his sides.

'Your face, Stanners! Your face! Oh, you really fell for that one!'

'But, C-S, I saw you hit! I definitely saw it.'

'You haven't heard the best of it yet,' Arthur announced gleefully. 'Or should I say the worst.'

With much slapping of his thighs, he divulged that there had been no battle earlier in the day. It had simply been an exercise using blank ammunition.

'But my report! It will be in the *Chronicle*!'

Robert's involuntary groan sent Arthur into fresh paroxysms of laughter. Carlton-Syms retained a superior, scornful expression, with just a faint glimmer of amusement that anyone could be so gullible. His obituary lay like a ton weight in Robert's pocket.

Robert turned to Arthur, trying to nurture his fading resentment. It was no good. There was no malice in what he'd done; his glorious enjoyment of life, his infectious laugh, were so irresistible.

≈

Arthur grinned at the two of them. 'It'll take more than a few blanks to get rid of you, Slogger, eh?'

'It was these damnable shakos,' Carlton-Syms said, lifting the elaborate headgear from the seat and placing it on Robert like a crown. It came down over his eyes, its forward brim resting on the bridge of his nose. So heavy was it that his head began to loll sideways.

More laughter. 'Come out of there, I can't see your feet!'

Robert lifted the shako.

Carlton-Syms said, 'There was a cross-wind. In that top-heavy contraption, anybody would have been unbalanced.'

'Even an expert horseman like Slogger,' Arthur said, winking at Robert.

'Precisely.' snapped Carlton-Syms.

The gallant Captain Trevellyn made a gracious bow to a passing senorita. Robert persisted. 'I saw men bayoneted. I saw it clearly through my telescope.'

Arthur stroked his moustache. 'Ah!'

'Ah?'

'Very much, 'Ah', I'm afraid. That bit wasn't supposed to happen. The fact is, it was an Irish battalion and an English battalion and they hate each other more than they hate the enemy.'

'Were many hurt?'

Carlton-Syms informed them: 'Sixteen dead and over thirty injured… And that's not for your blasted rag, Stanhope.'

'There you are, that's how it goes,' Arthur shrugged. 'Our first casualties of the campaign and we inflicted them on ourselves. Unfortunate.'

Carlton-Syms snorted impatiently. 'The very opposite to unfortunate! The men showed their mettle, they showed aggression and stomach for a fight. They displayed an excellent competitive spirit, a very proper eagerness to defend the reputation of their respective units. It was everything for which we have striven in our training of them. They'll all be flogged, of course.'

≈

Dear God, more floggings! Robert thought. On the voyage there'd been the episode with Carroty Kate; a young officer had been shot in a duel over cards; he'd seen men encouraged to bludgeon each other into unconsciousness with their fists; two men had died on parade, killed by army regulations which decreed they must wear their thick felt uniforms, fastened to the top button, with belts so tight that breathing was difficult, and tall shakos on their heads which must have weighed more than the crown of England. And now he had just learnt of more lives wasted in what had been merely a training exercise. What then should he expect when the violence began?

19

Thunder rumbled in the distant Andes, matching the sound of seven thousand men, four abreast, marching in step to the beat of the drums. Robert turned in his saddle to watch this snake, the British Brigade, undulating across the thirsty, thorn-sharp landscape. First came the main body of infantry, separated into blocks of colour by regiment and battalion, then the artillery with their horse-drawn cannon and ammunition trailers; behind them the baggage columns, the heavy ox-carts, the pack mules, the herds of cattle, and the llamas which served both as beasts of burden and as food. In the rear, tailing into the distance, was a second army, almost as large as the first—the camp-followers, mostly women—old hags who could produce a hot meal in the most unlikely of circumstances, washerwomen, common-law wives, prostitutes, and a host more, catering for the fighting men's needs.

≈

The British Brigade was several days out of Lima, under orders to reinforce the Patriot troops besieging the commandingly placed town of Cerro de Puna. It was a march of at least two hundred miles and most of it through rugged, mountainous country. On the way there, the brigade was to mop up any pockets of resistance and to root the Royalists out of any small towns they might still be occupying.

≈

On each flank of the main body, scouting ahead and to the sides, were the mounted troops of the British Light Horse. Walking beside Robert, holding Manco's bridle and perspiring mightily was Muldoon.

'My feet is quite out of breath, sorr.'

Following behind, attached to each other and to Manco by a rope, were Robert's two mules, Napoleon and Josephine. The latter had what Muldoon referred to as 'devotional habits'—which is to say that, occasionally, she would go down on her knees and refuse to budge. Strapped to their sides were Robert's tent, folding bed, bedding-roll, cooking utensils, clothes, his pigments and oils, half a dozen blank canvases stretched on frames, several boxes specially designed to carry and protect any paintings finished or in the process of completion and the basket cages containing the homing pigeons.

'Sorr, begging your pardon, sorr.'

'What is it, Muldoon?'

'It's Josephine, sorr. I think she's about to hold one of her jawbations with the good Lord. She's as stubborn as a mule, sorr, so she is. It's thirst, sorr. Both man and beast can work up a powerful thirst in this heat.'

He licked his lips. 'Man and beast… particularly man.'

Remembering Arthur's advice to be firm with Napoleon, Josephine and Muldoon… particularly Muldoon, Robert said,

'We'll wait till we get the order to halt.'

'Lord knows when that'll be,' Muldoon grumbled. 'Old Cockroach hardly notices we're here these days.'

'Cockroach?'

'The Brigadier, begging your pardon, sorr.'

There was no denying, Robert thought, that Cochrane-Dyat shut himself away more and more. And there had been a noticeable increase in his eccentricities. His adherence to military tradition had become obsessive.

Robert extracted two oranges from his saddle-bag, offering one to Muldoon.

'Well, Muldoon, you're the old timer. What are the dietary rules when on campaign?'

'Rule number one, sorr: try not to die.'

'No, I mean rules about eating, what to avoid and so on.'

'Avoid anything that will eat you, sorr, especially the heavy cavalry.'

'Cavalry?'

'Yes, sorr, the gentlemen in brown, sorr, the bed-bugs and the fleas. Not that they worry me. One bite o' me and they're legless… And talking of legs, the old trotter-boxes is killing me, sorr.'

'I dare say you'll manage at a pinch.'

≈

A group of the Light Horse cantered by, their scarlet jackets with silver-braided facings worn as cloaks from one shoulder, flying out like wings, exotic birds, rivalling the emerald green humming-birds in the bright blue flowering cacti.

The drums kept up their steady beat, the ground vibrating as thousands of booted feet stamped in unison.

'How goes it, my Prussian Blue?' It was Arthur, accompanied by Dickon, the Very Minor Major Minagh.

'And you, Muldoon, have you been giving Mr Stanhope any of your balderdash and blarneyfied botheration?'

'No, sorr!'

They gossiped about Major Maitland who had been fatally stabbed by a jealous husband in Lima. The vacancy had gone to C-S, the highest bidder. The illness of some of the senior command and plain incompetence on the part of others, had allowed Carlton-Syms to manoeuvre himself into a position where he was almost openly challenging Colonel Summers-Cox as to who was really in charge of the Light Horse. Arthur related how, at every opportunity, C-S undermined the authority of his rival and encouraged his fellow officers in despising their Colonel—a state of affairs which the enfeebled Brigadier did nothing to prevent.

'Splendid cricket captain, though,' Arthur concluded.

Robert managed an amused laugh. 'But what if the Spanish Royalists have some other game in mind?'

Arthur saluted the Very Minor Major. 'If you'll excuse us, sir, I'd like a private word with Stanhope. I'm sure you'll have no difficulty thinking up questions for Muldoon here.'

They trotted ahead, leaving Muldoon walking beside the Very Minor Major's largish chestnut.

'I brought the infant here by a route that took in a jump or two.'

'And?'

'And he fell off at every single one! But I'll give him this—he never said a word. As soon as his horse was caught, he just gritted his teeth and got back on.'

Arthur gripped Robert's arm and leant forward in his saddle, assuming his about-to-ask-a-favour posture. 'I say, be a good chap and look after the VMM for a bit, would you? I've been landed with him for the whole day—you know, showing him the ropes and all that. The beastly infant never stops asking questions! It's prodigiously tedious!'

'You mean you can't answer his questions.'

'Well, do you know why we don't have the new breech-loading muskets when they're ten times faster than our muzzle-loaders?'

'Why don't you suggest he asks the Brigadier that question?'

Arthur slapped his thighs with delight. 'By Jove, Stanners, a topping idea!' His laughing countenance gave way to an expression befitting a cornered animal. 'But you'll take him off my hands for a bit, won't you? You know, change his nappies, spoon-feed him, that sort of thing.'

'Well, just for a little… '

'Eternally indebted and all that,' Arthur declared, wheeling his horse and cantering off.

'Eternally is the word, since you never pay back what I lend you…' Robert cared nothing about recovering his loan, but it seemed the right sort of manly banter. Arthur raised his hat by way of response.

≈

When Robert returned to Muldoon and the Very Minor Major, the latter was drilling the former, making him march back and forth, wheel and turn.

'Pick those feet up! Swing your arms! Head up!' he piped, in imitation of a drill sergeant.

Muldoon was red in the face, more with rage, Robert suspected, than exertion.

'Stop that!' Robert shouted.

Dickon stared at him defiantly. 'I can do it if I want. He has to obey me because I'm an officer.'

They argued while Muldoon, having received no order to halt, was marching away into the distance.

'Well, go on, Major, say the proper words, whatever they are. Turn off your clockwork soldier.'

His expression was sulky. 'Only if you say 'please'.'

'Please.'

'Trooper Muldooooon… halt!'

Muldoon continued marching.

'I don't think he heard you. Try again.'

But his very minor voice did not carry and he had to ride after Muldoon, his order becoming more pleading with each repetition. Robert caught them up. Muldoon was standing to attention, breathing hard.

Robert rounded on the boy. 'Get down off that horse! At once!'

Startled, he dismounted. Robert dismounted too and drew him away. No longer astride his large chestnut, Dickon was just a boy. Robert addressed him as the child he was, upbraiding him for his inconsiderate behaviour towards Muldoon. Rank, Robert lectured him, might give the right to issue orders, but that was not the same thing at all as leadership.

'Do you think Muldoon is going to willingly follow you after that petty abuse of authority?'

≈

The Major burst into tears. 'I drill my toy soldiers every night,' he blubbed. 'I wanted to do it with a real one.'

It seemed to Robert that Dickon was relieved to have been stopped. Robert manoeuvred Manco so that the tears could flow unobserved. He passed Dickon his pocket handkerchief. 'If you're half the man I think you are, Dickon, you'll apologise to Muldoon.'

Horror, stubborn refusal, contrition, pride, all marched across Dickon's face.

'The worst thing you can do to your dignity is to stand on it,' Robert said. Removing his travelling hat—the straw one he'd purchased in Panama, the one Arthur referred to as his 'donkey's breakfast' —he threw it on the ground and jumped on it. The very minor Major Minagh let out a yell of delight. A fresh battalion tramped past, headed by their drummers. Robert and Dickon pranced and capered round the hat to the beat of the drums. Then, breaking away, the diminutive major walked up to Muldoon. Robert deliberately turned away and did not hear what was said. But, from that moment on, as far as Muldoon was concerned, no praise was too high for 'the young occifer.'

Shortly after that, a message came calling Dickon to a meeting at Staff HQ—a rather pretentious name, Robert thought, for a tent no bigger than the one used for the annual village fete.

≈

The daily march, it seemed to Robert, was some kind of contest between the British Brigade's thraldom to tradition and the South American climate. Nobody with any sense, as Cadey had commented more than once, would march through the mid-day heat. And yet the regiment did and men had died in consequence. However, the officers here who had served in India finally persuaded the traditionalists into granting a three-hour rest at noon. So, with the sun high in the sky, a bugle sounded, the brigade halted and Robert sat in the shade of an awning which Muldoon had fixed up for him, working on his painting of 'Battle at Rimac Ford.' As he worked at the canvas, he became aware that Rainbow had joined them. He often dropped by, sometimes with Jacko, when he had finished watering the horses or rubbing down their sweaty bodies, or whatever it was grooms did.

≈

Rainbow sat propped against the prone mule, Josephine. He stretched out his arm and picked up Robert's telescope. He had looked through it before during the voyage. He liked the way it brought everything nearer, particularly the clouds. It was as if you had seen an elephant in the distance and walked towards it for an hour or more to get closer to it, except that this instrument in his hand was able to compress time so that things were instantly in front of you.

Muldoon was sitting on an upturned bucket, polishing a pair of Robert's top boots.

'Is Rainbow asleep?' Robert asked.

Muldoon breathed hard onto a toe-cap. 'Difficult to say, sorr. Even awake, he's in a dream.'

Rainbow opened one eye. 'The Great Spirit is dreaming the Universe and, inside that dream, every living thing is dreaming its own dream.'

Muldoon winked at Robert. 'If he's in my dream, then it's a nightmare, that's for sure.'

≈

Rainbow looked long and hard at Robert's canvas. 'You understand the sky, Mr Hope.'

Robert laid down his brush, stood back and surveyed his canvas with a critical eye. 'I don't know what's wrong. It's somewhere inside me, but I can't find it! The sky is good, though. Some artists don't pay enough attention to the sky. It's what determines the way the whole picture is lit, the mood of it. 'I've studied the sky, heard thunder roll through dark clouds, seen their lightning flashes, watched huge columns of rain deluge the earth. And I've thought, 'Lord! Of all the clouds that ever existed in the whole history of the world, no two have ever been quite the same. I love clouds.'

Rainbow gave a cry of joy. Arthur had looked straight at him and spoken the words 'Skyherd' and 'Lord of the Clouds'!

Robert saw that the exploding shells in his painting mimicked the shape and colour of the flowering jacaranda bushes of the Rimac Valley. Muldoon's elbow was moving steadily to and fro as he polished, with the same action as that of a man bayoneting someone in the stomach—an action not unlike a wing about to unfold, the wing of an avenging angel. So many things suddenly seemed to fit, to connect, to be uncannily relevant to the painting. Robert felt Rainbow's intense gaze upon him.

'The power is flowing through you, Mr Hope.'

'It seems to me that when we are creating something, we're in touch with our Creator.'

Rainbow nodded. 'Everything connects, does it not?'

'Yes! Yes, it does!'

'We are both healers, you and I, Mr Hope. You of the land, the grass, the trees. I of my people... At least, I try to be.'

Skyherd made no reply.

'Your canvas is like a shaman's crystal. Through it we see our problems, our souls.'

'I suppose so, in a way.'

'Monkey has taught me much about walking the narrow beam, Mr Hope.'

Skyherd applied paint to the white clouds. 'What beam, Rainbow?'

'The one we both walk, balancing between opposites.'

'Yes... Yes, I see that. When I paint, I want both freedom and discipline at the same time!'

'As does any shaman, Mr Hope. We need both chaos and order.'

Muldoon sighed heavily. 'What I wouldn't give to be able to order a tankard of fresh, foaming beer.'

≈

Josephine's stomach rumbled beneath Rainbow's ear. Rainbow thought of thunder and rain and flowing water and of Yansam, who was walking towards him. She was wearing what was now her normal garb of riding britches and top boots.

She said, 'Dickon's caught up in some meeting. May I join you, Robert? It looks so cool under there.'

'Please do.'

≈

A column of ants was advancing across the dry, brown grass a few feet from where they sat.

'Here we have the ideal soldiers,' Cadey said. 'They obey their orders implicitly, without thought.' She pushed a stick into their path. They swarmed over it, undiverted.

'Ah, obedient ants, what general wouldn't prefer you to human beings? And yet, Robert, disobedience is man's original virtue.'

'It is?'

'When I say 'man', I include women, of course.'

'Oh... Yes... I'm glad of that.'

'It is through disobedience that progress is made... breaking free from the strait-jacket, challenging assumptions.'

Rainbow was listening with interest. Muldoon was muttering to himself and shaking his head. Robert said nothing. He couldn't imagine he'd ever be that sort of person. He would never find the sort of courage she had to be herself, whatever anyone else thought of her.

20

Framed in the entrance to Robert's tent, Muldoon's square bulk blocked out the evening sun.

'A note for you, sorr... hinvitation to a nosh up with Major Flogging-Syms, sorr.'

'You're not supposed to know what it says.'

'No, sorr.'

The competition to 'run a good table' far from base was intense. C-S had already demonstrated that he was determined to put any potential rivals for promotion to shame, even to the extent of commandeering space on the supply wagons for his private marquee, his crates of wine and hampers of preserved foods—space which could have been used for the woefully short medical supplies and basic rations.

'Any reply, sorr?'

'I'd better go, I suppose. But why would he invite me of all people?'

Muldoon brushed down Robert's favourite yellow waistcoat and hung it up. 'I'll put money on it, sorr, he'll be wanting himself pictured off.'

≈

Robert walked on a red carpet down an avenue of potted palms into the marquee. Trestle tables covered in white damask were laden with what the invitation had termed 'a cold collation'—a variety of game in aspic, potted meats, marbled jellies, piles of crystallised fruit, chilled consommé. Robert tried to imagine what went into achieving chilled anything in this baking climate. It was a buffet meal, it being deemed a luxury to eat standing after a day in the saddle. The officers mixed freely, except that Carlton-Syms had cordoned off an area of the marquee for Very Important Persons only—which, of course, included himself, but not his colonel, Summers-Cox, whom he regarded both as his social inferior and as an obstacle on the way to the top. Brigadier Cochrane-Dyat was absent, having taken to his bed.

≈

On one canvas wall hung a portrait of King George, mounted on a stallion. The artist, in Robert's opinion, had made a better job of the horse than of the king. Robert noticed that Rainbow, who had been pressed into service as a waiter, stared at it suspiciously every time he passed. And where was Arthur? Robert stood, champagne glass in hand, with waves of chatter washing over him, thinking how it had never failed to disappoint him when a mixture of the brightest hues in his paint-box produced, not some extra-magnificent colour, but a muddy brown. So it was with the conversations in the marquee. Each group might have its bright little topic—the merits of the pigeon v the heliograph for sending messages, the doings of those dangerous radicals back in England, the prospects for a good hunt while on campaign, but taken together they made a kind of dull hub-bub. What diverse motives had brought them all here to this god-forsaken wilderness? In one corner sat Cadey, known throughout the regiment as 'Nanny' Thomson. She was dressed in her usual britches. C-S would have some ulterior motive, of course, for inviting her. After all, Lord Hawksmoor was an influential person in the War Office. Robert was on his way over to join her when Arthur, who was passing by the edge of 'the paddock' as he named the VIP area, raised his glass to C-S.

Carlton-Syms affected not to see him, but when Arthur stretched a hand across the cordon, touched his friend on the shoulder and said 'Your good health, Slogger!' Carlton-Syms turned a cold stare on him. 'You will address me as Major Carlton-Syms at all times. Is that clear?'

Arthur's mouth hung open.

'Is that clear, Captain Trevellyn?'

'Perfectly clear... Major Carlton-Syms.'

Robert edged away so that Arthur would not know he had witnessed his humiliation. How he hated C-S!

≈

Cadey greeted Robert with a smile. 'How nice! Dickon, be a good boy and... ' She reached out to ruffle his hair, then withdrew her hand like a thief nearly caught in the act. 'Be so kind as to get us something to eat.'

Her eyes were soft as they followed his small erect back. She said, 'Until a few months ago, that boy believed in Father Christmas.'

Robert said, 'Can you imagine the derision if he'd arrived here still thinking it was true? Did you tell him?'

'No, he announced this revelation himself. I think people believe things or stop believing them when they're ready to and its no good trying to tell them if they're not ready. It's not so long till his birthday now. What would you have wanted as a present at that age?'

'He'll be eleven, won't he?'

'Yes.'

'I wanted a paint-box, which is what I got... and an illustrated book of Greek myths. Mama used to read them aloud to me.'

'I'm glad you see something of Dickon now and then, Robert. At least it redresses the balance towards civilisation a bit... I've been meaning to tell you, Robert, how much I enjoyed your recent set of caricatures.'

'Thank you.'

'It has always intrigued me how politicians become more and more like their own caricatures. A combination of power and vanity, I suppose. Power exaggerates people's faults and vanity can make those same people crave the recognition, notoriety or whatever it is that caricatures give them.'

'I think you're right, Cadey. I see it happening with Carlton-Syms, Cochrane-Dyat and a few others too.'

≈

An orderly offered Robert a cigar from a silver box. He declined. As the orderly moved on, Cadey called him back.

'Aren't you forgetting something?'

'Madam?'

'You didn't offer me one.'

Poker-faced, the orderly held out the box. She took a cigar and put it in her bag.

'Because of Dickon,' she said. 'For his sake I'll not smoke it here. Only for his sake. Do you know what men like most about cigars?'

'No. What?'

'The fact that they fondly imagine they're too strong for women. Cigar smoking is a 'men only' club, women excluded. I sometimes think men go to war for much the same reason.' She gave a short laugh. 'But, from what I've seen of you, I think you know what it's like.'

'What what's like?'

'To be excluded.'

An imperious rapping held their attention. Carlton-Syms, as host, proposed the toast.

'The King!'

They faced the portrait and raised their glasses. Carlton-Syms, in his fine tenor, led the singing of the National Anthem.

'God save our gracious king…'

When they got to the line 'Long to reign over us,' a tray and glasses crashed to the ground.

'Yes!' Rainbow shouted. 'Long to rain on us!'

≈

With the party still in progress, Robert walked out into the night. Small fires glimmered almost as numerously as the stars above. Around them hunched the soldiers and their women.

'A fine night, Mr Stanhope, sir.' It was Carroty Kate with a warm smile for him.

'How's your back, Kate?'

'Oh, long mended, thank you, sir.'

'Is that Jacko I see curled up there?'

'The very same, sir. He can sleep just about anywhere, that one.'

'Any news of Smithy?'

She shook her head, her unruly red mop catching the firelight. 'Meg always did find her John, didn't she, sir? Real life's not quite so obliging… oh, I was forgetting, you never saw Barnaby's show.'

Carroty Kate ladled an evil-smelling mixture out of the pot and into three bowls. Robert shuddered. 'What on earth's in that pot?'

'You wouldn't want to know,' Carroty Kate answered. 'Got to make the meat go round somehow.'

Their meat allowance, Robert learned, was one carcass of beef, or the equivalent weight in sheep or llama, per thirty men. Those drawing the rations from the regimental quartermaster, however, seldom got the full amount. As Robert made to move off, Carroty Kate plucked at his sleeve.

'Won't you stay, sir. The dolls are out tonight.'

'What?'

'The puppets, sir. A show.'

Robert hesitated, then caught sight of Rainbow standing in the shadows. Rainbow stepped forward and nodded as if to reassure him he'd be safe.

'Thank you. I'd love to stay,' Robert said.

≈

Several hundred camp-followers squatted on the sloping ground, looking down on the puppet booth. Sitting amongst them, Robert surveyed the faces around him—women from the back streets of Lima or the poverty-stricken countryside through which the brigade had marched—all under the spell of Golpetina, the little figure on the stage. Robert recognized the hand-puppet as one he'd seen Rainbow carving; and the booth looked suspiciously as though it had once been an army tent.

≈

One side of Golpetina was dressed as a soldier, the other half as a female camp-follower. Carroty Kate, rasping through her swazzle in the rough Spanish she'd picked up in the Peninsular War and on the march from Lima, had Golpetina strutting about the stage, defying army officers, Spanish officials and priests alike, downing rigid, uniformed authority in all its forms.

≈

Out sprang Rainbow, dressed as Golpetina. Leaping and swivelling, he flickered from male to female, sometimes the one, sometimes the other, sometimes both at once as he battled with Snake. The hissing serpent which had coiled round Golpetina's neck was the hidden menace beneath the stone, the thief that stole in the night, the dread invader of dreams, the secret terror, whatever it might be. Gyrating through his awe-struck audience, Rainbow silently marvelled at the cleverness of Snail. Through the androgynous spirit, Golpetina, Snail was showing the camp-followers they could be like soldiers, like warriors as well as being women. Already Snail had led them in several excursions and ambushes against the enemy, securing much-needed supplies for themselves and their men. With a somersault and a sudden twist, Rainbow threw off Snake's coils. The crowd rose with a roar of triumph.

21

With a deft movement of his knife, Robert took out Carlton-Syms's eyes. They weren't right. What he was trying to show on the canvas was their fanatical self-absorption. Muldoon had been right. C-S had been angling to have his portrait painted. He should have refused. C-S's behaviour to Arthur had been unforgivable. But C-S was a fascinating subject to paint. When the brigade was on the march, C-S usually demanded short sittings during the midday siesta. Today, however, was a rest day and they had fitted in a longer session. C-S sat in a chair which had ambitions to be a throne, his hand on the hilt of his sword. He sang softly to himself while Robert painted. As always, his voice was rich, melodious and perfectly in tune. For some reason this warrior of the moment, this would-be-charismatic-hero sang a nursery rhyme.

Ride a cock horse to Banbury Cross
To see a fine lady on a white horse.

He broke off to bark, 'Leave plenty of space on my chest for the medals and decorations.'

'Naturally.'

'And don't forget, Stanhope, I want you to paint a cocker spaniel sitting at my feet... My aunt kept spaniels, you know.'

Robert busied himself preparing his palette. He guessed that C-S was about to say more. When people sat for their portraits they revealed all sorts of things about themselves. There was Captain Hollis who had told him that he'd loved his nanny far more than his mother. There was an old sailor on the Charlotte Anne who had suddenly blurted out that he'd been afraid of the sea all his life. And...

'I was packed off to my aunt when my mother died.' C-S said.

Carlton-Syms' grip tightened on the hilt of his sword. 'A puppy, make it a puppy.'

Robert said casually, as if preoccupied with his brushwork, 'You had a puppy once?'

The puppy had been taken from C-S and thrown to his father's hounds for food. The little spaniel had been spoilt by too much love. It would be useless as a working dog.

C-S gave a harsh laugh. Dogs have to learn to obey. Men too. And if you want to be the one who gives the commands there's no room for... for... ' He broke off and snapped, 'Don't do my epaulettes just yet.'

'Mm?'

'No point in showing me as a major when I might soon be a colonel or even a brigadier.'

Robert said nothing 'Floggings by the daily dozen if that ever happens!' he thought..

'I can spare you another ten minutes, no more,' C-S informed Robert curtly. 'Got to get ready for the do this evening.'

≈

While out hunting, Brigadier Cochrane-Dyet and some of the other officers had met a group of Spanish Royalist officers who had slipped out of Aposa for the same purpose. They found that they knew each other. They had fought on the same side against Napoleon's army in the Peninsular War. Brigadier Cochrane-Dyet had invited them all to a drinks party in the Brigade camp.

'Yes, I'm going too,' Robert informed him.

'What! A drip, like you? My God, the army isn't what it used to be!'

22

Jacko spent his night in the soldiers' encampment, round a fire with
Carroty Kate and Rainbow. But he kept his smart red jacket and blue
trousers with a red stripe in Robert's tent. These he wore when he
served in the officers' mess or at special occasions such as the one
tonight. Jacko was already changed. His hair was tied back army fashion
—greased with candle wax, wound tightly round a pad filled with
sand and the whole tied with a leather thong. So tightly was the skin
of his face drawn by this pad in the back of his neck that he could
hardly blink. When he tried to swallow, the pad went up and down
like a sledge-hammer. There was still an hour to go before the Spanish
officers arrived.

≈

Ever since boarding the Charlotte Anne Cadey had been aware that
Dickon lacked the company of boys of his own age. After discussing
it with Robert, they'd come up with a plan. Jacko had been invited to
Robert's tent to play with Dickon. Cadey decided it would be better
if she didn't come.

'It will seem too much like having Nanny there to supervise his
play.'

≈

Muldoon had lovingly carved for the young Major a set of wooden
soldiers. Twelve British Brigade and twelve Royalists. Robert had then
added the colour. Dickon had brought the set with him.

'Inside my tent there are no ranks,' Robert announced. 'You are
simply Dickon and Jacko.'

'Toss for who gets to be the British,' Dickon said. 'You call, Jacko.

'Tails!'

Muldoon flipped the coin. 'Bad luck, Jacko.'

Dickon distributed the soldiers. The two sides were to be lined up
opposite each other, then Jacko and Dickon would take turns in trying
to knock over the other side with pellets. The one with the most left
standing was the winner.

'I'll be the umpire,' Muldoon volunteered.

'Yeah, I know who you'll be favouring,' Jacko grumbled.

'And I'll be the war correspondent,' Robert declared. 'And I'll write an account of the battle for you. Would you like that?'

'Does a mouse like cheese!' Jacko exclaimed.

'Good show, Boser!' Dickon cried.

'You sounds like Cap'n Trevellyn, bless you,' Muldoon commented.

Robert smiled. 'Boser' had grown out of a short-lived 'Uncle Bob' which had turned into 'Bob's yer Uncle,' then 'Bobsyer' and finally 'Boser'.

≈

The battle progressed, accompanied by shouts of glee and groans of disappointment. At one point, due to an extra strong flick of the pellet by Dickon, the legs and stand of a Royalist were knocked off. While they played Jacko recounted some of the pranks he got up to—like putting cactus juice in his sergeant's tea. The juice, which the soldiers used as an insect repellant, was also a powerful laxative. Another time, he had smeared fresh horse dung on his sergeant's right hand while he was sleeping off a heavy drinking bout, then tickled his nostrils with a feather.

Robert made notes and sketches, pretending to watch the action through his telescope. Eventually, when there were hardly any soldiers left standing, he said. 'I declare a draw! And it's time for both you to go. I'll be along to the party later.'

'That was fun!' Dickon said. 'Can we do it again sometime?'

'I expect so,' Robert replied.

'I'd like you to have this,' Dickon held out a British soldier to Jacko. 'It will even up the numbers on each side.'

'Thanks, Dickon! Thanks!' Jacko gulped, the pad at the back of his head hammering up and down.

23

Brigade Headquarters, from which the military campaign was directed and where the party was being held, was a tent somewhat smaller than the marquee which was the current centre of Carlton-Syms's promotion campaign. Inside the tent, beneath his stuffed arm, which hung in its case from the main pole, Brigadier Cochrane-Dyat raised his glass. 'Gentlemen, I give you a toast: to The Code!'

'The Code!'

Robert surveyed the flushed faces round the table. New treaties, new rallying cries and former opponents donned the same uniforms, while former comrades-in-arms were set to slay each other. But here they all were, drinking, reminiscing, joking and laughing together. One thing was clear, on whichever side in the present conflict these officers found themselves, they still had more in common with each other than with the troops they commanded. Cochrane-Dyat was saying something about the cold steel of a bayonet and the whites of the enemy's eyes.

Robert, who was sitting next to Dickon, whispered in the boy's ear, 'I'm afraid I have no tales of that ilk to tell... unless you count seeing the reds of Muldoon's bloodshot eyes as he tries to shave me with a cut-throat razor in his shaking hand.' He didn't say that Muldoon insisted on shaving him every morning, even though he only needed to do it once a week. It was part of camp ritual that officers sat outside their tents in the morning being shaved by their batmen, and Muldoon wasn't going to have Robert being any different.

'When did you start shaving, Boser?'

'Oh, quite late. Your time will come, never fear.'

≈

Arthur was leaning across the table and hissing at the Very Minor Major, 'Ask the Brigadier your question... You know... about the breech-loaders.'

The earnestness of the question, as much as the boyish voice, pierced the general conboberation of booze and bonhomie. There was a silence, almost a shocked silence.

The Brigadier spluttered like a live fuse on its way to a keg of gunpowder. 'Because... because... it's a lot of nonsense!' He forgot himself and tried to thump the table with a fist he didn't have. 'Because it's against the Code!'

The Very Minor Major Minagh looked at him with wide-eyed innocence, awaiting some elaboration on this pronouncement.

The Brigadier glared. 'A gentleman instinctively knows these things. However, since you seem not to... there are very good reasons... ' He cleared his throat, a sound not unlike a rutting stag. 'Which Major Carlton-Syms will explain.'

A minor war broke out on Carlton-Syms's face—the urge to squash the Very Minor Major versus the desire to win the favour of the boy's uncle, the influential Lord Hawksmoor. Robert didn't think it possible to sound both supercilious and ingratiating at the same time, but C-S managed it. He explained that breech-loaders would bring indiscipline and chaos. The breech loader fired five times faster than the muzzle-loader, which would mean there would be opportunity for individual fire rather than the controlled volley.

Robert said, 'And that would mean the common soldier thinking for himself. We couldn't have that, could we?'

Whereas charging cavalry, C-S said, could cover the intervening ground faster than it took a foot soldier to go through the complete drill of loading his musket from the muzzle end, this would not be the case with a breech-loader.

'It would be the end of one of the most glorious and noble aspects of warfare—the cavalry charge.'

He sat back with a smug smile, satisfied there could be no more conclusive argument against the introduction of the new weapon than that.

'Well spoken, sir!' The Brigadier declared. 'Tradition, that's the ticket. There's some johnnies around these days who know as much about tradition as my backside knows about snipe shootin'!'

There were nods and murmurs of assent all round, except from Colonel Summers-Cox, who stared at the table and said nothing.

'And another thing!' The General growled. 'This gathering of military information that goes on.' He threw a dark look at Summers-Cox. 'Damned unsporting! Like looking at a fellow's hand at cards!'

Summers-Cox continued to stare at the table.

≈

The Brigadier's 'cellar' was well stocked. His clarets were 'passably good', so Arthur said, and the assembled company did them full justice. After manfully struggling to finish his fourth glass of wine, the V-Triple M laid his head on the table and went to sleep. Arthur was swapping tales of practical jokes with a couple of the younger Spanish officers to their great merriment. The talk drifted into a discussion of the comforts and discomforts of the present campaign. Aposa, said the Spanish guests, was a dump, full of filthy Indians. Defending it was a real bore. Only one thing could be more boring, said their British hosts, and that was trying to take a dump like Aposa. Meeting on the field of battle would be a quicker and more honourable way of settling it.

'How about Wednesday of next week?' suggested the senior Spanish officer there. 'I am sure our general will be of the same mind.'

The Old Diehard scratched his wig. 'Thought we might all go hunting on Wednesday. My hounds will be rested and at their peak by then. What do you say we hunt Wednesday and have our battle Friday?'

The Brigadier was never too ill for hunting, it seemed.

'Done!' cried the Spaniard.

They shook hands all round.

'Five thousand men each?' the Brigadier suggested.

'Agreed, but we have no cannon.'

'Never did like cannon anyway,' the Brigadier growled. 'Not in the spirit of the Code. Make an awful mess of a horse. We won't use ours—that makes it fair, eh?'

≈

Soon after that the Spanish officers departed with much back-slapping, mutual good wishes and the exchange of tokens of esteem. To the Brigadier, their senior officer presented a hawk—a kind of feathered version of the Brigadier himself, with beady eyes and fierce, curving beak.

≈

When they were gone, Colonel Summers-Cox raised his objection to making it a fair fight.

'What you propose is tactically unsound,' he declared. 'Logistics, the movement of men to the right place at the right time, superior firepower—this is what modern warfare is about. Why, Clausewitz in his treatise on war says… '

Carlton-Syms snorted with disgust. 'Really! You're such an old woman! Stanhope here has more stuffing in him than you!'

This was blatant insubordination to a senior officer. All eyes were on Brigadier Cochrane-Dyat to see if he would reprimand Carlton-Syms.

There was a long silence. Somewhere in the lines a bugle sounded. The Brigadier tapped the table with his fingers. Carlton-Syms and Summers-Cox stared at each other.

'In my time,' the Brigadier said, 'I have fought three duels. As we all know, duelling between officers of different rank is forbidden at any time and, in time of war, even between those of equal rank, it is an offence which merits a court-martial… but I fought my three duels none the less.' He paused and looked straight at Summers-Cox. 'If a gentleman is insulted, there is only one honourable course he can take.'

Summers-Cox went white. 'I would have thought there was only one course a brigade commander could take when one of his senior officers was insulted in front of him.'

'Damn your impudence! Do I have to remind you, the colonel of a cavalry regiment, that honour comes above all else?'

'Sir, I will not fight a duel with one of my own officers. As colonel of the regiment, I will deal with this matter in my own way.'

Brigadier Cochrane-Dyat's eyes bulged, sweat started from his forehead, his whole body bristled. 'You are relieved of your duties, sir!'

Summers-Cox gripped the table and fought to control his voice.

'On what grounds?'

'Lack of moral fibre, weakness of character. In short, sir, you are a ninny! A confounded ninny!'

The Very Minor Major Minagh woke with a start. 'Nanny? Did someone call Nanny?'

Robert took the sleepy boy by the arm and helped him to his feet, hoping to get him out of the tent before the Brigadier's wrath turned on him.

As they reached the entrance, Robert heard the Brigadier say, 'As of this moment, and until such time as a permanent appointment is made, Major Carlton-Syms is in command of this regiment.'

24

Rainbow basked, lizard-like, on the smooth rock slabs. A pinkish glow suffused the bare landscape. The sun was still strong, but once it dipped behind the white-capped mountains, the temperature would plummet. A stream chuckled between boulders at the foot of the slabs, belying the fact that, within a spear's throw, it became no more than a trickle, evaporating in the dust. Even within sight of Skyherd's domain the drought held sway. All around him the British Brigade was setting up camp for the night. None of the usual banter bounced from one group to another as they built their fires and busied themselves with the evening meal. Tomorrow was the day they called Friday, the appointed day for the battle. Rainbow had asked Jacko several times what the war was about and why the battle had been arranged, but even wise Monkey did not have many answers. There were so many things in the Other World which were not as he had imagined they would be. Why, for instance, was Carlton-Syms, who was clearly in league with Nataxale, on the same side as Skyherd?

'Reckon he's their secret weapon,' Jacko had remarked and Snail had agreed with him.

But why hadn't he achieved command of the regiment by a fight to death with his rivals? Wasn't that how it was meant to be done? Rainbow had asked Mr Hope's ally, Yansam, about it. She'd said that, through back-stabbing and character assassination, the rival officers murdered each other's reputations if not their actual bodies.

≈

Rainbow's drifting mind snagged on the bleating of a goat, a familiar sound amidst alien smells. The earth, the wind, the people, the cooking food, nothing smelt the same as in his village. He tried to conjure up the sharp tang of the red earth of home; in the background, women would be singing as they pounded the maize, rhythm and counter-rhythm. He longed for the familiar. So many things in the Other World were strange and inexplicable, with layers of meaning. Perhaps he would come to understand these things one day. Maybe they would be revealed to him slowly, step by step. Wasn't that what Xango the Thunder God and wise Monkey had been telling him through that wooden doll? You opened one and found another inside it, and then yet another.

The goat bleated again. Twelve goats had been sacrificed to bring the rain, without success. Skyherd was not like the god, about which the dung-beetle had spoken, who sacrificed his own son. He felt sure the Lord of the Clouds hated bloodshed. Why, then, if Rainbow's mission failed, would twelve villagers be killed so that their blood could wet the earth like the rain? Why would Skyherd want or allow such a thing? Supposing Yaba was one of the 'privileged' twelve? Or any of his friends? So much had happened that he hadn't thought of them in a long time—not that he had many friends. Rainbow had always been on the outside of any laughing circle. The moment Ikpoom had chosen Rainbow as his apprentice his path had become a lonely path which went a different way from the one taken by his peers. Not even Yaba could follow him along that path, although she understood him better than anyone. He had opened his heart to her and she had responded. Would things be the same between them when he took a second wife? She had mentioned the subject several times. Well, more than several times. She was insisting he took another wife, in fact. It was shaming, she said, not to be a senior wife by now. None of her friends had to fetch the water or sweep the compound like she did, not when there were one or more junior wives to do it. It was only right and proper, she said, now that Ikpoom was dead, that he assume the dignity of the village shaman and extend his household. A shaman with only one wife lacked authority. Yaba had even offered to choose a docile, hard-working young girl for him. Rainbow smiled to himself. Yaba was so irresistible when she pouted. But it hurt that she seemed not to share his dread that their intimacy would be lost. Was he, as he'd heard people say, simply a romantic fool? Was he clinging to something which, by the nature of things, was bound to fade, like youth and life itself? Eventually, he would have to accept the inevitable. He had even half-promised to do something about it once the drought was over.

≈

On the other side of the outcrop on which Rainbow lay, Jacko was saying, 'I've never been in a battle before, Carrots, what will it be like?'

'Thinking about it, that's the hard bit. They all say that. Once it starts... Smithy used to say... '

'What? What did he say, Carrots?'

'He said there weren't no other feeling like it. Made me mad, that did. He said he weren't really alive 'cept for when there was a good chance he'd… er… Look at you, standing there! Get cutting that meat! And thin, or it won't cook proper.'

'What was it when it could walk?'

'Don't ask. And when you've done that, chop more firewood.'

Fuel for the camp-fires was a constant problem in this barren, almost treeless, landscape. Cattle, lamas, oxen and horses were all a source of fuel as well as food and transport. Every single dropping was seized by the camp-followers and carefully dried. And there wasn't a village through which the brigade had passed which had not found itself missing barn doors, fencing, even a four-poster bed.

'Are these what I think they are?' Carroty Kate demanded, unable to hide her glee.

Jacko pushed a heap of wooden tent-pegs out of sight. 'If Carlton-Floggin'-Syms' tent collapsed last night, I don't know nuffink about it.'

≈

'Come and get it, Rainbow!'

Rainbow scrambled to his feet and walked round the outcrop to where Jacko and Carroty Kate were doling out some kind of stew into wooden bowls.

'Not that you deserve any,' Carroty Kate grumbled. 'You did damn all to help.'

Jacko sniffed the contents of his bowl suspiciously. 'How many legs did this have?'

'Who said anything about legs?'

Jacko grimaced and swallowed. 'We had some good grub-ups when we was wiv Thackston's, didn't we? Those was good days… Our sarge says our officers has got more barrels to their names than all our artillery!'

Carroty Kate turned to Rainbow, 'A Patriot squadron came in this morning. There was a man like you with them, Rainbow, you know, a darkie, an Ethiope.'

'What tribe?'

'Said he was a runaway slave from Brazil. That's what you are, isn't it,

Rainbow, a runaway slave?'

'Why do you say that? I don't know what you mean.'

'What was his name, Jacko? Oh, what was it?'

'Search me, Carrots.'

'Anyroad, Rainbow, I asked him if he was the same sort of cove as you... Er, you know, if he did spells at the crossroads and all that. He said no. Said he came to this land as a slave and arrived at a port called... fuck me, forgotten that one, too!'

Rainbow's heart had stopped beating. The bowl slipped from his hands. What could Snail have meant? For a terrible, black moment, a nameless monster had been about to swallow everything that gave meaning to his life. Then he heard Ikpoom's voice reminding him there would be many things he wouldn't understand. Only the most experienced shamans and the most venerable ancestors were privileged to glimpse the wider pattern.

'An aphid knows only its own leaf. It knows nothing of the branch, the tree, the forest.'

Besides, Nataxale had many tricks for sowing doubt and weakening his enemies in subtle ways, many secret weapons, as Monkey had so cleverly warned him. But, how could this fellow Mortal be here if he was not a shaman? How could he have travelled the dark tunnel? Unless, perhaps, his mission was so secret he could not reveal it. Either that or the poor man was under some terrible delusion. Rainbow frowned and shook his head. He had thought the Other World had only one place of entry, the place they called London. But this person claimed to have entered at some other place. He must find this misguided man and talk to him and show him into what a swamp of errors and misunderstandings he had fallen.

≈

'Well, whatever's in this stew it ain't even first cousin to one o' them cattle,' Jacko was saying.

'Was it so bad you had to chuck it in the dirt, Rainbow?'

'What?'

'The stew.'

'I am sorry to have offended my most esteemed Orisha Animal.'

'Come orf it, don't start that again!'

Carroty Kate laughed and started telling Jacko how a women's raiding party, led by herself, had rustled a whole herd of cattle from the Royalists.

Rainbow said, 'There's a scouting party two days ride from here, heading this way.'

'The lot Smithy's with?'

'It is possible.'

'Did you see him?'

'I am not sure. I was looking down on them from a great height and could not see their faces.'

'Where exactly was this, Rainbow?'

'Somewhere on the other side of the dark tunnel, somewhere between waking and dreaming. I saw them while returning from a forest where Fear lurks in the deep undergrowth.'

Carroty Kate stared at him. 'Gawd knows why, but I believe you. I... I came so close to getting him back once before, I hardly dare hope... Yeah, it's just come to me... that Ethiope, he said his name was Edetaen.'

'Edetaen... That's a Yoruba name. They are not so different from us. Not scoundrels and murderers like the Ijeru.'

'Anyroad, Rainbow, he'd like to meet you. Said he'd drop by when he's got time. That'll be nice, won't it? Something to look forward to. Christ, two days' ride, did you say? Smithy could be here day after tomorrow.'

Jacko leant against Carroty Kate, his head resting on her shoulder. She stirred uneasily and pushed him away. Blank-faced, Jacko chewed in silence, then, spitting out his mouthful, he hurled his bowl to the ground.

'Effing muck! Effing maw-wallop!'

'For fuck's sake! Doesn't anyone want my stew?'

≈

Rainbow watched Monkey's hunched figure stomp off. Monkey's flickering aura streamed sideways as if in a hurricane. And, in it, Rainbow saw the noiseless, reverberating roar of rejection, and its colour was black.

Carroty Kate glared at Rainbow. 'Whatever you're going to say, I don't bloody want to hear it!'

She scooped the stew off the ground back into the bowl and offered it to him.

'Here, it landed a bit kinder'n yours. If that moping mizzler don't want it, you might as well have it.'

Rainbow shook his head. The sun had set. It was darker and colder. He moved nearer the fire.

'I'm scared, Rainbow. That's the long and short of it. Scared of loving the little bugger too much. He's got his thieving hooks on my heart, gawd 'elp me.'

Rainbow nodded. There wasn't a day when Obobo's little hand didn't reach out across the Great Water to grasp his finger or explore his face or tug at his hair.

'I cannot begin to imagine how I would feel if I lost Obobo.'

'My Bill, my Smithy. I couldn't go through something like that again, I just couldn't. I know Jacko needs a mother, but the closer he gets, the more scared I gets of losing him. It could happen all too easy in this mad war. And there's Smithy, you see. What if he were to turn up? How do you follow your man to the ends of the earth with a kid in tow?'

Rainbow looked up at the stars before replying. That was Snail for you, hard on the outside, soft on the inside. 'If you could have a second chance, if Smithy could come back again, would you push him away because you were frightened of loving him?'

'No, of course not.'

'Maybe Jacko's your second chance, Kate... a second chance for both of you.'

25

'Dearest Mama,

Today is the day for the battle—not the Friday, as arranged, but Sunday. On Friday the rain was so heavy the powder wouldn't ignite in the flintlocks' firing-pans and the wind was too strong for the tall shakos worn by the cavalry of both sides. So the fixture was postponed until today. Muldoon was not impressed. As for Rainbow, he was wild with joy, splashing about like a child, but then he went very quiet when it stopped and the sun began to beat down in its usual relentless way. Despite his strange ways, there's a dignity and wisdom about that man which inspires confidence. Anyway, Brigadier Cochrane-Dyat agreed to put back the starting time by two hours so that church services could be held before the battle. Muldoon's opinion of this is that 'The cool o' the mornin's for fighting, not praying.' He says he can't help being an atheist, it's the way God made him! As for myself, both sides asking the same god for their blessing doesn't seem right somehow.

I mentioned confidence just now. Well, what with Cadey's friendship and the dashing Arthur finding me not absolutely beyond the pale, and Rainbow's near worship of me, I was beginning to feel less of a failure. But I have to tell you that I rather blotted my copybook with Cadey. She was not pleased when I allowed Jacko and Dickon to have a pretend battle with toy soldiers. 'I don't want you teaching Dickon that war is a game!' However, we agreed that, on this campaign, that is exactly how many of those in command regard it. I think I am forgiven and, as they say, quarrels that are resolved often strengthen bonds.

Last night I, the war correspondent, the would-be peer of hardened officers, lay and groaned aloud in my bed, thinking about all the bereaved, broken hearted wives, mothers, fathers, sisters, brothers, sweethearts and children there will be as a result of this rather pointless encounter... I think I'd better stop for the moment. Here comes Cadey Thomson, striding towards my tent... '

≈

Cadey brandished a bottle of gin. 'Playing truant from Church Parade, I see! I'll keep you company, then!' She banged the bottle down on Robert's writing table. 'The day a woman steps into the pulpit is the day you'll see me in church and not a moment sooner… What's the matter, Robert?'

'Nothing.'

'Yes, something's the matter. What is it?'

Robert showed her his unfinished letter. Cadey read it in silence, then read it again.

'I feel honoured, Robert, that you let me see this, that you have trusted me with your true feelings. As far as I'm concerned, everything you have written here makes you more of a man than any of these emotionally stunted, immature stuffed uniforms. At least you have a complete range of feelings, not just the ones that fit you for war. Every line shows that you're sensitive and caring and responsible. As to being terrified—I'll bet there isn't a soldier on either side who doesn't secretly feel the same. You're simply more honest about it, that's all.'

Robert tried to speak through the lump in his throat. 'Do you really think so?'

She took his hand and squeezed it. 'Yes, I really think so.'

≈

Robert and Cadey sat together, drinking gin and listening to the litanies and responses being barked out like another army drill.

'By the end of today,' Cadey said, 'Most of the congregation will have broken most of the ten commandments… and all in the name of a just war.' She gulped down her gin. 'And by the end of today he might be dead. I should never have agreed to it. I shouldn't have given in to Lord Hawksmoor. I should never have let Dickon come. Do you think he'll be all right, Robert? He's so young… too young for all this.'

≈

The assembled company had been blessed and the Church Parade dismissed. The brigade reassembled in readiness to march to battle. The officers of the Light Horse partook of a glass of toddy, sitting in their saddles, as is the custom before a meet Robert and Cadey hovered on the edge of the ceremony, the latter trying to signal to Dickon not to drink too much. He edged his mount towards her.

'Don't fuss, Cadey!' he hissed. 'And don't try to hug me or anything when we go.'

Arthur raised his glass to him. 'To valour!'

'To valour!' the boy responded.

Cadey's voice trembled. 'As far as I can see, valour is a lethal mixture of masculine vanity, blind duty and a gambler's hope. It's the kind of heady nonsense that'll get Dickon killed.'

Robert nodded dumbly.

In a whisper that only Robert could hear, Cadey said. 'Please don't do anything heroic, Dickon. Be a coward if you have to. Just come back alive.'

≈

As the brigade marched out of camp, Robert, on the flank of the column, glimpsed Cadey's tense, white face, watching Dickon ride to battle at the head of his squadron. Those brave smiles... Robert knew what they masked.

≈

Somewhere behind them, the bagpipes of the Highland Regiment put a swing into the step of the marching men... the five thousand men and no cannon, as agreed.

'Who needs cannon, sorr, when we've got those sodding pipes?'

Robert tried to force a laugh. 'There's you, Muldoon, a double-breasted water-butt smasher, astride little Josephine, and I 'a mere rasher of wind' as I heard you call me, atop Manco. I suppose so simple a solution as swapping mounts is out of the question.'

'Rules is rules, sorr.'

Robert reined in Manco and pulled out his sketch-book. A line of drummer-boys drew level with them. Jacko was on the outside of the line. He turned his head as far as his stiff high stock allowed and winked at Muldoon. Brigadier Cochrane-Dyat cantered down the line, showing himself to his men, waving his cocked hat in friendly, pre-battle camaraderie, a feat which necessitated letting go the reins with his one arm. A cheer rippled down the line, keeping pace with him.

'Oh there's a conk! There's a smeller!' Jacko exclaimed. 'I'll tell you one thing for free... there's none of us would send up a hurrah for Carlton-Floggging-Syms.'

'Wouldn't even give him a fart,' said the drummer-boy next to him—a remark which unloosed a torrent of obscenities from all at hand.

Muldoon turned to Robert. 'They mean no harm by it, sorr. Us common sojers need to cuss same as we need food.'

Robert fondled Manco's neck, not knowing what to say. Everyone seemed so unconcerned with the prospect of imminent death.

'How do you think it will go today, Muldoon?'

Muldoon shook his head. 'There'll be plenty put to bed with a shovel afore the end o' the day. If you ask me, begging your pardon, sorr, what's been agreed to is a killing match. But don't fret your giblets, sorr, you'll be safe enough. I'll take care o' you.'

Robert blushed and muttered his thanks. But it was Carlton-Syms who scared him most. How many lives would he spend in his quest for glory?

≈

Over the crest of a low hill appeared a column of marching men—the Royalist force from Aposa. Swinging to their right, they marched parallel with the British Brigade, separated only by a narrow field of maize, towards the field of battle.

≈

Robert had obtained permission to attach himself to the brigade high command. Not only was it the centre for all outgoing and incoming messages, it was also the safest place. Cochrane-Dyat had chosen to operate from one of the more elevated undulations on the plain. Using Manco to steady his telescope, Robert watched the two sides draw themselves up into battle formation—a series of straight lines, double banked, standing in the tall, straw-coloured grass. The front lines of the opposing factions were barely a furlong out of musket range. An officer from the Royalist side cantered across the intervening space and addressed one of the British colonels who was trotting up and down in front of his men.

'He'll be asking whether we're ready, sorr,' Muldoon said quietly in Robert's ear.

≈

As soon as the Royalist officer regained his lines, bugles sounded. The drummers, in a line at the front, beat out their steady rrrat-tat-tat, rrrat-tat-tat. At a slow walk, the British Brigade and the Spanish Royalists advanced upon each other.

'Go on!' roared the Brigadier. 'Give it to the damn Frenchies! Let 'em have it!'

They passed the point at which they were within range of each other. On the command, the British Brigade halted. The drummers retired six ranks to the rear. The first of the double-banked lines brought their muskets to the ready, the front row kneeling.

'Fire!'

With well-practiced drill the lines waiting their turn to fire stepped past the reloading men. The drill was repeated over and over, pouring volleys of lead into the close ranks of the enemy, thinning their lines. Even more would have been hit had it not been for the high stiff collars the infantrymen wore, which prevented them from lowering their heads to the sights on their muskets. In places the grass was alight, adding to the smoke.

≈

The Royalists opened fire.

'God help the poor bastards,' Muldoon muttered.

Banks of smoke drifted across the scene of carnage. Above the bang of the muskets rose men's screams, hoarse shouts, urgent orders.

'Fire!'

'Fuego! Adelante!'

'Fire!'

'Fuego!'

A spent musket ball struck a rock within inches of the Brigadier's horse, causing the animal to whinny and rear.

'Coward!' the Brigadier roared. 'I shall stop your corn three days!'

In mid-discussion with a breathless, bleeding and smoke-begrimed captain, the Brigadier looked up, saw a terrified hare break cover, and spurred his horse in pursuit. Half-way down the slope he recollected where he was and came trotting back.

'Hrrumph! As I was saying, Mowbray, my compliments to Major … er… Carlton-Syms, and he's to sweep down on the right there and take the Frenchies in the flank.'

≈

The eight squadrons of the Light Horse charged the Spanish Royalists. The sun was in the Royalists' eyes. Stifled and blinded, they fired uncertainly into clouds of smoke. Before they could reload, out of the gloom rode the Light Horse. A whole battalion was cut up and dispersed by their shining swords. On they went towards the heart of the enemy, where fluttered their standard, smashing another unprepared formation. But the inner ring was ready for them. At ten paces distance the Royalists fired their first volley. Fully a quarter of the galloping squadrons dropped, but the impetus of the charge, though checked by fallen horses and men, carried the cavalry on to the bayonets. Hacking and stabbing, the British and Spanish fought it out amid the flash and crackle of muskets, the screams of maddened horses and the gasping shouts of men as they hewed and lunged for dear life in the choking smoke and dust. In the confused circle of his telescope, Robert saw Hollis go down, the Royalist standard almost in his grasp. Of Dickon and Arthur he could see nothing. Then the odds became too great for the Light Horse and the retreat was sounded.

≈

Across the plain the slaughter continued until, as if obeying some signal, the nerve and morale of both sides cracked. The front formations of the two armies broke and fled. They met face to face with their own rear-guard whose most important duty was to shoot deserters and turn back the faint-hearted. Robert watched with disbelief as the fiercest hand-to-hand fighting of the whole battle took place, both sides hotly engaged with themselves. So ended the battle for Aposa.

≈

Robert wandered with his sketch-book over the scorched, bloodstained plain strewn with the crimson ruin of men and horses, the air filled with moans, screams, sobs and curses. The camp-followers were there, searching for their menfolk; some were stealing from the stiffening corpses, despite the guards who had orders to shoot looters on sight. Weary soldiers were beginning to lift their comrades onto stretchers and carry them to the carts. Others were collecting reusable ordnance. Robert froze, staring at a body in the uniform of the Light Horse, the back of the head... the hair... Oh, thank God, thank God! It wasn't Arthur.

≈

Muldoon hailed Robert. He had hitched Josephine to an abandoned supply cart. Sitting in the back in his multicoloured coat was Rainbow.

.'Mr Hope, have you seen Monkey or Snail?'

'Who?'

'He means Jacko and Carroty Kate,' Muldoon said, tapping his head and rolling his eyes.

'No… Have you seen Arthur or Dickon?'

'No.'

≈

With Manco in tow, the cart bumped along behind a line of other carts loaded with the wounded. Muldoon and Rainbow sat together at the front of the cart, sharing a bottle of fiery aquadiente.

Muldoon said, 'I hear tell Jacko's been in hot water these last couple o' days.'

Rainbow nodded. 'Fighting and disobedience.'

Muldoon flicked the reins with one hand and took a swig of aquadiente with the other. 'Mischief's one thing. Fighting and insubordination, that's a different kettle o' fish. Not like him, not like him at all.'

≈

Robert was sitting in the back, flicking through the sketches he had made. In the paintings which grace the mansions of England, or lend a sense of history to the seats of power, in these canvases which look down upon scenes of gracious living, the dead always lie in heroic poses, an arm flung out dramatically, faces serenely lifted to the heavens. In real life, Robert had discovered… that is to say, in real death, they lie in twisted, agonised shapes, in deformed bundles of torn flesh, often face down in mud and blood; and the wounded have more than an arm in a sling or a rakish head bandage, they have guts spilling out, faces shot away, quivering stumps. Sir Charles would never print his sketches. His public wanted glory, romance, adventure, heroics. Robert crumpled the thin paper in his hand. His job, it seemed, was to give the bitter pill a sugar coating. But the sugar was what contained the poison.

≈

Blood-encrusted, shuffling men with drawn faces filled the road, slowing the cart to walking pace. Rainbow recalled Ikpoom saying that, although spirits might suffer temporary death and defeat, they were always there, waiting to return. So where was Jacko? Surely he had come to no harm, not him, not Monkey. Rainbow glanced at the frowning and silent Bat beside him.

'They'll be all right, won't they, Bat?'

Bat raised his eyes. 'You reckon?'

≈

Rainbow tried to think about anything, anything except Jacko. Now the battle was over, would Edetaen, the Yoruba of whom Snail had spoken, turn up? He wasn't sure whether he wanted to meet him or not. Perhaps the joy of talking to someone of his own kind, albeit of a different tribe, would be outweighed by the pain. There were days when separation from Yaba and Obobo and everything familiar receded into a dull throb. Did he really want to awaken that awful sense of loss? And, ever since Snail had first mentioned Edetaen, he'd felt the presence of danger. He couldn't think what threat the man might pose, but his instincts were seldom wrong.

≈

In this river of suffering there was now a group of horsemen. Skyherd stood up in the cart, scanning their ranks. He sat down again, his face drawn and anxious. Rainbow was certain he'd seen the horsemen before. Yes, in his spirit journey.

'Are you the scouting party?' he shouted.

They agreed they were.

Skyherd said, 'Is there a William Smith with you?'

One of the scouts bent forward in his saddle to hear better. 'Bill Smith, did you say?'

'Yes.'

'Otherwise known as Smithy?'

'That's the one.'

'Got himself captured. We thought we were ambushing a patrol, only it was us that was ambushed.'

They moved on.

Skyherd said, 'Poor Kate. Her Smithy always seems just out of reach.'

Like the completion of my mission, Rainbow thought. He had pondered the meaning of Snail many times. He had been tested, forced to prove that he desired the success of his mission more than anything else. And now a new lesson—not to be in such a hurry. He must accept the snail's pace at which he was moving towards his goal. He had yet to find Nataxale, let alone discover what his gift to Skyherd should be.

'At least Smithy missed the battle,' Skyherd remarked. 'Kate should be thankful for that. At least he's comparatively safe.'

Rainbow's heart lurched. His mind went back to the fair in London, the one he'd been to with Jacko, and he saw the broken clockwork drummer-boy lying limply on the ground.

26

Robert sat with Cadey outside her tent. She was dressed in her riding boots and britches and the scarlet jacket of the BLH. Robert had obtained the jacket for her so that she could sit for him while he got the details of the clothing right for C-S' portrait. A pile of tissue-thin papers lay on the table in front of Robert—an unfinished letter to Mama and his uncompleted report on the battle. He pushed the report aside, weary of trying to find the narrow path between the truth as he saw it, and what would be acceptable to Charles Makepiece and the readers of the *Chronicle*.

Cadey offered him a cigar.

'No thanks. You know they're too strong for me.'

She thrust a large glass of gin into his hand. 'So's this, but it's what you need right now. What we both need.'

She lit a cigar for herself. 'He should have been back by now. Dear God! How could I have let Dickon come out here?'

She made an effort to pull herself together. In her military jacket, sitting erect and straight, she reminded Robert of Dickon.

She leant forward, appealing to him. 'Surely they've revised the casualty list by now.'

Robert said, 'Hollis was on the earlier list.'

'I know. I can't feel anything at the moment for any of those young men... except relief they're not Dickon.'

'I know what you mean.' Robert replied. 'Not Arthur! Please not Arthur!' he thought.

≈

Robert called across to the next tent, his own.

Muldoon emerged. 'Sorr? ...Again sorr? I've only just got back, sorr, and no mention of Cap'n Trevelly or Major Minagh on the list.' He hesitated. 'Maybe it's not my place to say it, sorr, but the butcher's bill was too high today. Too high by far.'

He turned and set off at a lumbering trot.

Cadey's voice quivered. 'It's the waiting and the... '

'My stars! Dickon... How could I not have seen it before! ...Er, that is... You really care for him... I mean, more than if you were just his tutor. Cadey, do I know you well enough to ask you something?'

'Yes, Robert, he's my son. I'm glad you know. His father is Lord Hawksmoor's brother, Peter Minagh.'

'Minagh?'

'Yes, the title of Hawksmoor was taken because of the estate in Scotland.'

'Sorry. Go on.'

' I loved him. Oh yes, I loved him, fool that I was. Men can be such swine... Not you, Robert. Oh, Robert, it's such a relief to be able to talk about it.'

≈

Their affair had lasted five years, she said. In the end, unwilling to marry beneath him, he'd sailed off to India, leaving her pregnant. When her father had died, Peter's brother, Lord Hawksmoor, had taken her and his young nephew into his household, establishing the fiction that she was the boy's nanny and that Dickon's parents had died. Indeed, Peter might as well have been dead, as far as she was concerned, for Hawksmoor was paying him handsomely to stay in India and not return. She was grateful for Hawksmoor's help, particularly at a time when radicals were being arrested and harassed. She gave a low, self-mocking laugh. 'I, who attack privilege at every turn, was glad of its protection... for Dickon's sake. You'll hardly credit this, but I wore his ring for five years after he left me. I didn't really believe he'd send for me. I'm not even sure I wanted him to... I don't know.' There was a bitter edge to her laugh. 'Women can be such... such slaves to their feelings, to love.' She flicked the ash from her cigar. She twisted in her chair, looking to see if Muldoon was returning. ''What haunts me is that I came out here, to Peru, or at least, part of me did, to escape all those memories of Peter. Maybe I didn't resist Lord Hawksmoor's plans for Dickon hard enough because... '

'Nonsense!' Robert said firmly. 'You've done wonders in the circumstances. It must be very hard for you... Keeping it from him. Being something other than his mother to him.'

'It's not easy. God! Where's Muldoon? What's keeping him?'

'If you dislike men so much, why do you dress like one?'

She examined the lengthening ash on her cigar. 'Apart from the fact that it's eminently practical, you mean?'

'Yes, apart from that.'

'Well, it's not going over to the enemy, if that's what you think. It's more a matter of infiltrating their lines in order to bring about their downfall.' She raised her glass. 'And down with the Code! For without the Code there can be no glory, no treating war like some damn fool boys' game.'

'But there can be no glory without an audience,' Robert said, 'And that's exactly what I'm helping to provide.'

Cadey waved her hand. Robert wasn't sure whether it was his guilt she was pushing aside or the cigar smoke.

'You're not responsible for human nature, Robert. Have you ever watched respectable folk at a fair, paying their penny to smash as much crockery as they can? All that violence and mayhem conveniently legitimised. That's what the *Chronicle* is offering its readers, with a good dose of contempt and hatred for good measure.'

She stubbed out her cigar, grinding it into the ground with her booted foot. 'They're exciting emotions, contempt and hatred. And war allows us to enjoy forbidden feelings in the name of patriotism… You know, Robert, just for a moment I almost forgot. Oh God! Where are they?'

Tilting her head, she gargled with her gin. 'Glo-o-o-orrrry… Only when wars are the very opposite to glorious will there be no wars. Well, at least, perhaps, we wouldn't rush into them with quite such enthusiasm… Summers-Cox was killed, too, you know.'

Robert nodded. 'I think he almost courted death after his humiliation and losing command of the regiment.'

Carlton-Syms and a retinue of officers walked into view through a gap in the lines of tents. Cadey's back was to them.

'Glo-o-o-oo-rry!' she gargled.

'Very lady-like, I must say, Mrs Thomson,' C-S sneered. 'And while we're on that subject, you are not entitled to wear that uniform. Oblige me, madam, by changing into something more suitable.'

'Sir, since this isn't the King's uniform, but something concocted for a fancy-dress party, I'll wear it if I damn well please.'

C-S leered at her, his face awash with insincerity. 'But, madam, if I may say so, you look so fetching in female garb.'

'And if I may say so, sir, you only seem capable of seeing the world through the sights of a gun or the hole in your prick!'

C-S stiffened. 'Your reply, madam, displays a distinct lack of breeding.'

'And your conduct throughout this campaign, sir, has displayed a distinct lack of regard for anything except your own career. Men have died, been sacrificed, on the alter of your ambition. And that is despicable, sir, despicable!'

C-S took a step towards her, his face purple with rage. 'If you were a man… '

He spun on his heel and stalked off, followed by his retinue.

'Well done!' Robert breathed. 'Well said!'

'I'm not so sure, now,' Cadey replied with a worried frown. 'He won't forget or forgive and it'll be Dickon he takes it out on… that is if… if he's survived.'

Robert put a comforting arm around her and she was happy to let it stay there.

≈

Rainbow, in his coat of many colours, crossed their line of vision, leading a lathered, riderless horse. They both straightened with an intake of breath.

'It's not Dickon's,' Robert reassured her.

'Strange man.'

'Rainbow?'

'Mmm. Did I ever tell you, Robert, about his shameful treatment in that asylum? How he was locked up for… what was the phrase that pompous ass used? …For 'an insufficient hold on reality'?'

'No. I've heard Arthur's version, of course… Here's Muldoon! Well, what's the… ?'

'Missing, sorr. Both posted as officially missing.'

'Missing?' enquired a cheerful voice behind them. 'What are we missing? Nothing good I hope.'

A smiling, but weary Arthur sat astride his horse with Dickon up in front of him, grippinp the pommel.

'Where have you been, Dickon?' Cadey demanded. 'Didn't you realise I've been worried sick about you?'

Arthur turned and winked at Dickon. 'Didn't I tell you this would be the most hair-raising part of the day?'

Dickon said, 'Don't be cross, Cadey. Arthur saw my horse shot from under me and came back for me and then... '

'Oh my pippin!'

A sudden gust of wind caught the thin leaves of Robert's report and his unfinished letter and whisked them away. He chased after them, but they scudded along the ground, always out of reach, before taking off and disappearing in a swirl of dust. But it didn't seem all that important. Arthur was safe! Arthur was safe!

≈

Rrrr-atatatat-rratatat... The drummer-boys, fewer in number than before appeared out of the same swirl of dust. Robert searched the begrimed, dazed faces, some blood-spattered, others tear-stained.

'Mr Stanhope, sir!'

'Jacko! Are you all right?'

Jacko grinned. 'No holes in me, 'cept what's meant.' His expression changed. 'Not that anyone cares. Nobody'd miss me if I snuffed it.'

'Keep in step, Drummer Jackson!' the sergeant bellowed. He caught Robert's eye. 'Been a right pain in the backside, that one. I mean more than usual and that's saying something. Don't know what's got into him.'

Carroty Kate was beside Robert and Jacko, keeping pace with the marching boys.

'Thank Christ you're safe, Jacko.'

'What do you care?'

'Jacko... I thought you was... I thought... ' She reached out for him.

The sergeant bristled. 'And who said you could fall out, Drummer Jackson?'

Carroty Kate glared at him. 'Well, effing say so, or it's you and me is going to fall out.'

The sergeant blinked and waved his hands in surrender. Carroty Kate opened her greatcoat and took Jacko inside. Jacko clung to her, burying his head in her bosom. Robert left them standing there, Jacko with his eyes shut, a smile of utter contentment on his face.

Muldoon greeted Robert's return with, 'Sorr, I've sent your report off with the pigeons.'

'You can't have. It's just blown… '

'Yes, sorr. It was on your bed all ready and waiting.'

'Oh my pippin! Oh my stars! That was the one I wrote for the toy battle, for Dickon and… '

Robert rung his hands in despair and groaned. And his letter to Mama, the one he'd begun just before the battle started, it had been at the bottom of his pile of papers. It, too, had blown away.

'The others are in with Mrs Thomson, sorr, getting a good feed.'

Cadey's head emerged through the flap in the tent. She was laughing. 'I heard all that. What with your report on the non-existent 'Battle at Rimac Ford' and now this, maybe you're the one who should be locked up for 'an insufficient hold on reality'. Either you or the British public for believing it.'

Robert nodded sadly, remembering his vow to only report the truth as he saw it. The fact was, the exploits of wooden soldiers who felt no fear or pain made much easier reading than those of men made of frail flesh and bone.

27

In the grey dawn, Robert stirred in his narrow folding bed, listening to the faint tramp of booted feet and the distant, unfamiliar cry of a wild animal. The marching feet drew nearer—about a dozen men, he guessed. A sharp word of command and the platoon stamped to a halt close by. Raised, angry voices… Cadey's voice. Robert jumped out of bed and flung on an overcoat. He was half way out of the tent when Cadey met him, still in her nightgown, a shawl over her shoulders.

'I'm under arrest.'

'Arrest? …Can they… What on earth?'

She was shivering. Robert drew her inside his tent, sat her on the bed and put a blanket round her.

'What's going on, Cadey?'

The officer in charge of the platoon stood by the entrance. 'You have twenty minutes, Mrs Thomson.'

Cadey was shivering again. 'I can't take it in… Undermining the discipline and morale of the regiment… that's the official charge. In other words, C-S didn't like what I said to him yesterday. I'm being sent back to Lima.'

'Right now? At this hour?'

'Yes. Minimum fuss. They won't even let me say goodbye to Dickon.' She clutched Robert's hand. 'It's all so sudden. No time to… You'll look after him for me, won't you?'

'You know I will.' Robert pointed to his writing slope. 'At least you can leave a note for him.'

≈

With the blanket clasped around her, Cadey sat at the table, quill in hand. 'You will make sure he knows I haven't just abandoned him? Oh, Robert, I'll miss him so much.'

The quill scratched across the paper. 'I'm trying to explain it in a way that won't cause too much trouble between him and C-S. Oh dear, he's so young.'

Feet shuffled outside the tent. 'Ten minutes, Mrs Thomson!'

'I've written two notes, Robert. The second's for his birthday. He'll be eleven exactly two weeks today. My present's in my tent. Wrapped and ready.'

Robert knew what it was. She had discussed it with him at length and changed her mind three times about the wrapping.

'There's a present from 'Uncle Hawk', too. His ceremonial sword.'

Robert nodded dumbly. 'I'll take care of him, I promise... I'm going to miss you, Cadey... Terribly.'

They embraced and clung to each other.

The officer coughed. 'Please return to your tent, Mrs Thomson, and attire yourself for the journey.'

≈

Before the sun had risen and the sleeping camp come to life, Cadey had departed, escorted by an officer and ten mounted troopers of the Light Horse. An hour later, Robert visited Dickon in his tent, further down the lines, gave him the news and handed over Cadey's note. Rather to Robert's surprise, he didn't seem too upset.

'Did she make a cake for me?' he asked.

'No. There wasn't time. But I'll make one for you.'

'Thanks, Boser.'

Robert relived the moment of his and Cadey's embrace. Apart from Mama, it was the first time he'd held a woman. He didn't know what he'd do without her company. How well she had played her part as nanny, then tutor, Robert thought—the way she'd kept the proper distance between herself and Dickon. How well she had protected him from scandal, from any hint of illegitimacy. And how much it must have cost her, having to disguise her true feelings for her own child. Robert wondered if he'd perhaps detected a fleeting expression of relief on Dickon's face. The young major must have taken a fair amount of ribbing on account of his 'nanny'; and maybe he was glad of a bit more independence, a chance to prove himself on his own.

'I'm worried, Boser.'

'She'll be all right.'

'I know. I mean about my squadron's rations... We're just about out of everything.'

≈

Incompetence on the part of some officers and a complete failure on the part of all to grasp that campaigning in Europe was no preparation for the harsh, empty wastes of Peru had led to severe shortages amongst the regiments of the British Brigade.

'The only fat things in this country, Boser, are the flies.'

Robert scratched his leg. 'And the fleas.'

'We've been ordered to form foraging parties to scour the countryside for food.'

Robert grimaced. 'Using force if necessary, no doubt.'

'How else?'

Robert remembered how the gypsy women could wheedle for food in the village when their menfolk had doors slammed in their faces.

'It won't work, Dickon. You'll never get anywhere like that. The local people will simply hide everything. Why don't you ask Carroty Kate and her lot to do it?'

'Is that what Cadey would have said?'

'Yes. The woman's way—negotiating, bargaining, showing some understanding of these poor people's situation.'

Cadey had expressed her views on this in her usual forthright manner only two days ago. How long ago that seemed. The army's way of foraging was so typical, she'd said, of the way men went head on at things. Everything had to be some sort of aggressive confrontation. Parliament had to have an opposition party; the Law was adversarial—two sides fighting it out, with Justice the inevitable casualty; and doctors and surgeons, all men of course, were on the attack with strong drugs and sharp knives when gentler ways existed.

≈

A cold, dust-laden wind harried the lines of yellowing tents as Muldoon, Rainbow and Robert rode through the camp. As far as Robert could make out, Rainbow had volunteered himself for this expedition. Whenever his duties as a groom allowed, he appeared outside Robert's tent, ready to be of service to him. They were setting out to see how Carroty Kate's 'progging parties' were getting on in their search for eggs, chickens, flour, corn, the cheap local wine, a bit of pork or 'grunting-peck'—anything to supplement the rations and make a change from the diet of tough beef which had been the sole and unvarying ration for the past six weeks. It was an aspect of war seldom reported, and one, Robert thought, which might interest the

Chronicle's women readers.

≈

On the altiplano, the high plateau country, the mountains were a belittling presence. It had taken Robert several days to realise it was not clouds high above him, but snow-clad ranges of breathtaking scale. A member of the Brigade Hunt rode past them.

Muldoon turned to Rainbow. 'You may think you're seeing a man in a red coat on a white horse, but you're not.'

'I'm not, Bat?'

'No. You're seeing a man in hunting pink on a grey.'

'Powerful magic, Bat'

Muldoon took a pull at a bottle of cachaca, an evil white rum made from the local Indian corn.

'This sodding country!' he muttered. 'Either too hot or too cold and often both at the same time!'

A volley of musket-fire at the far end of the camp made him turn in his saddle.

'Another poor bastard down with a dose of lead poisoning!'

Robert said, 'In this regiment, if Justice is blindfold it's because she awaits the firing-squad.'

≈

Clumps of tamarind trees and pinion shrubs with brilliant red flowers brightened their path as they wound between head-high anthills.

Muldoon rode up beside Robert. 'The young major, sorr. He's given too much to do for his age.'

'I know, Muldoon. We'll all have to help him as much as we can now that Ca… Mrs Thomson isn't here.'

C-S deliberately heaped upon Dickon enough work to tire a grown man, and always the least popular tasks—patrols in the thickest scrub, overseeing the floggings, and piles of paper-work. The boy was persecuted, Robert guessed, because C-S felt threatened by his growing popularity and because, quite simply, C-S was a bully—the kind of man who would always get more pleasure from breaking a man's spirit than from winning his heart. The only thing which prevented Dickon being bullied even more was his connection with Lord Hawksmoor. Arthur took the burden from Dickon when he could, as did Robert who now did most of the paper-work Cadey had been doing. For all Dickon's pluck, Robert didn't know how much more of this treatment the boy could stand.

≈

They arrived at a crossroads. Rainbow sprang from his saddle, water-bottle in hand, and emptied its contents into the dust.

'Jasus! What are you doing?' Muldoon howled.

'I pay tribute to Exu.'

'Exu?'

'Exu, God of the Lost Crossroads.'

Rainbow's face shone as he spoke, seeing in his mind the meeting of forest tracks in his native land, with the sun filtering through a leafy canopy. The fabric of life, he explained, was woven from the criss-crossing of events. A decision to follow this route or that in life was always best left to Exu, the keeper of all their might-have-beens, attended by the ghosts of their other selves whom they had encountered or departed from at one crossroads or another.

'Well, jaw-me-dead, sorr! That's too deep for me. As long as there's an inn at the crossroads where a body can get a modest quencher, I'll not fret.'

≈

With the sun high in the sky, the three of them retired to the shade of a tree. Rainbow sat down beside Robert. On the other side of the tree Muldoon was already snoring loudly. Robert took out his sketch-book and looked enquiringly at Rainbow. Rainbow's flashing teeth signaled his delight.

≈

Rainbow wondered how Skyherd would cope without Yansam's support… she who wore men's clothes. Ikpoom sometimes had worn womens' clothes. He knew that to be both male and female, to unite these two aspects of nature, is to restore harmony between Sky and Earth, gods and men. Such boundary-crossing rituals were best done at a crossroads, of course. Rainbow stirred uneasily, thinking of Exu.

'Keep still!' Robert implored.

Perhaps he had not paid sufficient respect to Exu—he who is the meaning in coincidence, he who is the force of nature which makes communication between humans and orishas possible and who brings magic into the realms of ordinary life. Rainbow eased his boots off. He still found them uncomfortable, but they were a symbol of his transition to the Other World. He didn't like them, all the same. They gave him the same feeling as trying to speak the language of the Other World. It was as if his thoughts were being squeezed into a new mould. His language, he had come to appreciate, was a way of dreaming the world, and this was a different dream. The hot air shimmered above the arid landscape, distorting the shape of things. Do we ever see things as they really are, Rainbow wondered. Indeed, was there such a thing as reality, or only everyone's different versions and interpretations of how things were? What was it he had overheard Yansam say? She'd been discussing something Skyherd had written for the *Chronicle*. 'Maybe fact is simply all our fictions put together,' she had said.

≈

A group of Peruvian peasants, hoes in hand, were walking silently past them, staring at the three foreigners. Every single one of them, young or old, wore an identical pair of reading spectacles—expensive, fashionable, European spectacles.

'Buenos dias!' Robert called to them.

'Buenos dias, senora,' returned an old man. Then, removing his spectacles, he corrected himself. 'Senor.'

'Ask him about the spectacles,' Robert said to Rainbow.

Rainbow had picked up Spanish with a rapidity which astonished Robert. This same gift, he supposed, was why 'the George' had made Rainbow his interpreter.

≈

It was the repartimiento, the old man said. It had started, he said, as a privilege granted to the superintendents of districts to barter goods with the Indians in exchange for gold and silver. This soon turned into a compulsory exchange in which the peasant Indians had to take whatever goods the superintendent chose to offer—dying mules, reading spectacles for the illiterate, razors for men with no beards, silk stockings for barefoot women, any goods, in fact, which merchants in Spain or Lima couldn't otherwise dispose of.

'Sorr! To your left!'

Approaching them through the scrub was an upright rectangular wooden box. It swayed and weaved between the bushes, singing as it came. A break in the scrub revealed that the box had a pair of bare legs. The box reached the road, tripped and lay with its legs kicking, unable to regain its feet. Muldoon crossed himself.

Robert said, 'Cadey... Mrs Thomson was telling me about something like this. It's a restraining device for the insane.'

'We had something similar at my elite school,' Rainbow said.

≈

They got to their feet and walked up to the box. It addressed them loudly in a strange tongue. Muldoon and Rainbow turned it over. There was a window in the box through which they could see the face of a Peruvian Indian who was probably of middle age, although Robert found it difficult to tell with native Peruvians. This time the face addressed them in Spanish.

'I am Fernando Tupac Amaru, direct descendent of the Inca chiefs. I am Emperor of the Inca realms, Lord of all Peru. I have returned to free my people.'

Rainbow's intake of breath droned through his teeth. He turned to Robert. 'Mr Hope, this great shaman was at my special training school. As you know, only someone of his advanced powers can change bodies when on a spirit journey.'

'Change bodies, did you say?'

'Yes, Mr Hope.'

Muldoon looked at Robert for guidance. 'Should we let him out, sorr?'

'I don't suppose his delusions of grandeur are any greater than those entertained by C-S and he's allowed to run free.'

Picking up a big stone, Rainbow broke the lock with one blow. Muldoon lifted back the hinged lid, revealing the fact that the Emperor of all Peru was naked and with a sizeable erection. Muldoon slammed the lid shut. The Emperor let out a yell, leapt from the box and hopped about like a demented toad.

'Bless my boots if it isn't Jumping Jack-in-a-box himself!' Muldoon laughed and then laughed even more when Rainbow stepped up to the Emperor and embraced him.

With help from Rainbow, Robert understood Tupac Amaru to say that the local asylum for the insane had been hit during the bombardment of the town and all the inmates had escaped. Even now, he told them, lunatics were running all over the landscape.

'We already know that,' Robert commented. 'They're wearing hunting pink, blowing horns and chasing a hare which they're pretending is a fox.'

The Emperor pointed at Rainbow's coat of many colours. 'When your rainbow is complete, your journey will be over.'

Then he turned and loped off into the scrub.

≈

Out of a cloud of dust and a clatter of hooves Arthur emerged, shouting friendly insults to one and all.

'Been searching for you high and low, my Prussian Blue! And here you are, the very last place I looked!' he declared, looking at Rainbow. 'The fact is… the fact is, the battle for Aposa has been officially declared a draw, so, to settle the matter, they've come up with another idea.'

Robert let out an anguished moan.

'No, it's all right, Stanners, not the same again. It's… well…,' He dismounted. 'The Spanish have proposed a boxing match. Seems they've got a man they fancy we can't beat. And that's where you come in, Rainbow… why I was sent to fetch you back to camp.'

'No,' Rainbow said.

'I think it's an order,' Arthur said gently. 'If you refuse you could be in a lot of trouble.'

'Only Nataxale. I came to fight Nataxale and no other.'

Arthur looked baffled. He appealed to Robert and Muldoon. 'Can you make him see reason?'

Muldoon shook his head. 'Not a hope in hell, sorr. And there's a certain colonel would love an excuse to put him up against a wall.'

28

In the distance, Robert could hear the Brigade's artillery bombarding some town or other. The British Brigade had lost interest in Aposa... but not in the boxing match which would settle the matter one way or another. He worried about Rainbow, who was still refusing to step into the ring with the Royalist's champion. C–S had taken charge of all the arrangements and he was not a man to thwart or cross. He had offered promotion to Rainbow who had refused it. It was in his power to have Rainbow flogged or even shot for disobeying an order—not that a dead pugilist would be much use in the ring. But if another person had to be found to take Rainbow's place, and that person lost, C–S would exact his revenge. In the meantime another town was under bombardment—an unusually heavy bombardment, Robert thought. He hoped they had got it right this time and were pounding foe and not friend. He had discovered that, whereas the Creoles, the white settlers, were clear that they wanted to manage their own affairs, independent of Spain, there were others, the local Indians for example, who were not so sure they had anything to gain by exchanging one set of white rulers for another. They were ambivalent about where their allegiance lay. Groups of local militia had been known to change sides three or four times and a village friendly in the morning might be hostile by nightfall. Sometimes it was simply a matter of who was winning, the Patriots or the Royalists. Robert recalled that shutters and doors in the pueblos they had passed through were always painted blue. But, often, the paint was still wet and an enquiring finger might uncover yellow.

≈

The town, whose name nobody seemed to know, duly capitulated. On entering it, Robert found that it had surrendered both to the Patriots and to the Royalists since it had been bombarded by both sides at once. And now both sides were looting it at the same time.

'It gives you hope for the future, doesn't it,' Robert said to Muldoon, 'To see troops from opposing armies plundering the same house in perfect harmony?'

Muldoon pointed out Carroty Kate and Rainbow, who were

searching through the ruins of what had once been a butcher's shop. Robert hailed them.

'Can't you talk some sense into this man, Kate?'

'Do you think I haven't tried?'

Muldoon said, 'He's more stubborn than Napoleon and Josephine put together and that's saying something.'

Dickon and Arthur were clambering over the rubble towards them. Muldoon sprang to attention and saluted. Dickon squared his little shoulders and returned the salute.

Arthur waved an agitated hand vaguely in the direction of his head. 'Have you heard the news... The Brigadier, he's dead. Took a tumble during the hunt. Landed on his head. You realise what this means?'

'What?' Robert said, a leaden weight in his heart, because he already knew the answer.

'C-S will get the Brigade. He'll be in charge of the whole show. With his influence and money he's bound to get it.'

'Holy Mother of God!' Muldoon exclaimed.

There was a long silence, a mixture of respect for Cochrane-Dyat and dread of what was to come under Carlton-Syms. Like Arthur, he had started out as a Captain. In a matter of months he had been promoted to Major, then to Colonel of the BLH, and now he was likely to be made Brigadier. Rather than satisfying his lust for power, each step upwards had only whet his appetite for more.

Dickon pulled a handful of hot baked potatoes from his pocket.

'Have one, Boser. The smouldering ruins do an excellent job on them! Really excellent!' He offered them round.

'Shouldn't you be stopping the looting?' Robert asked Arthur through a mouthful of hot potato.

Arthur shook his head. 'Orders not to. They haven't been paid, you see... I say! Major Minagh... Your boots have stopped squeaking!'

'So they have,' Dickon said, looking down at them.

Robert caught Arthur's eye, frowning and shaking his head to stop him blurting out that he'd had a bet with his fellow officers as to which would stop squeaking first—Dickon's voice or his boots.

Arthur pulled Robert aside. 'There's more news,' he said in a low voice.

'What?'

'About Nanny Thomson.'

'What about her?'

Robert realised they were within earshot of Carroty Kate, who was dusting plaster and fragments of brick off a joint of meat. He rolled his eyes towards her.

Arthur laughed. 'There's nothing goes on that she and her lot don't know already.'

A party of Spanish Royalists, Arthur said, operating behind Patriot lines, had waylaid the group escorting Cadey back to Lima and taken her prisoner.

'Oh my pippin!'

Arthur grinned. 'Not to worry. 'I'll wager they'll be begging us to take her back before too long.'

Seeing that Robert didn't find it amusing, he added. 'She'll be well treated. Decent bunch on the whole... You'll tell Dickon, will you? Don't suppose he'll take it too hard.'

Carroty Kate straightened and Robert could see from her expression that she knew Cadey was Dickon's mother.

'Er... excuse me, Arthur, I just want a quick word with Carroty Kate.'

He motioned her round the back of the ruined building.

'How long have you known?' he hissed.

'About Cadey and Dickon? ...Oh, ages. I'm not blind, you know. I had a little boy too. You think one mother can't spot another? Poor bloody woman.'

Some of the women camp-followers approached Carroty Kate, baskets of loot slung across their backs. They went into a huddle, talking in Spanish. Carroty Kate thanked them and walked away. 'Hey, Rainbow!' she shouted. 'I've heard something what will make you jump out of your skin, my Shallaballah!'

Rainbow approached her. Carroty Kate crowed with delight and punched him on the chest. She caught Arthur's eye. 'Maybe you didn't know, Captain, but the women of Aposa slip out and trade with the villagers all around, just as we do. There's even some of them here today.'

'I say! They're not meant to do that!'

Carroty Kate chuckled. 'Well, they do. And they talk to the same folk we talk to. And do you know what… they know who this effing fighter is what the sodding Spaniards think can't lose.'

'Who?' came a chorus of male voices.

'Only someone what's on the run for murder, someone what's got a Spanish mother, someone what signed up with the Royalists in England to get as far away as he could.' She punched Rainbow again. 'Now who could that be, Rainbow, my Lion of Africa?'

29

In the dusty main square of Aposa, the ring had been roped off. Just about the entire forces of both the town garrison and their besiegers crowded into the square, leaned out of windows, packed the balconies or sat atop the roofs of the surrounding buildings. Both sides had come unarmed. If either high command had planned treachery, this would have been their chance, but a gentleman's agreement was stronger than any considerations of military advantage to be gained. Carlton-Syms, with a triumphant, self-satisfied smirk on his face, and the senior officer in Aposa sat side by side in a specially constructed pavilion which overlooked the ring. They were there to see fair play. Outside the ropes, men with staves had formed a cordon. In this clear zone between the ring and the crowd stood two closed carriages.

≈

Inside one of the carriages Rainbow received his final instructions from Arthur.

Broughton's rules allowed each fighter two helpers in his corner—a 'second', who would be Arthur, and a 'bottle holder', who would be Jacko. Rainbow had had a week to prepare for the fight. With Arthur's and Carroty Kate's help it was enough. He had come to Peru looking for Nataxale. He had kept himself fit and his hands hard in readiness for this supreme moment.

≈

Just audible above the excited hornets' nest that was the crowd, was a slow, dull thudding emanating from a tall tree in the corner of the square.

Rainbow cocked his head. 'What's that?'

'Are you listening to me?' Arthur said. 'You mustn't let him get in close.'

'Is it a drum?'

'Never mind what that is. Listen to me.'

'It's important.'

Arthur sighed, 'Kate, much obliged if you'd go and find… Now, about Jem's left hook… '

A roar burst from the crowd as Jem Ashley stepped from his carriage, stripped to the waist, his torso shining like old ivory in the afternoon sun. He vaulted the ropes and paced up and down inside the ring, flexing his muscles, acknowledging the shouts from the crowd.

Rainbow started forward, bristling. 'Is that him? Is that Nataxale?'

Arthur put a restraining hand on him. 'Not yet. Let him wait. Let him bake in the sun a bit.'

Carroty Kate returned. 'It's that lunatic what we met out progging. He's thumping a branch with a rock.'

'Tupac Amaru!' Rainbow exclaimed, overjoyed.

≈

On the pavilion balcony a white silk handkerchief fluttered in Carlton-Sym's raised hand. His hand dropped and another mighty roar went up as the two pugilists circled each other, sparring for an opening. The first round lasted twenty-three minutes, Rainbow's pent-up rage and hatred for the devil who threatened everything dear to him more than matching Jem's savagery. It was Jem, shaken and bleeding from the nose, who dropped to one knee, thus ending the round.

'By Jove!' Arthur shouted into Rainbow's ear, 'Ease up on the attack. You've got to pace yourself.'

≈

Three more rounds went by, of eighteen minutes, thirteen minutes and six minutes. At the end of each, Rainbow was the one still standing, his speed of hand and foot and his amazing anticipation making Jem, known for his whirlwind rushes, look leaden-legged.

≈

In the fifth round, Jem got in close for the first time, ramming his head into Rainbow's stomach before grabbing him in a bear hug and sinking his teeth into Rainbow's eyebrow. Through the pain Rainbow remembered Carroty Kate's instruction—'If he's biting you, his swazzle-box ain't far off.' He jabbed hard for the voice box. Jem reeled back, clutching his throat, gasping and croaking. In a flash, sooner than Rainbow expected, he leapt in close, gouging at Rainbow's eye. Again Carroty Kate's experience came to his aid. Seizing the thumb with both hands he forced it into Jem's own eye. Rainbow danced forward. His foot slipped on a patch of loose sand and down he went. As he rose,

Jem smashed a knee into his face and followed up with a chopping blow to the back of the neck.

≈

'He's a goner!' Arthur was groaning as Rainbow swam back into consciousness. He'd been dragged back into his corner. He knew his nose was broken.

'He's not finished!' Jacko insisted, putting the bottle to Rainbow's lips. 'Not by a long chalk. Not the guv.'

Rainbow rinsed the blood from his mouth and spat. Everything was black and white, drained of colour.

'Don't worry, guv,' Jacko grinned at him. 'If you could see him through that eye, you'd know he looks a lot worse than you.'

And then the wind shifted, bringing a new sound… water flowing… a promise of sweet, life-giving water, flowing in the River Itzuwala once more, if he defeated that evil henchman of Famine and Pestilence leering at him in the corner opposite.

'Call 'Ready'', he hissed at Arthur.

'Not yet.'

'Call it!'

'Ready this corner!' Arthur called, raising his hand.

≈

Jem prided himself on his ability to punch toe to toe with any prize-fighter in the world and never give ground. But the ferocity of Rainbow's attack drove him onto the ropes. Momentarily, Jem slipped onto one knee, then, leaping up, he slung a punch at Rainbow's head. It missed, but the fistful of dust struck Rainbow full in the eyes. Three unseen hammer blows felled Rainbow for a second time.

≈

The throbbing in his temples became a drum beat with the same tempo as that used by Ikpoom on the start of a spirit journey. Boom, boom, boom! The insistent noise became his heartbeat, the mantra inside his head, his footsteps taking him further and further into another tunnel.

≈

He emerged into a trampled, blood-spattered forest glade. Nataxale had shifted shape. Now he was a giant iguana. He himself had become a lion. The monster was bellowing for blood, the sound seeming to surround him and break over him in waves. He sprang at the reptile, his whole body charged with animal strength. Although the iguana sustained a broken rib from a blow of almost superhuman force, it fought on. Even half-blinded by blood and swelling, it fought on. For one hour and ten minutes the iguana battled with the Lion of Africa until Nataxale collapsed on the ground and was unable to get up.

≈

Together, C-S and the Royalist general stepped into the ring. The announcement was made by an interpreter, first in English, then in Spanish.

'By the full agreement and acknowledgement of both senior officers here present, the winner, in the seventh round, after two hours, thirty four minutes of combat, is the chosen champion of the British Brigade!'

Wild cheering broke out all around the square. Both besieged and besiegers glad that the stalemate had at last been broken.

≈

Arthur and Jacko helped Rainbow back to his carriage. He was exhausted, in pain, but wildly happy. For the first time since leaving his native land—and that seemed a long, long time ago—he felt he'd accomplished something of his mission. In the gaunt, dust-smeared faces of the village elders he thought he detected something close to approval, a grudging admission that perhaps he had not let them down after all... not yet, anyway. And Yaba's dulled eyes shone with a new light. He never ceased to be surprised and grateful for her love. Did he now see hope and respect there too?

'I shan't never see a fight as good that,' Jacko declared. 'Not never, not in my whole life. I'm proud of you, guv.' And he burst into tears.

'Amen to that,' said Arthur. 'You were magnificent, Rainbow, truly magnificent. I have to confess, I thought you were finished at the end of the sixth. What a come-back!'

But Rainbow had swooned away into a state somewhere between fainting and sleeping.

Martial music rolled across the square of the little town of Huahuajin
—for that was the name of the town which had been looted by both
sides. Robert wished he didn't have to attend these boring parades.
But as Muldoon would say, 'Orders is orders.' He leafed through the
sketches he'd made of the fight a week ago. They had been done
afterwards, in fact. He'd spent most of the contest with his eyes tight
shut and his head buried in his hands. How elated Arthur had been,
though, his face flushed, his eyes sparkling. After the fight, C-S had
sent for Robert and forbidden him to send the sketches to the *London
Illustrated Chronicle*, reminding him that, as long as he was attached
to the Brigade, he was subject to its rule and that he had signed a
document to that effect. The English public did not want to know
about 'some nigger' winning fights for his white masters. Any report
of the fight must say that Rainbow was a true-born Englishman. In
other words, he was to say that black was white. To C-S' absolute fury,
Robert had refused.

'You'll do as I tell you soon enough. I'll make sure of that. You'll see!'

≈

After Rainbow's triumph over Jem Ashley, the Royalists had honoured
the agreement and marched out of Aposa, glad to be quitting a nasty,
smelly town that nobody in their right minds would want to occupy.
Huahuajin was much more attractive, despite large parts of it being
reduced to rubble. The martial music reached a clashing climax. The
newly appointed Brigadier Carlton-Syms climbed onto a podium.
'What's he up to now?' Robert wondered. Perhaps it was something to
do with the death of Cochrane-Dyat.

A sergeant bellowed, 'Step forward the common law wife of Trooper
William Smith!'

A low moan rumbled through the lines.

'Silence in the ranks!'

It wasn't a flogging which a very surprised Carroty Kate received, but
a medal for bravery on behalf of the captured Smithy. And none other
than C-S himself pinned it to her chest with a smile which Robert
thought was about as genuine as an old master on a costermonger's

barrow.

≈

The day before yesterday a package had arrived from Mama, containing
three scarves of blue and white wool, knitted by Gwen, the cook—
one for Robert, one for Muldoon and one for Rainbow. In the
accompanying letter there'd been a bit Robert had puzzled over until
he remembered he'd developed a habit of referring to the common
soldier of the British Brigade as 'Bill Smith', a collective name, it being
easier to write that Bill Smith did this or that, rather than specify
individuals each time, or say 'someone whose name I don't know.' Thus,
to Bill Smith was accredited, as well as tales of humour and cunning,
many a deed of fortitude and courage. It seemed Mama had taken this
rather too literally and thought that this catch-all Bill Smith actually
existed and had personally done all these things. She had written to
the *Chronicle* and to the *Times,* drawing attention to this unsung hero
who had received no mention in Robert's more formal and generalised
accounts of the campaign. Such was the public's interest in the man that
a subscription had been got up and a special medal struck for the hero,
which awaited his return to the shores of England. There was even a
music hall song about 'Brave British Bill'.

≈

Reports of Bill Smith's fame must have reached Carlton-Syms. Now,
as he pinned a medal to Carroty Kate's chest, he was merely ensuring
the facts were in line with the fiction. No doubt he'd also make sure he
got most of the credit for having a national hero under his command.

≈

'Capital! Capital!' Arthur exclaimed, slapping his thigh, when, after the
parade, Robert explained how Carroty Kate's Smithy had managed to
become such a popular figure. 'Damn shame about Rainbow, though.
He's the one who should've had a gong stuck on him today.' His face
brightened. 'Tell you what… we'll have our own medal ceremony for
him! Gather your little gang and meet me here in half an hour.'

≈

Dickon, as the senior officer present, pinned the medal to Rainbow's
chest, standing on tiptoes to reach. Rainbow beamed and smiled as
widely as his bruised and swollen face allowed. It was Arthur's medal,

a silver one with the head of King George IV on it, attached to a broad yellow ribbon. Robert, Carroty Kate, Jacko, Cadey and Arthur applauded and Rainbow smiled even more widely when he learned that it was the face of The George on his new talisman.

'What did you do to get your medal?' Jacko asked Arthur.

'Oh, Peninsular War. Anybody would have done it. Just happened to be the one there, that's all,' Arthur mumbled and refused to say any more.

Robert stepped up to Rainbow and put the blue and white scarf around his neck.

'You only need red now, Rainbow.'

'Is this a riddle, Mr Hope?'

'What that madman in the box said… about completing your rainbow… Your violet coat, orange sleeves…'

'Carrots put those sleeves on, I remember that,' Jacko said.

Arthur said, 'And the green badge from the asylum, I remember that.'

'Your indigo sash the auxiliaries wear,' Robert continued, 'And now the yellow medal ribbon and the blue in your scarf…'

'I know, Mr Hope. But the colours must come unbidden. You cannot deliberately seek them.'

Blue and white, Skyherd's colours, Rainbow thought. White for the clouds that will soon gather in the sky, heralding the rain to come. But when would that be? After defeating Nataxale he'd thought, he'd hoped, that something important would immediately happen such as it being revealed to him what gift he should make to Skyherd. That Yoruba person Snail had mentioned… Edetaen, yes that was his name … he must be here, in the Other World, on a similar mission. Perhaps he would know how these things worked. Maybe he could explain what was what and put him on the right path. Rainbow decided to get word to Edetaen and arrange a meeting.

≈

Arthur and Robert strolled down Huahuajin's twisting main street. Arthur was telling Robert that, after a long meeting in a private room of Huahuajin's best hostelry, with the mayor paying for the wine, the senior officers of the opposing factions had agreed that the British

Brigade would stay and the Royalists withdraw.

'At least it's not another boxing match,' Robert said.

'Probably tossed a coin for it,' Arthur laughed. 'How do you pronounce this place, anyway?'

'Pretend you're about to sneeze, then stifle it at the last second and you've just about got it.'

They both laughed. They talked about Cochrane-Dyat's funeral which had been held the day before yesterday. There had been some speculation as to whether the Brigadier's arm would be buried along with him, or whether the Brigadier would be stuffed and join the arm in a glass case. The coffin, mounted on a gun carriage, had been pulled by the Brigadier's pack of hounds. Several high-ranking Spanish officers from the Royalist's side were there, paying their last respects to a former comrade-in-arms and seeming more ill-at-ease as Roman Catholics in a Church of England ceremony than they did at being in the enemy camp.

'Many's the time the Old Die-Hard would get the chaplain to gallop through the Sunday service, so we could start the meet a bit earlier.'

'Gives a whole new meaning to the Sermon on the Mount,' Robert said.

'I'll miss the Old Cockroach in a strange sort of way… I say, Stanners, old fruit, I wonder if you could… '

Robert's heart sank. Was he going to ask for another loan of money. 'Could what?'

'Well, I need some advice… about Dickon's birthday. I mean, to you he's a boy, to me he's my immediate superior in the chain of command. Should I give him anything or not?'

'Yes. Nothing too big.'

Robert waited to be asked what he had got for Dickon, but Arthur was distracted by a soldier with a face swathed in soiled bandages who lurched across their path on crutches.

'A word with you, Captain.'

'Ah, Tommy! How goes it?'

'Mustn't grumble, sir.'

Arthur turned to Robert. 'This poor fellow is one of our wounded who, because he can't fight any more, can no longer draw pay or rations.'

'That's disgraceful!'

'So, if you don't mind, Stanners old fruit, I'll talk to him for a bit. May be able to take up his case with the new colonel.'

'Yes, of course.'

'Good show.'

≈

Outside a small printer's shop Robert stopped to look at the posters displayed in the window. After all, he told himself, the printing department at the *London Illustrated Chronicle* had always interested him… Besides, a bunch of British Brigade officers was approaching from the opposite directions and there were tears in his eyes. Clearly Arthur only saw him as a friend and no more than that. And it would never be different. Robert bent closer to the window. He noticed that, on all the posters for forthcoming events—a horse sale, a visit to the town by a travelling puppet theatre, the monthly cattle market—the bar on the capital As was missing and the left-hand prong of the y had lost its top half. 'Donde Hay Amor Hay Dolor,' was the name of the puppet play, echoing the Spanish proverb: where there is love there is pain. The officers passed by. Robert straightened. He would rather have the pain than not be in love at all; not have Arthur to love.

≈

The householders of Huahuajin were obliged, by military decree, to quarter the Army of Liberation. So it was to rooms above a bakery owned by a mestizo family that Robert tried to find his way—no easy task because many of the streets had been re-named since yesterday. King Ferdinand Street had become Bolivar Street; Royal Square had become Independence Square. A better choice of name, Robert couldn't help thinking, would have been Victory Square, a name for all seasons, or even Freedom Square, since conquerors always claim to have liberated the places they occupy. Perhaps the inhabitants of Huahuajin knew something he didn't, because, in some parts of the town, the names were already changing back again to those favoured by the Royalists. Yesterday, the street in which his bakery was situated had been Little Madrid, this morning Little Colombia, and now it was Little Madrid once more. Boys, named after successful generals on the one side, found themselves answering to the names of the other side's heroes.

'Papa, who am I today?' Robert had heard the baker's son asking.

As a would-be-reporter of this conflict, had he hit upon an instant barometer of how the war was going? …Simply walk into the street and ask a boy his name.

31

Dickon's birthday party was held in Robert's room because it was bigger and because the floor didn't slope quite so much. Muldoon, hearing of 'los tremblos' which frequently shook the area, had selected a house whose walls were cracked and 'slantendicular'. A sure sign, he said, that it was safe because it had remained standing after the last quake. At Dickon's request, Jacko was there, again scrubbed to within an inch of his life. Because both boys would suffer if favouritism were suspected, their occasional meetings were conducted with more secrecy than a lover's tryst. Muldoon had been invited, too. Arthur had wanted to be there but regimental duties had prevented him from coming.

Jacko picked up a book and flicked through it.

'Nivver had a book in me 'and before. What's it about?'

Dickon pulled a face at Robert. 'Boser makes me do my lessons, even though Cadey's not here... It's boring geometry.'

'What's that when it's at home?'

'If angle A equals angle B... that sort of thing.'

'Oh that. Did that climbing chimleys. Best way to squeeze a square chimley? Angle it, of course.'

Robert offered Jacko a plate of sandwiches. 'Still liking the army, Jacko?'

'Ain't as hard as being on the street, sir,' he replied, grabbing six sandwiches at once. 'Nor as many beatings as when I was a chimley faker.'

'What do you like best about it?'

'The drumming... and the uniform. Makes you feel like you're someone, does the uniform.'

Robert refilled Jacko's glass of sherbet. 'And what do you do with your pay?'

'When we gets paid,' Jacko said with heavy emphasis on the 'when'. He shrugged. 'Baccy, rum... it's not like... not like your old man takes it off you to get legless, then bashes your mam. Carrots ain't like that. She ain't easy, though. Always fretting about her Smithy.'

'You see quite a lot of her, don't you, Jacko?'

'I share a camp-fire wiv her. Rainbow's there quite a bit, too. But he says …'

'What's he say?' Dickon wanted to know.

'He says he might not be here much longer. Says he has to go back to his own country and he can't take me wiv him.'

'Well!' Robert exclaimed, trying to sound jolly. 'How about lighting the candles?'

Although Robert had promised to bake a cake for Dickon, the birthday-boy had agreed that it was much more likely to be a better cake if the baker was asked to do it. Eleven icing soldiers marched around its perimeter, holding candles. Dickon extinguished their flames in one long puff. Jacko, Muldoon and Robert clapped and cheered. The cake was cut and the two boys stuffed themselves with huge slices.

'Look what Arthur gave me,' Dickon said, putting on a pair of spectacles—repartimiento spectacles such as the Indian peasants had worn. Arthur had somehow given the lenses a rosy tint.

'Everything's pink, Boser! The icing, Jacko, everything!'

He passed the spectacles to Jacko.

'Friggin' magic! Everyone oughta wear 'em all the time!'

'And here's my present,' Robert said. He had put together a collection of cartoons and caricatures , the ones he thought would amuse Dickon most, ones in which C-S figured large. At the end of the booklet Robert had included a pencil portrait of Cadey.

'Something else for you, sorr.' Muldoon handed Dickon a gold fob-watch. The insignia of a Royalist regiment engraved on the back gave Robert a good idea of how Muldoon had come by it.

Dickon flushed with pleasure. 'Thanks a lot!'

Jacko held out a small wooden figure, obviously well used.

'It's a little-get-up-man,' he said, demonstrating the way it bobbed up when pushed down.

The two of them played with it for a while.

'And now Uncle Hawk's present,' Robert said, producing the ceremonial sword from under the bed.

Dickon seized it, his eyes shining. He drew it from its scabbard and held it aloft so that it caught the light. Slash! Slash!

'Off with their heads!'

'Let me have a go!' Jacko cried.

Dickon ignored his plea, running a finger over the Hawksmoor family crest engraved on the blade just below the hilt. He flourished the sword. 'Have at you, sir!'

Clouds of feathers arose from Robert's mortally wounded pillow.

Robert said, 'Put the sword down, Dickon and let me give you Cadey's present.'

The Very Minor Major reluctantly sheathed his sword and took the packet from Robert. He tore it open. A leather-bound copy of 'Don Quixote', beautifully illustrated with engravings. It was a work Robert would have been glad to possess. With Jacko looking over his shoulder, Dickon flicked through it, then put it down. He drew his sword again, his eyes absorbed in its glittering curve. Cadey had deliberately chosen a present appropriate to a tutor rather than something more intimate. So intensely did Robert feel the agony she must have gone through, that he snatched the sword from Dickon's grasp.

'Tell you what, Dickon. Jacko has to be back on duty soon. Let him cut the cake in half… what's left of it.'

He handed the sword to Jacko who split the cake asunder as if it were a Royalist head. Robert wrapped one half for Jacko and saw him to the door.

≈

Jacko was hardly in the street before C-S burst into the room without so much as a knock on the door.

He scowled at Robert and Dickon. 'When I arrange a sitting with you, I expect you to be ready for me.'

'Five o'clock was the appointed hour,' Robert said.

With a great flourish, Dickon drew his newly acquired watch from his pocket. 'And the time now is precisely nine minutes to five.'

C-S glared. 'Now is when it suits me to be here. And if I want to know the time, I'll ask, you insolent puppy!'

When Dickon had withdrawn, C-S unrolled a poster and thrust it at Robert's face.

'Do you see this? Whole bundle of them found on a Royalist courier we captured.'

'You'll have to translate for me, I'm afraid. What's it say?'

Without reversing the poster to read it himself, C-S recited:

'Wanted! Brigadier Carlton-Syms, Commander of the British Brigade. His Excellency, the Viceroy of Peru empowers any senior official of his administration or senior officer of the Royalist army to pay the sum of 100,000 piastres to whomsoever delivers this brave but dangerous ally of the rebels, dead or alive, into the hands of the rightful rulers of Peru.'

In the centre of the poster was a rather poor likeness of C-S astride the grey stallion which had formerly belonged to Cochrane-Dyat.

'They must want me pretty badly, eh? I've been advised to form a bodyguard to accompany me at all times.' C-S coughed. 'Do you think it would add a certain something to the portrait? Lying on the table… like that, beside these maps?'

'Mmm, maybe… Like this, perhaps?' Robert rearranged the poster so that the size of the reward was obscured.

'No, like this,' C-S said, making sure the price and name clearly showed.

Robert shrugged. C-S took up his pose, one hand on his sword, the other resting on his breast in a manner reminiscent, but not too obviously so, of Napoleon Bonaparte.

≈

The portrait was nearly finished. Reluctantly, Robert had to admit to himself it was the best thing he'd ever done. At first he'd thought he would be able to forget his intense dislike for the man in front of him and lose himself in the challenge presented by composition, shape, the subtleties of tone and colour, the application of the paint itself, its texture, its flow, but he was wrong. And he thought he could forget he was painting the most unpleasant person he'd ever met if he tried to see him as a representative of something grander and more impersonal than his greedy, ambitious little self. This would be a portrait of 'Mars, God of War' in modern uniform; a portrait of 'the Glory and Responsibility of Command'; a portrait of the Trinity, 'Dignity, Authority and the Established Order Made Flesh'; a portrait of the Nation. But he was wrong. He could not forget that behind the paint, behind the symbols and archetypes was this loathsome man. And therein lay the power of the painting, its ambivalence, its tension, its struggle with itself, its irony.

'Well, Stanhope, have you composed your report yet on the boxing match between the heroic Bill Smith and that evil, traitorous, dago half-breed?'

Robert tried to control his breathing. If only Cadey was here to back him up. Inside his head he replied, 'Oh, Bill Smith, was it? Strange, isn't it that even Carroty Kate thought it was Rainbow. And, by the way, should I mention that you once wagered a considerable amount of money on Jem Ashley winning a certain contest that never took place?'

'Well, have you?' C-S demanded.

'What's the point? You know very well my pigeons have been impounded.'

The brigade vet had insisted that Robert's carrier pigeons had some rare disease which might infect the army's stock of birds unless immediately quarantined.

'You could use the brigade pigeons... Provided I approved the message they carried.'

Robert said nothing, carefully wiping a brush that needed no wiping.

Carlton-Syms abandoned his grand pose and stood hands on hips. 'Use your head, Stanhope! It would be the making of you as a reporter. It's just the story the readers of the *Chronicle* are craving for. Think how pleased old Charlie Makepiece would be, how proud you'll make your father!'

Robert stared into the canvas. He was tempted.

Carlton-Syms strode towards the door. 'You'll be sorry if you don't! And you're not the only one who'll regret it, just remember that!'

As he stalked past his portrait he tried to feign indifference, to sweep by without so much as a glance at the canvas. But the quick sideways flick of the eyes turned into a long stare of increasing absorption.

''I'll leave the poster with you. Make sure you can get all the details right!' C-S instructed. 'And have the whole thing sent to my quarters when it's done!' he barked as he slammed the door behind him.

≈

Robert began to put in some of the background jungle vegetation... Not that they had seen any jungle on the campaign, but C-S had demanded jungle. To the English public, his audience, South America meant jungle, so jungle they must have. Robert wanted his father to be proud of him, but he wanted to be proud of himself, too. Tiger, tiger burning bright in the forest of the night. Dickon's copy of 'Don Quixote' had been illustrated by William Blake, Britain's most imaginative living artist, in Robert's opinion. What would C-S do to try to force him to send a false report? Supposing he tried to put pressure on him by bullying Dickon? In the letter from Mama which had come with the scarves there had been mention that Lord Hawksmoor was out of favour, sacked from the government, his influence considerably reduced. No doubt C-S was aware of this too and would know there was no longer anything to be gained by going easy on the boy. Robert knew he hadn't stood up to C-S in the way he should have. He wished Cadey was here to support him. She was the only person he could talk to properly. Arthur seemed to think she'd be treated well as a prisoner of the Royalists. He'd forgotten to ask Jacko whether that other African... Garden of Eden... Edetean... had met up with Rainbow. Rainbow, on one of his frequent visits to Robert, had mentioned him. They kept nearly meeting, he said, then not doing so... like Carroty Kate and Smithy.

≈

Robert turned his attention to the poster, studying the text and the lettering. He drew in his breath. The same faults were in this poster as in the ones in the window of the printer's shop! No bar on the capital As, a faulty y. It was too much of a coincidence. This poster in front of him had been printed recently in Huahuajin, not in some Royalist-held town. Could there be another reason, beside vanity for faking a 'Wanted' poster? C-S was so hated by the men under his command that he needed an excuse to form a bodyguard. He was in more danger from his own side than he was from the enemy.

≈

That evening, Robert kept Dickon company in his room. Dickon, seated at a table lit by candles in a three-headed candelabra, was working on the minutes of Carlton-Syms' meeting with his senior command. He raised a troubled, frowning countenance.

'I've got so many notes here. Should I put everything in, Boser?'

'Rule one,' Robert advised, 'If C-S so much as coughed at the meeting, he is deemed to have made a significant and penetrating contribution to the proceedings.'

Dickon laughed.

'Rule two,' Robert continued, 'All statistics of casualties, if they're our own, must be halved and, if they're the enemies', doubled. And sour facts disguised in sweet words.'

Dickon was grinning with delight. 'Like calling a deserter an absentee, you mean? Or a retreat a strategic withdrawal?'

'Exactly,' Robert said and groaned inwardly. Most of the information in his reports to Sir Charles had been based on minutes and reports such as Dickon was writing. When would he learn that not everything that was written down happened, and not everything which happened got written down?

'What are you doing, Boser?'

'I'm writing to my mother. Not that it's likely to be sent for some time yet.'

'It must be nice to have a mother. I don't even have a picture of mine.'

'Perhaps she looked like you.'

'How do you spell 'audacious', Boser?'

Robert handed his dictionary across to Dickon. 'Look it up for yourself.'

The scratching of two pens, the flickering candlelight, the changing of the guard outside C–S's headquarters across the square.

'Do you think you could do one of her, Boser?'

'What do you mean?'

'A portrait of my mother. You know... using me to... to sort start you off on the right track.'

'Perhaps. I'll have to think about it.'

'And I could chose what she wore, couldn't I? And how her hair would be.'

'Shouldn't you be getting that report finished?'

≈

'Finished,' Dickon announced, about an hour later.

'It's about time you went to bed, isn't it?'

'Oh, Boser, not yet! Let's get a breath of fresh air first. You could wear your new scarf. Where shall we go?'

'I think we should see how those who didn't get a chance to stuff themselves with birthday cake are getting on. I mean your squadron, Dickon.'

≈

Number Five Squadron of the British Light Horse ate and slept in the cattle-shed next to the slaughterhouse, there being no more rooms available in the houses. They sat round a meagre fire in the middle of the mud floor. Normally, their numbers would have been doubled by the female camp-followers who had attached themselves to the fighting men. Tonight, however, there was only one old crone and a heavily pregnant woman to be seen.

'No, don't get up,' Dickon said as the men began to rise wearily to their feet. 'I've just come to see how you're faring.'

'Well, we are keeping fine company tonight!' jeered the old crone. 'And not a razor needed between the two of them.'

Dickon grinned. 'We get enough close shaves in battle, don't we?'

A rumble of laughter ran through the shed. The men relaxed.

'Where's everyone gone?' Robert asked.

'Las Golpetinas are out tonight, sir.'

'Las Golpetinas? Like in the puppet, Golpetina?'

'The same, sir.'

Robert was aghast all over again at finding how much was going on that he, the war correspondent, knew next to nothing about— things never mentioned in the official reports or written up in the minutes Dickon laboured over. He'd heard of the occasional raid on enemy supply-lines conducted by the camp-followers, usually led by Carroty Kate, but he hadn't realised these little bands had grown into what was virtually an unofficial female brigade. In the last few weeks, it seemed, a new leader had emerged, a newcomer to the ranks of the camp-followers. This woman, to whom Carroty Kate acted as second-in-command, answered only to the name of Golpetina and her well-organised force had become known as Las Golpetinas.

'What's that you're cooking?' Dickon asked.

'Skilly,' replied a soldier. 'Water'n oatmeal… Well, what might have passed for oatmeal once.' He held out a wooden spoon. Dickon took a tentative sip and spat it out. The men around the fire laughed.

'Have you men complained about this?' Robert wanted to know.

'And risk a flogging? Not frigging likely!'

Robert dipped a hand into a small bag of flour, fingered it, smelt it, then tasted it. Gwen had taught him what to do when the millers delivered their full sacks to the kitchen door.

'This flour ration, Major Minagh, has been kept up to weight only by a liberal addition of chalk and dust.'

'He's on the mark there,' said the old crone, a note of respect in her voice.'

≈

There was a loud knocking on Dickon's door. Robert, sitting in his own room, heard a military voice, the kind of voice that makes a bellowdrama out of the most ordinary statement, say, 'Brigadier Carlton-Sym's compliments, sir. He wishes to know the hour, sir, and you're to report in full dress uniform to tell him the precise time, sir.'

Robert paced the floor of his room. So it had started already.

≈

The town clock was striking three in the morning as Dickon clattered down the stairs and out of the house. This little ritual was repeated at four o'clock and again at five. On this last occasion, to give him some kind of moral support, Robert walked with him across the square to where C-S was quartered. One of the bodyguard received the Very Minor Major's announcement of the time with a cynical sneer. Robert could see the boy was exhausted and near to tears. He accompanied him back to the door of the bakery, then wandered through the town, raging against C-S, hoping Dickon had the same kind of resilience as his newly-acquired little-get-up-man.

≈

Robert passed heaps of rubble. So much of the town was in ruins as a result of the dual bombardment. He was reminded of something Cadey had said about disobedience being the agent of change. Traditions, laws, beliefs were what held society together and without which it would become just a pile of rubble. But they were also the shackles which prevented progress. He came to an intersection of four streets. Squatting in the middle of this crossroads, beside a bowl of blood, was Rainbow. He was cradling a drum, not a military drum, but one made from a tropical gourd, over which was stretched what might have been a monkey's skin.

'Whose blood is that?' Robert asked.

Rainbow indicated the slash he had made on his wrist. 'From a wound comes healing blood, from a dividing of the flesh comes wholeness.'

Rainbow wet a finger in the blood and drew the sign of the cross on his forehead.

'The cross,' Robert said, pointing to Rainbow's forehead. 'What's it for?'

'It has many meanings, Mr Hope. It is the bridge which connects, the four quarters of a whole, the moment of decision.' He began to drum softly. 'The crossroads is the meeting of tears and laughter, hatred and love, illusion and reality, male and female, unity and diversity and the point where all aspects of Exu, God of the Lost Crossroads, join as one.'

One of the four avenues led the eye to a mountain pass which framed the tip of the rising sun. Rainbow's gaze was on the snow-capped peaks.

'Now that I have defeated Nataxale, we can go to the realm of eternal whiteness, can't we, Mr Hope?'

'We must wait and see, Rainbow. Who knows what our orders will be?'

The tempo of Rainbow's drumming increased. The sun rose higher. On a sudden whim, Robert dipped his finger in the blood and made upon his own forehead the sign of the cross.

32

On a cold, clear morning the British Brigade filled the four sides of Huahuajin's cobbled square. In the distance, amidst the white-capped peaks, an active volcano raised a plume of vapour. Once again Robert marvelled at the intense blueness of the sky, which almost exactly matched the vase of Bristol glass in the kitchen of Beechwood House. The British Brigade was drawn up in readiness for marching out of town. The A & S—the auxiliaries and supernumeraries, amongst whom Robert and Rainbow were classed, were at the back. Robert sat astride Manco with Rainbow standing beside him, holding Napoleon and Josephine. The bruises on his face were beginning to fade.

'Mr Hope, there is still so much I have to learn about the Other World! That piece of cloth with magical markings in red, white and blue ...'

'The Union Jack they're hoisting?'

'What gives it the power to make people go rigid, unable to move, for minutes on end?' Robert sighed. 'Unfortunately it's a very powerful force, Rainbow. It can make people burst into song, cheer madly, and even go to war.'

Through his telescope Robert searched the assembled ranks, trying to see how Muldoon was faring. A company commander, loth to admit to yet another desertion, had slipped Muldoon a coin to stand and be counted. Over the past few months the distinction between one regiment and another had become blurred. As uniforms became torn and blood-stained and boots fell to pieces and no new issue was made, the men wore whatever they could find—a civilian pair of breeks looted from a shop, boots stripped from a Royalist corpse, a blanket covering near-nakedness. Many were barefoot. Ah! There was Muldoon, looking rather the worse for drink. Robert swung the telescope along the line—a man wearing a pair of boots made of cardboard; another holding a lump of wood crudely carved in the shape of a musket—not that some of the so-called 'real' muskets were any more effective, having been designed and developed in Europe for very different combat conditions. And there was a woman, a camp-follower in the uniform of her man, no doubt standing in for him while he slept off last night's drinking spree. Could that be a tailor's dummy, or just the effect of the local food and a tight collar? It was a kind of phantom army, an army which existed in far greater numbers and with far superior equipment in ledgers, in brigade reports, in the politicians' rhetoric than it did in reality.

≈

The sergeant-major's hoarse shout brought the parade to attention. The band struck up. Brigadier Carlton-Syms, seated on what used to be Cochrane-Dyat's charger, took the salute. Orders rang out, bugles blew, company by company, regiment by regiment, the British Brigade marched out of the square, heading west towards the besieged town of Cerro de Puna. Before each company received the order 'By the right, quick march!' the soldiers lucky enough not to be barefoot removed their boots, helping each other to stuff them into the tops of their packs. If you were down to your last pair of boots, it seemed, they were not for marching in, but for parades and ceremonial occasions. When Muldoon showed no sign of turning up to lead Napoleon and Josephine, Rainbow offered to take his place.

'Don't you have your own duties, Rainbow?'

'The others will do it for me, as I do it for them when they cannot be there.'

≈

Ahead were the clouds of dust raised by the Patriot brigade; which had been encamped outside the town and which had left twenty minutes earlier. And beyond that a jumble of peaks and valleys, all blue-grey and golden brown—the highest, the steepest, the broadest, the deepest, the most barren, the most isolated, the most exhausting landscape Robert had ever seen. Army engineers were dismantling a wooden bridge and re-erecting it half a mile up-river. Robert learned later that they'd discovered their map-makers had made a few errors. Instead of calling in all the maps and altering them, it was deemed easier to change the landscape.

≈

To the slap of bare feet on the march, the thud of hooves, the jingle of harness, the creaking of wheels and shouted orders, the British Brigade proceeded through a village whose inhabitants were still rehearsing its new name. Whether this was the map-makers' doing or a change of loyalties on the part of the villagers, Robert wasn't sure.

≈

On the other side of the village, the marching column ran into an ambush. The Royalists were hidden in a field of hemp. The British Brigade halted while a detachment was sent to flush them out. The field began to burn. Clouds of smoke drifted over the stationary troops. Without being ordered to, the band straggled into a ragged semblance of a tune to which the pipers of the Highland regiment added a disjointed wailing, almost drowning out the crackle of the muskets.

≈

Men began to dance and sing and to prance about on either side of the road. Feeling unaccountably light-headed and pleased with life, Robert joined in. The soldiers detailed to deal with the ambush threw down their weapons and rolled on the ground howling with laughter. The enemy did the same. Robert heard Arthur's joyous shout and caught a glimpse of him cavorting in a manner not so very different from his usual self. A soldier climbed slowly on top of a cart. It was quite the funniest thing Robert had ever seen. Perceived as if through the wrong end of a telescope, this species which swarmed here and there so busily, in a comedy of errors in which it had no idea it was cast, was hilarious in its antics, side-splittingly funny.

≈

Gradually it seemed less funny until it ceased to be even mildly amusing. Robert sat in the middle of the road, wondering what he had been laughing at, feeling that something wonderful, he didn't know what, had eluded him. People stared around them sheepishly and reformed their lines. Bugles sounded. The march resumed.

'What was that about?'

'Hemp,' said Muldoon.

'Oh, so you've decided to put in an appearance at last. What about the hemp?'

'Yes, sorr... the effect of the smoke, sorr. I doubt we'll sight Cherries and Prunes tonight, sorr, not after this delay.'

≈

Later in the day, Arthur rode up to them and announced, 'I've made a wager that we're in Cerro de Puna by this time tomorrow.'

Robert gave a mock groan. 'Wager?'

'Don't worry, Stanners, it's my moustache I've bet. My moustache against Ferguson's. And I shall win!'

'By a whisker, no doubt.'

'And when we enter Cerro de Puna, keep your eyes peeled.'

'Why?'

Arthur tapped his nose and winked. 'Oh, just a little surprise I've arranged.'

The thought of it, whatever it was, made him slap his thigh and rock in his saddle with laughter.

≈

The Royalists had deployed several divisions to intercept the Patriot advance. They were waiting on the other side of the river, at the only bridge for miles in either direction. The Patriot brigade were already drawn up opposite them. Their commanding officer, General Garcia, was the senior officer in the field. It was up to him to decide the overall battle plan. But Carlton-Syms, without conferring with him, ordered the British Light Horse to take the bridge and hold the bridgehead on the far side.

≈

The cavalry assembled in close rank.

'Why, damn me!' Robert heard Arthur joke. 'If it isn't Vauxhall Bridge! And there's Fitz's Club on the other side!'

'Good luck, Arthur!' Robert called out, but the regimental band struck up, drowning out his words. To the same rollicking tune to which the officers and their ladies had swirled around the ballroom floor not so long ago, the Light Horse charged, swords drawn, hooves thundering on the wooden planks. The vanguard reached the other bank. Had the element of surprise carried the day? Had the audacious plan succeeded in securing the bridge? Then the bridge exploded with a bright orange flash. Men, horses, fragments of timber were tossed high into the air. What remained of the bridge collapsed into the river. The Patriot cavalry tried to cross the river by swimming their horses across, but the current was swift and the Royalist musket-fire deadly. The current, tinged red with blood, carried the struggling, thrashing mass downstream. Men fought against the weight of their breast-plates, their heavy uniforms and emblems of glory only to be dragged beneath the surface. Those stranded on the far side were hacked to pieces. A few tried to surrender, but in the heat and frenzy of the moment, they too were killed.

≈

Sick at heart, feeling utterly helpless, Robert scanned the churning river. Then he saw Jacko running along the bank, shouting... and a pale young face rising and sinking in the turbulent water... Dickon. Robert started forward. Hadn't he promised Cadey he'd take care of Dickon? He sprinted towards the river, without knowing what he would do, trying to catch up with Jacko who was now level with Dickon. Jacko flung off his jacket and boots and plunged in. Robert tugged at his own boots. He was a poor swimmer, but he had to do something. Dickon was sweeping past now, gasping for air, drowning in front of him. He hurled himself forward... only to be caught from behind by a pair of strong arms.

'No, Mr Hope, no! Leave it to me.'

Robert struggled and kicked out. 'I must help him! I must! Let me go!'

He felt a blow on the back of his neck. His knees sagged. He slumped to the ground, just conscious of the splash as Rainbow dived in.

≈

Robert sat up shakily. There was nothing he could do now. He pulled out his telescope. Heads and half-submerged bodies were bobbing downstream. He couldn't make out who they were. None of them looked like Dickon or Rainbow or Jacko. Where was Arthur? Robert traversed upstream with his telescope, searching the far bank, the wrecked bridge. No sign of him. It seemed clear enough C-S had ordered the charge because he saw a chance of glory and wanted to grab it before General Garcia could snatch it from him. Angry with C-S, angry with Rainbow, angry with himself, Robert stumbled towards the field hospital. He'd offer his services—anything to keep his mind occupied.

≈

The makeshift hospital was no more than a roped-off bit of ground in which the stretchers were placed. The wounded lay in the blazing sun, their wounds thick with flies. Officers galloped by on urgent business, raising a whitish dust which settled on the supine figures, rendering their faces a deathly ashen colour. As if a door had closed, the groans and sobs faded from Robert's hearing. He was looking at the broken and burned body of Arthur. His moustache had been singed off. Robert knew he was dying and that there was nothing he could do to prevent it. Arthur turned his head. A flutter of recognition crossed his face.

'Last fence, old fruit!'

His cold hand found Robert's. 'Don't let me die alone.'

Robert squeezed his hand. 'I'm here, Arthur. I'm with you. I won't leave you.'

Arthur began to quiver and moan. Robert leapt to his feet and seized a passing orderly by the arm.

'He's in pain! Can't you do something?'

The orderly wrenched free. His hand slid over the label on the bottle he was carrying.

'What's in that?' Robert demanded. 'Let me see!'

'It is to dull pain, sir.'

'For God's sake, give him some then!'

The orderly shook his head. 'Reserved for the rank of major and above, sir. Almost empty, anyway.'

Robert grasped him by the lapels and shook him. 'You must! You must!'

The orderly pushed him away.

'I'll pay you for it!' Robert panted.

The orderly waited. Robert ransacked his pockets. Another moan escaped Arthur's clenched teeth. Robert thrust a handful of coins into the orderly's hand and snatched the bottle. He knelt beside Arthur again, pressing the bottle to his lips. He stroked Arthur's matted hair. Arthur let out a gurgle. It might even have been a laugh. Looking into Arthur's vacant face, Robert knew that he was cradling a lifeless body.

33

Yaba's breasts were brushing Rainbow's eyelids. Now the erect nipples, set in their deep purple areolae were teasing his lips, inviting his tongue to lick them. Yaba moved on down, pressing herself against his chest before enclosing his penis in her cleavage. Rainbow clasped her buttocks, shifting her so that he could enter her pulsating, vibrating body—vibrating so hard that flakes of stone fell from the ceiling onto his face. He sat up. A faint yellowish light seeped through the barred grille above his head. Next to him, on the straw-covered floor of the damp cell lay Monkey and Yansam's child, Dickon. Rainbow hugged his knees. There were so many things he still didn't understand. Any shaman, whose senses were properly trained, would know that Dickon was Yansam's son, so why did she pretend it was not so? If it was an attempt to conceal him from her enemies it had failed. Powerful influences were abroad, magical forces which reduced warriors to helpless laughter and produced violent explosions and made Skyherd, a god whose element was air, not water, try to plunge into a raging torrent. Rainbow banged his head against the wall. He had struck Skyherd. What else could he have done?

≈

The shadows of the bars, cast upon the stone floor, were like the tall, straight trees of the forest. A slender young woman, a basket balanced on her head, was approaching him along a narrow forest trail. He stepped aside to let her pass. Their eyes met, her arm brushed against his, then her erect back and swaying hips dissolved into the filtered forest light. His first sight of Yaba. But the shadows on the floor were not trees, they were bars—bars and bolted doors that shut out many things and kept others locked in. How he envied his fellow shaman, Arthur. Rainbow had seen him being lifted from the river. Clearly his mission in the Other World was over. He was returning to his real body in the Mortal World. At this very moment he was probably waking from his trance, being greeted by his family and friends.

Jacko stirred. 'If we was back in the Old Smoke, this'd be a cushy lurk and no mistake. Slept in plenty worse. We had some good times there, didn't we, guv? Remember the fair? And the Wild Man of Borneo?

You saw him, too, didn't you, Dickon? …You awake, Dickon?'

'I am now.' He started to shiver. 'We shouldn't have charged. We should never have charged!'

His shivering became worse. Rainbow removed his violet coat and laid it over him.

≈

'Tell us another story, Rainbow,' Dickon said. 'It helps the time go by.'

'One day,' Rainbow began, 'Exu came walking along a path between two fields. Seeing a farmer in either field, he donned a hat which was red on one side and white on the other. When the two farmers went home to their village at the end of the day, the one said to the other, 'Did you see that old fool go by today in the red hat?' To which the other farmer replied. 'It was not a red hat, it was a white hat. I saw it with my own two eyes.' 'You must be blind,' declared the first. 'You must have been drunk,' retorted the second. The argument became so heated that they came to blows and had to be brought before the headman of the village. At the trial, Exu was in the crowd, enjoying his prank.'

'Oh yes! I like Exu!' Jacko exclaimed. 'We'd see eye to eye and no mistake!'

'Is that one of those stories with another meaning?' Dickon asked.

'Maybe,' replied Rainbow. 'If you can find one, then it has.'

There was a distant rumble. The cell vibrated. Bits of stone rattled to the floor.

Rainbow sat down with a thump and began rocking to and fro.

'What's up, guv?'

'Don't you feel it? Don't you feel the current of power, the earth's energy? Don't you hear the birds fly up from the trees?'

A massive roaring judder shook he cell. With a noise like gunshot, a crack opened up across the floor, through which water spurted. A large block fell from the ceiling. More rubble followed. The shaking stopped.

Rainbow looked up at the gap where the grille had been. Even with one of the boys standing on his shoulders, it was out of reach. The straw was afloat now in the rapidly flooding cell. Waraqocha, God of the Shaking Earth had broken the grille for them and soon the rising water would float them up to within reach of the opening. It was to be expected, of course, that Water would come to the aid of the son of the

Water Goddess. Perhaps she had sent it.

≈

Rainbow calculated that within his next one hundred heartbeats the brand he held aloft to light their way, the one which had been in the passageway above the grille, would burn itself out. They had tried to retrace the route by which they had been brought to their cell, only to find the way blocked by a rock-fall.

Jacko whispered, 'We passed a kind of shaft a little way back... above that heap of twisted metal. We could give it a go.'

≈

It was a narrow, vertical shaft, connecting one level of passage with another. Rainbow peered upwards. The twisted metal, he realized, was what had once been the lower half of a fixed ladder. The brand burned out. This was not the darkness of the night with its moon and stars and reflections, this was blackness so black as to have substance.

'Reckon there's only one person around here, guv, what can climb a chimley in the dark... Need a rope. Can't help you up wivout one, can I?'

Dickon said, 'Cadey read me a story once, in which the hero escaped out of a window by knotting his clothes together.'

≈

Between the three of them, with every piece of clothing put to use, they had about thirty feet of twisted, uneven, knotty line. Monkey disappeared into the cavity. Echoing sounds of struggling and gasping reached Rainbow as the rope inched upwards, then a weird, sharp, cracked call.

'Root-a-toot-toot!'

'Are you all right, Monkey?'

'Oh dear! Am I in a coal-hole?'

Rainbow laughed softly. 'No, Mr Punch, you are in a prison.'

≈

It was so like those awful days with Grimshaw, his chimney master, Jacko thought. There would be something about that in his letter. He missed its reassuring pressure in his pocket. It had been getting too worn and creased, so he now kept it in his small army-issue back-pack,

'Drummer-boys for the use of.' Just as well he hadn't been carrying it when he jumped into the river, or it would be a right soggy mess. . He'd never forget the day his mother had taken him to Grimshaw's yard. To see an uncle, she'd said. And then she'd slipped away while he wasn't looking. She'd tricked him. But the letter would explain it all—how she'd been deceived herself by Grimshaw in some way he couldn't quite... that came later in the letter. And there was a whole page where she begged for his forgiveness. What about the drinking? She must say something about that. He couldn't bear it if Carrots went the same way. She was nothing like as bad yet, but supposing...

Loose stones rattled down the shaft, followed by curses from Jacko.

The bottom end of the rope rose from the floor, higher and higher. A shout from above. Then silence.

'Monkey?'

'Found the friggin ladder... Seems... safe enough... ' A shower of grit descended. 'Well, almost. Send up Dickon.'

By standing on Rainbow's shoulders, Dickon could just reach the end of the makeshift rope. He, too, faded up the shaft.

≈

'I been thinking,' Jacko said as Dickon's head appeared dimly at the top of the shaft.

'What?'

'You know how your mum has been captured by the Royalists... they probably got her in a cell somewhere.'

Dickon untied the rope with trembling hands. 'My mother? What do you mean?'

'Mrs Thomson... Cadey.... She's your mum, ain't she?'

'What! I... I... Why do you say that?'

'You're having me on, Dickon! Of course she is! Rainbow thinks so. And Carrots spotted it donkey's years ago. Wasn't fooled by her giving herself a different name, oh no. Let it slip one night when she was a bit rat-arsed.'

Jacko lowered the rope again. 'Like fishing, isn't it?

Dickon gripped his arm. 'What did she say?'

'Nothing much. Just that it was bleedin' obvious if you thought about it and had two eyes in your head.'

Dickon's cry echoed down the tunnel.

≈

Alone and naked in the dark, Rainbow waited... Like he'd waited in the darkened hut, while Ikpoom drummed softly outside the entrance, on and on... waiting for the force to suck him into the long, dark tunnel, waiting to make his first spirit journey, miserable that he was a disappointment to Ikpoom.

'If only your Orisha Animal would come to you,' Ikpoom had said. 'Once you have an Orisha Animal you can feel it pulling you through.'

What would Ikpoom think of him now? Would he be pleased with him? But why was it all taking so long?

≈

Fully clothed again after a desperate struggle with knots, they moved slowly forward. A rat scurried past. They came to a fork in the tunnel. Rainbow stopped. He could hear the breathing of the other two behind him.

Jacko spoke, his voice echoing along both ways. 'What was that friggin' lump in the rope, Dickon? Wasn't the little-get-up-man was it?'

'Uh? What?'

'The little-get-up-man. Have you got it?'

'Yes. It's my lucky charm. Why?'

''Cos you're forgettin' it's a tinder-box. We can get a light off it, see.'

'What good would that do?'

'Dunno. Better'n nuffink.'

Dickon found it in his pocket, fumbled with it, dropped it, found it again, then fumbled some more.

'Here, let me do it,' Jacko said and Dickon didn't protest.

≈

The tinder flared up long enough for Rainbow to see the true message wise Monkey had been sending him when he explored the wooden figure in the darkness, opened it, found another hidden inside and yet another until the source of light was discovered. The tinder flared again and Rainbow saw the vertebrae of some small animal, picked clean, scattered on the ground.

'Ah! Now the gods will light the way for us!'

Kneeling, he gathered three of the bones and cast them on the ground, studying the way they fell by the light of the flickering flame in Jacko's hand.

'We go left.'

≈

The left-hand tunnel took a steady upward incline.

Jacko said, 'Think I hear something above us, guv.'

They stopped and listened.

Rainbow said, 'It sounds like a herd of cattle.'

'Or the Thames when it's really flowing,' Jacko said.

They moved on, cautious and uncertain.

34

It mattered nothing to Robert that the British Brigade was marching into Cerro de Puna, feted as conquerors and heroes and that he was part of it. It was of no importance to him that the carnage at the river had not been the military set-back it seemed. He could raise no interest in the fact that the really decisive engagement hadn't involved the military at all, but the two opposing armies of camp-followers. Led by the mysterious Golpetina, Las Golpetinas had crossed the river further upstream and fought a pitched battle with their counterparts. The Royalist camp-followers had been routed, leaving behind their cattle and a great many essentials for providing food, shelter and comfort for their fighting men. The sudden loss of the support they relied upon for daily existence in this harsh terrain and the threat of being outflanked by fierce amazons had been too much for the Royalist general. Instead of continuing on to Cerro de Puna with his reinforcements, he had ordered a retreat. The Royalist garrison in Cerro de Puna, on learning that the expected reinforcements were not coming, had surrendered. None of it seemed to matter or to pierce Robert's grief. Arthur was dead and Dickon was missing—that was what mattered.

≈

They entered the city to the cheers of the inhabitants. Throughout the ranks of the British Brigade snatches of 'Brave British Bill' started up. How Arthur would have loved it, Robert thought. He would be slapping his thighs and laughing that boyish laugh, enjoying the absurdity of it all.

Muldoon took Manco's bridle. 'Begging your pardon, sorr, if… when the young major turns up, he'll need you all cheerful-like, sorr.'

'No news of him and the others?'

'No, sorr. Maybe the occifers high-jinks tonight will cheer you up, sorr.'

Robert gave a bitter laugh. 'You mean the impromptu banquet General Garcia has ordered the mayor to give? I don't think I could face it.'

Dear God, when the Royalists took Cadey prisoner, they would have brought her here. And she would have been set free by now. She'd be waiting to greet Dickon. And he, Robert, who had promised to look after him, would have to break the news that her son was missing, presumed drowned.

'He can swim, can't he, sorr?'

'Yes, but we shouldn't clutch at… Oh, this is awful! Terrible! Talk about something else, Muldoon.'

'Do you think Smithy will be here, sorr?'

According to military intelligence, the majority of Patriot and British prisoners had been taken to Cerro de Puna.

Robert said, 'There's a good chance, I suppose. Kate's counting on it, I know.'

With any luck Smithy was still alive. But not Arthur. His grave was beside the river, just a mound of earth in a row of other mounds, each with a simple wooden cross on it.

≈

The banquet was in full swing in the spacious central courtyard of the mayor's residence—a beautiful quadrangle with hanging gardens, tinkling fountains and numerous little alcoves, all open to the starlit sky. Robert sat with his unopened sketch-book on his knee, wondering how Muldoon had cajoled him into going. He knew he should be recording it all for the *Chronicle*. It was just what Sir Charles would want—titles longer than your arm, gold braid by the mile, medals by the ton. He just hadn't the heart for it. He toyed with his food, the eleventh of fourteen courses, and stared at C-S, seated at the top table. His satisfied smirk so clearly announced that the loss of life which his own overbearing self-importance, his arrogance and his lust for glory had caused, perturbed him not one jot.

Robert's table vibrated gently. An elaborate edifice of jelly shivered on a plate. The wine in his glass slopped from side to side. A minor tremor. They didn't amount to much, Robert had discovered, when you were out in the open.

≈

Over the rim of his wine glass, C-S's eyes were boring into Robert's. From his waistcoat pocket C-S drew several sheets of thin rice-paper. Robert's mouth went dry. The paper was very like the kind he used for writing to Mama. Exactly like, in fact, and the handwriting looked like his own and was in the same shade of blue ink that he used. Was it his letter to his mother which had blown away at the same time as his report on the battle for Aposa? Had someone found it and sold it to C-S? Maybe his host of informers had heard it had been found and C-S had gone out of his way to acquire it.

≈

C-S unfolded the paper, a contemptuous sneer on his face. He half turned to his neighbour. Robert was on his feet, a scream of protest rising in his throat, when C-S folded the letter again. C-S stood up, pocketed the letter and strolled towards the screens behind which were rows of chamber-pots and basins. Robert followed him.

'From now on, Stanhope, you'll write in your reports exactly what I tell you to. Is that clear, you pathetic apology for a man?'

'What if I don't?'

C-S held up the letter.. Oh what fun I'll have with it! With you! I can read it out in the mess.' C-S assumed a high-pitched prissy voice. 'Dearest Mama... I feel such a cissy compared to the others... I am terrified! ...And I've never told you or anyone this before, but... '

'All right! All right! I agree!'

'Good. You'll get your first note from me tonight.'

C-S returned to his table. Robert knelt over a basin and heaved up his meal. Worse than the vomit was the taste of failure. Sheer panic had taken over, his budding confidence in himself had deserted him and he'd run for safety. Someone came in. Robert pretended to be unbuttoning his britches. The man relieved himself and left. On the other side of the screens, in the banqueting area, a Patriot officer was reaching the end of a recital of General Garcia's many honours. Now the general was rising to his feet to propose a toast to Simon Bolivar... a lengthy business since the Great Liberator was even better endowed than his general with titles and honours. Then, while Robert sat amongst the chamber-pots, Carlton-Syms launched into a long and vainglorious speech in which he gave himself all the credit for the British Brigade's occupation of Cerro de Puna—the sort of thing, Robert realised, he'd have to send to the *Chronicle* and call his own.

≈

Through a gap in the screens, Robert's listless gaze alighted on a flagstone in the centre of the quadrangle. It shifted slightly, then slowly rose upwards. Dickon's mud-spattered head appeared. He clambered out, looking around as if searching for someone. Robert stepped out from behind the screens and raised a hand. Dickon saw him, but his eyes moved on past him. C-S paused, mid-sentence, to stare at him.

Dickon saluted. 'I thought you might want to know the time, sir.'

Rainbow and Jacko emerged, blinking like moles, as waves of laughter broke over them. Carlton-Syms' speech was forgotten. Dickon's fellow-officers crowded round him to shake him warmly by the hand and hear his story. Still Dickon's eyes roamed the courtyard.

'Where's Mrs Thomson?' he demanded, cutting through several questions at once.

There was an awkward silence. People looked at each other, only now remembering she should have been here in Cerro de Puna. Dickon turned in Robert's direction, his expression clearly an appeal to be rescued. Robert pushed through to him.

'You must be exhausted, Dickon.'

Dickon turned and shook Jacko warmly by the hand. 'Thank you, thank you, Jacko.' He put his small hand into Rainbow's huge fist. 'And you, Rainbow. I wouldn't be standing here, but for you two.'

Jacko was looking around in wonder. 'There's going to be rich pickin's in the bins in the back of this place tonight!'

Dickon laughed. 'And even richer pickings if you sit down right here, Jacko.'

He gave instructions that his two companions be treated to the feast they so richly deserved.

But Rainbow shook his head. 'You stay, Jacko. I shall find Snail and tell her you are safe.'

Dickon allowed Robert to lead him away, without so much as a glance at the dishes which had been set before them.

≈

'What's the matter, Boser?'

'I'll be all right in a minute.'

Robert steered him out of the quadrangle and along a shady veranda which looked across a well-watered ornamental park with a large glasshouse in the middle of it. At the end of the veranda was Robert's allotted suite of rooms.

≈

Inside Robert's quarters, Dickon burst into tears. Robert sat with an arm around the boy.

'I thought she'd be here. Why isn't she here, Boser?'

'I don't know. I thought she'd be here, too. I'm sure she's all right.'

'I hate her!'

'No, you don't.'

'I thought I was one person and… and I'm not. I'm someone else.'

'How did you find out, Dickon?'

Dickon explained.

'Why didn't she tell me, Boser? She obviously told you. All that stuff about telling the truth and she was lying to me all the time. She knew how much I wished I had a mother!'

'And she's been longing to tell you, to call you her son, to be a proper mother to you, to hold you and hug you.'

'Why didn't she, then? She can't have wanted to all that much.'

'Believe me, Dickon, she does. If you only knew how hard it's been for her, pretending all the time, trying not to show how very, very much she loves you.'

'Then where is she now? Where is she, Boser?'

'I wish I knew.'

Dickon blew his nose, sucked in air and gave way to fresh tears. Robert gave him another hug.

Dickon looked up at him. 'Arthur… he wasn't there at that banquet thing. Is he?'

'He's dead, Dickon. He died of his wounds.'

Dickon buried his face in the pillow and kept it there. Robert thought he'd fallen asleep, overcome by nervous and physical exhaustion. Then the boy raised his head.

'I think I knew.'

'Do you mean about Cadey… about your mother, or about Arthur?'

'I… I meant Arthur… Cadey… no, I had no idea. I… I still can't take it in, not really.'

'Say it aloud, Dickon. Say 'Cadey is my mother and she loves me.' …Go on, say it.'

Dickon fiddled with his watch. ' Hasn't worked since I got a ducking in the river… And another thing—if all prisoners were set free when Cerro de Puna surrendered, why weren't we?

'I don't know, Dickon. Maybe because the official prisons were full and you were put somewhere else and were then forgotten about in the panic to get away. And don't try to change the subject!'

'Do you have the book she gave me?'

'Say it, Dickon.'

'I feel… I don't know… shy or something.' He punched the pillow, keeping time with his words. 'She's my mother. Cadey is my mother.'

'Louder!'

'Cadey is my mother!'

'And?'

'And she loves me.'

Robert drew him close. 'It must be terribly hard for you, Dickon. I think you're managing wonderfully well.'

There was a knock on the door. Muldoon's head appeared. 'Glad you're safe, sorr,' he said gruffly. 'I'm not sure you two gents should be allowed near the fireworks—you might put 'em out! But if you're interested they'll be starting soon.'

Robert shook his head. 'An early night's what the young major needs. A good long sleep will do wonders for you, Dickon. I'll stay with you.'

≈

Robert tossed and turned in his unfamiliar, wide bed, trying to curb the violence of his movements so as not to wake Dickon. On the other side of the park fireworks whizzed and banged. Cerro de Puna was famous for its fireworks. The town contained several establishments which manufactured them for the carnivals, festivals and fiestas which… how had Arthur expressed it? Which dotted the Peruvian calendar more liberally than lead shot in a poacher's bum. Oh, Arthur, I miss you. Tonight the factories were vying with each other to produce the loudest and most dazzling effect. Robert flung himself onto his other side, jack-knifing his body, tense with his scalding anger with C-S, his disappointment with himself that he'd been too weak to resist blackmail. A hand covered Robert's mouth. Carroty Kate's face was close to his.

'Get up, but don't wake the young major,' she hissed in his ear. 'Someone outside to see you.'

Robert followed her onto the veranda. Waiting for him was the same wounded soldier on crutches and with a bandaged face to whom Arthur had spoken in Huajuahin. The soldier stared steadily at Robert.

Robert said, 'I deeply regret to have to tell you Captain Trevellyn was killed in action at the bridge.'

The soldier nodded and continued to stare. A firework burst overhead.

Robert said, 'But if I can help in any... '

'You don't recognise me, do you, Robert?'

'Cadey? Is that you, Cadey?'

'Sh! Not so loud! Yes, of course it's me.'

Robert rushed forward and hugged her. 'Cadey, I've missed you!'

Cadey dropped her crutches and returned the hug. 'Me too.' She pointed to the open door and Robert's rooms. 'Dickon's in there, I'm told.'

'Yes. He's sleeping.'

'Is he all right?'

'Depends what you mean. He's come through the disaster at the bridge and his capture and escape without harm, But... He knows.' Robert glanced uneasily in Carroty Kate's direction.

Carroty Kate thumped the butt of her musket on the tiles. 'If it's me knowing Cadey's his mother that's worrying you... guessed it even before she told me.'

'How's he taking it?' Cadey asked.

'The poor boy's very confused.'

Robert related how Dickon had found out.

'And what about you, Cadey? Why are you dressed like that? I'm sure C–S would find it very unbecoming.'

Cadey laughed. While fireworks flared and exploded, she told her story. The party escorting her to Lima had not been intercepted by Spanish Royalists, but by Arthur and a group of friends, disguised as Royalists. The business about her being held prisoner in Cerro de Puna was to cover the fact that, all the time, she had been with the British

Brigade's camp-followers.

'Oh my pippin! You're… You're Golpetina!'

'Best friggin leader we could 'ave!' Carroty Kate declared.

Cadey's eyes were on the open door. 'Sleeping, you say?'

Robert nodded. He could see what an effort she had to make to speak of anything or anybody but Dickon.

'Robert, I promised Rainbow I would speak to you at the first opportunity.'

'How did he know who you were?'

She shrugged. 'He seems to have ways of knowing things. He came to me because he is desperately worried you won't forgive him for hitting you. He saved Dickon's life in the river. The least I could do was promise to speak to you on his behalf. It's all he seemed to want.'

'Of course he's forgiven. I'll tell him so.'

Cadey began to unwind the bandage from her face. 'I… I won't wake him. Just a peep. But just in case he does, I don't want to frighten him.'

≈

Robert and Carroty Kate remained outside.

'You'll keep this under your hat, her being Golpetina, won't you, sir?'

'Yes, of course. I dread to think what C-S would do if he found out.'

'She'd make a better job of commanding the Brigade than Carlton-Friggin'-Syms, that's for certin.'

'Did you get word that Jacko is safe?'

Her face softened. 'Yeah. And I seen him, too. Pretended he was starving the little bugger, but I'd heard how he'd laid into the grub at the officers' do.'

Cadey appeared in the doorway. She turned for another look, her face tender.

Dickon's voice, sleepy, uncertain, hopeful. 'Cadey? …Mother?'

'Oh Dickon, my very own, darling boy!'

Carroty Kate took Robert by the arm. Tears were running down her freckled cheeks.

'Time for us to bugger off and leave 'em to it.'

≈

They sat together on a park bench.

≈254≈

'I should have asked sooner, Kate. Was Smithy among the prisoners released today?'

'No, he wasn't. He bloody wasn't.'

'I'm so sorry.'

'Yeah, me too. I'm about ready to give up. How long can a body go on hoping and waiting?'

35

Rainbow sat on a bench outside the heated glasshouse in the grounds of the Mayor's residence. Overhead, fireworks crackled and banged and flooded the night with cascades of light. His attention, though, was not on the fireworks, but on the thwack of water on waxy leaves. He could almost believe it was rain drumming on the high forest canopy, dripping and splashing through the foliage. Spray issued from overhead pipes, wetting the plants. The glasshouse was filled with specimens collected from the Peruvian jungle, a place very different from the high, arid plateau of the Western Andes. Leaves and flowers and human skin glistened in the moonlight. Rainbow turned. Carroty Kate was standing beside him.

'Like washday in the workhouse in there,' she said.

Rainbow could see from her expression that she had not found Smithy.

'No sign of him, then?'

She shook her head. 'There's three prisons in this effing town where our men were kept and he ain't on the list for none of them. He's not here and that's that. Feels like all I ever done is wait for him to come back to me. But he ain't coming, is he?'

She sat down next to him and began to cry. Rainbow put a comforting arm around her. Someone was running towards them. Jacko appeared out of the dark.

Guv! Carrots! I think it's Smithy. Come quick!'

≈

With fireworks banging and blossoming in the sky, they raced through the wealthy part of Cerro de Puna, past the high-walled gardens and patios and windows guarded by ornamental ironwork. To a boy who could climb like a monkey, a window left open and an adjacent drainpipe made an irresistible combination. The house Jacko had entered seemed to be deserted. In his pocket he still had the little-get-up-man which he had used in the dungeons—now Dickon's, but he had forgotten to return it. He found a candle, lit it and began exploring the house. An eerie whining filled the gloom, rising and falling. Out of the corner of his eye, Jacko saw something move very fast into the shadows.

'I might have let out a yell,' Jacko panted. 'You know, just to scare it off, whatever it was.'

And then a voice, a man's voice, weak and thin, had called out. 'Who's there? Is anyone there?'

The voice had come from the other side of a locked door.

Jacko had shouted, 'Who are you?'

'William Smith.'

At that point, the ghostly noise began again, much closer, and Jacko had fled back to his open window.

'Is he a prisoner in there, or what?' asked Carroty Kate.

'I don't know, but he got strange company in that house and no mistake.'

≈

The outer doors of the house were all locked. The open window on the second floor was too small for anyone but a child to squeeze through.

'I ain't going in there alone a second time,' Jacko declared.

Carroty Kate pulled a pistol from the pocket of her greatcoat. 'How about this for company?'

Jacko hefted the weapon in his hand, his eyes shining. As he moved towards the drainpipe Carroty Kate caught him by the arm.

'Jacko... if... if it is Smithy in there, I want you to know... it don't make no difference to you and me.'

She drew Jacko to her. He nestled in her embrace for several minutes before saying,

'Carrots... I... I was scared to let on about him.'

'It's all right, Jacko, I understand. And thanks. Ow! For fuck's sake watch what you're doing with that pistol!'

Jacko stuck the pistol in his belt, patted his pockets to make sure he still had his candle and his little-get-up-man, grasped the drainpipe in both hands and swarmed up it.

'Good luck!' Carroty Kate called.

≈

Rainbow and Carroty Kate waited on the street.

'Where the fuck's he got to?'

≈

After what seemed a long time, they heard a key turning in the front door and bolts being drawn back. Jacko, lighted candle in hand, beckoned them in.

'This is a toff's house all right,' Carroty Kate said.

'There is something dead in here,' Rainbow said.

Jacko let out an oath. 'And here it is! What in Hell did this?'

The remains of a dog lay in a corner. Something had devoured it, leaving only the paws and scattered bones. In another corner was an empty cage.

'That might have been me,' Jacko said and his hand trembled so much that Rainbow took the candle from him.

Carroty Kate eased the front door open a crack. 'Who knows but we might want to get out extra bloody quick.'

≈

Two flights of wide, curving steps led up to opposite sides of a gallery. With Rainbow holding the candle aloft they cautiously mounted the stairs, passing waist-high Inca vases.

'That's it,' Jacko said, pointing to a door at the head of the gallery.

'Smithy?' Carroty Kate called.

No answer. She called again.

Jacko slapped his forehead 'Friggin' 'ell, I remember now!' Jacko said. 'It was the other stairway, t'other side. A darker door!'

≈

The deep claw marks in the varnished wood were plain to see. Strong teeth had gnawed away the bottom corner of the door. Jacko drew the pistol from his belt.

'Smithy, are you in there?'

'Kate? Am I dreaming? Is it really you?'

'Oh Jesus! It's you, Smithy! It is, it bloody is!'

'Kate! My Kate!'

Rainbow called out, 'How do we open the door?'

'I think there's a key on the ledge above. Be careful… there's something out there and it's hungry.'

Rainbow felt for the key, found it and unlocked the door. Smithy, wearing a black cassock which was much too big for him, emerged holding a lantern. Carroty Kate rushed forward into his arms.

Some instinct made Rainbow turn. Two large yellow eyes reflected the lantern's gleam.

'Behind you, Monkey!'

Jacko whipped round, let out a yell and fired the pistol. A vase exploded into a hundred pieces. Spitting and snarling the beast, no more than a dark shadow, streaked down the stairs and out of the front door.

'Whatever it was, it's not my idea of a household pet,' Smithy grunted.

Carroty Kate removed one arm from round Smithy. 'This young crack shot here is Jacko.'

Smithy gripped Jacko's hand. 'You're the one brought Kate to me. I owe you, Jacko. I owe you big.'

Carroty Kate beamed. 'And this is my friend, Rainbow.'

'Much obliged to you, too, Rainbow,' Smithy said, offering him his hand.

≈

As they started down the stairs, Rainbow stooped and picked something out of the sand which had acted as ballast in the shattered vase. He held up an emerald. They passed it around, speculating whether it had been hidden there or had fallen in by accident. When Carroty Kate tried to hand it back to Rainbow, he wouldn't take it.

'Keep it. Green is the colour of new life. It marks the new life you will have with Smithy.'

'But you'll need it, Rainbow, to get you back to Africky.'

He shook his head. 'Your help in completing my mission is all I need and I have that already.'

'Thanks, Rainbow.' She grinned at him. 'Like I said before, you're a good man.' Two beefy arms hugged Jacko and Smithy close to her. 'It's a new beginning for the three of us.'

Jacko said, 'There's something else in the sand.' 'Seven stones!' A thought struck Smithy. 'Er... how old are you, Jacko?'

'About eleven, I think, near enough.'

Carroty Kate laughed. 'Yeah, Smithy, he's more than seven, anyroad.'

'I think,' said Jacko, 'There might be some grub and maybe some grog downstairs.'

≈

Smithy recounted how he had been taken out of the prison where the other soldiers were and brought to this house. The owner, he gathered, was a rich merchant by the name of Mario Valentes. It was a private deal, as far as Smithy could make out, no questions asked, no official records of the transaction. He had been locked in a room in which were bricks, mortar, a ladder, buckets of water—all that was needed for building a false wall at one end of the room. He was fed only if the wall progressed each day to the satisfaction of Mario Valentes. His prison was, in fact, a private chapel. Smithy passed a hand over his cassock. 'At least this kept me warm at nights.'

He was only guessing, but he reckoned what he was building was a hiding place for the merchant's wealth if the town fell to the Patriots. And Valentes didn't want a local person doing it—someone who might betray his secret. A British prisoner, unknown to anyone, who could disappear afterwards and not be missed, suited Valentes much better. However, Cerro de Puna had surrendered unexpectedly and Valentes and his family had left in a hurry, leaving Smithy locked in the chapel and a starving wild animal at large in the house.

'After it done in the dog—and it weren't a pretty thing to hear—the only thing worth eating in the house was me.'

'Weren't you starving too?' Carroty Kate asked.

'Bet you never thought your Smithy would take the holy sacraments. Well, I did. I drank the holy wine and scoffed those thin pancake things, a whole box of 'em.'

And then, tucked away in the confessional, he'd found a bottle of cognac and half of a large fruit cake, and the water in the flower vases was drinkable—just.

'Even if I wasn't locked in, reckon I'd have stayed put with that thing roaming about. You was lucky it didn't get you, Jacko. Maybe its heart was set on me by the time you showed up.'

≈

Carroty Kate and Jacko brought Smithy up to date with what had been going on in the Brigade.

Carroty Kate winked at Jacko. 'And somebody you knows very well got himself a medal for bravery.'

'Who would that be now? Can't say as I knows anyone that stupid.'

'You, Smithy, that's who!'

She produced the medal from her pocket and handed it to him. 'Maybe you didn't do all them things they said, but you could of.'

'Yeah, could of,' Smithy said, slugging some cognac from a cut-glass decanter. 'I've been thinking,' he said. 'Even with that Carlton-Syms person in charge, I'm going back to the regiment. I couldn't desert on my mates, tempting though it is.'

Carroty Kate nodded her assent. She lifted one of the several lanterns Jacko had collected. 'Back soon.'

≈

When she returned, she was wearing a full-length evening gown.

'Wow, Carrots!' Jacko breathed. 'You're like one of them ladies what step from the carriages.'

Smithy stared at her open-mouthed. 'Maybe I won't go back to the regiment till tomorrow... or perhaps the day after.'

'For you,' she said, tossing a bundle of clothes at him.

They danced in each other's arms, Carroty Kate in a gown too small for her, split at the waist and undone at the back where the fastenings would not reach; Smithy in a brocade evening coat that could have accommodated two of him. On the polished parquet floor of the entrance hall, they slowly gyrated, keeping time to a rhythm only they could hear.

Rainbow said, 'I had a look outside. The firework display is reaching a... what is the word? ...a... '

'The best bit?' Jacko said eagerly.

'Yes. Do you want to come and watch it with me, Jacko?'

'Do I? Does a snossage want mustard!'

Over Smithy's shoulder, Carroty Kate threw Rainbow a grateful glance.

≈

To obtain a better view, Jacko and Rainbow walked up the small hill on which the Mayor's residence was situated. The fireworks had brought Robert onto his veranda. The three of them watched while Jacko gabbled out the tale of Carroty Kate, Smithy and the mysterious beast.

≈

Rockets invaded the sky, trailing animals in coloured tissue-paper. Whoosh! A condor. Whoosh, whoosh! A crocodile, a monkey. Whoosh! A jaguar.

Rainbow said, 'Here they call him Jaguar, but my people call him Shoshobi, the Leopard. He is the spirit of Trickster and of Exu. Shoshobi, the Leopard who does not know himself, is one of the many forms assumed by Exu.'

Shoshobi represented the unknown, hidden things. It was Monkey who had driven the leopard out of the house and into the open. It was Monkey who had told Dickon that Yansam was his mother. The jaguar twisted through the sky and began to dip.

'Exu, when he is Trickster, never brings only good or only bad, but always both together. He… '

≈

Muldoon hove into sight, a concerned frown across his brow.

'Bad news, sorr.'

'What now?'

'The carrier-pigeons, sorr. All in one compound, sorr. All killed by a wild beast what broke in. They say the paw marks were made by a jaguar.'

'All dead?'

'The lot, sorr. Not you nor anybody can send off reports, sorr.'

Robert jumped up and down on the veranda, waving his arms and shouting with relief.

'I can't send my fake reports! Do you hear that, C–S? Do you hear that? Thank you, Trickster, whoever you might be! Thank you, gods of the Lost Crossroads!'

36

Three weeks after the burning of Cerro de Puna, Robert was in a mountain village making potato soup, while an old woman sat outside, singing. Across a steeply terraced valley on whose slopes grew maize and quinoa, was the Royalist-held town of Santa Rosa. Robert looked around the stable which was his temporary quarters. Everything was in order—his camp-bed, his writing-desk, his stacks of canvases and paintings. He fanned the fire which smouldered beneath a blackened pot. The soup was for Dickon. Normally, Muldoon would have been making it, but Robert had given him the day off.

'It's the ancient ruins, sorr, I'm keen to inspect them.'

'If I know you, Muldoon, you'll be the only ruin around here by tomorrow morning.'

But Muldoon's expression had been that of a dog waiting to be thrown its favourite slipper and Robert had let him go. Besides, he was glad of a chance to cook for Dickon, whose own batman had been pressed into military duties, such was the shortage of fighting men. The boy, Robert thought, had adjusted with remarkable speed to the discovery that Cadey was his mother. Since she could not reveal herself as long as C-S was in command, the two of them, with the help of Robert, Carroty Kate, Muldoon and Rainbow, met in secret.

Robert put his head out of the stable door and called to the old woman, 'Is that you, Cadey? Come in.'

'You're not supposed to recognise me, Robert.'

Robert smiled. 'I've heard you singing that song to Dickon.'

She saw the soup simmering. 'Is he coming?'

'I hope so.'

'How's he doing? I see so little of him now. I do what I can to help him, but it's never enough.'

Robert reassured her, telling her that she had seen more clearly than anyone how appallingly inefficient the British Light Horse and the Brigade as a whole were in their catering arrangements compared to the average household run by a woman. Her influence had made a difference in Dickon's squadron, at least. They were better fed and in better health than anyone else in the Brigade.

Cadey flushed with pleasure. 'And thanks to you, Robert, there are fewer casualties in his squadron than in any other.'

When they were out on patrol, away from the prying eyes of C-S and his yes-men, Dickon's squadron put net and sacking over their scarlet uniforms. As Robert had explained to Dickon, any wild animal in Beechwood Chase knew the advantages of blending with the landscape.

'Strictly against the Code of course,' Robert said to Cadey with a grin.

Cadey slapped her thighs. 'Capital!' She realised what she'd done. 'Sorry, Robert, so sorry.'

'It's all right… I do miss him… I miss him more than I can say.'

'Maybe one day you'll find that you can say. It can never be wrong to love someone.'

They stared into the fire until Cadey broke the silence. 'Did you hear we captured an American gun-runner this morning?'

'No.'

'He had a couple of Kentucky long-range rifles on him, although it was obvious his mules had been carrying a lot more. We traded him his freedom for the information that he had sold one hundred of them to the Royalists in Santa Rosa. It was meant to be a military secret, a nasty surprise for the British. You see, Robert, they have a range half as long again as our muskets..

'I hope you've passed on this information to C-S.'

'Not yet. We—Las golpetinas, I mean—may be able to use it to our advantage.'

'I think you're right, Cadey.'

'And we took a pile of money off him too. And that will certainly come in handy. You know, with those rifles you can tear up the army training manuals, and you can burn the rule books. And another thing… What are you laughing at, Robert?'

'Oh, nothing. Just the way you're striding about in so un-crone-like a way.'

She stared out angrily at Santa Rosa. The town, well equipped with canon, guarded the approaches to Puerto Grande, the only sizeable pass through the mountains for hundreds of miles. To gain access to the high passes and so cross this branch of the High Cordillera, the British Brigade had to go through Puerto Grande, and to do that they must first take Santa Rosa. General Sucre and a Patriot force were on the other side of the mountains, soon to engage the main Royalist army. The British Brigade had orders to cross the Cordillera and attack the enemy in the rear—assuming that they could first take Santa Rosa.

'I don't like what C-S is planning,' Cadey said. 'A frontal assault on Santa Rosa is sheer madness. It will be a bloodbath. His mind's on glory, not on the lives of his men. He doesn't care whether Dickon gets killed. He might even hope he does.'

≈

Preparations for the assault had begun and were likely to continue for at least another ten days—the building of emplacements from which to bombard the town, the construction of scaling-ladders, the training of the men.

≈

Robert sighed. 'How much longer is this war going on? When can we go home?'

'Soon, I hope. I've had my fill of killing and death. Violence doesn't solve much in the long run. I want to fight for liberty, but not like this.'

Robert tasted the soup and added salt. 'Like your father did, with public meetings and demonstrations?'

'In a way. I'd like to return to England and set up a free press; the kind of press that would expose poverty and inequality and rouse public opinion against slavery and say what really went on in this campaign.'

Robert grimaced. 'I haven't done very well in that department, have I?'

'Hardly your fault.'

'And what about Dickon?'

'This is no life for a boy his age.'

'I know that, but does he?'

'You see, Robert, while all this is going on, neither of us can… well, Dickon can't be a proper son to me and I can't be a proper mother to him. I think he wants that more than anything. I know I do.'

Robert cut slices of maize bread and put them on a wooden platter. 'You often talk about your father, but not about your mother. Tell me about her.'

'She was a devout Catholic. It was hard for her having a husband and daughter who didn't share her beliefs. My father could never understand how she could believe what she did when it seemed to him the evidence to the contrary was all around her. To have lost her faith would have killed her... And what about you, Robert, what will you do when all this is over?'

'I'm not sure... paint, of course, but what else or where, I'm not sure.'

'Robert, what's the matter?'

'I feel such a failure, Cadey.'

'That's nonsense! What on earth can you mean?'

'Oh, you know... I didn't stand up to C–S. I let him blackmail me.'

Cadey faced Robert and took him by the shoulders. 'Listen. You've been further from home than nine out of ten people in England; you've travelled through terrain that's tested hardened soldiers; you've been closer than most to blood and death... But, above all, you've got a special kind of courage, Robert—the courage to remain vulnerable. That's strength, not weakness. People respect you, Robert, yes, don't look so surprised. I know Las Golpetinas do, and the men of the regiment, too, and it's not because you're a poor imitation of what somebody thinks a man should be, but because you are yourself.'

She pushed Robert into his folding chair, the wooden soup spoon still in his hand. 'So don't let me hear you talk such bilge again!'

'Do you really think so?'

'I know so.'

'But, when C–S threatened me, I caved in.'

'Well, you haven't yet, not really. I mean you haven't actually sent off any false reports yet, have you?

'No, but only because the carrier pigeons were all killed.'

' There's bound to be a few setbacks, Robert. The difficulties of the internal journey we all make are every bit as real as this one we're making through Peru. Believe me, you're getting there slowly but surely... Oh! And talking of getting there slowly, I have to tell you, Robert, I heard this morning that a new supply of pigeons is on the way. Several dozen of them. It might be several weeks before they reach us yet, but… Oh my God! The soup's burning!'

She seized the wooden spoon from Robert and began vigorously stirring the pot. 'I think it'll be all right.' She laughed. 'Both you and the soup!'

'Thanks, Cadey, for saying all that.'

'And I'll tell you something else…'

Carroty Kate banged on the lower, closed half of the stable door. 'Thought you ought to take a gander at these,' she said, holding out some rather soiled papers.

Cadey took them. It was a complete list of the garrison of Santa Rosa. Carroty Kate explained that a small party of Golpetinas had caught a Royalist soldier sneaking over the town's outer wall and heading for a narrow mountain track behind the town. At first they'd thought he was a deserter, but he turned out to be a messenger.

'Thank goodness for bureaucratic inefficiency,' Cadey said. 'Their headquarters should have known that sort of thing.'

'Probably lost the file,' Robert said, thinking of the piles of paperwork he tried to keep in aorder for Dickon. 'I suppose we ought to hand it over to C-S.'

Carroty Kate grinned. 'Yeah, but not quite yet. Could be useful to Las Golpetinas. Not sure how, but you never know.'

'What did you do with the messenger?' Cadey asked.

'We let him go… after he'd satisfied Carmelita—a fate worse than death, if you ask me.' She held up a newspaper. 'There was this, too.'

Cadey skimmed through *El Tiempo*, occasionally asking Carroty Kate for assistance in translating a word.

'Strange how life goes on, even in the midst of war. Marriages and births… And there's going to be a bull-fight and an amateur production of 'Figaro' and… ' She stopped, her eyes wide with horror.

A horse was plodding towards them. Slumped in the saddle and covered in blood, was Dickon. Cadey rushed out. Dickon sat up with a jerk. For an instant he didn't recognise her. Then he said, 'Must have fallen asleep… Oh, this isn't my blood. It's… It's Tom Walker's. One of my best men. He was standing right by me and… ' It was horrible. The whole side of his face …'

'Hush, my darling. Come and change those clothes and there's hot soup waiting for you.'

Dickon sniffed the air. 'Smells good. Hunger makes the best sauce. Don Quixote said that, you know.'

Cadey's face lit up. 'You've been reading it, then?'

He smiled wearily. 'It's fun the way he can't tell what's real and what isn't... Tom... that was real enough. The bits that are like bad dreams seem to be the real bits now.'

'It will end soon.'

'Mother, this evening, will you go on telling me about my father.'

'If you want... Here's your soup, my love.'

≈

Dickon fell asleep at the table before he'd finished his soup. Cadey gently removed the bowl and placed a towel under his head. Beside him, she placed a wooden soldier and the little-get-up man she'd extracted from the pockets of his blood-soaked clothes.

'His lucky mascots,' she said. 'I feel his childhood has been cut short and, somehow, it's my fault. It should be some kind of magical other world and it hasn't been, not recently, anyway.'

Robert said, 'You're too hard on yourself, Cadey.'

'Yeah, that's not something Jacko's had much of, either.' Carroty Kate pushed the little-get-up-man down and watched it rock up again. 'He got it off Jacko then, I see. At this rate, our two lads are going to get knocked over any day now and they ain't going to bob up again, are they?'

Cadey waved a hand over Dickon's bloodied garments. 'And this was just a skirmish! What's going to happen when the assault on Santa Rosa really gets going?'

'It'll be Badajoz all over again,' Carroty Kate growled. 'And I don't mean Barnaby Thackston's version of it.'

'We have to do something.' Cadey said. 'We'll take the town ourselves, that's what we'll do! Las Golpetinas will take Santa Rosa! Only we'll do it our way, the women's way.'

Carroty Kate said, 'I reckon the Brigade will make its first assault ten days from now. So whatever we're going to do, we got to do it before then.'

'Exactly what do you have in mind?' Robert asked.

'I don't know,' Cadey replied, stroking Dickon's hair. 'But we'll think of something.'

Robert picked up the toy soldier which lay on *El Tiempo*. 'I think I have an idea,' he said.

37

In the shadow of the walls of Santa Rosa, a Punch and Judy show was in progress. Faces were beginning to peer over the battlements. Rainbow danced to the rhythm of Jacko's drumming. Robert and Cadey were squeezed inside the booth with Carroty Kate.

'In my way, that's what you are,' Carroty Kate barked. 'But you're worse than useless out front, the pair of you. Not what I'd call natural performers. Give the game away in no time flat, you would.'

'Sorry,' Cadey said meekly.

'Let's hope the place ain't full of swatchel omis or we'll be rumbled. They'll know you don't need three to manage the dolls.'

The dance ended. Coins rained from on high. Jacko yelped as one bounced off his head, bringing down a fresh shower upon himself. Punch began weeping as the hangman erected the gallows.

Carroty Kate shouted out her lines in her harsh, backs-street Spanish. 'Oh my wife and sixteen children, all of them twins!'

Try as he might, Punch could not get his head in the noose. 'Well, I never was hanged before and I don't know how to do it.'

'Well, Mr Punch, observe me. In the first place, I put my head in the noose... so.'

The battlements were now lined with soldiers, laughing and straining for a better view.

'Bugger this!' Punch shouted. 'I'm tired of yelling myself hoarse for you lot up there. I'm not doing the next bit until either you come down to me, or I come up to you. Don't you have any manners in Peru?'

An officer leaned over the battlements, 'How do we know it's not a trick?'

Punch leaned out of the stage. 'Of course it's a trick! I'm not real, you know. I'm only a puppet, you wooden head!'

Amidst laughter, the officer disappeared. After a while, a large basket was lowered on the end of a rope.

'One at a time!' the officer called down.

≈

Cadey scrambled out of the booth and was the first to be pulled up.

It had been decided between the five of them that she and Rainbow were to do all the talking. They would explain their foreign accents by claiming to hail from Brazil where the main language was Portuguese. They were touring parts of Chile and Peru and had recently come from Arica in Chile. With the help of Las Golpetinas, they were dressed for the part in an assortment of bright rags. Rainbow, it was agreed, was perfect for the part as he was.

'Where is it we're from?' Jacko whispered. 'Is it Africa?'

'Not, Africa,' Robert hissed. 'Arica.'

As the basket with Cadey in it ascended, Carroty Kate gave Robert a nudge.

'Men! They'd have bombarded and attacked all day and not gained entry. And here we are being helped in as nice as pie and without even breaking sweat.'

≈

Carroty Kate was last to be hauled up, having first sent up a basket full of the dismantled booth and the puppets. Even though a small boy, a half-mad former slave, two women and a slight young man hardly posed a threat, the Royalist guard on the battlements were taking no chances. Each was searched for weapons. Robert held his breath as the puppets were examined to see if they concealed a pistol, a knife or a bomb. One of the searchers fingered the papers lining Judy's head. Robert clung to the parapet, weak at the knees. Those papers were a key part of the plan. But the soldier was clearly looking for something bigger and ignored them. The examination of their props completed, the officer instructed them, since they were new to the town, that a curfew was imposed from half past eleven at night to half past five in the morning. 'In case of night attacks,' he said.

≈

Having completed their performance for the soldiers, they performed twice more in the town square, gathering good crowds on both occasions. And, in between, they managed to locate the premises of *El Tiempo* and unobtrusively reconnoitre it. Now they were sitting in a nearby café. In half an hour it would close to enable its patrons to reach home before the curfew started.

'Huh,' scoffed Carroty Kate, 'Night attacks my arse! To stop deserters going over the wall, more like.'

'And sabotage by Patriot sympathisers,' Cadey added.

'Reckon I could put away another of those pie things,' Jacko said.

'Well, we're spanking flush and no mistake,' Carroty Kate said, jingling a bag of coins at the waiter.

'I'm sorry we couldn't bring Smithy with us,' Robert said.

Carroty Kate nodded. She knew very well that five were as many as would seem credible for a small, itinerant puppet show. Obviously, the three involved in the actual performance had to be included, and Cadey because she alone amongst Las Golpetinas could read and write, and Robert himself because he was the only one who knew how to set up the type and operate a printing press.

Carroty Kate laughed. 'Smithy'll be quite happy yarning round a camp-fire about his adventures behind enemy lines.'

'Yeah, I heard some of them,' Jacko said. 'It's no wonder he's called Brave British Bill.'

'Sh! Not so loud! You're speaking English!' Cadey warned.

≈

Robert went over his plan one last time. Tomorrow, being a Thursday, *El Tiempo* would be on sale. According to information gathered by Las Golpetinas, the newspaper was printed on Wednesdays. The latest edition should be stacked and waiting at this very moment for Robert's 'supplement' before being sent out for sale throughout the town tomorrow morning.

'Are you quite sure you'll know how to work their printing press?' Cadey wanted to know.

'I hope so. I've watched them doing it at the *Chronicle* often enough. They even let me help sometimes.'

≈

In a dark side street they pressed themselves against a wall as a patrol tramped through the empty square. Shot on sight, they'd been told, was the penalty for breaking the curfew.

'All clear!' Rainbow called.

The reconnaissance had shown the building to be well defended against illegal entry. Then Jacko had spotted a chimney on the roof whose covering grille had come loose.

'Reckon I could squeeze that. Worth a try.'

Carroty Kate said, 'You don't have to do it, Jacko. We can find another way.'

'No, I'll give it a go.'

'Are you sure?'

'Yeah, one last time.'

Once inside the building, Jacko would make his way down to the ground floor and look for a door or a window which he could open from the inside.'

≈

The building was in the ornate Spanish colonial style, affording good holds for Jacko, so that he quickly gained the ledge directly above the large clock which dominated the façade. A pair of armed soldiers entered the square and stood talking on the steps of the opera house. Jacko flattened himself on the ledge. An almighty crash shattered the night. Jacko half rose, all but fell off the ledge, then lay still, covering his ears. One of the soldiers glanced up at the clock as the second stroke boomed and reverberated across the square. Robert held his breath. The accusing midnight hands seemed to point straight at Jacko. The soldier continued to gaze at the clock while fumbling for a watch in his pocket. He looked down to check its accuracy. His companion said something at which they both laughed. Still laughing, they strolled out of the square. As the twelfth stroke died away Jacko rose to his feet. Swinging up on a carved bunch of grapes, he was on the roof, sauntering, with hands in pockets, across the steeply sloping tiles.

'The little bugger's showing off!' Carroty Kate breathed into Robert's ear. 'He knows we're watching him.'

Jacko reached the chimney and climbed into it.

'He ain't as skinny as he used to be,' Carroty Kate said in an undertone. 'S'posing he gets stuck? Maybe I shouldn't of let him. He still gets nightmares about it.'

'That's why he needs to do it,' Rainbow said.

≈

They moved round to the back yard and waited. An hour passed.

'Christ. Where is he? He's got stuck, I know he has.'

Cadey said, 'If ever a boy could take care of himself, it's Jacko... I wish I could say the same of Dickon.'

Rainbow raised a hand. 'Listen!'

A window was being eased open. Rainbow stepped out of the shadows and helped push it up. Jacko, covered in soot and grazes, grinned out at them. Once inside the building, they heaped praise on Jacko until he glowed with pleasure.

'A bit tight in places,' he said, 'But nothing like as bad as I thought it was going to be. Nothing like... you know.'

'Nothing like your dreams,' Rainbow said. 'They won't come again, now.'

Carrroty Kate had a damp rag ready. She seized Jacko and gave him a good rub all over.

'Ow, Carrots! I ain't one of Smithy's boots what you're polishing for parade!'

≈

On the ground floor of *El Tiempo*, behind drawn curtains and by the light of a lantern turned down low, Robert, with Cadey helping him, began creating his special supplement. It was an account of the taking of Santa Rosa by the British Brigade on this very Thursday. In it was a graphic description of how the British appeared, not from the side they were guarding, but from the undefended East. Despite the Kentucky long-range rifles used by the Royalists, the British infantry advanced upon Santa Rosa with fanatical determination and scaled the walls.

'I like that bit about the Kentucky rifles,' Cadey said. 'That will really be a blow to their morale that their secret weapon is not a secret anymore.'

Robert's report described how the ferocious, bloodthirsty British inflicted heavy casualties on the Royalist garrison, showing little mercy to those who did not immediately surrender. Thanks to the captured list of the garrison, the fictitious account carried gory details of those who had been killed and wounded which were correct in every particular of name and rank.

While Cadey acted as compositor and set up the print for her translation of Robert's original version, Robert worked on copper plate illustrations of the carnage, bearing captions in Spanish such as 'Capitan Carlos Gomez losing both his legs.'

Robert turned to Rainbow. 'You once told me that if you can make people believe they're cured, then they will be. Well, this is sort of the opposite to that.'

'I can't see what I'm doing,' Robert said. 'I'm sorry, but I must have more light.'

Despite the curtains, they'd kept the lantern low, afraid some tiny gleam or chink of light might arouse suspicion.

'There'll be plenty can't read as will look at the pictures,' Jacko observed. 'Worth the risk, I say.'

'You're right, Jacko,' Robert said and turned up the lantern.

≈

The clock struck three as the first copies of the 'supplement' on the fall of Santa Rosa began to come off the press and were inserted into the waiting edition of *El Tiempo*.

'When do you think people arrive for work here?' Cadey asked, surveying the piles of newspapers yet to receive their extra pages.

'Curfew lasts till five thirty, so six at the earliest, I should think,' Robert replied. 'We've got maybe another three hours yet.'

'Looks like we're going to need it,' Carroty Kate observed.

Robert said, 'And we must leave time to put all the type back in the proper trays and make everything look as if we've never been here.'

As they worked, Robert explained to Rainbow what would have to be done. Rainbow, who was full of wonder at seeing a new story made in front of his eyes, was awed that it could then be taken to pieces and made to tell an entirely different one. It confirmed what he already knew—that who has power over the story, over what is told and how it is told, has power indeed.

'It is like Xango, the Thunder God's gift to Yansam's son,' he said. 'There are hidden things in this.'

Robert turned to Jacko. 'I appeal to his official 'interrupter'. What on earth is he talking about?'

'He means the little-get-up-man.'

Dawn was breaking as they left the building. In their earlier reconnaissance they had picked the tower of a disused church in which to keep out of the way during the day and from which they could observe what transpired. They dozed on the wooden floor of a dusty belfry, listening to the sounds of the town awakening. In a garret across an alley, a man and a woman, unaware that the tower opposite was occupied, were making love in full view of Jacko. Carroty Kate pulled him away from the narrow window.

'Carrots! They was almost at the winning post.'

≈

From the tower they could see boys with barrows taking bundles of *El Tiempo* in all directions.

Cadey said, 'Won't be long before the garrison learn whether they're going to die today or merely lose a limb.'

Jacko said, 'Reckon that Carlos personage will be off his breakfast!' He picked up a broken piece of shutter, snapped it in two and beat a tattoo on the floor.

Carroty Kate sighed. 'Give it a rest, Jacko, for pity's sake!' She glanced in Cadey's direction, exchanging silent messages of long-suffering motherhood. 'Boys!'

≈

Robert gazed across the rooves of Santa Rosa, alive to the tiles in many shades of orange and their resonance with the steeply-terraced fields beyond, thin strips of green against burnt sienna browns. It seemed ages since he'd done any serious painting. A pigeon fluttered up from a nearby roof and Robert's heart fluttered with it—the whole humiliating scene with C-S over his letter to Mama... He'd had a reprieve when the carrier-pigeons were killed by the jaguar at Cerro de Puna, but, before long, when a fresh supply of pigeons arrived, he was going to be put to the test all over again. He sat down on the bundle that was the folded booth, the flame of his newly found hope for himself guttering in the wind of doubt.

≈

Carroty Kate drew Jacko aside. She took a deep breath. 'Something I been meaning to tell you, Jacko... Had to give me babby away. Ten year ago that was. Still like a raw stump when a leg gets cut orf.' Tears were washing her begrimed face. 'Reckon I found out that starving a broken heart of love don't mend it. Only more love can do that.' She put an arm round Jacko.

Jacko felt his anger towards his mother melting away. If Carrots could love her baby so much, but still be forced to give it away, then perhaps his own mother had felt the same. Perhaps she had loved him after all.

≈

Not so long ago Rainbow would have thought he had not earned the right to bother Skyherd with any details about his particular mission. But after the defeat of Nataxale, and being so close now in this small belfry, the time seemed right. He told him about the underground water and how they had been unable to break through the rock to reach it.

'Gunpowder could be the answer,' Cadey said.

Now Rainbow understood! If gunpowder had the power to propel a lead ball with such force that it could break skulls and bones, it could also split rock. It had been put in front of him and he had been too blind to see. The water beneath the surface was stored up rain. It still lay within Skyherd's domain. How then would Skyherd bring about its release? How would he make this thing with the magical substance Gunpowder happen?

≈

'Watch your arse!' Carroty Kate yelled, suddenly wide-awake. 'The dolls is in there!'

'Sorry… Do you think you'll go back to the puppets one day, Kate?'

'Shouldn't think so. But the circus… now there's something! Might look up Barnaby Thackston… if we ever gets back.'

'Wonder if Joey's still there. Remember Joey and his cigar, guv?'

'I do, Monkey, I do.'

'We could do like the Storming of Badajoz, Carrots, 'cept it would be the adventures of Brave British Bill. The real Bill Smith doing the real stories! That would be something, wouldn't it, Carrots?'

'Well, I wouldn't say they were exactly the real stories.'

'Becoming more real by the day,' Cadey laughed.

'You should hear Smithy tell 'em, guv!'

'I have, Monkey, I have.'

'As a matter of fact,' Robert said, 'Bill Smith plays quite a big part in the fall of Santa Rosa.' He quoted from the report in *El Tiempo* in which Brave British Bill, with the strength of a lion, tossed men from the battlements as if they were dolls.

'You see,' Robert explained, 'At Cerro de Puna I heard a Royalist prisoner whistling the tune of the music-hall song about Brave British Bill and I knew a myth like that was worth any number of canon.'

Jacko burst into song:

Brave British Bill!
Our hero they'll never kill!
Oh, we will, we will, we will
Of vict'ry have our fill,
'Cos of Brave British Bill!

Jacko was about to start the second verse when he broke off and pointed.

'Hey, look at this down below!'

'If it's that man and his woman, I told you...'

'No, Carrots, look!'

In the street below, a little knot of people had gathered round someone reading out bits from *El Tiempo*'s special supplement. A young woman wailed and flung her arms round her uniformed sweetheart.

'Am I to lose you so soon?' she cried.

On the other side of the tower, several healthy young soldiers were accosting a priest and demanding the last rites. On the balcony of a house, an officer was having a perfectly good arm bandaged in preparation for the wound it would receive. Bugles were sounding the alert, soldiers were trying to haul cannon from the front battlements to the other side of the town.

'Too late!' Robert crowed. 'They'll never do it in time!'

Whereas no body of troops could hope to reach the undefended rear of the town undetected, it was a different matter with collapsible wooden soldiers. Flocks of goats being herded up to the higher pastures along the mountain paths outside the walls of Santa Rosa were a common sight. The guards on the ramparts thought nothing of the women with packs on their backs who were herding the goats. In planning the deception Robert had made use of the knowledge that the Royalists possessed Kentucky long-range rifles. Cannon would send up showers of splinters and fragments of cloth when they hit the target and the deception would be discovered, but not so with the rifles. Moreover, being long-range, for the first twenty mintues or so, it would not be obvious, even through a telescope, that the soldiers were not real.

≈

At twenty-five minutes past eight, as reported in *El Tiempo*, row upon row of British soldiers appeared over the crest of a hill to the East of Santa Rosa—the undefended side—and moved down the hill towards the town. One hundred Royalist marksmen opened fire with their Kentucky rifles. Despite terrible casualties in the ranks, the British Brigade did not waver, advancing slowly and steadily upon Santa Rosa.

≈

Robert smiled to himself, thinking of the hours he had spent supervising his construction team which had built life-size silhouettes of soldiers—light wooden frames stretched with canvas, sacking, calico, anything they could lay their hands on. To simulate the scarlet of the jackets, they had stolen paint from the quartermaster and, when that had run out, they had dug red earth and collected berries for their juice. Even Carmelita's voluminous pantaloons had been pressed into service, renowned as they were for turning anything washed in the same tub a bright red. Twenty or more of the 'light infantry', attached to one pole, could be 'marched' by only two people, so that a mere fifty volunteers from Las Golpetinas were sufficient to manage five hundred of these fearless warriors who were indifferent to death.

'The next ten minutes will decide it,' Cadey said.

Robert nodded tensely. In a few minutes the wooden soldiers would be close enough for the ruse to be spotted through a telescope.

'Slow down! Slow down!' he implored them under his breath.

The marksmen stopped firing. Men were running along the battlements and down the stone stairways into the streets. They were joined by other soldiers who were throwing away their weapons as they headed for the main gate. The guards at the gate, instead of turning back the would-be-deserters, opened the huge double portals and joined the exodus. The garrison poured out of Santa Rosa, fleeing in all directions, to be absorbed by the vast landscape within a matter of minutes.

'Congratulations,' Cadey said, throwing her arms round Robert. 'A brilliant plan, truly brilliant, one which deserves to be recorded in all the military manuals, but probably never will be.'

Robert beamed with pleasure. 'I must say, I do wonder what the history books will make of it!'

Cadey said, 'I think you've just invented a whole new kind of warfare. I think you should be in charge of a new branch of our operations. Let me see, what should we call it?'

Robert said, 'How about WORDS …Warfare of Rumours, Disinformation and Stories?'

'WORDS … Yes, I like that. Women have always used words as a weapon and, if it needed proving, you have certainly proved that the pen is mightier than the sword, that the story is what counts. As Commander of Las Golpetinas, I officially appoint you Head of WORDS.'

'Thank you. I accept.'

≈

Two hours later, Cadey, as Golpetina, stood on the steps of the opera house in the main square. To conceal her identity she wore a carnival mask purchased from a trembling shopkeeper. Around her were Las Golpetinas, who had been the first to enter the fallen town. Robert stood apart from Cadey on a lower step. He didn't want to become a clue that might help C-S or his cronies guess who Golpetina really was. Next to him were Rainbow and Jacko. As the British Brigade marched through the gates and into the main square, Las Golpetinas greeted them with an ironic cheer. Leading the brigade on his charger was Carlton-Syms.

'Look at his face!' Robert breathed in ecstasy. 'Just look at his face!'

Utter fury contorted his features. As he passed the opera house, he cast a thunderous look at Golpetina. Cadey gave a mocking bow in return. Behind Carlton-Syms marched the drummer-boys.

'I should of been wiv 'em,' Jacko said. 'I'm in trouble and no mistake.

It was worth it though. What a lark we had, eh guv?' He laughed. 'Difficult to tell our sojers from the wooden ones, isn't it?'

Robert said, 'Except these ones aren't quite so easy to nail and glue back together.'

'There's talk of mutiny,' Jacko said.

'I'm not surprised,' Robert replied. 'With every flogging C-S is making a rod for his own back.'

'Or a noose for his own neck.' Jacko broke into a high cracked voice. 'Come on Mister Punch, put your head in this noose.'

Rainbow said, 'Mr Hope, now that we have captured Santa Rosa, the way is open to the mountains and the Land of the Clouds, is it not?'

'Yes, that's right. It will be your first experience of snow, I fancy.'

On the opposite side of the square, the civilians of Santa Rosa had gathered to watch the rather less than triumphant entry of their liberators. Rainbow stared distractedly at the banks of multi-coloured capes. He'd waited for his rainbow to find its last colour, as spoken by Tupac Amaru, so that his mission might end, but nothing had happened. Nor did he yet know what gift he should make to Skyherd. He'd listened through the cracks in his skull; he'd listened through his skin, but he had heard no voice, received no sign. Yes, he had helped Skyherd to the best of his ability, but it was not enough. Ikpoom had told him he would know when the time came. Surely, as they neared the Land of Clouds, the true domain of Skyherd, that time must be very soon.

38

The rope bridge swayed like a giant's empty hammock. Below Rainbow, a torrent churned through a rocky gorge. A few feet behind him was Skyherd, clearly apprehensive about the crossing. To help him feel safer, Rainbow had tied a rope round Skyherd's waist, with the other end round his own. A wave of awe and gratitude surged through Rainbow as he marvelled that one of the most important gods should show such humility, such love for the Obolu people that he was willing to assume human form, with all its limitations, frailties and fears, in order to have direct contact with one their shamans. With Jacko's help Rainbow was leading the three cavalry horses for which he was responsible. Ahead of them, and already on the other side, was Muldoon who was leading Manco, Napoleon and Josephine. Trumpet notes, the distant cries of men and the neighing of horses echoed from the cliffs. They were eight days onward and upward from Santa Rosa. Way below lay the thorn scrub and the cloud-forest known as 'the jungle's eyebrows.' Now they were in the cold, precipitous wastes of the high cordillera where narrow tracks across perpendicular cliffs, deep gullies and numerous waterfalls had strung out the column so that its end was lost to view in the bottom-most ravines, while its head was scaling the crest of a ridge.

≈

There was always one more ridge, one more summit, upwards and upwards. Rainbow was gasping for breath in the thin air, his heart pounding. He was surprised that Skyherd was experiencing the same difficulty. He had imagined that the Lord of the Clouds would be at ease so near to his true domain. They climbed in single file. Men struggled and panted and cried out for a rest, their strength exhausted by lack of proper food, their vitality sapped by the intense cold against which their threadbare clothing afforded scant protection. The chilling rain came on again, glazing the steep trail with ice. A buzzard circled overhead.

'I'd eat even that, if I got the chance,' Muldoon panted.

≈

Momentarily the line paused while a mule, loaded with the barrel of a cannon, tumbled headlong from a precipice, struck some rocks, bounced, bounced again and plummeted from view into a deep ravine. That morning Rainbow had watched a young soldier do the same.

'Even a mule will lose its balance if overloaded,' Muldoon panted in Robert's ear.

He had not been pleased when Robert decided to take his canvasses with him. He had taken them off their frames and rolled them up. Even so, Napoleon and Josephine had quite enough to carry without them. But Robert had found himself unable to abandon his paintings. There was nowhere he could safely leave them, nowhere to which he could be sure he would return. The portrait of Carlton-Syms, in particular, he could not be parted from.

'Manco's limp is much worse, Mr Hope!'

The sharp, stony trails had lamed at least a third of the horses, Manco amongst them. Iron was in such short supply that the regimental farriers had been busy melting down muskets and swords to make horseshoes and nails, but to no avail. For several days now, despite the poultices applied by Rainbow, Manco had suffered agonies with every step he took. For an hour he struggled on, snorting with pain, coaxed, pulled and pushed. Then the poor beast lay down in the trail, refusing to budge, obstructing the march of those who followed.

'Get that damned nag out of the way!' an officer shouted. 'Corporal Higgins, shoot the damned animal!'

The corporal edged his way past a line of soldiers who were only too glad of the rest. He raised his musket. Skyherd snatched it from him.

'Nobody shoots him but me!'

Skyherd put his arms round Manco's neck; the horse sighed softly into his ear and looked at him with his large brown eyes as Skyherd's tears wet his piebald head. Then the Lord of the Clouds, who had never knowingly harmed a living creature, shot Manco.

≈

With the shot still echoing from one cliff to another, several ragged, hungry-eyed soldiers started forward, knives in hand, prepared to carve up the fallen animal. The first to approach was seized by Rainbow and lifted bodily from the ground. He felt Muldoon's restraining hand upon his arm and lowered the terrified soldier. The men retreated, muttering. Muldoon, Jacko and Rainbow cut as much meat as they could carry from the dead horse before letting the soldiers behind them fall upon the corpse, tearing and hacking at it, some pulling the flesh from the bone with their teeth, others lapping at the blood.

≈

At one of the delays caused by some stoppage higher up, Skyherd took out his telescope to study the long line of struggling men and women above and below.

Rainbow asked, 'Can you see Yansam or Dickon or Snail?'

'Mrs Thompson or Carrots,' Jacko interpreted.

Skyherd shook his head. 'But way below I can see a string of mules, each with the same kind of panniers strapped to their sides as I used for my own carrier-pigeons.'

≈

When night descended, one third of the brigade was still on the steep mountain face. Ahead of Rainbow and his three companions, the line pressed on, following the sounds of the bugles into a blackness which as Muldoon put it, 'was as black as the Earl o' Hell's riding boots'. Less than an hour ago yet another man had fallen to his death. The dreadful cry, the thud of flesh and bone on rock, the flailing, bouncing body, the avalanche of dislodged stone had left them all shaky, unnerved and reluctant to continue in the dark. Thus, when Rainbow spotted marks on the rock indicating a route leading diagonally downwards, off the track to which they were committed by the press of those behind, they decided to follow it.

≈

It started to snow. The track widened into a level platform on which was a small round construction rather like an oversized beehive made of stone. Rainbow tethered his three cavalry horses and Napoleon and Josephine. Wet and shivering Robert, Muldoon, Jacko and Rainbow squeezed inside the shelter. Had there been room for the animals, they would have taken them in with them for the warmth of their bodies. Muldoon produced a candle and a tinder-box from his pack. They surveyed their den by the light of the flickering flame. The place was filthy.

'I don't care as long we're dry and out of that icy blast,' Robert said, trying to control his chattering teeth.

'As long as the dirt doesn't wriggle,' Muldoon said. 'Jasus! My stampers are freezing!' He pulled Gwen's scarf closer round his ears. 'Looks like we'll be eating the meat cold and raw tonight, sorr. By the Holy Poker, what I wouldn't give for a good fire and a good hot meal!'

'Me too!' Agreed Jacko.

≈

Robert could see that Rainbow's dark skin, normally alive with fascinating highlights and deep, deep blues that plumbed the depths of blueness, was a dull ashen grey. Rainbow's shivering became more and more violent and uncontrollable. Outside the stone shelter the wind was blowing some piece of harness against the wall. Rattle, rattle! Tap, tap, tap! A red-hot wave surged up Rainbow's spine and exploded in his head. Energy like liquid radiance saturated every part of his body.

≈

Something shifted in his mind and he suddenly understood many things which had been puzzling him. He understood that every visitor to the Other World had their own unique and special experience of it because, for each person, what took place was staged for their benefit alone, to instruct them, to lead them towards the solution to whatever problem had made them cross the Great Divide in search of an answer. That seemingly inexplicable battle he had witnessed, which had been deliberately arranged—unmistakably it had been a ritual human sacrifice on a grand scale. He knew, with a sudden and absolute clarity what he was being told. The time had come for a deep-rooted custom to change. The ritual killing of the twelve to bring the rains must cease. He had been so blind! The message had been there all along for him to see. The war between the Patriots and the Royalists had many meanings for him, it had been enacted so that he could see the waste of life and tragedy involved in human sacrifice. He had listened, often enough, to Yansam and Skyherd deploring the awful sacrifice of the British Brigade, made to Glory, to the gods of Trade and Commerce and to the Toffs in London to restore their declining powers. It was like a puppet show, staged for his benefit on a vast scale in case he failed to see it—like some novice hunter being stood in front of fresh, clear tracks. To make sure he understood, Snail and Monkey had even involved him in a puppet show. But, stupid mortal that he was, all this time, he had missed the point. The earthquake at Cerro de Puna had brought down a solid construction which had endured for centuries; Yansam had spoken of disobedience being the instrument of progress; the George had warned that others like him would follow and that change was inevitable. Ikpoom had known this and that it was better to change from within than to have it forced upon you from outside. When he returned to his village he must persuade them that tradition was their guide, not their captor. He must tell them that Skyherd was not swayed by the symbolic act of draining life-giving blood into the dry earth, indeed, he was angered by it. The Great Rainmaker had said, 'When you are creating something, you are in touch with your Creator.' What Skyherd wanted was new songs, new dances, new stories, not blood, and this was what he, Rainbow, must tell his people.

'I, shaman of Mwanza will be the instrument by which the Obulu people no longer make human sacrifice. This I vow!'

He began to feel cold again. Supposing he was unable to carry out his vow? He might die, or remain trapped in the Other World. A spasm of shivering and a fresh doubt swept over Rainbow. Was his vow his gift to Skyherd, or was it, perhaps, a pre-condition of the nature of the gift being revealed to him?

'He's in a bad way,' Jacko said.

Robert stared anxiously and helplessly at Rainbow who was crouching on the floor of the shelter, clutching himself for warmth and mumbling incomprehensible things about Skyherd. Every night in these mountains, weakened men had died.

'If only we could light a fire,' Muldoon moaned. 'If only we had something to burn.'

'We have.' Robert said. 'My paintings.'

He tore 'The Battle at Rimac Ford' into thin strips. But the canvas was damp and would not ignite. They hunted around for dry kindling and found none.

'Cadey has got all my writing-paper,' Robert said. 'I didn't have room for it.'

Muldoon drew from his breast pocket his portrait of Mary. 'I've got this.'

Jacko knelt and opened his back-pack. Slowly he drew out his letter. 'And I've got this.'

Robert saw the initial 'J' on the letter and the intact seal. 'Would you like me to read it to you before we burn it?'

Jacko hesitated. 'No, I know what it says.'

≈

They huddled over a fire fuelled by the canvases torn into strips. 'The Battle at Rimac Ford', 'The March of the Heroes', 'The Gallant Bill Smith Sore Pressed', and finally, reluctantly, inevitably, the portrait of Carlton-Syms—they burned fiercely, giving out a fine heat, particularly those parts to which the oil-paints had been generously applied.

Robert held a slab of horse-meat over the fire, skewered on a stick. 'Thank you, Manco,' he muttered.

'I do believe, sorr, this is the first time I've ever warmed to our commander,' Muldoon observed, extending his hands over the embers of Robert's masterpiece.

Rainbow, revived by the food and warmth, watched the portrait burn. As the canvas curled and the paint blistered, it seemed to him that Ikpoom's face appeared in the undergrowth behind Carlton-Syms and smiled at him.

39

They dozed fitfully until dawn, then made their way back to the main track and started the ascent. Ahead of them a half-frozen line of men dragged upwards. The mules with the carrier-pigeons, they learned, had passed through this point soon after dawn.

≈

Just in front of them was an officer wearing a thick overcoat of a lighter blue than the standard issue to the British Brigade and with a modish little belt at the back.

'All right for some,' muttered Muldoon. 'Bet it's a lot warmer than what we got.'

At a point where the mountain path crossed sloping icy rock, the officer slipped and skidded on his back down the steep slope until his fall was arrested by the belt on the back of his coat catching on a protruding rock. There he hung, suspended over a precipice. Jacko leapt towards Robert, untied the rope round his waist and fastened it round himself.

'Lower me down!' he yelled.

'Take this with you!' Rainbow thrust his long knife under Jacko's belt.

Rainbow paid out the rope until Jacko reached the helpless man. Jacko cast about for somewhere to stand while he untied himself and put the rope round the officer. The fashionable little belt looked as though it migh not hold much longer. Jacko could find nowhere to stand safely. Spotting a horizontal crack in the rock, he drove the kinife into it up to the hilt, then stood on the handle. Very carefully, so as not to unbalance himself or dislodge the coat belt, he tied the rope round the officer, who remained motionless and speechless, paralysed by terror.

'Haul away! And don't friggin' forget I'm still down here!'

≈

Back on the path, Captain Dacey thanked Jacko profusely for rescuing him.

Robert said, 'You're one of Brigadier Carlton-Syms' bodyguard, aren't you?'

'Yes, and you're the artist who painted his portrait, aren't you?'

Captain Dacey shook hands with everyone. 'Thank you again. I owe my life to you, Drummer Jackson.'

Jacko gave a smart salute. Dacey, still quite shaken, rejoined the group he had been with and was soon lost to sight round a bend in the path.

≈

At last they reached the top of the pass where the brigade was gathered. Rain swept through the gap in the mountains. On the other side of the pass three major valleys came to a head. Robert could see why this high mountain crossroads was of strategic value. Muldoon did his best to warm some broth over a meagre fire, using the last remaining strips of canvas. Robert gulped at the broth, grateful for the glow inside him, for the warmth in his cupped hands, the steam thawing out his face. On the snow-covered ground groups huddled round tiny fires. Amongst them were the hardier female camp-followers who would follow their men and Golpetina through hell and back. Robert admitted to himself that he had felt much the same about Arthur. But Arthur wasn't here anymore.

≈

Robert stared into the pinched faces of the underfed, ill-clad mass and at the sick and the wounded who lay on the ground in neat military rows, wrapped in their greatcoats like newly-turned furrows of earth. He surveyed the shivering figures, one quarter of the number which had started out from Tilbury, and remembered how grand they had been in their new uniforms, how the bands had played and the pride and the swagger with which the men had marched through the streets in front of the cheering crowds.

As if reading his thoughts, Rainbow said, 'Look at us, Mr Hope. Once we were a full set of gleaming teeth, and now we are the mouth of an old man.'

≈

Muldoon and Jacko sprang to attention at the approach of an officer.

He addressed Robert. 'You're to report to Brigadier Carlton-Syms. At once.'

'Do you, by any chance, mean he requests the pleasure of my company, if it is convenient?'

The lieutenant reddened. 'He means now.'

'Tell him I'll be along when I've finished my broth.'

So the moment had come. Robert followed the lieutenant to a shelter built out of bales of hay with a tarpaulin for a roof. Inside, the effect was rather like being in a small barn. Carlton-Syms, Stringer and another officer, Smeaton, who had ragged Robert mercilessly ever since Tilbury, sat at a table. Others of C-S's elite gang, his flatterers and favourites, lounged about at the back. C-S and the other two at the table were drinking red wine from crystal glasses. The thought of the lives put at risk to carry such unnecessary luxuries all this way gave Robert the anger he needed.

C-S thrust a folded piece of paper towards him. 'This is to go out, in your hand and signed by you before this evening.'

Robert didn't need to read it to know the report would give C-S all the credit for the victories won by Las Golpetinas, while saying nothing of the suffering caused by his own inadequate leadership.

C-S tapped his pocket. 'I am sure I needn't tell you what will happen if you refuse.'

Robert took a deep breath. In a loud voice, he recited his letter to Mama, staring defiantly into any eyes that would meet his. Where were the jeers, the howls of laughter, the derisive shouts? Only an amazed and uneasy hush.

Carlton-Syms hurled his wineglass at Robert. 'Silence! I order you to be silent!'

'Silent? Not so long ago you were gloating at the thought of everyone knowing!'

'I… I… Well, I mean… '

Robert turned and walked out.

Carlton-Syms shouted after him, 'You'll end up doing what I want, you'll see!'

A sudden burst of sun made the ice-clad slopes glint and glimmer. If Rainbow were to tell him that an aura radiated from his whole body, blazing bright, shooting meteors, he would have believed him. Until this moment, until it was lifted from him, he had not known the true weight of the burden he'd been carrying, nor understood how much of himself had been consumed in the effort of pretending to be other than he was. The released energy, the strength of wholeness, surged through his body so that he let out a shout of joy. He sang at the top of his voice, stared at by weary soldiers slumped in the snow, while his song eased into tears of relief.

≈

Rainbow found him sheltering behind a rock, glowing with an inner light like a pregnant woman.

'It won't be long now, will it, Mr Hope... Hope of the rain to come? The drought is nearing its end, is it not?'

'Guv! Guv! And you, Mr Stanhope, sir, come quick!' Jacko, white-faced, stood before them, breathing hard in the thin air.

'What is it, Monkey?'

'It's Dickon and Muldoon.'

Jacko poured out the story, tumbling over his words in his agitation. It seemed that Muldoon had been drawing double rations for himself. He'd made friends with the quartermaster's clerk and persuaded him it would be an easy matter to retain the name of a dead or missing soldier on the list against which rations were drawn. For the past eight weeks Muldoon had been purloining the food, and more to the point, the drink, of a Corporal O'Leary, who was not unlike Muldoon in appearance. O' Leary, it transpired, had not been killed in action, but had deserted—a fact which army bureaucracy had only just caught up with. And desertion was punishable by death. And then came a second terrible blow—the person whom C-S had made responsible for seeing that the execution was carried out was Dickon. But Dickon had refused to do his bidding. Dickon had been charged with mutiny. There was no question of any kind of trial, court-martial or hearing. This was not the British army, but the Patriot army and the commander had absolute power to enforce discipline while in the field—and the penalty for mutiny, as for desertion, was death by firing-squad.

'When?' Robert shouted.

'Friggin' now! The squad's being got together this bleedin' minute as ever was.'

Robert was already running towards the shelter of hay. 'I know what C-S wants. I'm pretty sure I can get him to stop it. You two go and find Cadey.'

But Carlton-Syms wasn't there. Only Smeaton was in the barn-like place.

'You're late,' he sneered. 'The Brigadier expected you before this. And he's not pleased you didn't come. Not pleased at all. He might just go ahead with it.'

'I didn't know until... Where is he now?'

'The little plateau on the East side of the pass.' He laughed. 'Better hurry.'

≈

There was a long way round on flatter ground and a short way which cut across a steep snow slope. Somebody had already crossed the slope. Their steps, kicked in the snow, curved round the slope and out of sight. Robert was halfway across when, without warning, he was hurtling downwards amidst a choking white flurry, ending in a heap about a hundred feet below. He fought his way to the surface of the loose snow. He was shaking all over. He shouted. He shouted again, but nobody looked over the edge. He began the ascent, each step, each handhold having to be kicked and gouged out of the ice which the avalanche had laid bare. Gradually he gained height. Then he slipped and was back where he'd started.

'Help! Please, somebody hear me! Please!'

He stumbled forward and trod on a body buried in the snow. He dug it free with his hands, hoping to find a knife, a bayonet, anything to help him cut steps in the ice. The man wore a Patriot uniform. Slung round his neck was a Peruvian horn. Robert's first attempts at blowing the horn produced little more than squeaks and groans. Then, suddenly, deep, resonant notes were issuing from the instrument. He paused for breath.

Away to his left, he heard the sharp order, carried on the wind, 'Load!'

The wind dropped. He blew the horn again and again with all the power of desperation until a volley of shots echoed around the peaks.

40

Rainbow was certain he would recognise Yansam whatever disguise she adopted, but he couldn't find her, nor did Carroty Kate or any of Las Golpetinas know where she was. He raced towards the place of execution. It began to snow more heavily. The long, quavering note of a horn filled the sky, reverberating from cliff to cliff. Skyherd was calling the clouds to assemble.

≈

He reached the area of level ground where the firing-squad, well muffled against the cold, was lining up. A cordon of soldiers, bayonets fixed, was keeping a growing, muttering crowd at bay. Dickon and Muldoon stood in front of their executioners, side by side, blindfold and with their hands tied. Mounted on his grey charger, watching from a position behind the firing-squad, was Carlton-Syms. Captain Dacey was the officer in charge—the man whom Jacko had rescued. Dickon and Muldoon had been stripped to their shirts, but Dacey was wearing his distinctive French overcoat, topped by a thick scarf and shako. A grey mist hung in the air. The horn sounded again. The sound seemed to come from somewhere beyond the edge of the flat ground where it fell away in a steep slope. Rainbow ran to the edge and looked over. About a hundred and fifty feet below was Skyherd, the Great Rainmaker, blowing his horn and standing upon a surface of pure white.

'Load!' came the order from Captain Dacey.

'About face!'

The squad turned in unison, their muskets levelled at Carlton-Syms.

'Fire!'

Carlton-Syms' charger reared and plunged. C-S crashed to the ground and lay still. A lieutenant in his guard ran forward and knelt beside him.

'He's badly hurt… But… But there are no bullet wounds!'

Captain Dacey removed his scarf, then his shako. It was Yansam.

'We fired blanks,' she said. 'I simply meant to warn him he'd gone too far.'

'He struck his head when he fell,' the lieutenant said. 'And… and I think his spine may be broken.'

The semicircle of guards stood, weapons lowered, unsure what to do. The crowd pressed forward.

Cadey mounted the grey charger. All eyes were on her.

'Release the two prisoners!' she commanded.

Men as well as women ran to do her bidding. Hundreds were pressing round her, cheering, trying to shake her hand, kissing her booted feet. She raised an arm for silence.

'Who is now the senior officer in the brigade?'

'Colonel Lithgow,' said one of the guard.

'Killed in an avalanche on the ascent,' someone called out.

'Major Crammond, then.'

'He died during the night.'

The throng parted to let through a skeletal figure on an equally emaciated horse. 'I am Colonel Digby of the Highland Regiment and I believe I am now the senior officer here. And I believe you, Mrs Thomson, are Golpetina, the leader of Las Golpetinas.'

'Golpetina! Golpetina!' shouted her followers, a shout swelled by more and more male voices until almost the entire throng was chanting the name.

Colonel Digby tried to say something, but his voice was too weak to be heard above the crowd. Cadey raised a hand again.

In the ensuing silence, Colonel Digby said, 'I am too exhausted, too enfeebled by this campaign to take command. I... I don't know what else to say to you. I am a broken man.'

'Then I say, let Golpetina take command!' All heads turned. Robert stood at the top of the slope, horn in hand. A huge cheer went up, a shout of assent.

Cadey was standing up in the stirrups, seeking out the faces of Carlton-Syms' elite.

'Does anyone disagree?'

Nobody spoke. It stopped snowing. A weak and watery sun filtered through the mist.

'In that case,' Cadey declared, 'I propose that the British Brigade and Las Golpetinas join forces and operate as one united group.'

As Cadey, with Dickon beside her, received the acclaim of both the

British Brigade and her camp-followers, there was a sudden break in the mist. A light could be seen flashing from a lesser peak down the other side of the pass. Somebody was sending a message. Cadey turned to Dickon. 'What does it say?'

'I don't know, it's a new French system used by the patriots.' He called for a signalman to take down the message, which was being repeated over and over.

≈

Cadey read the written message. She looked up with a smile. 'We've won!'

General Sucre had inflicted a crushing defeat upon the Royalists at a place called Ayacucho. Nine Royalist divisions, including their crack cavalry regiments, had been routed with heavy losses; La Serna, the Spanish Viceroy, had been captured. The communiqué ended: 'The chains binding Peru are broken. The war of liberation has been won.'

41

Outside their adjacent tents which overlooked slopes of deciduous forest, Robert and Cadey were sitting in folding canvas chairs, drinking coffee. Muldoon was hovering in the background. Robert was reading a book of essays by William Hazlitt which he'd borrowed from Cadey. She was catching up on Brigade administration. Strands of mist lingered in the treetops and in the gorge which sliced through the mountainside, dividing one village from another. Three days ago the combined forces of Las Golpetinas and the British Brigade had crossed the high pass to the other, less precipitous side of the mountain range. After two days of descent down reasonably good paths, they were below the snowline and on good camping ground near one of the two villages. The next three days had been set aside for rest and recuperation before returning to Lima by a longer, but easier, route.

Robert tapped the book. 'Listen to this, Cadey.' He read aloud: 'Life is the art of being well deceived, and in order that the deception may succeed it must be habitual and uninterrupted.' He put the book down. 'What do you think of that? Would you say we were well deceived?'

Yes, most of the time probably, and mostly by ourselves. We invent the reality that suits us best.'

≈

Cadey's gaze wandered across the surrounding fields, packed with rows of tents. She frowned. 'Do you realise, Robert, we've completely flattened their hay crop? We'll have to compensate them. They'll die of starvation if we don't.'

'And they'll die of surprise if we do such an unheard of thing… Talking of which, I hear you've banned flogging.'

'Yes. Some of the senior officers are predicting an outbreak of indiscipline and chaos. I've told them, as far as I'm concerned, if an officer can't manage his men without resorting to the lash, he doesn't deserve to be one.'

'Dickon has never needed to, nor did Arthur.'

Robert saw in his mind Arthur's simple grave beside the river where the bridge had been blown up. All along the bank there'd be mounds where the grass was thicker and greener.

'I wonder who's buried on either side of him. Whoever they are, you can be sure he'll be borrowing money from them!'

Cadey banged the folding table in approval. 'Do you remember that time in Lima he tried to ride bareback round the plaza, while standing on one leg and downing a flagon of wine?'

'As I recall it, he didn't get very far.'

'I wonder if his parents have received the news yet.'

'I wrote to them, you know, Cadey.'

'What did you say?'

'That… that he was the best, truest friend anyone could possibly want.'

Cadey leant forward and kissed Robert on the cheek. 'Donde hay amor hay dolor,' she said. 'But love will remain long after the pain has gone'

'Forever, I think.'

≈

Robert returned to his book, Cadey to her paper-work. .

Cadey looked up from her lists. 'I've been so busy, I haven't had a chance to say I'm sorry you had to burn your paintings. I know they meant a lot to you… How is he, by the way?'

'Hasn't fully sunk in, but devastated. In a matter of seconds his power vanished. He's confused and frightened. For the first time since I've known him I caught glimpses of a person I could relate to.'

'A person you could paint …. Because I know you're going to do another one of him. You are, aren't you?'

Robert nodded. 'I like it that you know me so well.'

Cadey said. 'Right now, C-S is the man who put my son in front of a firing-squad. I have no regrets about what I caused to happen to him. Maybe, just maybe, sometime in the future, with the help of the portrait you're going to paint, I will see a human being and not a monster.'

Muldoon refilled their cups. 'Good riddance, I say! Fell off his high horse good and proper, so he did.'

Robert lifted his cup to his lips, then set it down again. 'I'm worried about Rainbow. He tells me more about himself these days. Did you know that, in times of drought, they make human sacrifice to bring the rain?'

'No. I knew there was a drought there.'

'The awful thing is, Cadey, that Rainbow must have left his country… what, six or seven months ago. The time on the slave ship, the time in London, the time spent getting to Peru and all the time since… Yes, at least six months.'

Cadey leant closer. 'You mean it's pretty certain twelve people have been sacrificed—unless the rains came.'

'But Rainbow won't admit that time has gone by.'

'I know what you mean, Robert. It's as if he's battling to keep a whole lot of fears and doubts at bay. Things I don't even begin to understand.'

'Perhaps this other African in the Brigade, the one from much the same area, will open his eyes to things.'

'I don't know,' Cadey replied. 'But if he succeeds, if he delivers too big a dose of reality, it could be an awful shock for Rainbow.'

≈

They sat side by side, watching the clouds pouring through a gap between two peaks.

Cadey bit into a guava. 'It's such a relief not to be in disguise all the time.'

Robert looked her in the eye and grinned. 'So I am discovering … only it's taken me all my life to find that out.'

'Not disguising things from yourself, that's the most important thing, Robert.'

Robert waited, knowing there was more to come.

'You've never known a woman, have you Robert? Sexually, I mean.'

Robert shook his head.

Cadey said, 'Perhaps it's not in your nature to want to.'

Robert was silent for a while. 'I think I'm still finding out what my feelings are about that. I loved Arthur. I'm sure about that.'

Cadey reached towards him and put a hand on his arm. 'And one thing I am sure of, Robert… you won't hide from the answer, you won't be frightened to be the person you really are. Once you might have been, but not now.' She laughed. 'Well, to change the subject… will you live in London or at Beechwood House?'

'London,' Robert said, smiling back at her. 'But Muldoon has agreed to go to Beechwood House and help out old Dan, our ageing gardener.'

Cadey cocked a booted leg across her knee. 'And have you thought about where you're going to live in London?'

Robert hesitated.

'Because,' Cadey continued, 'I'd like it to be somewhere close to us …to Dickon and me… when we've found somewhere suitable.'

Robert said, 'Dickon…Won't he want you to himself?'

'No, of course not! He loved the idea.'

≈

Cadey turned to look in the direction of a path which crossed the valley. 'I'm expecting Rainbow any minute. This may be a rest day for some, but I've got a hundred and one things to see to.'

Rainbow, who had been assigned to the charger which had been ridden by Cochrane-Dyat, then Carlton-Syms and now Cadey, was due to bring it round to her.

'Ah, here he is!'

Cadey clicked her booted heels and sprang up. 'I have to go.'

Robert said, 'I'm giving a little party this afternoon. Can you come … and Dickon, too?'

'I'll do my best. Dickon will have to answer for himself.' She swung into the saddle. 'See you later, I hope.'

≈

Robert stood on the wooden bridge which spanned the gorge, staring into the rushing water below. How many weeks or months till the tumbling waters in the gorge reached the distant ocean to be evaporated and return as clouds… like the ones streaming over the shoulder of the mountain? He began sketching the scene, imagining the painting which would grow from it, one line suggesting another.

≈

On the other side of the bridge, on flat ground, men of the British Brigade were kicking about an inflated sheep's bladder, laughing and shouting. People have such resilience, Robert thought. But then, he already knew that from Dickon and Jacko—little get-up-men, the pair of them. Other soldiers were washing their clothes in a rock-pool further downstream, or sitting cross-legged outside their tents, mending their tattered uniforms. Forgiveness was like that—mending something broken, washing clean something soiled. He thought of his father. Until this moment, he'd never wondered what his father's childhood had been like, whether he was happy, or what sort of relationship he'd had with his father; nor had he ever stopped to think why Mama married him, why she fell in love with him and what she saw in him that he had been blind to. Now he recalled that mama had said in one of her letters that he was not taking well to retirement, that he was bored and felt that he was no longer pulling his weight.

'Mr Stanhope, sir.'

Robert turned. A soldier was standing on the bridge.

'I served with your father, sir. I wanted to say…'

The coincidence of his own thoughts and this man's words came as no surprise. There are no coincidences, Rainbow would say, only harmonies of which we can be part, if we know how.

'General Stanhope is a fine man.'

'Kind of you to say so. Might I know your name?'

'Higgins, sir. Corporal Joe Higgins. And he was a brave 'un, sir. Never asked us to do anything he wouldn't do himself.'

'I appreciate you coming to speak to me. Thank you, corporal.'

'It's us should thank you, sir.'

'Me? What did I do?'

'We reckon most of us would be dead, but for you. A frontal attack on Santa Rosa would have been murder, sir, sheer murder. Not even your father could have taken that town. We're grateful to you, sir. Just wanted you to know.'

He turned and walked off the bridge. Robert leant over the railing and let the tears flow.

≈

Carroty Kate and Smithy, Dickon and Jacko, Muldoon and Rainbow, Robert and Cadey were gathered on the grass outside Robert's tent. Smithy was proudly sporting the medal that had been specially made for him on the orders of Carlton-Syms, fully convinced that it was no more than his due. Cadey's grey—that is to say, white—horse waited close by. The cake which Robert and Muldoon between them had put together and baked in an open-air oven built by Rainbow was a small, soggy, half-baked affair, covered in bullet-proof icing.

'I decree this recipe to be a military secret,' Cadey declared. 'Nobody must hear of it.'

But Jacko and Dickon thought it wonderful and devoured the lot.

'Shall I mix more punch, sorr?'

'Punch is the right word for it, Muldoon. What on earth did you put in it?'

'That's the way to do it!' Carroty Kate squawked. She continued in her puppet voice, 'This is an hofficial hannouncemint... Jacko, what hain't nivver 'ad a birthday in his whole life, has now got one!'

'Third of November,' Jacko said. 'You'll know why, guv. Just before Guy Fawkes day, the day we first met up with Carrots.'

Everyone congratulated Jacko and shook him by the hand.

'Smithy!' Dickon called. 'Give us a story!'

Smithy needed no second bidding. He launched into a vivid description, recounted with utter conviction, of how he had been the first one up the ladders at Santa Rosa and had cleared the battlements of the enemy practically single-handed.

Dickon turned to Robert, his eyes shining. 'Wow! What do you say to that, Boser?'

'I'd say the account in *El Tiempo* hardly does justice to Smithy's truly incredible heroism.'

'Kind of you to say so, Mr Stanhope,' Smithy replied. 'Very kind.'

'It'll go down great in the circus!' Jacko cried.

Carroty Kate held up the emerald Rainbow had given her. 'With the dosh we'll get for this little beauty, we can work up the act proper, hire extras for the Royalist sojers, flashy uniforms, the lot.'

'A gift from Exu, God of the Lost Crossroads, in his guise as Shoshobi the Leopard,' Rainbow said.

'How so?' Carroty Kate wanted to know.

'It was Shoshobi who made Jacko's shot shatter the big pot where it was hidden.'

≈

Then, at Jacko's request, Rainbow performed his Monkey dance, whirling and stomping. As Robert watched Rainbow's athletic leaps, he marvelled that he should feel so at one with a tough, strong man who could have been a famous prize-fighter. He owed so much to

Rainbow and to Cadey and Carroty Kate and Arthur, of course, and Muldoon, too. Without them he would not have survived, physically or mentally. Even C-S was part of the grand scheme which had brought him to this point, where he was happy.

In the distance, a carnival procession was approaching the bridge across the gorge, its brass band just audible.

Cadey remarked, 'It won't be their liberation they're celebrating. The Indians, the original inhabitants, don't see much difference between the Patriots and the Royalists, they're both foreign rulers, conquistadores.'

Dickon shouted. 'Mother Cadey, look at that masked figure on the horse… in the middle of the procession… That's spooky!'

Cadey nodded that she'd seen it. 'I'm sorry, Dickon, Robert, everyone, but I think I'll have to go now. So much to do.'

Smithy held up his mug of punch. 'A toast from our commander! Give us a toast Mrs Thomson!'

Cadey smiled and raised her glass. 'Not a military kind of toast. Let's drink to love. To love in all its many forms!'

'To love!' they chorused.

'Don't go yet,' Dickon pleaded. 'Stay until the carnival's gone past, at least. We can go down to the bridge and watch them.'

Robert said, 'Do stay, Cadey, just for a little longer.'

'Tell you what,' Cadey said. 'Walk me to the bridge since it's on my way.'

Muldoon said, 'I think it might be quite cold down there, sorr.' He brought out of the tent the first thing that came to hand, which was the scarlet jacket he wore when sitting as a clothes model for Carlton-Syms's portrait.

Carroty Kate called out, 'Look, Rainbow, here's that Ed-What's-'is-name coming!'

'Edetaen?'

'The very same and it's you he's coming to see. You two will be having good jawbation I'll wager.'

Edetaen waved and signalled that he would meet them at the bridge. They walked towards it with Rainbow leading Cadey's big grey charger.

'Let me hold it,' Robert said, taking the charger's reins from Rainbow. 'I've always been frightened of it.' He addressed the huge animal. 'Time

I got to know you better, isn't it?' And, on an impulse, he said, 'Help me into the saddle, Rainbow.'

≈

They descended out of the sun and into the shadow of the mountain above. Trumpets and cornets of European origin joined sound with Peruvian flutes and Andean pan-pipes. The tune seemed familiar to Robert, yet strange—a hymn he had sung, many a time, in his own parish church, but changed almost beyond recognition by the different rhythm and tempo. The procession began to cross the bridge. Young men in brightly woven caps and capes carried a platform on which reposed a carved figure, garlanded with flowers and painted white.

'I think it's Our Lord of Bonfim, sorr,' Muldoon said, crossing himself.

'Or it might be the Inca god, Wiraqocha, Creator of the Shaking Earth,' Carroty Kate added.

'They are one and the same person as Oxala, Lord of Creation,' Rainbow said. 'And they celebrate the cycle of birth, death and rebirth.'

Dickon asked, 'So who's the masked figure in the middle, Rainbow?'

'I am not sure, but I feel we know each other.'

≈

Robert was in the act of dismounting so that Cadey could be in the saddle, above the press of bodies, when he heard the shot. At the same moment, Rainbow hurled himself in front of him. The bullet struck Rainbow in the chest. He sprawled on the ground, blood pumping from the wound, staining his violet coat, his orange sleeve and blue scarf. The masked figure, who had fired the shot, cast off his cloak and mask and leapt onto the railing of the bridge. It was Tupac Amaru. He dived into the torrent below and was quickly swept downstream. Beside the discarded cloak lay one of the posters offering a reward for Brigadier Carlton-Syms, dead or alive, with a picture of a man astride a charger and wearing a scarlet jacket.

≈

Rainbow was dying. On his face was a radiant smile. Jacko was beside him, tears streaming down his cheeks.

'Oh, guv, don't go! Please don't go!'

Rainbow lifted a feeble hand and stroked his cheek.

'Thank you, Monkey. Thank you for everything.'

His eyes swivelled to Robert. 'Skyherd… at last I may call you Skyherd. Ikpoom was right. He said, when the time came, I'd know what my gift should be.' He tried to sit up, but fell back. He was fading fast, his voice barely a whisper. 'I have waited so long to return to the world of the living… Yes, Yaba, my love, I hear the rain.'

THE END

POSTSCRIPT

Extract from catalogue of paintings by Robert Stanhope, exhibited at St James Gallery, London, December 1825:

The proceeds from the sale of these paintings will be donated to the fund for drought relief in the Upper Volta region of West Africa which has been organised by the artist's father, General Stanhope.

No 7: Rainbow (Sold)

This portrait is of an African who saved Robert Stanhope's life in the recent War of Liberation in Peru. It is regarded as one of Stanhope's finest paintings so far and one which justifies the claim of many connoisseurs and critics that this young artist should be counted amongst England's leading portrait and landscape painters. The gathering rain-clouds behind the standing figure are 'almost a spiritual experience' (The Times). And the interior feeling and subtlety of expression captured in the subject himself are generally thought to be superior even to Stanhope's much admired portraits of Hugh Carlton-Syms (No. 3) and Cadey Thomson (No. 10). Mrs Thomson, who met the subject of this portrait while in Peru herself, has reviewed this exhibition in her controversial liberal reform magazine, 'Golpetina.' Of this portrait she wrote: 'In *Rainbow* many opposites meet within one man—light and dark, spirit and body, mature wisdom and childlike wonder.'

Rainbow was purchased by Lord Hawksmoor at the private viewing, for a considerable (undisclosed) sum—one which will bring to the drought-ridden community of Upper Volta several wells to provide the area with a permanent water supply.

NB All of the author's profits from the sale of this book will be donated to Water Aid UK.

Previous fiction by Robin Lloyd-Jones

Red Fox Running (Andersen Press, 2007) – a novel for teenagers, set in the Arctic, looking at environmental issues. Short-listed for Heart of Hawick Children's Book Award; long-listed for Manchester Children's Book Award. Also published as a Collins Reader, and translated into German.

Fallen Angels (Canongate, 1992) – Linked short stories about the lives of street children in South America. 'Compassionate and deeply moving' (*Contemporary Review*); 'His commitment and empathy show. This book hurts' (*Books in Scotland*).

The Dreamhouse (Hutchinson, 1985) – A surrealist satire set in a remote nineteenth-century gold-rush town in Alaska. The arrival of a con-man turns the community upside down. A Booker Prize entry. 'Fantastic, funny and inventive, a tonic to read' (*The Guardian*).

Lord of the Dance (Gollancz and Arena; in US: Little Brown; in Spain: Argos Vergara, all in 1983) – A sixteenth-century English doctor on a quest to find a cure for leprosy in the India of Moghul Emperor, Akbar. Winner of BBC Bookshelf/Arena First Novel Award and a Booker Prize entry. 'A significant literary discovery' (*The Glasgow Herald*); 'Astonishing imaginative brilliance' (*The Times*)

Where the Forest and Garden Meet (Kestrel, 1980) – children's fiction (9-12). Short stories based on author's memories of a childhood in India. Short-listed for the Children's Librarians' Award UK.

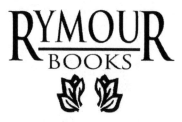

This book is set in Bembo, a typeface
cut by Francesco Griffo in 1495 for
the works of Pietro Bembo, a poet, a
Cardinal and lover of Lucrezia Borgia.